A Month of
MURDER

DAVID BAKER

authorHOUSE®

AuthorHouse™ UK
1663 Liberty Drive
Bloomington, IN 47403 USA
www.authorhouse.co.uk
Phone: UK TFN: 0800 0148641 (Toll Free inside the UK)
        UK Local: 02036 956322 (+44 20 3695 6322 from outside the UK)

This is a work of fiction. Names, characters, business, events and incidents are the products of the author's imagination. Any resemblance to actual persons, living or dead, or actual events is purely coincidental.

Published by AuthorHouse 06/16/2021

ISBN: 978-1-6655-9057-0 (sc)
ISBN: 978-1-6655-9058-7 (hc)
ISBN: 978-1-6655-9056-3 (e)

Print information available on the last page.

This book is printed on acid-free paper.

1

1 May 2019: Just Another Day

—⌀—

The train was late. *Northern Fail at their very best again. When will the government renationalise the railways?* Gordon Wright pushed past the schoolchildren dawdling in front of him, grimaced at a cyclist who should have been walking, not riding, his bike down the path to the road, and set off on his customary trek home from work. For once, it wasn't raining. *No, then, it's the scenic route today!* The walk back to *High Windows* along the cinder track would make a welcome change from the main road. He took off his tie, symbol of the civil service for which he worked and so hated. The squelch of his shoes showed him how wet the ground still was. Perhaps he could get into the garden this weekend if the forecast turned out to be true.

More trains passed, bringing the last cohorts of workers home. At least living in Holme Hill meant an easy journey to work in Leeds and back. Someone in a red hooded tracksuit passed by. Wright looked at his watch—twenty past six in the evening—then turned off the cinder track and down towards the cricket ground. He looked back at the jogger, but the athlete had disappeared.

I should take up running again.

Wright stopped to see if there were any vegetables or bits of fruit worth picking; only a few sticks of rhubarb remained in the free-for-all public allotment. He mused on the fact that the people who most needed this gift of nature's bounty were most likely to be stuck in front of the telly eating pizza and wondering how much more they could claim from the welfare state. He heard voices in the distance: young boys throwing stones at the chapel windows. Wright shouted at them, but they took no notice. He shouted again. They finally ran off when he threatened to call the police and took out his mobile and started to dial – or at least pretended to.

The sooner that building is converted to apartments the better! Ten years since it closed and what an eyesore it has become. How much will they cost? A bachelor flat – perfect! So near and yet so far away from mother. Is there time for a swift half before I go home?

Wright looked longingly over to The Bargeman.

It would be good to call in and power down. Joan would listen to his moans about work and living with his mother. If only…

The Bargeman beckoned. It was even warm enough to sit outside by Upper Lock; to sit and feel the warm sun on his face. Wright set off. He could always phone Mother and say that the train was late. After all, he was going to be spending the whole weekend with her.

Thank God for paperwork! And the garden!

She wouldn't know that the train was late; couldn't see the trains – hadn't been able to see them for years. Wright took the mobile out of his pocket and looked down the contacts list: E for Elsie - Elsie Wright. He was about to press the green telephone button when his stomach tightened.

*She can't **see** the trains, but she can hear; hearing as sharp as a piano tuner's, that woman.*

A change of plan: Wright picked up pace; began to stride home.

He looked over at The Bargeman once more. He thought of Joan. There would be hardly anybody in at this time of day. They didn't start serving meals until seven and business was slow on a Friday night. Nothing much ever happened in Holme Hill anyway: 'The Rip Van Winkle village of Yorkshire', the *Post* had once dubbed it. If there was nobody else at the bar, he could ask her. See what she said. He suddenly felt tired.

No, I can't do it to Mother. I ought to go straight home; she's been on her own all day.

He sighed then guffawed.

I could have had a pint: all this time thinking about it.

Wright stood for an instant longer, to give himself time to make the correct decision. He went home. If he cut across the cricket pitch, he could save five minutes and not be too late. He was just at the boundary edge when he caught sight of Ted Gelsthorpe standing at the door of his old lock keeper's cottage.

Hmmm, the old bugger will start shouting any minute now not to walk across his beloved square.

Wright took the long route around the ground. There was no way that he was going to incur Gelsthorpe's wrath. Gelsthorpe lived for that cricket club. Every day of the year, summer, winter, come rain or shine, he was out there doing something; cutting grass, mending fences, painting the pavilion.

Perhaps Ted would be interested in partnering up with mother.

3

Wright waved as he walked. Gelsthorpe took the pipe out of his mouth as if to speak but then raised his cap in acknowledgement instead. A dark cloud blotted out the sun; it had suddenly become colder. Wright chuckled to himself as it started to rain.

Mother's washing will be for it.

Wright began to jog towards the gate that led to Highgate Road. He could now see Mother at the window, her hands clutching the curtain.

One day; one day I will be free.

He looked back to see if Gelsthorpe was still watching him, but the groundsman had gone back inside now the square no longer needed guarding. Wright had not noticed someone else watching him. It seemed strange that on a warm day, despite the rain, there was a man sitting on a spectator bench in thick overcoat, scarf, hat and, as far as Wright could make out, gloves; and not trying to go for cover now that drizzle had become shower and shower might well turn into torrent.

The figure seemed familiar, but the trilby, muffler and dark glasses made it difficult to be sure. Wright motioned to his mother to give him five minutes while he investigated. He mouthed the words, knowing that she could lip read from the days when she worked in the mill and the sound of the looms made speech impossible.

Wright addressed the person sitting so silently on the bench.

'Hello. Are you alright?'

No reply; no movement; nothing.

'I say. Are you OK?'

Wright walked back down from the gate into the road and around to where the man was sitting.

'It's Gordon, your next-door neighbour. You're going to get wet if you don't get a move-on. Come on, I have an umbrella. Take it. I'll give you a hand to get up and walk you home. Better look sharp. Mother's waiting and she'll have my tea ready!'

By now, Wright was standing in front of the silent spectator. Even wrapped up as he was, and though wearing sunglasses, he could tell that it was Rhys Williams.

Crotchety old bugger! Why be kind to him? He never has a good word to say about anybody or anything. And mother hates him.

Wright tapped the old man on the arm; then squeezed it. How brittle it felt! He looked at Williams's face, tried to see if there was any movement behind the eyes. Nothing. Then he noticed the faint trickle of blood coming out of the corner of the mouth. Wright grabbed Williams by the shoulders and shook him. The body was limp; limp and lifeless. Then he took the hat and glasses off and unfurled the muffler. He did not notice the paleness of the skin.

Why did I never go on that first aid course at work? What am I supposed to do?

Wright undid the collar, slapped Williams' on the cheek.

'Rhys, Rhys, it's me. Gordon, your neighbour. Elsie's son'.

At which point, Williams' body slumped over and onto the ground.

Dead, without a doubt.

2

May 2, Morning: Coming Home

'Coffee?'

'What? Oh, er, no, thanks, Viv'.

'You're very quiet, sir. Is something wrong?'

'No, nothing'.

Which meant everything was wrong.

Detective Sergeant Vivienne Trubshaw knew her boss too well. Was it their affair? Was it his marriage? Or was it last night at Holme Hill? Unusually, he had driven to the crime scene. She liked to do the driving when they were together. It gave her a brief sense of equality with her DCI, but no matter. He had wanted to drive, and she would never counter him when he was in *that* mood.

She watched him staring out of the window of his office watching the rain. Her commanding officer, her muse, her mentor, and, since the previous Friday, her lover.

Or is this a one-off? A weak moment when they had both had too much to drink? What did he want of her? What did she want of him?

'I've changed my mind'.

'Sir?'

'Yes, please'.

Trubshaw felt relief.

What do I want from him? From this?

'Yes, please, strong and black'.

Just as DS Trubshaw was standing up, Charlie Riggs walked in.

'You're late, Detective Constable'.

Trubshaw shook her head, warning her junior partner to be careful. She went for the drinks. May kept staring out of the window. Riggs could tell that the SIO was angry by the way his neck muscles tightened as he spoke.

Riggs stood waiting in front of the DCI's desk. After a while he coughed in the hope that he would be allowed to sit down. Eventually May sighed, turned around and told him to go over to the conference table. Riggs was relieved to see Viv return with three mugs of coffee.

'So much for our May Bank Holiday weekend, eh, sir?'

May said nothing.

Riggs had another go at starting a conversation.

'DIY. It was meant to be DIY this weekend. New kitchen. Kate won't let me rest till I've finished'.

Still no response. Riggs hadn't seen the boss like this for a long time. But the DC had noticed a change over the last few weeks. He wasn't his usual self.

God knows what's the matter with him!

The silence seemed endless. Then May snapped out of it; became a different man.

'Well, that was a night and a half', he said curtly.

'Yes, sir'. May's two subordinates replied at the same time.

May opened the case file, such as it was, and studied its contents. He thought back to the previous evening. He had already left work when the call came through on his hands-free mobile. The scene of the crime was only ten minutes away. He had phoned home but there was no reply. Caz and Freddie must have been out somewhere, though it seemed an odd time. Freddie had to have his routines and it was surely teatime. May had not left a message.

A murder in Holme Hill of all places. May had not been back in ten years, since his father's death and the closure of the Methodist Chapel in quick succession.

Thank God Dad had not had to deal with the winding up of his beloved 'Salem'.

May remembered when he had first preached there as a newly qualified local preacher. The slight nod of Dad's head had told him all he needed to about the performance in the pulpit. The sign of approval, as always, made him smile. It did now as he pictured the scene. 'Salem Primitive Methodist Church, 1897': the text could still be made out on the engraved stonework above the pillared portico. Most of the windows in the lower part of the front face had been smashed in and then boarded over, but the upper ones still contained their stained glass. Someone had spray-painted 'Tracy I luv you' across the oak front doors, while either side of the entrance, 'Vote Conservative' posters had been plastered into place.

'What have you got for me, Charlie?'

'Not much so far, sir. Uniform were the first to arrive. They were in Holme Hill anyway. Reports of youths throwing stones at the chapel windows. It's a regular trouble spot where the local teenagers gather. Nothing else for them to do'.

May remembered his own youth and what he and his mates had got up to behind the cricket pavilion.

'The paramedics pronounced him dead at the scene. Suggestion is that he had been dead some time when the body was discovered'.

'Cause of death?'

'Well, sir, the PM is due for tomorrow morning, but Fizz said that it was almost certainly knife blade to the throat: side to side'.

Riggs made as if to demonstrate, then thought better of it.

'Are you both going to be there?'

Trubshaw nodded. Riggs hesitated, then decided that he should nod as well, despite his aversion to blood.

'Noted. 0915, as per?'

The two officers nodded once more.

'Time of death?'

'Interesting, sir', Riggs coughed. 'The victim was well dead by the time the body was discovered'.

'Well dead?'

'At least four hours'.

'He had been on that bench for four hours?'

'Apparently, sir'.

'OK, Viv. Tell us about the victim'.

'Rhys Williams, sir. 79 years of age. Born and raised in Cardiff. Moved to Holme Hill in 1970. Widower. Lives - lived - at number 35, in a row of terrace houses right by the cricket ground'.

May nodded. He knew exactly where Williams had lived. His father's house had been number 41: all two up two down, ex-millworkers' houses; each one now individualised inappropriately, spoiling any heritage that they might have otherwise possessed.

And he remembered Rhys Williams too. He had sung in the Chapel choir. Tenor.

'Worked at the local mill until it closed. He had ended up as factory manager'.

Riggs looked surprised.

'Yes, if you don't know already, you had better know now. I was born and brought up in Holme Hill'.

'I did know, sir. I seem to remember you telling me at one point'.

'I had forgotten that Viv'. May smiled gently.

'The victim was discovered by his neighbour walking the scenic way home from the railway station'.

'Scenic way home?' May snorted.

'That's what he said. The witness – or rather the man who discovered the body. Gordon Wright'.

'You'll find Wright's statement in the file, sir'.

'Any other witnesses?' May interjected.

'No–one has been identified yet, sir'. It was Viv.

'Sorry to interrupt, Charlie', she continued.

'That's OK, Viv', replied Riggs.

May burst out laughing; they all did.

'What's all this with the politeness?'

'We thought you were mad with us, sir. We didn't want to get across you'.

How could you get across me, Vivienne Trubshaw, when you look at me like that?

'No, nothing to do with you two. I think it was going back to Holme Hill last night. Anyway where's your Mr Wright?'

More laughter.

'Come on you two. Let's get the show on the road'.

'Oh, sir, one thing you should know. The victim had a piece of paper pinned to his lapel'.

'And?'

'Here it is, sir. No prints on it, though'. Riggs handed the paper over.

May stared at the note.

'Well, well, well. Interesting. Very interesting. And unusual'.

***

'Have you heard?'

'Heard what?' the old man croaked.

'Heard about Rhys?'

'No. What about him?'

'He's dead'.

'I thought he didn't look well the last time I saw him'.

'Not died, murdered!'

'Oh my God'.

'Do you think someone's on to us?'

'What? You mean he was murdered because of you know what?'

'Why else was he murdered?'

3

May 2, Afternoon and Evening: Frustration All Around

———— ⌇ ————

Wright wouldn't stop talking. May had rarely come across someone as garrulous as this. Periodically, Wright's mother told him to stop so that she could say something, but he soon got back into his stride.

Just occasionally, May and his Detective Sergeant looked at each other as they interviewed Gordon Wright and his mother in the lounge at *High Windows*.

Perhaps they could go for a drink at the local after this. Charlie would still be organising the door-to-door so they would have some time on their own together.

'So that's everything, Mr Wright?' the DS was eventually able to say.

'I think so, Sergeant. That's how it came about that I discovered the body. What a shock to the system. I dreamt about him last night. Woke up shouting his name. More tea, either of you?'

'He was no friend of mine. Nobody liked him, not around here, they didn't'.

'Mother! He was a respected member of this community, and you know that as well as I do'.

'I'm sorry, Mr May, Miss Trubshaw. Mother and he didn't get on. But that was six of one and half a dozen of the other, wasn't it Mother?'

'No, Gordon. It was his fault, and his fault alone'.

'Excuse me, Mrs Wright. What was his fault?' Trubshaw put down her cup and saucer (Mrs Wright's finest bone china, no less) as if to emphasise that she was all ears. May cleared his throat in support.

'The noise'.

'Noise?' May interjected.

'That infernal choir, those singers. What did they call them?'

'But Mother, they haven't practised in his house for years'.

'That doesn't matter Gordon, I still remember the nuisance they used to cause. What a racket. They couldn't even sing!'

'They could Mother. I thought they were rather good. I used to enjoy hearing them. They won prizes all over Yorkshire for their performances. And they used to teach some of the local children singing as well'.

'Well, I hated it. And still hate it. When he goes past our house singing at the top of his voice. He does it deliberately to annoy me. He knows I hate music!'

'Well, he won't be doing it ever again, will he, Mother?'

'That's very true, sir', May added.

'Mrs Wright, before we go, could we just confirm again that you saw nothing unusual during yesterday, the first of May?'

'No, I did not officer. And I would have seen it – or heard it at least. I know what goes on around here'.

'Thank you, Mrs Wright, Mr Wright'.

May and Trubshaw got up to leave.

'I am sorry that we had to disturb your Bank Holiday weekend like this'.

'Happy to help, Inspector, Sergeant. Let me show you out. I will be back to clear up the crockery in a minute, Mother'.

Gordon was only too happy to escape his mother and lead the two police officers into the hallway.

'It was built by the local magnate, this place, you know. Ernest Riddles: he could see across his village, down to his mill and across to his chapel. It's not like that now, of course, with the mill all turned into luxury flats and old 'Salem' next to be converted. But about time. The vandalism we've had in there. And the drugs and more. There'll be a better sort once those apartments are finished and occupied'.

'Thank you, Mr Wright. You and your mother have been very helpful. We may need to interview you again. Just one thing – how well can your mother actually see?'

Trubshaw looked at May. She had been thinking much the same thing.

'Not very well, Inspector, not very well at all. She suffered a stroke a while back and has glaucoma. But she hears very well. And she could see across the road and into the cricket ground. I waved to her from just by the gate last night when I was going to see what the matter with Rhys was'.

'And did you get on well with him?' Trubshaw asked.

'He was alright with me. I used to say hello to him every morning. He was as regular as the proverbial clockwork. Seven every morning to go and get his paper. I used to walk with him sometimes when I went on the main road to the station'.

'As opposed to the scenic way?' smiled May.

'Indeed, Inspector, as opposed to the scenic way'.

'And did you see him yesterday morning?'

'Funnily enough, I didn't. That was unusual, that was'.

***

Ted Gelsthorpe watched the man and the woman come out of *High Windows*. He saw them shake hands with Wright.

Gordon Wright! What a mother's boy, poor bugger! Only child. No wonder poor Ernest had drunk himself to death married to her.

Gelsthorpe didn't recognise the woman, but he knew the man. Willie May's lad. He still remembered some of Willie's sermons at Salem. And Donald wasn't a bad preacher either.

He could see young Don and the woman talking across at each other from either side of the car, opening the car doors as if to get in. But after a few moments of hesitation, they changed their minds, for they locked the vehicle (Gelsthorpe thought it looked foreign) and walked over Highgate Road and into the cricket ground.

Are they coming for me? I've already told them what I know – and that isn't much!

For a few moments, Gelsthorpe imagined that he was to have another visit from the police, but they followed the path away from his house and towards The Bargeman.

Fair enough, an after-work pint. I would have done the same!

The old groundsman let go of the lace curtain and turned back to his chair and his paper. He felt very tired. And cold, even though it was now Spring, had the central heating full on, and had lit a fire in the back room. He could hear the water surging over the top of the lock gates. He still worried about flooding, like the previous year.

Gelsthorpe turned on the television to watch *Look North*. It was the main item: a murder in Holme Hill. May 1st.

Then it came to him. The memory came to him so forcefully it hit him in the stomach and made him feel sick.

May 1st. That was the day she died. The day she was murdered. And Wright knew her. And he wasn't the only one either.

***

The Bargeman had hardly changed since May had last been in the pub, the day of his father's funeral wake. As the two officers entered, somebody was watching cricket on Sky. A young girl dressed in black shirt, skirt and tights lounged at the bar, looking at her silver nails. But it was not the gothic appearance that shocked May; the hair was a total mess, like something out of a horror movie – like a modern-day Medusa.

May ordered: a pint of the local brew for him and a gin and tonic for Vivienne. He told the goth that it had to be Plymouth.

She still hasn't got used to Yorkshire. God knows why she ever moved here.

May remembered the first thing that he had said to her when she arrived in his office. September 2016.

From Devon? People retire down there! Why do you want to come up here?

It had meant to be a joke, but she had taken him seriously. She always took him seriously – too seriously.

The Goth seemed to be taking her time with the pint.

'Sorry, sir, I think we have a problem. I'll be back in a minute'.

May was intrigued by the accent; as far removed from the image as it was possible to be. This was someone who sounded as if she was home from boarding school, somewhere like Benenden. He had gone out with a girl from Benenden when he had been at UEA doing his first degree.

Camilla was too posh for the likes of me though.

The Goth was nowhere to be seen. But the landlady was. May couldn't believe his eyes as she walked in behind the bar.

'Are you being served?'

Now this is what you call an attractive older woman!

'I am thanks, but it seems to be taking a while to get my pint'.

'I'm sorry about that, sir. She's new. Kids these days are useless. If only they taught them practical common sense!'

May smiled.

That's what Caz is always saying.

'I'm Linda, Linda Welch. I've not seen you in these parts before'.

The landlady held out a hand for May to shake. The rings and the tattooed heart on her wrist caught his attention.

What a strong grip!

'Detective Chief Inspector Donald May – but everybody calls me Don'.

He took out his ID, more through force of habit than because of necessity.

'And over there is Detective Sergeant Vivienne Trubshaw. Though we are off duty, I can assure you!'

Trubshaw nodded acknowledgement, giving no sign of her impatience at the slow service.

'So you're investigating the murder?'

'Yes. I'm the SIO, the Senior Investigating Officer, and Viv is my number 2. Have you run The Bargeman for long, Linda?'

'About a year. I've been out in Australia for the last 40, but I guess the pull of God's Own Country is too much for a Yorkshire lass like me. Just like you are a Yorkshire lad. I can tell just from your accent, even though you've been educated. Anyway, you go and join your Sergeant and I'll bring your drinks over to you'.

May nodded.

This woman has the most gorgeous eyes I have ever seen.

'What are you smiling at, Don?'

'I was just remembering my Dad's funeral wake here. We 'buried him with ham', as they say. He was very specific about that. That's proper Yorkshire for you!'

'Are you sure? The landlady seems to have made quite an impression'.

'Has she? I wouldn't have said so...'

Trubshaw cleared her throat to alert May to Linda's arrival with their drinks.

She really is very well preserved. What would Auntie Nell call her? Definitely a cougar?

'Here we are. Sorry about that. Here's your money back, Inspector. You deserve better than that'.

'But...'

'I insist'.

'Well, thank you'.

'My pleasure. I expect we may be seeing more of you over the next few weeks!'

'Did you know the deceased?' Trubshaw thought a publican – especially in a village – would hear lots of gossip. That was what she remembered from her time as a barmaid when she was at university.

'Not really, Inspector'.

'I'm only Sergeant'. May smiled at Viv's response.

'He never came in for a drink, then?'

'Very occasionally. Him and the old groundsman'.

'You mean Ted Gelsthorpe?'

Trubshaw was impressed with May's recall, not realising that he had known the man from the lock-keeper's cottage from when he was a child; had taught him to play cricket – not that his eyesight was good enough for him to play in the first team.

'Yes. That's the one. They used to sit in that corner over there. Seemed not to say much to anybody, not even to each other'.

May and Trubshaw looked over to where Linda Welch was pointing, as if for inspiration. It was just a table in a pub, the only thing distinguishing it from thousands of tables in hundreds of pubs up and down the county was the photographs on the wall.

'We call it "Memory Lane", that corner. All those pictures. I thought about taking it down when I arrived in Holme Hill, but I didn't have the heart. It's part of our heritage. Look at those two playing that odd game. We have the equipment from it above the bar. Nobody knows how to play it anymore'.

'It's called "billet"', said May, wistfully. 'I remember my Dad playing it. I can't have been above five at the time though. I only saw them play it once'.

Linda Welch looked at May quizzically.

'Yes', May added, 'I used to live here. Just over there, in fact. The third terrace house in that long row that goes right up to the chapel'.

'Welcome back to Holme Hill, then'.

'Thanks. Not the most auspicious of occasions'.

'No. Anyway, I'll leave you two to talk business. You're welcome back anytime. Both of you'.

Somehow Trubshaw didn't believe that last sentence, the way Welch looked at the DCI. No matter; she wasn't the jealous type. Not when the man she loved was already married.

May sipped his pint.

Mmm, that was good! Nothing like a good beer!

He held up the glass and checked the clarity of the liquid as he looked through to see the face of his detective Sergeant.

Viv laughed. It was the first time he had seen her laugh since they had been together that night after the conference. One thing had led to another...

'Viv, we need to talk'.

'I know we do, Don'.

'You know I have feelings for you, Viv'.

'I think I had guessed that'. Trubshaw mock smiled. 'After last week'.

'I always have had'.

'What?'

'Do you believe in...'

Charlie Riggs entered. May and Trubshaw put their drinks down hurriedly, as if the Detective Constable had found them out.

'Charlie. We didn't expect you here!' The two officers spoke in tandem.

'Ah, well. I finished organising the door to door and uniform have done combing the cricket ground. They'll expand the search into the surrounding woodland tomorrow. And I've put out an appeal for witnesses, including through the *Northern Rail* website. There may have been people on the train who saw something'.

'What are you having to drink, Charlie?'

'Thanks, sir. I'll just have a half of lager, please'.

'I'll get it, Charlie. Sir, would you like another?'

May looked up, irritated that they would not now have a chance to talk. Viv knew full well that Charlie would give her a lift back to the station and that May had to get home to see Caz and Freddie.

'No thanks, Viv. I'd better go. "Show a wife a good husband", as they say. You'll take Viv back to the station, Charlie?'

The DC nodded without enthusiasm, knowing that kitchen units were waiting to be fitted.

'See you tomorrow – at least for the morning – unless you're preaching, that is?'

'Not tomorrow, Viv. Not while I am on this case. 10.00 in my office, you two'.

May stood up and made for the exit, passing 'Memory Lane' on his way out. He studied the photographs. Most of the people were dead. One of the pictures was the Chapel choir. Dad was there, and Mum. Then there was another of the 150th anniversary celebrations of the Chapel. Memory after memory came back to him. Then he saw a group photograph that he had never seen before. And it made him wonder.

4

May 3, Morning: Not All Bad News; Some Dates for the Diary

May was late. And he had never been late before. Riggs looked at his watch for the third time in as many minutes. Or that's what Viv Trubshaw thought.

Where is he? It's not like Don at all. You can set your watch by him.

Fizz tut-tutted at Riggs.

'What's wrong, Charlie? Can't wait to get started?'

The Detective Constable gipped at this point but managed (he hoped successfully) to turn it into a cough. Trubshaw smiled, remembering how she had felt just before observing her first post-mortem.

'Sorry, Fizz, must have been something I ate last night'.

'Dr Harbord to you, matey. You don't know me well enough to call me Fizz. But you do know me well enough by now NOT to call me Felicity, I hope!'

'Yes, Dr Harbord'.

Riggs studied the medical examiner. She reminded him of Kate: diminutive, wriggly body, but packed with energy, ready to pounce. He wondered why Fizz had never married; no partner, apart from her cat. Not interested, so she had said. One of those people who didn't need anybody or anything. Apart from her work that is. She had won numerous awards – police as well as medical.

Another workaholic, just like the DCI! Except Don May had not been as scrupulous or as punctilious in recent weeks. What is going on with that man? It's affecting Viv, and it's affecting me. We aren't the team that we used to be.

Now even Detective Sergeant Trubshaw was looking at her watch.

Where the hell is he? Had there been another bust-up with Caz? It's never easy in two-career families where both are ambitious. That's why Phil and I split up. Two rozzers both trying to climb up the ladder. And then Phil wanting children. Why? When there are so many unwanted kids around anyway. Not for me, parenting, not after that time in Family. Thank God I'm out of that and doing real detective work! But Caz and Don: I thought they had it all until he told me last week. Was I meant to fall for the 'my wife doesn't understand me routine', or was he genuine?

The doors swung open. May flung off his overcoat and threw it onto a chair in the corner.

'Morning, Fizz. Sorry I'm late'.

Vivienne sighed.

You're OK! I was worried about you.

She really was trying to forget what happened at the Hull Conference, but it kept coming back into her mind. She and her DCI had made love.

We made love. And it was good; it was special; different; intimate! He looked tired. *Another argument with Caz perhaps?*

'Not like you, Don'.

May grimaced, then nodded. Dr Harbord decided not to pursue the line of enquiry.

'Anyway, shall we begin?' she queried.

'Ready when you are, Fizz'.

May looked at his colleagues.

'We all are'.

***

The brown envelope smelt musty. One by one, the cuttings were taken out and laid on the dining room table in date order. Twelve reports grouped into two sets. The folding and unfolding had taken their toll on the paper which, in places, had torn, and torn badly.

I should have protected them better. Put them into plastic wallets or something like that. I could always scan them and put them on my computer. But then somebody might find them and that would be a problem if they realised that I was linked. Best not. Let's just hope they don't deteriorate much more. They are the only thing I have left. They keep me going.

The pictures were grey. Nobody smiled on any of the photographs. Except on the twelfth one: the last to be taken out of the envelope and put in its correct place in the chronological sequence; right at the top, the first, the thing that started the chain of events that led to a gross injustice.

I will have my revenge now, while there is still time.

It was difficult to cut out the smiling face from the newspaper clip without any tearing; the rest of the group standing there looking out had to be preserved, for now. But apart from a slight serration, the deed was accomplished satisfactorily. The scissors were put away and the cuttings went back in their envelope. Once the flap had been closed, the envelope was placed in the bottom drawer. For a moment, the round face of Rhys Williams stared back from his greyscale hilarity. Then a match was struck and the cutting lit.

How I hate him. How I hate them all. They will burn in hell! I will see to that!

What day is it today? Where are we now?

The calendar on the dressing table had not been updated since Wednesday. Two days were torn off in quick succession.

May 3rd today: 4-5-6-7 – 8th May next.

***

'So, there you have it'.

Dr Felicity Harbord concluded her oral report to the three detectives. She smiled appreciatively at DC Riggs who, for once, had not left the room to be sick.

'So, let me get this straight, Fizz: the murder occurred somewhere else and the body was then moved to the cricket field at some point before Gordon Wright discovered him?'

'That's about right, Detective Chief Inspector. I reckon that he had been dead for at least four hours before he was moved to where he was found'.

May scratched his head.

'So, T.O.D. was when?' DS Trubshaw joined the discussion.

'Sometime before 13.00 on May 1st. And, as I've already said, a simple cut-throat job'.

'So, there must have been a lot of blood?'

May and Trubshaw were surprised that Riggs could even utter the word 'blood', given his aversion to it. The DC smirked triumphantly at his bravery.

'Almost certainly. Death by exsanguination. So, somebody had to clean up the mess; unless they still have that to do. The blood will have dried by now, of course'.

'And the murder weapon?'

'A very sharp and long knife, Detective Inspector. And you are looking for someone who is left-handed, given the fact that the attacker drew the blade right to left as stood behind the victim. But not a kitchen knife or anything domestic like that, I think; something more sophisticated. Perhaps even a ceremonial sword'.

'Well, that narrows the search down, colleagues!' May laughed wearily.

'What do you make of the piece of paper, Fizz?'

'Just an ordinary piece of lined paper that anyone could have bought from W.H. Smith's. No watermark or other distinguishing feature. There were no fingerprints on it. And the psalm reference has to be one for the preacher man here'. Harbord nodded over to May.

'Psalm 127 verse 3. I recognised the reference as soon as I saw the paper last night. Our murderer knows their Bible, by the looks of it'.

'And what about the dates, sir? 1 May; 8 May; 15 May; 22 May, and then a question mark'.

'I don't know what they signify Charlie. But we know what 1 May means, don't we?' May replied.

'There is one piece of good news, team'.

Trubshaw and Riggs hated it when Harbord called them 'team', as if they were about to go out and play jolly hockey sticks. May always let Fizz's frippery, as she herself called it, pass.

'Go on, Fizz, cheer us up!'

Harbord looked at Riggs as if she could kill him but decided against a second murder in one week.

'He was going to die soon anyway. Advanced prostate cancer. He only had a few weeks to live'.

'Did he know that, I wonder? Charlie, check with his doctor'.

'The thing is', Harbord concluded, 'did his murderer?'

5

May 3, Afternoon: A Case Review; a Last Visit; a Promised Revenge

'OK, let's do this'.

May looked up at the murder wall that they had now created. There was not much to see. Just a picture of Williams with links to the mill and the chapel.

'So let's look at means. He was killed several hours before the body was discovered. He was murdered away from the cricket ground then dressed up (according to Fizz) and placed on the seat, where he sat for most of the day, as we understand it'.

'He was not there at 0900 when Ted Gelsthorpe went out to water the cricket square'.

'And that took what, Charlie? Half an hour?'

'40 minutes, sir. Gelsthorpe said he was locking his front door to go and catch the train to Leeds at 0945'.

'And he knows it was that time because...'

'Because the chapel clock struck the three quarters'.

May had forgotten that Salem had a clock. How could he, given that his father had been left in charge of winding it up when Peter Smith was away on holiday?

'And the clock still works?'

'Yup. Gelsthorpe looks after it! Takes great pride in doing so, as he told one of the WPCs at great length'.

'The body was not there at 0945, but it was there when Wright got off his evening train and walked past the field and home?'

'And nobody saw anything in the meantime?'

May and Trubshaw quizzed Riggs one after the other. They smiled at each other for a brief moment. Then Trubshaw blushed while May turned towards the window. Riggs thought better of it than to say or do anything.

'Apparently not. There are only one or two places where you can see the cricket field from the houses in Highgate Road: too many bushes and trees. In fact, *High Windows* is the only one with a good line of sight. That's why it's called *High Windows,* I suppose. In any case, Williams was on the seat below the wall so even Elsie Wright wouldn't have spotted him'.

May wondered whether to tell Riggs about the Larkin poem, but decided that the literary allusion would be lost on his DC.

'Why do you say, "even Elsie Wright", Charlie?' May asked.

'Because, sir', said Trubshaw, 'she is a real busybody. Always looking out the window. Knows what everybody is doing. Sits in the bay window all day. God knows how her son manages to live with her!'

May thought back to his own mother's life after Dad had died. She always blamed May for Dad's death. God knows why! They had only gone to Headingley together for the day!

'And what about passengers on the trains going past? Surely someone must have seen **something**!'

May made a mental note to ask Freddie what he knew about the Holme Hill train timetable when he got back.

'Again, sir, the trees mask the field. Given the speed at which the trains would have been travelling, even if they had been slowing down into the station, there would only have been a split second to see anything; that's assuming as a passenger you were looking for something anyway'.

'Thanks, Charlie. And nothing from cyclists, dog walkers and the rest?'

'Not yet, sir'.

'And The Bargeman?' May decided he could do with a drink right then and there but saw from his watch that it was still way off opening time.

'No obvious view of the field, or at least that part of it, sir, and they were closed for lunch that day. Something about repairs to the bar after a bit of an altercation the previous weekend'.

Riggs put his notepad away, having finished his report.

'OK then. Let's focus on Williams himself now'. May cleared his throat and sat down after one last look at the murder wall.

'He had no close relatives, sir. No brothers or sisters, and no children. He doesn't seem to have had many friends either. We have checked around the area; neighbours and the like, but he kept himself to himself, as they say. You have Gordon Wright's testimony, and more importantly that of his mother re. Williams. The man lived on his own; had done since his wife died. He would go down to the newsagents every morning - same time, same paper. He had been a regular attender at the chapel, until it closed. It had been the centre of his social life after he had retired, his only social life in fact, according to the locals. Poor bugger'.

Charlie Riggs snorted, remembering how his own mother had gradually sunk into absolute nothingness. By the time she died, she could not even recognise him; could not even say his name. Except just once, the day before she died, he had gone to see her in hospital. The nurse had asked if he wanted to feed her and, too surprised to give a reason why he should not, had ended up spooning yoghurt into her mouth. As he aimed the last spoonful, she had looked at him and smiled, like she used to do when he was small. For one final moment they had understood each other; now the roles were reversed, and he was feeding her. 'Charles', she said. Then the flash of lucidity was gone. She never spoke another word. 24 hours later, she was dead, and he had not got there in time.

'What about when he was still at work?' May asked.

'Riddles was a typical heavy woollen mill. Closed when they couldn't compete with India and the Far East. They tried. Imported workers, put in new machinery that ran 24/7 and 'diversified'. They even started moulding plastic, but nothing would save them. Inevitable'.

Riggs stopped, realising that May and Trubshaw were not as interested in economic and social history as he was. But the DCI remembered the mill; remembered how his dad had said how he was grateful to have had a white-collar job as a bank clerk. Had Williams ever come to their house? Not that he recalled; but Dad would have known him from the Chapel, especially if he had sung in the choir. It would have been easy enough to remember the names of the singers in the last few years; there were only a handful left in the choir by the time the place closed down. 'Closed down before it fell down', his mother had said. Then there was that photograph that May had seen in the pub. What was it about those smiling faces?

'Thanks for the lesson, Charlie. Remind me to give your name to the local PROBUS club. They will enjoy hearing you lecture to them'.

Riggs could not work out whether May intended this as a serious suggestion or a piece of sarcasm. But that was what happened when your boss was on the Asperger scale. Or at least that was what the Detective Constable thought.

'No enemies, no fall-outs, no grudges, old scores to be settled; nothing like that?'

May wished he still smoked, for as he spoke, he felt the increasing tension between the three of them as they puzzled over Williams' death. A cigarette would have calmed him down now. Or a drink. But no, he had put all that behind him; ever since he had finished his PhD.

'You should know, sir, with your Methodist Church connections!' Trubshaw tried to make light of May's frustration but quickly realised that she had said the wrong thing.

'You'd be surprised, Viv. It's amazing what goes on in some churches. The infighting, the backbiting, the falling out. That's why that Chapel in Holme Hill was built: rivalry between two local wool magnates'.

'What about other avenues, sir? We've had reports about drug-dealing around there'.

'I guess so, Viv, but that's low-level stuff, don't you think? It wouldn't involve murder, would it?'

Trubshaw shrugged at her DCI.

'I agree, sir, but what if Williams saw something? Witnessed the trafficking, perhaps?'

'But the people who sell drugs behind the cricket pavilion are the bottom of the pile, Viv. They are expendable'.

Riggs almost felt sorry for them as he spoke. Little did they know what they were getting into; teenagers, most of them, like his flat mate at Uni – just a bit of extra money, no harm in it. Then he had gone on to bigger stuff; couldn't stop, either the dealing or the using. And then prison: that's where Riggs and his old flat mate had met up.

'I agree, Charlie; Sir. But what if Williams had discovered who was at the top of the food chain? You know we have been trying to catch the head of the OCG behind all this drug dealing in the borough. That would warrant murder, if Williams knew who was behind it all'.

May looked at her; then at Riggs, considering the option.

'Well, someone wanted him dead. I don't buy drug rings or any other OCGs, for that matter. Let's dig a bit deeper into his past. There must be something that made the killer want him dead; and a killer with a religious streak, if the Bible quotation is anything to go by. And what about these other dates?'

May looked at the Bible quotation, now written up on the murder wall along with the four dates.

'Thou shalt not kill', he mouthed quietly.

***

'Shall we go in one last time?'

Ted Gelsthorpe poured another cup of tea for his guest. He looked at Smith and wondered how he had aged so badly in recent years. They were the same age, born a month apart, but Gelsthorpe could still go for his long walks around Yorkshire. He looked up at the water colour of the Ribblehead Viaduct that he had painted himself. Maisie had been with him then; the last time they had walked the *Dales Way* together.

'If you like, but would there be any point? There's not much left to see. All the pews have been ripped out and the organ's next'.

'All the more reason to go and have a look, Peter. You could even play it. It was kept in good order until a couple of years ago, though the place wasn't used'.

'Ted, I haven't touched the organ for years. And in any case, I don't have any keys'.

'I do'. At which point Gelsthorpe took out a large key from his pocket and brandished it triumphantly in front of Smith.

'Come on, Peter. One last time. We'll never get another chance. Our lives are in that place. For good and ill!'

***

Joan Wilberforce liked working at The Bargeman. It gave her something to do now that bastard was finally out of her life. Just a few hours a week – occasional Saturday and Sunday evenings if Linda was short of staff – to give her a bit of extra cash. Much needed cash now that Captain Underpants had gone off with Dawn. *God, what a name! She is a Dawn alright.*

'Are you ready, Joan?'

'Yes, I'm ready, Linda!'

Linda Welch went to the front entrance, turned the key in the lock and freed the large bolts at the top and bottom of the door. The hinges creaked as she opened up. There were already a few of the regulars waiting to come in for a pint or more. One of them had been smoking outside. It wasn't the smell that irritated her, but the fact that the man had dropped his cigarette butts right by the front step.

I'll have my revenge on him before I have finished here. Just like all the others that are on my list.

6

May 3, Evening: Reminiscence; Replay; Reminder

'The lawn needs cutting'.

'I know. I'll do it on Sunday'.

'Aren't you preaching?'

May shook his head.

The microwave beeped.

'Here you are. It's not too burnt'.

'Thanks, Caz. Sorry I'm so late, *again*'.

'Don't worry. I'm used to it. I've always been used to it. But do try and spend some time with Freddie this weekend. He so misses you. He wants you to help him work on the model railway'.

'I'll go talk to him when I've eaten this'.

May looked at the stew and dumplings; his favourite, but not as good as his mother used to make it. He took his fork and began, savouring every mouthful, consciously attempting to slow down his devouring of food into civilised eating.

Caz looked at her husband. Don was so used to finishing meals in a hurry that she wondered if he ever enjoyed the process. For that's what it was: a process; something to be completed as effectively and efficiently as possible. Nothing to do with enjoyment or relaxation. He wasn't always like that, she thought. He had been the life and soul of the party when they were at university. *I chose him because he made me laugh. And I wanted him to be the father of my children.*

'When are we going to talk?'

'Not now, Caz. I'm shattered'.

'You're always shattered, Don. It used to be so good. And you know what I want to talk about'.

May grunted. His stomach rumbled, reminding him that this was his first real meal of the day.

'OK. This weekend. We'll talk about it this weekend'.

Catherine May put her hand on her husband's arm.

'Do you mean that?'

May nodded gently.

'You promise?'

'I promise'.

'OK. Here's the newspaper. And yesterday's. And the day before. You haven't read any of them. And I know you like to keep up to date. I'll be in the living room. There's some apple pie and custard in a bowl in the fridge. And make sure you go up and see Freddie before too long'.

'I will'.

Caz looked back at her husband, already engrossed in the newspaper.

Despite everything I still love him. I just wish…

May read about the local elections of the previous day: losses for Labour and UKIP; gains for the Greens, Lib Dems and independents. Dad would have grieved over what was happening to his beloved Labour Party.

What would Dad have made of Williams' murder? Did he know Rhys? I remember him talking about the choir. Was Williams a singer? He was in that photograph at The Bargeman.

May returned to reading the newspaper. There was more on Fiona Onasanya: an MP perverting the course of justice. *Not the first and not the last!* The DCI looked at his watch.

I'd better go and see Freddie.

***

'So, this is Salem now'.

Smith looked around the chapel. Paint was peeling off the ceiling where rainwater had seeped through. Plaster was coming off the walls. Light came in through holes in the glass where yobbos had thrown stones. Everywhere was dusty, dank, uncared for. The place smelt of musk. And charred wood.

I remember when some vagrants got in and burnt the Lord's Table to keep warm. Scum!

Standing in the pulpit, Smith looked down at the empty space where the pews had been.

'Do you remember, Ted, when this place was full – upstairs as well as downstairs?'

Smith pointed up to the galleries that went around three sides of the building, could almost hear the singing on one of those long-gone Sunday School Anniversary Services. *To God be the Glory, great things He hath done!*

Gelsthorpe remained silent, lost in his own memories of the place. Salem was where he and Maisie had got married, where their children had been christened, where their son and daughter had both been wed. But there wouldn't be any grandchildren baptised here. *Ten years; ten years since this place closed! It seems like yesterday.*

'Come on then, Peter. Give us a tune!'

Gelsthorpe wiped his eyes and tried to smile. He beckoned Smith to sit down at the organ console.

'There's still power to the blower'.

Gelsthorpe pressed the green button to the right of the keyboards. Both men could hear the bellows fill with air. Then the hissing began as the instrument leaked wind. A low moan came out of some of the big pedal pipes. Smith looked at Gelsthorpe.

'Don't worry, Peter, the moan will stop when she warms up'.

Smith laughed at Gelsthorpe's attribution of gender to the organ.

'I know, Ted. And I know how to look after the old girl. Or I used to be able to!'

Smith pulled out the loud stops on all three keyboards and the pedals and coupled them together. *I know what I'll play. Has to be Handel; has to be* Messiah; *has to be* The Hallelujah Chorus! *One last time, for everybody that worshipped here!*

Gelsthorpe wondered if the organ would take it. Even a non-musician like him could tell that the organ bellows were struggling to supply enough wind. But the instrument had been built like a battleship and she was still ship-shape enough for one last voyage.

'Sock it to 'em, Peter!'

Gelsthorpe joined in, much to Smith's irritation, given his companion's inability to sing. Smith added more stops in an attempt to drown out the noise. Gelsthorpe just sang louder. Smith gritted his teeth, determined to finish the piece before the organ gave out.

The final chord wavered: there was not enough wind left in the bellows and the triumphant final tones fell away into a final gasp.

'Well, I tried. But no more'.

Gelsthorpe gave Smith a tissue to wipe his eyes and blow his nose.

'What went wrong all those years ago, Peter? Is there something you want to tell me? Something about Rhys, perhaps?'

***

'He should be home by now. Where is he? I knew I shouldn't have let him go out'.

Elsie Wright was at the bay window. It was now dark, and Gordon had been out at The Bargeman for over two hours now.

Who does he think he is? I have rights. I am a widow. I am his mother. He should be looking after me.

She poured herself another gin.

Nectar. Pure nectar. That's what Ernest would have said.

Elsie turned to the wedding photograph on the sideboard. May 1955; a warm, sunny day, just like this.

But oh, the shame of it! The shame of having to get married. And in that chapel! Everybody pointing. Why had she let him do it? Her mother had made her have pink and blue strands in the wedding dress so that it was not all white. They were subtle colourings, but everyone knew what it signified. She had not been pure when she got married. And there had been a limit to how far they could convince people that Gordon was born prematurely. Not at his weight. And that had been it. No more children and no more sex. Her husband had found his pleasure elsewhere. 'What the eye doesn't see the heart doesn't grieve over'. But what Rhys Williams and his cronies had gotten up to was something else.

***

'So, what's she like, your new boss?'

'She's very, very well organised. I can tell you that!'

Gordon Wright could talk to Joan Wilberforce. She made him feel good; made him feel like a man. He could look her straight in the eye; could think of what to say. She laughed at his jokes; nodded knowingly at his comments; smiled at him with her eyes as well as her mouth.

As they got to know each other better, Joan would squeeze Gordon's arm from time to time. At one point, he thought he felt her foot stroke the bottom of his leg.

'She was in Australia for a long time, wasn't she?'

'She was. Hence the twang. If you listen very carefully, you can hear it, especially at the end of sentences when the intonation goes up'.

'I hadn't noticed. I'm more interested in listening to you, Joan'.

'Ha! Flatterer you! I'm interested in the way people speak. My Dad was a member of the Yorkshire Dialect Society and I suppose some of his interest rubbed off on me. And I did study English at York in my youth'.

'You're still young!'

'Young at heart, Gordon. Young at heart. Like Linda. She certainly doesn't look her age, does she?'

The two of them looked over to the bar where Linda Welch was serving a customer and giving instructions to the chef.

'Where does she hail from originally, Joan?'

'I don't know Gordon. Why do you ask?'

'No reason. She sounds more Yorkshire than Australia, if you ask me'.

7

May 4, Morning: Awake, My Soul; Vendettas in Riddles; Wright in Love

'It was sweet; so, so sweet. One last time, and then goodbye. At least it's going abroad. It will have a home. I'll have to go and play it when it's been installed. I have never been to France'.

Peter Smith often talked in his sleep but never before had he heard himself talking as he slumbered. *Who am I talking to? Apart from my wife's ghost!*

He did not remember leaving the chapel after the impromptu concert with Ted Gelsthorpe. Nor could he recall how he got home. Anyhow, he was home, and it was time he woke up and got some tea on the go. *I feel so hungry! Haven't eaten since lunch at* The Bargeman.

Opening his eyes, Smith decided he must have been asleep for hours, as it was now very dark. The sun had still been high in the sky when he and Ted had gone into the chapel. He thought of the light shining through the stained-glass windows as they had gone upstairs to the gallery and across to the choir stalls and organ loft.

But there was no light shining through the windows now. It was black in the living room. So black that he could see nothing. Absolutely bloody nothing.

Not only that, but he was on the floor. *God I must have been drinking! Did Ted and I go to* The Bargeman *after the chapel?*

Smith shook his head, trying to rouse himself. He ached everywhere. Where the hell was he? What had happened to the carpet? Just bare flags? *What am I doing in the cellar?*

He pushed himself up onto his elbows. It was at that point he realised that he was not at home, not even in his basement. Peter Smith was in a strange place; somewhere that he had never been before. Worse than that, he was in chains.

***

'So, Mr. Gelsthorpe, you arrived back on the 14.45 from Leeds, getting into Holme Hill about ten to four?'

'Give or take a few minutes. The train was late. It's always late'.

Gelsthorpe sipped the tea and munched the biscuit that DS Trubshaw had arranged for him.

'I sympathise Mr. Gelsthorpe. Northern Rail aren't known for their reliability or their punctuality, are they?

'Time was when you could set your watch by those trains! Gone downhill ever since privatisation!' Gelsthorpe grunted

'And you saw nothing on the way back to your cottage?'

'No. Nothing'. Gelsthorpe folded his arms and crossed his legs.

'You knew the deceased, I believe?'

'Yes, I did'.

'And how well did you know him?'

'Well, everybody knows everybody in Holme Hill. Or they used to, till the urban sprawl came. You know, the housing estate and the people who came from the towns to live in it. But they didn't mix; still don't. Out in the morning and back at night. They're just commuters. I don't know hardly any of them. Not like when everybody worked in the mill during the week and went to chapel on a Sunday. And all the kids went to the local school. But you don't want to know any of that'.

Gelsthorpe noticed that the DS had stopped writing.

'It's all very interesting, Mr Gelsthorpe. It gives us lots of local colour, and that's important with a crime like this. We need to build up the fullest picture possible'.

'So, how well did you know Rhys Williams?'

'Well enough. Sang in the choir, worked at the mill, had his Sunday lunch at the pub. Went on holiday to Scarborough, then Cyprus when they got more money and he had his promotions at Riddles'.

'And where did you work, Mr Gelsthorpe?'

'Same'.

'Same?'

'Yup. Riddles. We all did'.

***

This is ridiculous! Some kind of sick joke!

Smith cried out, but there was no reply. He looked around his prison. It felt cold. Large stone flags suggested that it was an old building. He recognised the flooring, so typical of older properties in Holme Hill. His own house was much like it. All those 'dwellings' – as the estate agents called them.

But this cellar was too big for a house. His eyes had grown accustomed to the light and he could see that wherever he was, this room was used for storage. Unopened crates, old furniture, cans of paint and rolls of wallpaper; a doll's house and a child's pram.

Could he still be in the chapel? Unlikely, for as far as he could remember there were no rooms like this at Salem. In any case, even the lower floor, where there had once been a school hall and classrooms off to either side, had windows.

No, it was not Salem, and there was no light.

Smith heard dripping. He could not see well enough to tell where the sound came from, but the regularity of the rhythm began to irritate him. He tried to shut it out of his mind by concentrating on other sounds and smells; anything that would help him to find out where he was.

He noticed a hum. He had heard that sound before: the sound of an electricity meter. So, somebody was using something electrical – light, heater, cooker – a house.

Smith heard a door being unlocked. At the far end of his prison cell a crack and then a shaft of light cut through the darkness. But only for a moment, for a silhouette appeared in the door frame and then just as quickly disappeared as the door slammed shut. Once again, there was nothing, apart from a dripping tap and a whirring meter.

'Do you know why you are here?'

Smith was startled by the strangest voice that he had ever heard. It could have been that of an alien.

'Who are you? Is this some sick kind of joke? I'm an old man. I can't take this kind of stress. I have a heart condition. I need my tablets'.

'Do you know why you are here, Peter?'

Smith could see the alien advancing toward him. He had always prided himself on his eyesight – near enough 20/20 vision, even in his 70s. But he couldn't believe what he saw now. The figure was dressed in black, with what looked like a World War II gas mask over the face.

Some kind of voice distortion mechanism! That's why the voice sounds odd; it's being filtered through that mask!

'Of course I bloody don't know why I am here!'

'Then sit back, Peter, because I want you to spend the last night of your life repenting of your sins'.

***

'So how did you get on with Gelsthorpe?'

'Nowhere, sir. He wasn't exactly the most cooperative witness I have ever interviewed'.

'How's that, Viv?'

Trubshaw looked at her DCI and wondered if he was making sure that the two of them had no time on their own together. *We need to resolve all this Don. One way or another. But you know how I feel, and you know what I want to see happen.*

'The only time he opened up was when he started reminiscing about Salem and the choir'.

'Chapel meant a lot to people of his generation – my Dad lived his around that chapel. Another week and it will be gutted and turned into luxury flats. Do we know who is buying it?'

'Rodney Halliday Enterprises'.

'That was excellent timing, Charlie. Where have you been?'

'Collating all the door-to-door reports, Viv. Nobody reported anything unusual on 1 May. Most people were at work. No witnesses on passing trains or people walking through the cricket ground – not that there were many of those – Gelsthorpe has warned people off going that way so often that people are scared. It is technically private land anyway. Used to be owned by Salem Chapel and then the cricket club bought it. And not that many use the scenic way to get over the other side. The path is overgrown and unsafe. In any case, most drive to and from the railway station and the pub these days. Would you believe it, as far as I can see, the only place that has a really clear view of the cricket pitch is *High Windows*, and even then Gordon and Elsie can't see what's going on immediately beneath the wall on the other side of the road'.

'Thanks for the update, Charlie. Add what you need to the murder wall and then let's see if anything emerges as we talk. Time for more coffee, I think!'

'I'll go, sir. The usual?'

'As always, Viv'.

DS Trubshaw gathered up the coffee mugs and made for the machine in the outer office. As she did so, she remembered something Gelsthorpe had said.

'Sir, I forgot to mention. Gelsthorpe and Williams both worked at Riddles'.

'That doesn't surprise me, Viv, it was the staple industry for miles around. After you left school you just walked down the hill and went through the factory gates – for a life of toil in the mill'.

'I know, sir. But he gave the impression that the two of them did not get on. Gelsthorpe said he wished he had never known Williams and wanted to forget all about Riddles'.

'Interesting. And they both went to Salem, didn't they?'

'They did indeed, sir. But apparently for the last couple of years they have never spoken, and Gelsthorpe wouldn't say why'.

'Did Gelsthorpe tell you that, Viv?'

'No, Elsie Wright did'.

***

'Are you alright, Gordon?'

'What... oh, yes, Sally, fine'.

'You've been on another planet today, Gordon. Very wistful if I may say so'.

'Have I?'

Wright smiled, looking across at his colleague.

'Oh, just a lot on my mind. My mother, and the murder in the village, and...'

Sally peered in between the box files that formed half a partition between their two desks.

'And?'

'Nothing, Sally. This murder has been very unsettling. Mother hasn't stopped talking about it. She knew the victim – man and boy, as they say. I even think that they went to primary school together. She never liked him much, though. Not that my mother is a suspect!

Now there's a thought, a murderer for a mother! But she's not going to kill me anymore. Not after last night with Joan. I want to live the rest of my life; not cooped up in that house with that bloody woman! Joan makes me feel so good. And she's so fit and agile. Still goes running every day, she was saying. Horse riding, swimming, fencing, the lot. She's the one for me!

***

The door opened again. It was the same shaft of light, the same silhouette and the same voice. Or was it? Smith felt that

48

the sound was lower; a different filter, presumably. *Why am I thinking about voice filters at a time like this? After what that thing has said to me? Is there no compassion? No mercy? What have I done wrong, can I not be forgiven? It was all such a long time ago!*

'Now then, Peter. Are you ready? Are you prepared? Any last words?'

Smith began to sing as the blade came down over his head.

Awake my soul, and with the sun...

8

May 4, Afternoon: Back to 1976; a Warm Welcome; Final Preparations for an Organist

'They were bad times'.

Ted Gelsthorpe sighed as he spoke to his wife in the chair opposite. He sat back and looked at the fire. The paper was burning well, and the kindling was alight. He reached over and threw a few small logs from the back garden into the stove and closed the door.

'What do you make of it all, Liz?' It's a rum do an' all, as Dad would have said!'

Gelsthorpe laughed as he remembered his father's broad Yorkshire accent. He looked across at the armchair where his wife used to sit and do her knitting. *If only she were still alive. He could have coped with all this! She would have told him what to do!*

He stared out of the window and across the cricket pitch. He lit his pipe and drew deeply on it. Liz had always loved the aroma, even though she complained about the way it yellowed the wallpaper and the linen. And she always turned up her nose at the morning-after smell.

Gelsthorpe inspected the cricket pitch from his vantage point. Nothing: no movement; no dog walkers; no joggers; no children playing. It was that time of day. Everybody at work or in school; or in the care home. That's what would come next. He already thought he had started with Alzheimer's. He tried not to think about that; about losing his mind; about nothing being up there; not being able to think or understand or feel. It was time to sort things out once and for all.

I was the last person to see her alive. Apart from the murderer, that is. How old would she be now? 1976 – she was thirteen then – it's 2019 now. Goodness, she would have been 56! 56 years old! She would have been married, with children. I bet she would have been a highflier as well, off to university and more. She could have gone to Cambridge, I bet. Her parents would have loved that. Arnold and Daisy were so proud of her! How they cried at her funeral! And I had gone to their burials within six months! What a waste!

It had been good to hear the organ one last time. Gelsthorpe wiped away a tear. He thought how Peter Smith could play 'like nobody's business'.

'You would have enjoyed it, Liz'.

Gelsthorpe turned back to the empty chair.

'I wish I hadn't asked him, hadn't asked Smith. And I should never have gone for drinks with Williams. I thought all that was in the past. You were right, Williams was evil – pure evil you said'.

He went across to their wedding day photograph, wiped away the dust with his fingers and drew around his wife's image.

'Those were the days. Before I started at Riddles. Before I got involved with Williams. And then Peter Smith as well'.

The phone rang. Gelsthorpe went into the kitchen, waited, and then, after several rings, picked up the receiver slowly. He said nothing but waited for the caller to announce themselves.

'Oh, it's you', Gelsthorpe sighed. 'I wondered when you would call. I am surprised you didn't ring sooner'.

***

Don May always let Charlie Riggs drive him when the two of them were in the car together. Viv had looked askance at the DCI when he had asked her to stay behind and research the Hargreaves killing of 1976. *Yet another chance gone to talk to you on your own!* Her eyes had said it all. But May couldn't cope with his feelings for Viv at the moment. Not with a murder enquiry going on. That was what he kept telling himself. And Freddie and Caz needed him – more than ever.

Riggs eased the BMW down into Holme Hill past *High Windows* and the terrace houses where Rhys Williams had lived, alongside the cricket pitch and into The Bargeman's car park. May thought back to his own early years in the village. His father had never been inside that public house – or any pub for that matter. As a good Methodist he had foresworn drink and told his children that they must do likewise. Donald May had been sixteen when he first touched alcohol and got very drunk in the process. His mother thought that he had been Mickey Finn-ed. He had tried to stay upright and talk coherently, but within minutes of eating – or rather trying to eat – his supper, he had thrown it all up. It was the first time that he saw his father cry. He did not see that again until his mother's funeral.

May got out of the car and headed towards the pub as Riggs gathered his file and notebook and locked the BMW. Riggs noticed that the boss always buttoned up his suit jacket at times like this, as if putting on a suit of armour before going into battle.

Linda Welch was at the door, waiting to greet them.

'Good afternoon, Inspector, Detective Constable'. The landlord nodded to Riggs but her eyes were on May from the start.

'We're just about to close for the afternoon, but there is some good pub grub left if you are interested!'

May smiled. Riggs was about to ask what was still on the menu when he thought better of it, knowing what the DCI's answer was going to be'.

'No thanks, Ms Welch. We've already eaten, though, to be honest, I am not a great one for lunch'.

Riggs snorted to himself. *That man's not a great one for food, period. No wonder he's so thin. I just look at a plate of stuff and I put weight on.* As if to concur. The DC's stomach rumbled audibly.

'A drink, then, gentlemen, or are you going to say, "not while on duty"? Welch laughed.

'Black coffee for me, please, Ms Welch'.

'And white coffee with two sugars for me', Riggs added.

'Of course. And stop this "Ms Welch" business. Linda to you two!'

The two men nodded in acquiescence as they followed the landlady into The Bargeman. A group of geese that lived by the lock tried to follow them inside in the hope of food. Linda shooed them away.

The two policemen sat at a table in the window as their coffees were prepared. Riggs looked across to the cricket field and Ted Gelsthorpe's house. The window rattled as a train went past. May smiled to himself as he knew what Freddie would have said if he had been there. He would have been able to tell what sort of train it was just by the sound, and whether or not it was stopping at the station or was a 'through' to or from Manchester and Leeds.

'Sir, have you noticed that there is a very good view from here, right over to the lock-keeper's cottage and up to *High Windows*? You can see the chapel and the old mill easily enough as well'.

'Indeed, Charlie, that's one of the reasons why we are here'.

The coffees arrived.

'There we are gentlemen, and just in case you were a little peckish, here are some biscuits. I made them myself this morning'.

Linda smiled at Riggs as she spoke. May noticed the upturn of her accent at the end of the sentence.

'So how long were you in Australia, Linda?'

'Oh, goodness, a very, very, long time', she laughed.

The Bargeman's owner went slightly pink as she tried to remember, counting back the years.

'It must be forty years now, give or take...'

'And why come back here, Linda?'

Riggs glanced out of the window as he spoke. It had started to rain.

'I went to Sydney on holiday a couple of years back. I didn't want to come home. Loved the weather, the people, the lifestyle'.

May raised an eyebrow at his Detective Constable. Welch smiled.

'A good question, Detective Constable. In some ways, I don't really know. I guess you can take the girl out of Yorkshire, but not Yorkshire out of the girl'.

May tilted his head as she answered Riggs's question.

'Don't I sound like a Tyke, Detective Inspector?'

'Hardly, Linda. No doubt one of our speech experts would be able to tell. I just about detect a Yorkshire accent in there – the short vowel sounds, I guess!'

'My late husband used to say that if you asked somebody you didn't know to say "bath bun", that would give them away every time!'

The three of them laughed, each wondering what the other would sound like if they attempted the test.

'I am sorry to hear about your husband, Mrs Welch, I mean, Linda', Riggs continued.

'Don't be. We split up a long time ago. He traded me in for a younger model while we were in Oz. I hadn't seen him for years when he died'.

'So why come back here – to Holme Hill, I mean?'

Linda Welch shrugged at May.

'Why not? I am from the West Riding, and I've always wanted to run a pub. The Bargeman was available, so I bought it. It's a free house, which is the way I like it, and I think there's a real potential for a place like this. Let's face it, there are so many pubs that have closed in recent years that if you can offer a good pint and a great meal, I think you are on to a winner. I drove into Hartley the other day and counted 19 – yes, 19 – pubs all closed. And that was on the main road alone'.

May and Riggs both nodded. Neither man could recall when they had last gone out to a pub for an evening drink. It was easier and cheaper to buy in bulk from the supermarket and imbibe at home.

'So, Linda, where were you on the day of the murder?'

'What, May 1st?'

Riggs nodded.

'I was here, I think. Yes, here all day'.

'But the pub was closed, right?'

'Yes. We were having some repairs done, but we opened that evening'.

'And who did the repairs?'

'Butch – Butch Butcher. He's our chef and also the local odd-job man. I try and use people in the village or the valley – even if it costs more. I do the small jobs myself'.

'And you live here on your own, Linda?'

'I do indeed, Detective Chief Inspector. I would have it no other way! I am happy in my own company and in my own space'.

'And you saw nothing, according to the statement that we got from you immediately after the body was discovered?'

'Nothing at all. It's very quiet around here, apart from weekends and in the summer, if the weather is good, we do a lot of trade during school holidays and especially when there is a cricket match on. But May 1st, not really. It warmed up a bit in the evening, but nothing earlier'.

'Any people in the pub in recent weeks that you hadn't seen before?'

'No, nobody that I can recall. As I said, we were closed that lunchtime anyway. You should also ask Joan as she was on duty that evening and had been all the previous week. She's just sorting things out in the cellar'.

'And you saw the victim, Rhys Williams, in the pub from time to time?'

'Yes, he normally drank alone, and never spoke to hardly anybody. But just recently he had been meeting up with Ted Gelsthorpe. Strange, when rumour has it that they can't stand each other'.

'Do you know why they didn't get on, or why they were now meeting up?'

'They both worked at Riddles, I am told. Perhaps they were trying to reconcile their differences while they still had time. Or settling old scores. One or the other'.

***

Peter Smith died almost immediately after the blow was delivered. There was a good deal more blood than expected, and the scene of the murder took almost three hours to clean. Once that was done and the body made presentable, the task began of ensuring that the old chapel organist was properly dressed and ready for transport to his final resting place – and what a fitting place it would be! But the body was heavier than that of Williams. Some assistance would be required...

9

May 4, Evening: A Holidaymaker Returns; Playing Trains; a Slow Evening Reviewed

'I don't think I'll be going again. I love the sun and the sea, but I could do without the hassle of the airport and the flight. All that queueing up. And then we were delayed by four hours coming back'.

The taxi driver nodded. Harry Metcalfe was not sure if he had heard or understood; or perhaps he just didn't care to listen to his fare's moaning.

'Anyway, how much is that?'

'Forty pounds'.

Metcalfe shrugged. *Not bad, to say they had to come all the way to Leeds/Bradford Airport to pick me up.*

'Here's fifty. Keep the change'. *I can afford it. I bet he won't ever get a pension anything like the one I've had for the last thirty-odd years.*

The driver became more energetic than Metcalfe had seen him since the greeting by the pick-up point outside the airport. His chauffeur even insisted on carrying his cases up the steps to the front door of the house, waiting until the front door was unlocked so that he could take them over the threshold.

'Thank you, that will be fine. I can manage from here'.

Metcalfe smiled, relieved that he had not had the bother of lugging his cases from the car. And he was happy to be home, as he closed the door behind him, picked up the post and the newspaper and went into the living room.

How many years have I been going to Cyprus now? When did Maeve die? Crickey, I have been going since 1999! But I'm too old. This was the last time. And I felt lonely. Three weeks out there, and nobody to share it with. It never felt like that before. But it did this April.

Metcalfe made himself a cup of tea; used the best china that his wife had been so proud of. It always made him think of Maeve. *Why ever did she marry me? She never really liked it in Yorkshire. She was a Belfast girl through and through.*

The tea tasted good. He had missed it in Paphos. But he had enjoyed the vino and the food. *No wonder my trousers are tight!*

The post all looked boring. Metcalfe decided that the mail could wait until the morning. As could the unpacking. The village laundry would be open in the morning. He could drive down and drop it all off, along with the dry cleaning that would need doing. Thank God he didn't have to do his own washing and ironing! Lightning Cleaners had kept Harry Metcalfe clean and clear for ten years now. He let the paper drop onto the floor by the side of his favourite armchair.

He switched on the television with the remote, looking at the picture of him and Maeve on their silver wedding anniversary.

He had put it there on top of the screen to remind him of how happy he had once been and as a caution about getting involved with anybody else. 'I won't mind, love, if you want to be with someone else after I'm gone, but don't rush into things. Take your time; get to know them, and just be friends, at least for a while. Remember John Tomlinson. He should never have married Mary six months after Hettie died. He lived to regret it big time!' *I know my love. But I have stayed loyal to you these twenty years. Always have and always will!*

'The Metropolitan Police says that the National Security Council leak about Huawei "did not amount to a criminal offence"'. Defence Secretary Gavin Williamson, who was sacked after allegedly making the leak, was unavailable for comment, as was his replacement, Penny Mordaunt'.

Metcalfe felt like throwing his empty cup at the television but thought better of it and grabbed the remote instead.

'Should be sacked, the whole bloody lot of 'em'.

Having finished his rant, Harry Metcalfe realised how quiet it was. Absolute silence. Now he remembered why he had gone away. Why he was always trying to go away. *Phone calls! I wonder if there have been any phone calls!*

Metcalfe went over to the telephone table by the front window. As he picked up the receiver to dial 1571, he looked out down Highgate Street. It was remarkably quiet for a Saturday evening. Was there a big match on television?

'BT call minder: you've two new messages'.

Metcalfe pressed '1' to listen. He recognised the voice on the first message'.

'We need to talk – and talk soon. Ring me back as soon as you get this. You **must**'.

Metcalfe was puzzled. What was so urgent? He pressed to retrieve the second message. This time he did not recognise the voice, because the voice was unrecognisable.

'Do you remember 1976, Harry? May 1st, 1976? I do. And I will be jogging your memory very soon now'.

Metcalfe put down the receiver. He felt sick. Then he saw the front page of the *Hartley Observer* lying on the floor where it had landed. He ran to the downstairs toilet and vomited'.

***

OK, Fred. What's the plan?'

Freddie May smiled at his father as the two of them pulled down the loft ladder and clambered up to where the half-built model railway was located. It was a warm evening, so Dad opened the window. As he did so, a train rattled past.

'That will be the 18.17 from Leeds, Daddy. It gets into Hartley at 18.52, or it should do, but it is two minutes late'.

Freddie May looked up at the replica station clock that his parents had bought him for his birthday, and tut-tutted at Northern Rail's failing, pointing out to his father that if a train arrived at a station less than three minutes after the stated arrival time, then it did not count as being late, unlike in Japan, when 30 seconds was the equivalent.

Don May smiled at his son. *Where does he get all this from? Why is he like this? Why us? He tries my patience at times, but I love him when he comes out with this stuff about trains. How could he possibly know the whole of the railway timetable off by heart?*

Freddie had begun running the model trains. Always to a fixed timetable. And once the sequence had started, it had to be finished. Otherwise, there would be an almighty tantrum and Freddie would not calm down for days. May felt guilty at the thought of being away so much and Caz doing all the schooling from home. No wonder she always looked so frazzled and said all those caustic things to him! *All the more reason not to have another child! What if we have another Freddie? And I am too busy to play my part? In any case, I am in love with someone else! I have been since I first met her three years ago.*

May tried to focus on his son and his model railways He had to admire Freddie for all the work that he had done himself on the layout.

'Look at the engineering works on this section, Dad. What do you think of it? It's just like what they are doing at Holme Hill'.

'What are they doing at Holme Hill, Fred?'

'A new car park and station lighting. They've already installed self-service ticket machines'.

'So there would be extra workmen about, around the station and the exits and entrances?'

'Of course there would. And diggers and machines. And the trains would have to go slowly past where they were working'.

Did we interview those workmen? Could they have seen anything? Did we even know that they were working at Holme Hill?

May's mobile rang. Much to Caz's annoyance, he always carried it around with him, even now, on a Saturday evening, playing trains with his son in their loft.

'We need to talk, sir'.

It was Vivienne Trubshaw.

'I think we may have a lead'.

'So do I', replied May.

***

'Well, that was hardly worth it, Linda!'

Linda Welch nodded back at Joan Wilberforce and laughed.

'Worst Saturday night since I took over six months ago'.

'I think it's the murder. It's unsettling people. Folks don't want to go out when they think they might end up being murdered. Found floating face down in the lock with their throat cut, perhaps'.

'Surely not, Joan'. The two women looked at each other.

'Let's leave the rest till the morning'.

Linda nodded at her colleague. The door to the kitchen opened.

'Well, I'm off home'.

'OK, Butch, see you tomorrow morning'.

Linda smiled at her cook; he smiled wearily back.

'I don't like being bored. I want to be busy; run off my feet'.

'You will be, Butch. Holme Hill will get over it. They will be fighting to get in to have one of your famous steak pies before you know it!'

Linda Welch tried to reassure 'Butch' Butcher, but he seemed less than convinced.

'I'll be in about 10.30, if that's OK. That should be enough time to get the kitchen up and running'. Butch sneezed as he spoke.

'Bless you, Butch', said Linda, worried that her star attraction might go off sick just when she needed to drum up business.

'I'm fine, Linda. Just dust or something'.

Joan Wilberforce snorted. *Dust when I have just been cleaning everywhere?*

'That'll be fine, Butch'.

'You off fencing first thing?' asked the cook as he opened the front door.

'Indeed. We both are'.

Welch and Wilberforce looked at each other in anticipation.

10

May 5, Morning: 'On Sundays I Take My Rest...'

―――――∞――――――

She wondered why. Here she was, outside his house. It was the first time: the first time in three years.

Vivienne Trubshaw remembered January 5th, 2016, as she reported in to Hartley CID and her new senior officer. It was not the most auspicious start to a relationship. She had spilt coffee over DCI May as she walked around the corner from the cafeteria. *It was his fault not mine! He wasn't looking where he was going! Nose in a file, as per.* But she took the blame. Her blouse – and his shirt – were both ruined. Fortunately for him, he had a spare shirt in his office. She was less fortunate; people looked slyly at her all day, smirking as they saw the dark grey stain across her front.

But things had got better. Donald May had been a good boss. Still was on his good days. He had trained her, mentored her, supported her, given her every opportunity to grow in the job. And now she had passed her inspector's exams with distinction and had just been offered another job, over in Lancashire. After the jokes in the office about 'going over to the dark side', everybody had been delighted that one of their own was being promoted. May had said how it reflected well on all the team when he announced the news to the assembled office. But there had been a note of regret in his voice as he said it.

And then the one-night stand at the Hull Conference. It had seemed the most natural thing in the world. They had been the last drink in the bar; she had invited him for back for a coffee; they had ended up sitting on the edge of the bed; he put his hand on hers; they had kissed.

It had seemed the most natural thing in the world.

And now she was outside his house. On a Sunday morning in May. They had hardly spoken since Hull. But she was in the area, and this was an opportunity to brief her DCI on developments overnight that couldn't wait until Monday. Or that's what Vivienne Trubshaw told herself.

***

'This is where they used to do it?'

Joan Wilberforce laughed. She had not had so much fun in years. And had got to go fencing again! Just like the old days. And now she and her new boss were back at The Bargeman. She looked across at Linda, and then around the 'upper room', as it had been known for decades. It looked as if it had not been cleaned for an age as well. The window frame was rotten; wallpaper was peeling off the walls; the floorboards creaked unsafely. Old and broken tables and chairs littered the place.

Joan went over to the corner by the small bar. She opened the piano lid and played a few chords. She was no musician, but even she could tell that the instrument was out of tune. Some of the notes gave out a metallic sound. One black key disintegrated in her hand.

'This will have to go, Linda. It's seen better days!'

'Just like everything else in The Bargeman'.

Linda Welch was too busy looking out of the window across to the lock to notice Joan opening the piano stool and rifling through the music. She sneezed uncontrollably as the scores fell apart in tatters.

Linda turned around and smiled at her colleague.

'I thought you had asthma'.

'I do, Linda'.

'Then what the hell are you doing with that dusty old stuff? It'll play havoc with your breathing. I should know, I've had to suffer it for long enough'.

'That explains all your coughing! I thought it was the cigarettes!'

Joan laughed and walked over to join Linda. Holme Hill was its usual peaceful self. Two narrow boats were moored just beyond the lock, the occupants no doubt waiting for the pub to open. Linda noticed how one of the boats had been damaged at its bow. Tourists who had never been on any kind of boat before, no doubt. It was only two weeks since one lot had got their boat stuck on the lock's cill. That nearly ended in disaster, though it had meant more business, given that no other boats could get through for a week and boaters passed their time in the pub. It had been the best takings since The Bargeman had re-opened.

Ted Gelsthorpe was out yet again, mowing the cricket square ready for the match that would start shortly: Holme Hill Second Team versus Mytholmroyd Seconds, according to the poster in the pub entrance.

The two women turned back inside as Gelsthorpe realised they were looking at him. He had stopped the mower, taken his pipe from his mouth, doffed his cap and nodded to them. Linda and Joan had feigned indifference.

Joan nudged Linda.

'Look up there'.

All around the room, between the ceiling and the picture rail, were paintings of lyres, harps, pan pipes, oboes, clarinets, a cello, a bassoon, all interlaced with musical quotations. Joan had no idea what they were, but Linda could read music – at least a little.

'Barber of Seville; Nabucco; Messiah... all the old warhorses. Yes, this is where they did it, alright. The Select Seven. Some selection!'

'And their followers', added Joan.

The two women paused, then turned back to the window. Gordon Wright could be seen in the distance, walking his mother's poodle. Linda mused on how Joan's admirer was going to help her implement her plans.

***

Harry Metcalfe had recovered from his 'travel sickness' (as described to his next-door neighbour) and just eaten a light breakfast when he heard a lawn mower in the distance. There was no need to look out of the front room window: the cricket pitch was being prepared for a match. Gelsthorpe was as regular as the proverbial clockwork.

But that meant that he would need to set off shortly for his meeting, as arranged the previous evening. He was not looking forward to it for sure. He felt nauseous again, but a swig of tea calmed him sufficiently for him to take his three blood pressure tablets. He stood up, went over to the fireplace, and made sure that his tie was straight, his waistcoat properly buttoned, and his hair combed back into place. The parting, as ever, was immaculate. It was as if the line that divided the head had been measured out by a ruler.

Harry Metcalfe smiled and sang a tuneless melody in a grumbling bass voice. The doorbell rang. He donned his jacket, picked up his walking stick from the hat stand in the hallway and went out to meet his taxi.

'It'll probably be nothing', he murmured to himself.

Little did he know what was in store for him. It was much worse than nothing.

***

Vivienne Trubshaw had just about decided that her news could wait until Monday when there was a tap at her car window.

But it was not who she thought it would be.

'Hello, I'm Freddie. Who are you?'

'Hello, Freddie. I'm Detective Sergeant Trubshaw. I have come to have a quick word with your Daddy. Is he at home?'

'Yes. Do you know that your car registration number is almost a palindrome?'

'A what?'

'A palindrome. It means...'

'That's OK, Freddie. I am sure that DS Trubshaw doesn't need a long explanation of what a palindrome is'.

'Morning, Sir'.

Vivienne Trubshaw got out of the car quickly, realising that she had left it far too late to escape. May must have seen her talking to Freddie.

'I'm sorry. I was just driving past to the supermarket and I thought I would call in with the information that I mentioned to you'.

May took a long time to reply. Then he spoke.

'Come in for a coffee. The kettle's just boiled. What's the break you want to tell me about?'

'I think there's an Australian connection, sir'.

'A message from Oz, DS Trubshaw?'

11

May 5: Three Sunday Lunches

—⌁—

'Why don't you stay for lunch?'

'That's very kind of you, Mrs May, but I only called in to share some new intelligence with your husband'.

'Call me Catherine or Caz; everyone calls me Caz. Come on, there's plenty to go round. My mother was supposed to be coming today but she'd forgotten about her lunch with us and accepted an invite out to lunch with one of her old school friends. They'll just be sitting down to their Sunday roast at The Bargeman round about now.

Vivienne looked over at her DCI for all sorts of reasons. Don had never talked about his mother-in-law; but that meant nothing, given that DS Trubshaw knew so little about her boss's family life.

'And Freddie will welcome having somebody else to talk to. We all will'.

Trubshaw looked at Catherine May. She and Don must be about the same age. Strangely, she was taller than her husband, something the DS always found odd, given that she had always been shorter than the men in her life. Until now that is. Caz reminded her of so many women who had given up their careers to become home-makers, as the Americans used to call it. She was pretty in a chubby kind of way, but her dress sense left something to be desired. The DCI's wife had such sad eyes, and the grey hair made her look old, especially when you looked at her husband's jet-black locks.

'Do you like working for my Dad, DS Trubshaw?'

Freddie appeared, carrying one of his model railway engines.

'This one is G gauge. G stands for Garden. Come, I can show you the railway we have in the back'.

'Later perhaps, Freddie. DS Trubshaw and I need to talk now'.

Caz took the hint and ushered Freddie out of the lounge. DS Trubshaw smelt the Sunday lunch as the door closed behind them. *Tempting to say yes, but far too awkward, especially now...*

'At last, we're alone together'.

'What?'

'At last, we have an opportunity to discuss the case together, sir'.

Donald May did not often blush, but he was bright pink now.

'I was surprised to see you here this morning, Viv'.

The two of them were on opposite sides of the room. May was sprawled in what Viv took to be his favourite armchair, complete with reading table at the side, while she sat politely on the settee. Neither of the Mays had especially good dress sense, Trubshaw thought, but someone has an eye for décor. *I could take their advice when I move into my new place in Lancashire.*

'We need to talk, Viv, I know. And I know that I have been avoiding you. But not now; not here. Let's find a time tomorrow – after work perhaps?'

Trubshaw nodded.

'I was surprised to find you at home, sir, then I realised that you had told us you weren't preaching this morning, and I was driving nearby, so I thought I would call in. I'm not sure why I did it, really. It's not something I make a habit of. In fact, I've never done it before with any of my commanding officers'.

May smiled ruefully at the *double entendre.* Now it was Vivienne Trubshaw's turn to go red.

'No. I'm not preaching at the moment, Viv. I have decided to take a break from it. I need to think through how I feel about the Methodist Church; and about religion in general'.

Trubshaw could see how sad her DCI was. *He has lost his faith. I can tell! Just like my parents did when my sister died. How they shouted out about God and His not caring. How my Mum cried out in church. She was only 19 when she died, for Christ's sake! Skin and bone when she finally said goodbye. We could only recognise her by her voice, she was so thin.*

'Come on, Viv. Let's talk business. What have you got for me? You said something about Australia?'

'Yes, that's right, sir. Well, I have been researching the backgrounds of Williams and his close connections. No remaining relatives – nobody local, no next of kin to inform. He was connected to Salem Chapel, as you already know'.

'I remember him vaguely; from the days when my Dad was the leading light there. But I was only a lad'. May nodded.

'And he worked at Riddles'.

'Yes, Viv. Tell me something I don't know...'

'Well, sir, they all did'.

'All?'

'There were seven of them. They were a singing group. They called themselves The Select Seven'.

'I know. They were a cross between a Barber Shop Group and a Glee Club. They sang for pleasure and they performed for charity. I was looking at a picture of them in The Bargeman the other night; in 'Memory Lane' corner. Even my Dad was in the picture! So? Everybody worked at Riddles in those days unless you went off to grammar school and then university'. Like I did. The only one from the village primary in my year to go to Hartley Grammar. The first in my family to go to university. It would be natural to sing together. There's still a great choral tradition in the north of England, especially in God's Own Country'.

'OK, sir, I accept what you are saying. But I have been following up on what happened to them, just to see if there was any other connection'.

'And?'

'Well, Williams is not the first one of them to die in suspicious circumstances'.

'No?'

'Thomas Hodgson was another of their number'.

'I don't recall him'.

You probably wouldn't, sir; he emigrated to Australia back in 1977'.

'So did a lot of people when the textile industries collapsed'.

'But not everybody committed suicide'.

'Committed suicide, Viv?'

'Well, it was an open verdict. Supposedly drowned, but no note and, according to his friends and co-workers, no reason to take his own life'.

'OK. Let's take it further'.

'But there's more, sir. You remember when Linda Welch was talking to us about her life 'down under' when we were having a drink the other evening?'

'Yes, I do. She said that she had been out there for most of her adult life'.

'Well, sir, at the time Hodgson died, Linda Welch was running a beach bar just yards from where his body was found'.

***

The taxi had taken so long to get to Micklethwaite Hall that Harry Metcalfe wondered if the man had done it deliberately to increase the fare. It was certainly more than he had paid the previous time. He had hoped never to come here again. But the telephone call had meant a second (and last?) visit inevitable.

'Thank you, sir'.

Metcalfe smiled lamely at his driver and decided to wait for his change.

'I'd like a receipt, please', he said curtly.

'Don't have receipt book, sir'.

'Very well, leave it'. Metcalfe grimaced.

'Thank you, sir. Have a good day, sir'.

Metcalfe snorted. That was the last thing that he was going to do.

He walked through the front doors of the Hall and into the reception area. The fresh coat of paint masked – but did not obliterate – the smell of urine: urine and cabbage. It reminded Metcalfe of his boarding school. *How I hated that place! Hartley Grammar for the Sixth Form was like Paradise after that!*

Metcalfe rang the bell; twice. Eventually a woman that he would have described as 'matronly' came out of the back office and greeted him with a beaming smile.

'I'm here to see the Reverend Graham Dooley. He should be expecting me'.

'And your name, sir?'

'My name? My name is Harry Metcalfe'.

'Thank you, sir. My Dad was called Henry'.

'And I am called Harry. Always was; that's what I was christened'.

'Ah, right, sir'.

'If you just take a seat, I will get one of the nurses to see to him. He'll be in the main lounge at the back of the house, I imagine'.

Metcalfe sat down on the leather settee set against the wall opposite the reception desk. He looked at the high ceiling, complete with paintings of gods and goddesses, attended by cherubs and satyrs, all naked apart from the occasional strategically placed drape. On a table by the settee was a book rack that advertised David Tomlinson's *History of Micklethwaite Hall, from the Sixteenth to the Twentieth Centuries*. A new edition was needed, thought Metcalfe, though there would not be much to add since the place became a nursing home. *Come on! Come on! I want to get this over with! Where's this bloody nurse?*

The nurse arrived.

'Mr Metcalfe?'

Metcalfe nodded, grudgingly.

'I will take you to Mr Dooley. Though I should warn you, he is not having a good day today. He has good days and bad days.

But then I expect you know that. Though I don't recall seeing you here before. Friend or relative?'

'Neither'.

The nurse drew breath.

'Er, well, sort of a friend, but not really. He was the Minister at our local Methodist Church. Salem Chapel in Holme Hill. But that was a very long time ago. And the place has been closed for at least a decade'.

'I forgot to say, Mr Metcalfe, Mr Dooley will still be having his lunch. Will you want something to eat?'

Harry Metcalfe remembered the last time he had been. It was lunchtime then. Like feeding time at the zoo, and worse.

'No, thank you. I will eat later, if I am hungry'.

Metcalfe thought he was going to be sick then and there. As they entered the lounge, he saw the rows of armchairs located around the walls. A further clump of seats faced out to the gardens and what remained of a large Victorian orangery. Some of the residents were asleep; others stared vacantly; a third group talked either at each other or to imaginary third parties.

The Reverend Graham Dooley still wore a dog collar on Sundays. He was deep in thought, or so it seemed, as the nurse led Metcalfe to his former minister.

'Mr Dooley? Mr Dooley?'

'I am not Mr Dooley. I am the Reverend Graham Dooley, B.D., M.A. And you will address me as Reverend Dooley'.

'That's right, dear, so you are. I will leave you and your visitor to talk now. Enjoy your lunch, dear'.

Lunch arrived just as the nurse left and Metcalfe sat down.

Dooley looked at Metcalfe.

'Do I know you?'

'I think you do, Graham'.

'Eh?'

'You rang me. Said we needed to talk'.

'Did I?'

Dooley turned his back on Metcalfe and started to eat his lunch.

'Graham?'

Dooley turned back to stare at Metcalfe.

'The Reverend Graham Dooley to you'.

'Reverend Dooley, why did you ask me to come here? What do you want with me?'

Dooley put his knife and fork down on his plate and pushed the meal away.

'It is time, Harry. It is time to put right a very grave wrong. You know it. I know it. God knows it'.

***

'That was a lovely meal, Elsie. Thank you! What a kind thought! And what a good old natter we have had. It's so good that The Bargeman has reopened. And the food is excellent'.

Elsie Wright smiled.

'We should do it more often. Why don't we make it a regular event? Once a fortnight, say?'

'Why not, Elsie. I don't have much else to do these days'.

Good. I'll book a table before we go. Oh, and how is your son-in-law getting on?

'What, Donald? Didn't you know? He's in charge of the investigation into Williams's murder'.

12

May 5, Afternoon: A Winning Draw

Vivienne Trubshaw had never understood why people liked cricket. Watching paint dry would be more fun. Mike had tried to educate her; she had gone to watch him play at the local ground in Hull, but likeable as he was, she could not take to the game and had never visited again. Her Dad had been upset when she split up with Mike; perhaps because the two men spent all their time talking about the sport. But then Dad had been a card-carrying Yorkshireman. He had laughed and laughed when she gave him a copy of Don Mosey's *We don't play it for fun.* Not that it told him anything he did not already know about Yorkshire cricket, but it gave him plenty of reminders of what he called the 'glory days' of the county champions – people like Boycott, Close, Illingworth, Trueman. And Mike had joined in.

Then there was the chance to leave Hull and come to Hartley as a DS. Viv had not hesitated to take the opportunity. And three years later she was a different person. Mike had visited to start with, but the encounters got fewer and further apart until one Friday evening he had telephoned so say he wouldn't be coming over. She knew that he must have found someone else – and had been with that someone for at least a few months since the move to Hartley. But he never told her; and Viv never asked. That was it. Work had been all-consuming since then. She had never had any time to meet somebody; Donald May had worked her too hard for that, and she had loved every minute. And now she loved him. And though he hadn't said it in so many words, he was in love with her.

In three months, she would be moving to a new post. Would Don be the new Mike: keeping in touch at first and then gradually fading away as distance made it easier to sever the tie that had so bound them together? Perhaps Don May as friend and lover but not as boss and mentor would be somehow less attractive. Should she not go across the Pennines? Her DCI had said nothing. But then he never would; Don would never ever stand in her way. Career came first and personal relationships second. No, she would go with his blessing and his encouragement to go even higher in due course. Just as he was looking for further advancement.

'Out!'

Trubshaw looked up to see the umpire raise a finger. Mytholmroyd's last batsman had been 'given' LBW. The visiting side had only managed a meagre 112 runs. Not that she knew much about the game, deliberately so after Mike and Dad, but even Vivienne Trubshaw could work out that this was Holme Hill's game to lose.

'What the hell am I doing here?' she said out loud.

'That's a very good question, Detective Sergeant. I would have thought you would have taken Sunday off. Or is this background research for the murder case?'

DS Trubshaw turned around to see who was trying to engage her in conversation.

'Harry Metcalfe. I live in Holme Hill. We've not met, but Linda Welch told me who you were so I thought I would come and introduce myself'.

Metcalfe offered his hand; Trubshaw took it, only for her arm to be gripped as if she were about to begin a wrestling match. Realising he had been overenthusiastic, Metcalfe let go and motioned to the Detective Sergeant to sit back down. She had no objection when Metcalfe asked if he could join her.

The two of them must have seemed to the casual observer like father (or even grandfather) and daughter, out for a Sunday afternoon tea. Metcalfe looked the part, with his panama hat and linen jacket, his tweed waistcoat and his summer trousers, his walking stick, and his English ring. His brogue shoes were just like the ones that William Trubshaw used to wear as part of his Sunday best.

'Are you a fan?'

'Not really, Mr Metcalfe'.

'Call me Harry, please. And I am Harry – christened as such, not as Henry, though when I did professional singing engagements, I was billed as Henry'.

'Very well, Harry'.

'No, I can't stand the game. But I was out for a Sunday drive and the car brought me here. I decided I would look around the area. And then I hadn't eaten since breakfast, and I am told the cricket teas are something to behold here'.

DS Trubshaw nodded towards the tea tent, from which Joan Wilberforce was delivering plated teas, as ordered at the start of the match.

'And here's mine. Have you ordered Harry?'

'Sadly, no. I am off food at the moment. Just got back from holiday abroad. I was fine while I was out there, but the travel doesn't do for my stomach'.

'I'm sorry to hear that, Harry'.

'It always happens. But I shall be as right as rain, as they say, in a day or two'.

'When exactly did you get back from your vacation, Mr Metcalfe – I mean Harry?'

Day before yesterday – er no, yesterday. Evening. The travel has addled my brain, obviously'.

'So have you heard about Mr Williams?'

'I read it in the paper when I got home; and saw it on the late news'.

'And you have lived in Holme Hill for how long?'

'All my adult life. That's my house over there. The right hand one of the two big semis. Not as big as *High Windows* of course, but big enough. Built for one of the factory managers at Riddles when it first opened in the nineteenth century'.

'And did you know the deceased, Harry?'

'Not well, DS Trubshaw. We sang together occasionally, that's all. In the chapel choir and that sort of thing, you know. Nothing else'.

***

'Well, this is one way to make a living, Joan'.

'If you like cricket, it's a hoot. I can take it or leave it'.

'It's a great game. My husband played when I was in Australia. He was thinking of turning professional at one point, but I don't think he was quite good enough. And he knew that.

Then he met *her,* and he became more interested in what he could do off the field than on it'.

'There'll be plenty of offers once you are settled in. I'll bet you'.

'Not interested, my love. Not in a man, anyway. I've had a lifetime of men. No, there are more important things than someone of the opposite sex'.

'Such as?'

'That would be telling'.

Linda laughed.

Joan Wilberforce looked at her boss. How immaculately dressed she was! She was perfectly turned out: just the outfit for a sunny Sunday afternoon; glorious hair, smooth skin (not a wrinkle in sight), precisely manicured nails, divine figure.

'Come on, Joan. We'd better serve the rest of these teas before the second half starts. You know how important it is not to be moving when the bowler is running up to the crease!'

'OK, boss! And we need to get some more kegs sorted once the food is all out'.

Linda Welch nodded back at her aide.

'What are you doing this evening?'

'Serving at The Bargeman, if I remember rightly', she laughed.

'What about afterwards? How about a late snack?'

'Very late by the sound of it! By the way, have you seen that one of those detectives is in the audience. I just served her tea. She's sitting with that Metcalfe man'.

Linda Welch stopped smiling. Biting her lip, she said:

'Perhaps another time, Joan. I've just remembered that there are other things I must do tonight. You know'.

'Of course, Linda. I understand'.

***

To say it was an easy target to reach, Holme Hill Second Eleven were making heavy weather of responding to Mytholmroyd's innings. Four wickets lost for only thirty runs and then three maidens in a row. Slow hand clapping began at one side of the ground and rapidly spread all the way round the oval.

'Why won't they bloody learn?' Ted Gelsthorpe took his pipe out of his mouth and spat onto the ground by the heavy roller. In order to reinforce his disgust at his team's shoddy performance, he kicked the side of the machinery.

The batsmen must have heard him, for the next delivery was hit for a straight six into the community vegetable patch at the far side of the ground. The fielding side ran over to where the ball was last seen. Gelsthorpe assumed that it would be only a matter of moments before it was found, but nobody had any luck. The slow hand clapping started again, but for a different reason this time: the home team's supporters sensed that Holme Hill could win the match from here on.

Still no ball, though. Gelsthorpe decided to join in the search. A number of the younger spectators also helped. But the red, round thing, as Joan Wilberforce suggestively described it to Linda Welch, was nowhere to be found.

Then a young boy – one of the batsman's lads, Gelsthorpe thought – said that he could see the ball stuck in the artificial marsh that had been created at the end of the patch. The groundsman pushed his way through the crowd that had gathered at the scene.

'Come here. I'll get it'.

At which Gelsthorpe took off his jacket, rolled up his sleeve and pushed his hand and arm into the muddy water. A moment later, having felt around for the ball, he pulled out what he thought was the missing item.

'Oh my God. What's this?'

13

May 5, Evening: Gelsthorpe Rants; Wright Is Saved; Two Hands Need an Owner

———⌒⌒———

Linda and Joan were doing a roaring trade in The Bargeman and Butch Butcher was now regretting his previous evening's lament about lack of business. But then, what else do you do with frustrated cricketers and their supporters when the Sunday afternoon match had to be abandoned, especially when Mytholmroyd and Holme Hale teams both thought that they would have won? The umpires had eventually awarded the 'winning draw' and the extra points to 'Royd, much to the home team's disgust. But everyone was now drowning their sorrows in drinks. So much so that Joan had ended up phoning her daughter to come and serve in the bar. Butch just managed to keep pace with the demand for his pub grub.

'It's an ill wind, eh, Joan?'

The two women laughed as Linda stroked Joan's arm.

The talk, of course, was all about what Ted Gelsthorpe had found in the swampy pond. The groundsman had never wanted the community area and the 'ethnic playground', as he sneeringly described it, at the edge of his beloved cricket pitch, but there was nothing he could do about it. The local council owned the land, and they were going to do something with it for the good of the people of Holme Hill. And the 'fancy types' who had moved into the mill apartments had all been in favour, so there had been no point in the locals putting up a fight to keep the land as the old recreation ground. And when the new owners of the mill had agreed to rebuild the cricket pavilion as a token of their support for the local community, Ted Gelsthorpe had suddenly become a lone voice. He remained implacable and would remind himself of his opposition when taking Midge out for a walk of an evening by urinating in the watery monument to big estate companies and touchy-feely tenants, provided, of course, that no-one was looking.

***

But Gelsthorpe would not be walking Midge on the evening of 5 May 2019, as the area had been cordoned off by the police. Having been interviewed by uniformed officers, Gelsthorpe and Midge had gone in a different direction. The canal towpath was a pleasant enough stroll, provided that the 'waccy baccy' brigade were not out in force. There was one boat that had some suspicious folk on it, but Gelsthorpe tried not to look through the window as he walked past. He saw two women smoking. *On speed, most like. I bet they get their stuff from that man who parks his car by the pavilion in the evening, then sets fireworks off. If I could catch him, I would kill the bugger. Pedalling that kind of misery, especially when it's youngsters that he's selling to!*

Gelsthorpe could see the arc lights that the police had set up around the swamp. He had warned them to stay well away from the cricket square, though he had accepted they might have to walk across the outfield; but they would still have to be careful.

It was time to turn back. The lights were coming on all over Holme Hill, even though it was now well into spring. Gelsthorpe looked around at the village: the canal, The Bargeman, Riddles, High Windows, Salem. Light everywhere; including the chapel. Had somebody left a light on? Was it when he and old Smithy had been in there trying to find *The Lost Chord* on the organ?

***

'Gordon? Gordon! Listen to me, Gordon!'

'Yes, mother?'

'What is happening out there?'

'I don't know, mother'.

'Well, go and find out!'

'Yes, mother; with pleasure, mother'.

It was the first opportunity Wright had been given to get away from her. As he put his coat and cap on, he began to wonder where it had all gone wrong. He had won a scholarship to London University, but his mother had persuaded him to accept the place he had been offered at Leeds so that he could stay at home. After all, he was an only child and his mother needed him to help her and his father. It would be wrong of him, selfish even, to go away from home at a difficult time. But Gordon had never found out what the difficult time was. He suspected that his mother and father had realised that they were ill suited long before he became a young man; his parents' time together had always been difficult.

I can never remember a time when they were happy; when they laughed together, when they did things as a couple. I used to look at other families and think: why are my parents not like that? I haven't been a son to her; I have been a substitute for a husband! That's what! And I fell for it; I said I would go to Leeds and not London. Biggest mistake of my life.

88

Wright was now on the canal towpath. His anger and bitterness had made him walk quickly. So quickly that he nearly lost his footing at one point.

'Are you alright? Here, let me help you'.

Gordon had tripped against one of the ropes that secured *Lancashire Lasses* to the side of the canal, just up from the lock.

'I'm fine, thanks. It's my own fault. I wasn't looking where I was going. Had my mind on other things. You know how it is'.

Wright hardly dared look at the two women who were expressing concern for his welfare. Both wore denim dungarees; one had hair shaved at either side with a mullet at the back while the other had rings in nose and mouth as well as several in the ears. Gordon wondered where else they might be. There was a strong smell of weed.

'You look awfully pale. I think you are in shock. Come on, come inside, Abbey will sort you out, won't you, Abbey?'

The accent made Wright think of the higher-ups on *Downton Abbey*. How incongruous!

'Oh no, I couldn't'.

'Oh yes, you could, Mr. My Abbey is a nurse, and if she says you are in shock, you are in shock'.

Gordon had little option but to accept the invitation of help.

'I'm Jaycee, by the way – it's my initials. I'm really called Janet Christine Harrison. And this is my wife, Abbey Harrison'. The woman giggled as she looked across at Abbey.

'Ah, OK. So, you are...'

'Yes, we are. Now come on'.

Wright found himself manhandled onto the narrow boat and sat in a chair by the warm stove. Abbey put another log on the fire.

'You're shivering. Definitely shock. Let's get a cup of tea inside you. And some of my medicine, I think. Let me loosen your tie and put this blanket over you'.

'I'm OK, thanks. I'll do it'.

'Very well. I'll go see to the kettle and the babe. It's about time he had a feed. You sort him out, Abbey'.

Abbey did not hesitate to roll Gordon's trouser legs up and look at the grazing.

'That's nasty. I've got something to help though, and it will stop the infection. You don't mind homeopathic stuff, do you?'

Wright had no time to reply. Jaycee had now returned with a mug of tea and the baby.

'By the way, what's your name?'

Gordon remained silent as he watched Jaycee put the mug down next to his chair, sit down opposite him, undo her shirt, take out a breast and push a nipple into the waiting child's mouth.

'This is Arthur, by the way. He's three months now'.

'Hello, Arthur. I'm Gordon'. *What a stupid thing to say! But how the hell did I get in here and how the hell do I get out?'*

Jaycee smiled.

'There's a good boy'. Arthur belched and broke wind, loudly and satisfyingly.

Gordon looked away and out of the porthole nearest to him, so that he faced the far side of the canal. Beyond the boundary fence, he could see two men talking. He knew them both well. They were gesticulating at each other; then one pushed the other and the first pushed back. He knew enough me-mo to pick up some of what they were saying, even from this distance.

He could at least make out two words:

'You murderer'.

***

'You three took your time getting here'.

Fizz always liked getting one over on May and his team.

'Sorry. I was playing trains with Freddie and my phone was switched off. But I knew that I could leave things in the capable hands of DS Trubshaw'.

Fizz and Charlie Riggs smirked at each other as May spoke.

'What were you doing here, Viv? I can't think you are a cricketing *aficionado'*.

'That's the last thing I am, sir, despite my Dad's best efforts. I actually wanted something to eat. I was starving and when I drove past I saw that they were advertising tea. And it was a good one'.

'Well, what do you expect if you turn down a May Sunday lunch?'

Riggs and Fizz again looked at each other. Trubshaw blushed and May moved on to a different topic.

'So what have we got here, Fizz?'

'Two hands, Detective Chief Inspector. That's what you've got. A man called Gelsthorpe found one hand when he was searching for a cricket ball that had been hit for six into the pond just there. A search was instigated when uniform arrived, and I had cleared it, and a second hand appeared just before you arrived. The search continues and now we have lighting I imagine we can have done it all by morning'.

'What can you tell us?'

'You lot are always so bloody impatient, aren't you?'

'Fizz!'

'Alright, alright. I will know more tomorrow, but I can tell you that the hands were severed *post mortem* and not *ante mortem*. And I know you will want me to say something about the person to whom they belonged. Well, DNA may tell us more, but in the meantime, an older person, possibly a man, probably married at some point – see the paler skin there on the ring finger of the left hand – never done manual work in his life, a clerical job perhaps, given the little bump on the middle finger of his right hand – so right-handed? And you see the bruising here? It looks as though he was restrained – something like handcuffs or chains – before death'.

'How about that for starters?'

14

May 6, Morning: A New Man Makes Decisions; Monday Review at the CID; Lancashire Lasses Has an Angry Caller

Mother would hate it; would hate them. But they're ordinary people – real people – it's a free country! If they want to live together, then fine! I think they rather liked me, as far as they like men. And I liked them. I even got to hold the baby! I WILL like them if I want to!

Gordon Wright had decided to walk the long route along the canal towpath to the railway station. He had been hesitant about taking the short cut since he had found 'the body'. He had only seen one dead person before and that was his father, laid out in his Sunday best in an open coffin in the drawing room (as mother insisted on calling it). Gordon had never seen his father so relaxed.

Finally, away from her; that's why.

Wright chuckled to himself and then slowed down as he saw *Lancashire Lasses.* He determined that he had two decisions to make that morning; neither would be easy, though in his heart of hearts he knew what he should do; but that was not necessarily what he wanted to do: *could-should-will-must.*

The grey-black smoke went straight up from the stove pipe atop the narrow boat. Strange to have a fire going in May, perhaps, though boats like a seventy-footer were cold, and Arthur would need to be kept warm. Gordon had never seen a child breast fed before last night. Initially repulsed, he had begun to realise what a wonderful, earthy, basic thing it was. And it made him happy and sad at the same time. Why was he not a father? A husband? A lover? And then he had looked at Arthur's unfocused eyes as he held him in his arms; had listened to the gurgling; had stroked the soft cheek.

I should have been a Dad! Not all families are as dysfunctional as mine was!

Wright made his first decision and laughed out loud as he did so.

This is the new me: no stopping me, mother!

He opened his briefcase and took out a small bouquet of flowers – flowers that he had gathered that morning from his mother's beloved garden.

How she will hate me for taking them! And, even worse than that, who I am giving them to!

Gordon Wright checked the note that he had written on his business card.

'Thank you for last night, you two. Much appreciated. Best wishes to Arthur!'

He got out his pen and decided to be daring, adding a 'x' to his signature. He stepped on to the back of the boat, hoping that he would not be noticed. He could hear the baby crying; one, or even both, of his mothers were singing to him. This only seemed to make the crying worse. Then he heard footsteps coming towards the deck.

Best that I go. I have a train to catch.

Gordon ran as fast as he could to get away from *Lancashire Lasses* and out of sight of its occupants. They had invited him back anytime for as long as they were moored there, and he might well take them up on the offer. When were they moving on? End of the month, he seemed to remember.

Once under the bridge, around the corner and in sight of the railway station, Wright slowed to his normal brisk walking pace. Cyclists coming the opposite way tinkled their bells to make him move out of their way. He did so grudgingly, shouting after them to remember the towpath code (which he had partly written). One of the cyclists put two fingers up at him, but Wright was too engrossed in looking at the poster on the community noticeboard by the station steps. Pauline Philbey and Wallace Walker were giving a talk on Holme Hill in the 1920s. The poster was dominated by a sepia illustration of Salem Chapel's Sunday School Anniversary. Wright even thought he could see his mother on the front row of children, sitting cross-legged in front of the sullen-faced teachers.

That place has a lot to answer for!

Gordon Wright made his second decision of the day. He would not tell the police about the conversation he had observed the previous evening. Not yet anyway.

***

'Have a good weekend'. Charlie Riggs always said that to everyone in the office on a Friday evening. And he usually did. Make the most of life was the Detective Constable's philosophy.

If you are going to be happy, then you have to work at it. Happiness has to be earned.

And he and Kate were happy, always had been, right from sixth form together. And they always would be. Once they got the children thing sorted out. But it was always the same when her period started: hoping against hope that she wouldn't bleed this time; and when she was late, beginning to think that this time maybe, just maybe, she was pregnant. But it never happened. Always the same disappointment. And Charlie's optimistic words no longer consoled either of them.

But they got on with their lives and Monday 6 May 2019 was no exception, even though Megan Markle was about to give birth to her first child.

Riggs walked into the office, putting on his happy face on top of his detective suit. Hartley Police Station was its usual hive of activity. Though on time (thirty seconds early, in fact) Riggs was the last person to arrive in CID. The DC had once resolved to set up CCTV in the office to see who was first to arrive and last to leave. He had never done so, but he knew who would win every bloody time: Detective Chief Inspector Donald James May.

Charlie admired May. The best on the force in West Yorkshire: and that was a big area, the whole of God's Own Country. The ultimate professional. In the 18 months since he had been with May and Trubshaw, he had learnt so much. The three of them made such a great team.

Riggs thought about May's recent demeanour. The boss had not been his usual self for the last few months. He had become withdrawn, not that he was ever a great talker, and less willing to share his thoughts on cases with his colleagues. Whereas once upon a time he would go for a drink at the Three Bulls around the corner from the station, now he would bid goodnight when the rest of the team left and stay behind to continue working. Riggs had not said anything to Trubshaw about the change, but she must have noticed it as well.

'So where are we on these railwaymen?'

May never started a case conference with pleasantries.

'We have a list of all personnel working at Holme Hill Station that day. I have organised interviews with them starting later this morning. I am not sure how useful it will be though, sir, as the new car park is being built on the far side of the track, away from the cricket ground, so it's unlikely they would have seen – or heard – anything. There are quite a few JCBs on site at the moment'.

'You never know, Charlie. Leave no stone unturned, as my old boss used to say! We will review the statements when we have them – say Wednesday?'

''On it, sir'.

'Now what about our lovely landlady, Linda Welch?'

'I've asked to see her later this morning at The Bargeman. I thought it better to do that instead of asking her here. We don't want her to feel under pressure – at least not at this stage'.

'Agreed, Viv'.

'I assume that you will want to come as well, sir?'

'Yes, please. And I think we might wander around the area, just to get our bearings again in the light of last night's find – finds, in fact'.

'Yes, sir. Shall we leave here at 1030'.

'1030 it is, Viv. I think it's time I renewed my acquaintance with Ted Gelsthorpe as well as talked to the lovely lady landlord'.

May laughed at his own alliteration. No-one else did.

'By the way, sir, it's a boy. Megan Markle has had a boy'.

'Thanks for the update, Charlie. I'm sure we all wanted to know that'.

***

'What do you make of him, Jaycee?'

'What a sad little man he is'!

'I rather liked him'.

'You would. I sometimes wonder about you, Jayce. And these older men. Are you looking for a father figure or something?'

The two women laughed. But then Jaycee turned towards the window and looked out over the cricket field.

My father. If only I could have helped my father. Taken the pain away from him. And mother as well. But she held it all together better than he did. I didn't know what being heartbroken meant until it all happened to us and our world came crashing down.

'He's a mummy's boy!'

'Abbey!'

'Well, he is. Have you seen his mother sitting in the bay window of that big house up there with those binoculars? What does she do all day? She must know everything that goes on in the village. I wouldn't be surprised if she films it as well!'

The two of them laughed as Arthur gurgled. Abbey and Jaycee wondered whose turn it was to change him.

'And wasn't it sweet of him to leave those flowers? They look hand-picked. From her garden, no doubt. And I bet it is *hers*. Have you seen her out there? That's when she's not filming, of course'.

More laughter.

'I don't want Arthur to grow up like that'.

'What utter, utter bollocks, Abbey. There is no way that will happen. I'll make sure of it. *We'll* make sure of it'.

Jaycee kissed her wife full on the lips.

'Come on. Let's get going. We have plans to finish. And I could murder a drink, if nothing else'.

More laughter.

Abbey was about to open the rear cabin doors when there was a tap at the window.

'I want a word with you'.

The man at the window barked much like his dog, though at least the canine was wagging its tail.

'Can I help you?'

The dog jumped onto the narrow boat and put its paws up at Abbey.

'Hello there, fellah! What do you want? You're a real cuddle-monster, aren't you? What's his name?'

'You don't need to know his name!'

'Don't I? Well, I'm Abbey Harrison and this is my wife Jaycee'.

'Well, whatever you are, I want you moving on from here'.

'But why? We have every right to be here!'

'24 hours mooring for visitors. Then you've got to move on'.

'But we have special permission'.

'From who?'

'From the owner of The Bargeman'.

'Well she shouldn't have given you it'.

'And what's your name?'

'Never you two mind. Just be warned. Stay away from here; stay away from my field. We don't want your sort. Or there'll be trouble'.

With that the man and his dog walked across the cricket field.

Abbey and Jaycee looked at each other in disbelief. Arthur gurgled.

15

May 6: A Liquid Lunch Brings a Turn-Up for the Books

———— ᴄᴧᴐ ————

Pauline Philbey poured herself a large gin. The clock had just struck 12 so she felt duly justified. It was a warm day, made cold outdoors by the strong wind. At least the washing would dry, she thought. The village looked peaceful from her house. She had chosen it because here was the highest point in Holme Hill and on a clear day, the view from the front room was second to none. You could even see Lancashire, if you wanted to.

Sinking into her old armchair, she opened up the file of photographs and other documents and began to sift through them. The drink tasted good, especially with not much tonic in it. The choirmaster at St Maurice's had introduced her to Plymouth Gin and how she had taken to it! So smooth that a mixer was not required. But it was only lunchtime, so some dilution was necessary, especially if the old pictures she had been given were to be sorted, catalogued, and added to the archive while she still had a clear head.

The folder was bulging with material. Why should Rhys Williams give it to her just before his death, or rather his murder? Should she give it over to the police? He had told her it was for the photographic archive; had given her a big, padded envelope when she was in the Post Office one day, without explanation, other than telling her that he did not want any of 'the stuff' back.

Pauline had not known Williams well – and not wanted to know him at all: she was church, and he was chapel. She had not liked him in any case. And those were the days when the village was divided between those who had money and those who did not. Williams thought himself a cut above 'the workers', even though he had only been a glorified office clerk at Riddles for most of his life; until he got the part-time job with the inspectorate, that is. He had acted like God Almighty after that. Pauline had stuck it for three months as his secretary and then left Riddles for a job in Hartley.

She took a large swig of her gin to help her forget Williams and his behaviour towards her; towards anybody, for that matter. That man was poison in the village. He seemed to have a hold over people at the chapel and the factory. What did he know about them that meant he could bend them to his will? Pauline smiled to herself as she remembered the rumours of strange antics going on in the village when she first arrived there. Surely the things that were being said could not possibly be true. Wife-swapping in a church choir? *Ridiculous!* Was Williams blackmailing people because they were playing away from home? Surely not! It was almost the 'done thing' in those days, though perhaps not for chapel folk. And Holme Hill wasn't that far from Hebden Bridge; there was lots to talk about there, especially in the 1970s…

Another large swig of gin. *Time for a top up, I think. That's the great thing about gin; only 250 calories a glass. And the tonic is slimline, of course…*

The village archivist hiccupped and then giggled. *That was another lifetime. How Holme Hill has changed in the last 50 years! Riddles was still open; Hartley had a grammar school; there were far fewer cars on the road; the bypass had not been built; and Salem was going strong!* A picture caught Pauline's eye: a forty-strong choir standing on the front steps of the Chapel. And there in the middle of all his admiring women, arms folded and baton in hand, was Peter Smith. *Now there was a ladies' man! Always cracking his* risqué *jokes. There was someone who would have indulged in wife swapping given half a chance.* Then she decided that was unlikely: he was a Methodist, after all.

She giggled again.

'Time for more gin, I think. But I'll go easy on the tonic. Got to think of the calories!'

The cat looked at her in disgust, as if to say: 'stop bloody boozing and feed me!'

The folder seemed bottomless. It was more like a loose document case with pockets in it. She had not observed until now that it had come from Riddles. The pseudo coat of arms on the front and the Latin motto reminded Pauline of her brief employment there. *Labor omnia vincit* – Labour conquers all. Just like Bradford's strapline, she mused. But in the case of Ernest Riddles, founder of the factory, that had meant his employees' labour as much as his own. *The meanest man in Yorkshire – and that was saying something! And his sons were just as bad. No regard for the workforce, right to the end!*

Pauline pulled out the next wodge of material: aerial photographs of the village taken as the new estate was built. The pictures were numbered, in a sequence that showed the progress from holes to houses. Each photograph was carefully dated. There was even the mayor cutting the red ribbon at the main entrance. She noticed how there was a gap in the sequence: no photographs for May.

May 1976! That was not a good month; not a good year all told! Minnie Hargreaves. We all remember her. And what happened.

The folder had more in it: newspaper cuttings – all to do with that fateful day in May, 43 years ago. Again, all were dated; names and comments in each of the reports underlined. One name had a double underlining every time it occurred. *Why them, I wonder?*

That was it. Or so the village archivist thought. As she got up to put the material on the dining table, a small book fell out of the last pocket in the folder. She picked it up from the floor and returned to her seat. Not noticing that the cat was now immediately behind her, she trod on his tail, heard him yowl and saw him scoot of the room and through the backdoor cat flap. She called after Boris to no avail.

'Never mind. He'll be back for tea'.

Back in the armchair, she looked at the pocketbook. It had black covers and a red tape down the spine. She opened it. Even after all these years she recognised the handwriting.

Pauline Philbey began to read.

'Oh my God!' She put her hand to her mouth. 'Now I really do need a drink'.

16

May 6, Afternoon and Evening: Intruders Break into Salem; Philbey Loses a Book; Welch and Gelsthorpe Are Uncooperative

'We've got until tomorrow to sort this out'.

'I know. It wouldn't have been so bad if Gelsthorpe and Smith hadn't been nosing around. We'd have had more time then. What were they bloody doing in here anyway?'

'Playing the organ one last time. You can understand it in a way. All their lives attached to this building. Every Sunday'.

The two intruders walked carefully on tiptoe through the chapel just in case someone else was intent on talking a final look around.

'Anyway. Best get it done. Old Philbey and her crew are down to do a tour on Wednesday'.

'What bloody tour's that?'

'Local history society. She's doing a guided tour of the chapel before the builder starts work. That's if she's sober enough!'

The other figure coughed.

'God, it's dusty in here?'

'Indeed, it is. Come on, you. The deadline will be good for us. After all, what did Dr Johnson say?'

'Dunno. Haven't been to the doctor's in years'.

'No, the great Dr Johnson'.

'Never heard of him'.

'He said – oh never mind what he said. Come on. Where is the equipment and all the other goods?'

'Down in the basement. There's a secret staircase down to the back of the stage where they used to have the plays and stuff. And the Sunday School. I used to go when I was little'.

'You? You went to Sunday School?'

'Yeah, mi mum sent me. I was in one o' them nativity plays'.

'What were you, then? The Virgin Mary?'

'No, I was Joseph'.

'Poor you! I'll never look at you in the same way again'.

'It's not funny. I loved Sunday School'.

The two intruders made their way behind the pulpit. There they found elegant pine panelling, but no obvious entrance to anything. In the middle of the central panel, immediately below the pulpit floor, a large wooden statue of John Wesley looked straight at the two people who were now studying him. The founder of Methodism looked as though he was admonishing them – like every other person who had chosen to inspect the statue – to repent of their sins and turn to Christ. There he stood, pointing accusingly with his right hand, while the left held an open Bible. Underneath his preacher's robe was a long waistcoat, buttoned up to the very top, where his starched, high-necked tabs covered his throat.

One of the intruders went right up to Wesley and pulled on the outstretched arm.

'Just like pulling pints, eh?'

The other intruded guffawed.

'Highly unlikely in a Methodist church, I would have said, unless it was Ribena!'

Wesley's right arm was now down by his side. Then there was a click and the whole panel became a door and the statue a handle. The wood had swollen, and the hinges were rusty, but between them, the two intruders managed to move the panelling to its open position. Behind was a set of narrow steps to an underground room.

The two looked at each other then went carefully down the secret staircase. It was dark. There was no light fitting anywhere. The only sure way of descent was to grab the rope-rail and take the steps one at a time. The intruders did their best, but both ended up stumbling down to the bottom step and crashing into the half open door at the foot of the stairs.

A dingy grey light came through the arched windows with their tattered and torn curtains.

'It was a perfect place to make the stuff. Nobody knew where it was – until last Friday, that is – apart from Williams'.

'A pity about him'.

A very great pity indeed. But he found out too much. It was either us or him. Except I didn't expect it to be done so quickly and – well – like that! It seemed a bit melodramatic somehow. You know, the actual way he died'.

'Don't look at me. I'm just a fetcher and carrier. I don't ask questions. Come on. Let's get this stuff sorted. If we get it ready now, then we can shift it tonight after dark'.

***

Rodney Halliday looked over the plans one more time. This was going to be good; very good. Riddles' Mill had already made him a handsome profit and now it was time for Salem Chapel to pay a nice dividend. He had got the building for a bargain. The Methodist Church authorities had jumped at his offer. After all, what else could you do with a 1,000-seater building? Pull it down? That was not an option because it was grade 1 listed. But then it did look more like a Graeco-Roman temple than a place of worship.

And now it was going to be turned into luxury apartments, starting at £350,000, with the penthouse suite going on sale for £950,000. Halliday laughed to himself. *What a beauty! If only my Dad could see me now! Except he wouldn't approve of where the money was coming from. No sirree!*

Halliday decided it was time for a cigar and a whisky. Barbara had served up a good lunch and what better way to round it off? But she hated smoking and drinking so he would have to have his pleasure on the balcony. What did it matter? It was a warm sunny day and he could look out over his growing property empire. It had been a good decision to move into the penthouse at Riddles. What better way of demonstrating the quality of your work than to buy one of the apartments yourself? Barbara had not been convinced at first, but now they had the place in Spain, a big house in Yorkshire was less important, and she was won over by the time and effort that he had lavished on the furnishings. For a London barrow boy, he had quite an eye. *You've got taste, Halliday. You've got class.*

He looked out over the village. St Maurice's clock was chiming two. The cricket ground was empty after the recent drama that had ended the match with Mytholmroyd, save for the groundsman mowing the square and repainting the white lines. The Bargeman was still busy; it was too good a day not to be drinking outside by the canal. Not that the lunches were anything like as good as Barbara's. Two women were sitting on their narrow boat playing with a baby. A BMW car drove into the pub car park and a man and a woman, dressed very formally and, as far as Rodney Halliday could make out, looking serious.

Not much going on, Halliday thought. But then it was a Monday. Just like any other Monday. He looked over to Salem Chapel and wondered if his last-minute instructions were being carried out correctly.

***

'Archie Harrison Mountbatten-Windsor. That's what they are going to call him'.

Vivienne Trubshaw smirked at Donald May and the DCI nodded in return. Neither of them was much interested in news of the Royal Family, though both were intrigued by the choice. The rest of the occupants of The Bargeman were much taken with the baby's names as they watched the announcement on Sky News.

'We're here to see Linda Welch. Is she available?'

'I'll go get her for you. You are?'

'DS Trubshaw and DCI May'.

'Ah, right. Perhaps you'd better come through, then'.

The barmaid let them behind the bar and into the corridor that ran along to the back of the pub and out towards the courtyard that abutted the end of the lock.

Linda Welch was standing looking down at the water, a cigarette in her hand. She was wearing a black leather skirt and a Breton stripe T-shirt. She turned to greet the two police officers as she heard the crunch of feet on gravel.

'Hello, DCI May, DS Trubshaw. We meet again. What can I do for you? Terrible business about the hand; *hands*, in fact'.

Linda Welch seemed unperturbed by the thought of severed hands.

'Holme Hill is gaining in notoriety. But it's not bad for business. And I need to raise cash to do this place up'.

She looked around the courtyard and up at the roof.

'That lot needs to be replaced for starters'.

'We'd just like to ask you a few questions about your time in Australia'.

'Australia? What's that got to do with anything?' Welch threw her cigarette into the canal and walked past Trubshaw as she spoke.

'Just a few words, please, Linda'.

'Very well. Let's sit down'.

Linda guided May and Trubshaw to the bench that overlooked the lock itself. It had been put there in memory of a local worthy. She had paid to have it restored after the last bout of vandalism.

The three of them sat down, with Welch in the middle.

'You've only recently come back from Australia, Linda. Is that right?' Trubshaw asked, wondering where the T-shirt came from.

'That's right. I told you all that the other day'.

'What did you do when you were out there?'

'In Australia? What do you mean what did I do?'

'What did you do for a living, Linda?'

May took over the questioning.

'Supported my husband most of the time. He became successful; not that it did me any good in the end. He traded me in for a newer model. She was twenty years younger than him'.

'And then what did you do, Linda?'

Welch turned back to look at Trubshaw as the DS asked the question.

'What did I do? Tried to screw him for every penny but didn't manage to. Bummed around for a while, then picked myself up and decided to get on with the rest of my life'.

'And what did you do for a living?' May asked.

'I ran a bar. That's what I did. It was the only think that I could afford with the payoff I eventually got from my ex. Then, when I had saved up enough, I decided to come home and buy this place, such as it is'.

'Does the name Thomas Hodgson mean anything to you, Linda?'

'Thomas Hodgson? Thomas Hodgson? Nothing at all, I am afraid. Should it?'

'We just thought you might have come across Mr Hodgson, given that his body was found near your beach bar; very near, in fact', said Trubshaw.

'And he came from Holme Hill', added May.

Don May looked at Linda Welch. There was silence; not a flicker of emotion on her face.

Then she replied.

'No, nothing. Sorry I can't help you. I must be going now. They'll need me to help clear up after lunch'.

***

Boris was busy with his ablutions. Pauline Philbey watched as her cat stuck one of his legs straight up in the air so that he could get to the more intimate parts of his anatomy. As a result of this repositioning on the windowsill, he looked more like a champagne bottle, with the whiteness of his leg giving a passing imitation of some Bollinger.

The local archivist looked at her grandfather clock as it chimed 3.00 pm. Her head felt hollow, and her mouth was dry.

'I must have dozed off. I shouldn't have had so much to drink'.

As she came round, she remembered what she had been reading. But the little black book was no longer in her hand. She looked down between her legs to see where it must have fallen. But there was nothing. She looked across at the folder that contained Rhys Williams' papers.

'I must have put it back in the folder. It must be there'.

Pauline Philbey rummaged through the cardboard folder. Like the good archivist that she was, she had replaced all the other documents exactly where she had found them, ready for cataloguing by one of her volunteers when she was next in the archive. But there was no sign of the notebook.

By now Boris had decided to stop washing himself. He looked down at his owner accusingly. She looked back at him.

'What have I done with it? It must be here! Things like that don't just disappear'.

But on occasion they do; and this was one of those occasions. Williams' jottings were now safely in someone else's pocket and out of harm's way; at least for now.

***

'I have nothing more to say to the police. I have said everything that I am going to say. If you want to question me again, then I require that my solicitor be present'.

Gelsthorpe was adamant. He had kept May and Trubshaw standing at his doorstep for nearly fifteen minutes but to no avail. He had done talking to the police about Williams, about hands, about anything.

May decided that there was no point in trying to persuade the groundsman to let them in. His father had often said how awkward Gelsthorpe could be, so that was an end of it.

'Very well, Ted'.

'Mr Gelsthorpe to you, young May'.

'Very well, Mr Gelsthorpe. We may be in contact with you again, but we will not bother you further today. I am sorry that we troubled you'.

'Yes, you did. So that's it now'.

The two police officers turned away from Gelsthorpe and back to the BMW. Just as they arrived at the front gate, he shouted after them.

'If you want to make yourselves useful, find Peter Smith. I haven't seen hide nor hair of him since we went into the chapel last week. Nobody has'.

Trubshaw looked at May and May looked at Trubshaw.

17

May 7, Morning: Riddles Begins to Give Up Its Secrets; May and His Team Remain Unconvinced; Dooley Receives Another Visitor

———— ❧ ————

Jo Bishop looked out of the window as she turned on her laptop. She had resisted connecting to the Internet since the previous Friday and her flaming row with Bill. *The ungrateful so-and-so! All that work on those transcriptions and not a word of thanks! That's the last time I do a favour for him!*

And yet, as the machine powered up, she hoped there would be an email from him asking her to do more. She had so enjoyed the research into Riddles's mill and the stories of the workers in particular. And she welcomed the interaction with Bill. He might be a selfish bastard when it came to acknowledging assistance, but Professor William Harker was one hell of an academic. And signing up for that part-time MA in Local History had been one of the best things Jo Bishop had done for a long time. She had to be grateful to him for the way he had guided her towards researching the industrial heritage where she now lived. And as Harker had said, delving into the building's past might help with the dispute over the heating system, especially now that the owner had moved in as her next-door neighbour.

'What if he has used my research in his own work? It doesn't matter. I wanted to do the studying anyway'. Jo looked down at Nib; the cat ignored her.

She surveyed the pile of documents that needed transcribing. The Riddles family had been scrupulous about keeping every piece of paper ever generated in that mill; there were even clocking in documents and carbons of payslips. She looked through the folders that she had created for each decade. She was now up to the early 1940s and World War II had started. Thank goodness she had taken photographs on her phone when she was looking at the bundles in the archive centre in Hartley.

The laptop was now powered up. She logged in to Facebook, like she did every morning. Staring back at her was a picture of a pig-tailed blonde in school uniform; and another; and a third. *It was a hell of a fancy-dress party at* The Bargeman*! That Linda Welch knows how to organise a great bash!* Jo looked through the pictures. *Who were the people in the Darth Vader outfits? It was weird seeing four of them!*

'Come on, Jo, let's get going on these transcriptions. Move yourself!'

She took one last look out of the study window down across the cricket field and over to the canal. There by the pub would have been the place where raw materials were unloaded ready for transfer across to the mill and finished garments packed in their place to go to all parts of the country and abroad. Then when the railway arrived, the distribution system would have changed, and goods carried into and out of the factory via the sidings specially constructed for the purpose. Nothing remained now. That was the area on which the housing estate had been built back in the 1970s. For the last years, no doubt everything was transported by road.

Jo studied the detailed maps of the area, as it had been in the 1930s. There was much that remained the same: mill, pub, chapel, canal. But much had been completely obliterated. She turned her attention to the records of the factory workers. That was the real interest for her: perhaps some of the younger ones might still (just) be alive; or at least their children would be around if they had stayed local and they could remember what life had been like in the mill and the village all those years before.

She turned to the files marked 'employees, 1940-1980'. Not surprisingly, almost three quarters of the people listed were women. *Of course, the men were away at the war. That would account for it. And then, when they came back, the women would have gone back to cooking, washing and child rearing so that the men could have their jobs back!*

She opened up the Excel spreadsheet where she was collating all the details about the workforce, cross-checking it against other records that she had got hold of, whether from the archives or *Ancestry.co.uk*.

'I'll work till eleven and then coffee', she said to herself, 'that's if Nib here lets me. Come on, you'.

That's the thing about cats: what a marvellous knack they have of knowing exactly where to sit so that you can do absolutely nothing!

Jo began work in earnest. The next two hours flew by; more than two hours, in fact. But by the time she realised that she had missed her coffee break and it wouldn't be long before her Skype call with Harker, a clear pattern had emerged on the spreadsheet in front of her, especially when she manipulated the entries into a particular date order.

'Well, I never. Professor Harker will have something to say about this'.

***

'She's lying and he's hiding something'.

DCI May sighed.

'I agree, sir. I can't believe that Linda Welch knew nothing about Hodgson's suicide – if that's what it was. Anything more from Australia yet, Charlie?'

DS Trubshaw turned to her colleague at the conference table, hoping for some answers.

'Nothing whatsoever, Viv. But I will chase them today'.

Riggs winked at Trubshaw, trying to cheer her up. She smiled weakly back at him.

'When you do, Charlie, could you check if Hodgson was living there under another name at any time?'

May nodded in agreement with the Detective Sergeant's request.

'Noted, Viv, but everything I have so far points to him being called Thomas Hodgson from the moment he disembarked to the time he washed up dead, next to Linda Welch's beach bar'.

'There's no reason why she would have known him before they each moved out to Oz, is there? It isn't as if she came from Holme Hill. Yorkshire is a big place!'

Trubshaw noticed May smiling as he spoke. She had known from day one how proud he was of his roots. But then so was she in a way; especially when it came to moving out and up from her two-up, two-down terrace house.

'But then, not to remember somebody who died on your doorstep seems a little strange', the DS replied.

May got up from the conference table and walked over to the murder wall. He surveyed the scene, his arms folded, his foot tapping. Nothing came to him.

'And what about Peter Smith? What was Gelsthorpe saying? He seemed pretty agitated last night'.

'We also have a complaint about Gelsthorpe harassing two women on a barge'.

'They're called narrow boats, Charlie. They are only barges when they carry freight. And I assume these two were either pleasure-cruisers or live-on boaters'.

'The latter, sir. They complained that he had been shouting at them to move their boat. He keeps knocking on their windows and making a nuisance of himself, as well as hurling abuse at them'.

'Interesting. I wonder what they have done to make him behave like that. I don't think I ever saw him be agitated when I lived in the village. But then he is an old man now'.

'Perhaps we should get uniform to check on Smith, sir'.

'OK, Viv, given what happened in Holme Hill last week, I agree with you. Any family, or close friends?'

'Well, there's Gelsthorpe, but I don't propose we start with him, given his reaction to our questioning last night!'

'Agreed. Charlie, could you sort it?'

'Will do'.

'Oh, and Charlie, get someone to take a statement from the women on the boat and then see what Gelsthorpe has to say about it all'.

Riggs nodded. May returned to his office as the Detective Constable left to organise a visit by uniform to Smith's house. Trubshaw followed him.

'Close the door, Viv'.

Trubshaw did as she was told.

'I know this is just about the worst time to say this, Viv, but...'

'Don don't say it. I know how you feel, and you know how I feel. But you have your family and your career, and I have ... well I have my career too. And I will be gone in three months at most. We just need to wrap this case up now, that's all. I'll do my best – like I always have done for you, Detective Chief Inspector'.

'But I've been thinking...'

'No need to think, Don. Let's just do it'.

'That's one of the things I love about you. Straight to the point'.

'Don't say any more, Don, just do as I say'.

'But...'

Charlie Riggs knocked on the door and entered without waiting.

'Sir, we now have a missing person's report on Smith. Gelsthorpe was right. He hasn't been seen since last week'.

***

'Mr Dooley? Mr Dooley?'

'I'm afraid he's usually like this now, sir. I don't really want to wake him up. It wouldn't be good for him. Best that you sit here and see if he comes around of his own accord, as he would say. He likes using that phrase 'of his own accord', or 'of one's accord', you know'.

The visitor nodded and sat down next to the retired minister. Dooley was very thin; shockingly so when compared with the old days when he had been at Salem. He was positively rotund then. But now his clergyman's suit was far too big for him and his dog collar went loosely around his neck. There were food stains down his waistcoat and his trouser zip was half open.

The reverend's mouth was half open as he slept. This allowed anyone passing to see that the man still had all of his own teeth, with hardly a filling. From time to time, the nose twitched. In his right hand was a small Bible, open at the psalms.

The visitor stood up and leaned over Dooley, trying to find out which passage of scripture he had been reading.

'Psalm 127', the man said out loud.

'Psalm 127 verse 3, in fact. "Children are a heritage from the Lord; offspring a reward from him". I wondered when you would be back. Sit down and tell me all about it'.

'Yes, Reverend Dooley. I am glad that you have woken up'.

18

May 7, Afternoon and Evening: Philbey Confesses; Metcalfe Runs Off

cᴐ

May tried to look enthusiastic, but the thought of talking about the new baby filled him with horror. He had never been much of a royalist; neither had his father. There was something incompatible about being a Methodist and yet a supporter of the Queen. She might be head of the Church of England, but there was no place for a sovereign in the non-Conformist hierarchy. But then, there was no real hierarchy: the movement had been built on democracy; on ordinary people having a say. That was why it had spawned the Co-operative Society and the Labour Party. May thought of life in the 21st century. Perhaps there was no need for Methodism now: it had done its job; got people the vote and improved living standards; helped to abolish slavery and evened up the odds. What would John Wesley say if he came back now? *He wouldn't be best pleased, as his Dad used to say.*

Detective Chief Inspector May did his best to smile as the WPCs in the station gossiped about Harry and Meghan, and

Archie. Having run the gauntlet of the outer office chatter, he strode into his office, threw his briefcase onto the desk, put his jacket over the back of the swivel chair and switched on his computer. 32 unread emails; none of them urgent or serious, as far as he could see. Except one, that is, from Fizz. He was about to open it when he was interrupted. *I should have known; the only way to clear your inbox is to be in the office before everybody else or be there after all the others have gone!*

'There's someone to see you, sir. Says she will only speak to you'.

WPC Ellis knocked on the open office door and spoke without waiting to be spoken to.

'Thank you, Ellis. Who is it?'

'She wouldn't give her name, sir. But insisted on seeing you. A Mrs Philbey, I think she's called; says she knew your parents'.

May sighed as he looked at the young policewoman: small, slim, her long hair immaculately tied up; the shiniest shoes in the station. She even made a uniform look like something from a Boden catalogue; or so Viv kept saying. But the Detective Chief Inspector was only interested in what people wore as a way of finding out who they were as people. Georgiana Ellis had only been at Hartley for a few weeks but had already impressed with her intelligence and attention to detail; and that was clear from the way she wore her uniform. She had come from North Yorkshire with glowing references. Perhaps she was future CID material. If Riggs becomes a DS when Viv leaves, then she could take his place as a DC. *But that's for another day; let's make the most of DS Trubshaw before she goes to sunny Lancashire.*

'Very well, Ellis, show her through'.

Ellis disappeared back down to reception. A few moments later she returned with May's visitor.

'Thank you, Ellis. Carry on. Please close the door behind you as you go'.

Ellis smiled thinly and did as she was told.

May gestured to the woman to take a seat.

'How can I help you, Ms...'

'Mrs. I don't believe in any of that feminist nonsense! Mrs. Mrs Philbey. Pauline Philbey. I need to talk to you about riddles, or rather Riddles; Riddles Mill, that is. I have found something that may be of interest. Except that I have now lost it. Or it was stolen. But I can remember what was inside'.

'Slow down, Mrs Philbey, a book that you have – that you *had*, that is – would be of interest to me?'

May studied the woman now sitting on the opposite side of his conference table. Long, curly, white hair; red cheeks, so red that May assumed she was a drinker, and a heavy drinker at that. The DCI made the sign of a 'T' with his hands to Ellis in the outer office. The WPC nodded back.

Mrs Philbey was very smartly dressed, with a large handbag, whose handles she twiddled incessantly. The large rings on her fingers must have been worth a fortune; diamonds and rubies bulging out everywhere.

'WPC Ellis said that you knew me: or rather knew my parents?'

Pauline Philbey became less agitated.

'Yes, officer. Mr May, I mean. I knew your father; not well, but I used to organise the joint services between St Maurice's and Salem when your Dad was in charge at the Chapel.

May narrowed his eyes and played with his pen as if it were a cigarette.

'Philbey? Yes, I remember; at least, vaguely. But it's a long time since Salem closed and even longer since my Dad died'.

'I know. How times have changed! But I thought I should tell you about a book that I found. Well, that I was *given*, actually'.

May tried to look interested, noting the email from Fizz that still needed his attention. The fact that there was a red exclamation mark next to the header made it all the more frustrating that Mrs Philbey seemed incapable of getting to the point. May cleared his throat and interrupted the good lady in mid flow.

'So, Mrs Philbey, in a nutshell, who owned this book, and what was in it?'

May realised that he had been more than a little rude with his visitor, but it worked. Mrs Silver Hair (as May had mentally nicknamed her) stopped in mid-sentence. There was a pause while she looked down at her handbag, then inspected her immaculately manicured nails and then, as if to be sure, opened and closed her handbag.

'It belonged to Rhys Williams and contained a list of people that he was blackmailing'.

***

Harry Metcalfe was noted in Holme Hill for his sartorial elegance: the perfectly buffed shoes; the choice of outfit, always so well matched; the dress handkerchief in the breast pocket; the carnation in the button hole; the waistcoats; the walking stick; the hats for every occasion. Everything about the man's appearance oozed class; or so he liked to think.

Elsie Wright begged to differ. Metcalfe was a pretentious, stuck-up boor; a nobody who thought himself better than all the rest when he had been nothing but a jumped-up little overseer at Riddles. Her husband had hated him as well. Just because his mother had sent him away to some tin-pot boarding school, all because he flunked his 11-plus and was afraid of what the lads at the secondary modern would do to him; because he went to Sawby School for Boys he thought he was a gentleman and deserved to be treated as such.

Elsie would watch him walk past *High Windows* every morning on his way to the paper shop to get his copy of *The Telegraph*. Metcalfe would be singing in that low bass voice of his, no doubt trying to perform excerpts from his beloved Wagner operas. Sometimes at night, she could hear him playing his record collection (he only ever bought vinyl), volume turned up to maximum. Gordon thought that he could detect Metcalfe singing along when it was a bass solo.

Today was different. Metcalfe was not singing; nor was he the dapper, confident man that Elsie Wright had come to hate: no, she had not *come* to hate him; she had *always* hated him. The grandfather clock in the hallway of High Windows laboriously struck 7 o'clock. Elsie was looking out for Gordon, who seemed to get later and later coming home from work; assuming, that is, he had been at the office all this time in the first place. *Why had he started talking about those two women on the boat and their baby?* Gordon should have been on the same train as the previous week, when he had discovered Williams and their lives had been turned upside down.

Elsie Wright thought that there was a lot more to come before this business was over; if Holme Hill's dark secrets all came out, that is. And then she noticed one particular dark secret run past. Dishevelled, unkempt, hair out of place, no tie, no stick, no carnation, no graceful, striding, manner. Metcalfe almost ran past the front gate. Despite his years, he was able to make rapid progress down the hill, past Riddles Mill and across the road to Salem Chapel. At that point, she lost him. There were too many overgrown trees in front of the Greek columns for her to tell whether or not he had gone into the building (he would probably still have a key, being one of the trustees) or whether he had used the graveyard side of the Chapel as a short cut to the newer part of the village and the shops. The Co-op would still be open if nothing else.

She had never seen Metcalfe like this before. And she would never see him again.

19

May 8, Morning and Afternoon: Boris and a Book; an Organist Turns Up

'I thought she was never going to shut up about Boris'.

'Boris Johnson?'

DCI May laughed.

'No. Boris the cat!'

WPC Ellis laughed as she brought coffee and biscuits for the 'inner cabinet' as the office called May, Trubshaw and Riggs. It was a morning ritual for the three detectives; the communal eating and drinking somehow got the case conferences going and Wednesday morning, 8 May 2019 was one of those days when stimulation was required. It was a week since the discovery of Rhys Williams' body and the progress had been limited. Then Peter Smith had gone missing. But as Donald May always said, 'each day brings a new opportunity; we just have to make the most of it'.

'Thanks, George. We'd better stop talking about Boris and get on with the case in hand. By the way, you two, I have just forwarded an email that Fizz sent me yesterday. We need to talk about it before we've finished today'.

Georgie Ellis stayed a moment longer than she should have done after leaving the tea tray on the conference table. Dare she ask to sit in on one of their discussions? She had a first-class degree in Criminal Psychology from Plymouth Marjon University, after all. There must be more to policing that being a tea girl.

It was as if DCI May sensed what she was thinking.

'Perhaps you would like to sit in on our case conference, George, unless you have something more pressing, that is?'

May smiled.

'Of course, sir. I would love to!'

'Close the door and pull up a chair, WPC Ellis. Better get yourself a coffee first, though, if you want one!' May nodded to the outer office as he spoke, beginning to wonder if he and George might be working more closely together before long.

'No, I'm fine thanks, sir. Thank you all for letting me observe'.

Viv Trubshaw smiled at Ellis, noting that it was now two against two in the case conference.

'We'd better talk about Peter Smith first. Any news since the missing person's report was filed?'

'None, sir'.

'Charlie? Who reported him missing?'

'Err, would you believe Elsie Wright?'

'Blimey! Mother and son are obviously in this together, sir!'

'Many a true word spoken in jest, as my mother used to say, Viv. First the son finds a dead body; then the mother reports someone missing'.

'Why her and when did she report it?'

'Near neighbours, sir. He often pops in to do odd jobs for her. Gordon is at work for long hours and is useless at DIY anyway, apparently. Peter Smith is a 'dab hand' according to Mrs Wright. And I got the impression that they were quite fond of each other'.

May laughed.

'Elsie Wright fond of Peter Smith? I don't think that woman has ever expressed any kind of positive feelings towards anybody!'

'Well, sir, she spoke very warmly about him on the telephone. And she insisted that he should have been around to her house at least twice since she last saw him'.

'And Ted Gelsthorpe was also telling us to try and find him. Very well, Viv. Put uniform on it. If nothing turns up by the end of the week, then we will go big on the story with the media'.

'OK, sir', will do, as soon as we have finished here'.

'So what's all this about Boris?'

'Well, Viv, as George will testify, I had a visit yesterday from a certain Mrs Philbey – Pauline Philbey. My parents knew her vaguely and, many years ago, she briefly worked at Riddles'.

'Boris is her cat, DS Trubshaw'. May nodded and smiled.

'Ah, right. Now I understand, I think. Personally, I hate cats!'

'Back to work, you lot'. May snapped.

'Philbey is the local archivist. Shortly before his murder, Williams gave her a whole set of documents. They were in this folder'.

May went over to his desk, coughing as he opened up the pockets of the musty document holder. He came back and emptied the contents onto the conference table. The other three began to pore over the photographs and papers that had spilled out.

'Most of this stuff is photographs of the new estate at Holme Hill as it was being built in the 1970s. 1976, to be precise'.

'Why did Williams give Philbey this stuff, sir?'

'No reason given, Charlie. Presumably for the archive that she looks after. When she's sober, that is!'

'Sir?'

May looked at Ellis.

'I think George will confirm that she likes her drink. She even took a swig from a hip flask while she was here, though she was very, very nervous, I'll admit that'.

Ellis smirked at May.

'As if she had something to hide?'

'No, Charlie, as if she was cross with herself'.

'How so, sir?'

'Well, inside this document case, folder, whatever you call it, there was a little notebook. She doesn't know whether Williams meant to give it to her, or if he had forgotten about its existence. Anyway, it fell out – or so she says – and she began to read it'.

'And what was in it, then, sir?'

'According to Mrs Philbey, Viv, it contained a long list of times, dates, amounts, of people who were paying Rhys Williams to keep his mouth shut'.

'You mean he was blackmailing them?'

'Yup. Blackmail. Members of a church circle associated with Riddles and all living in Holme Hill'.

'So where is it, sir?' All eyes were on Ellis as she spoke.

'Good question, George. She lost it, or rather it was stolen from her'.

May saw the look of disbelief on his colleagues' faces.

'I know. Can you believe her?'

Shrugs of shoulders suggested negative replies.

'And how was it stolen, sir? Who might have stolen it? Boris, perhaps?'

Trubshaw and Riggs laughed at the WPC's comment and the formality (mock or otherwise, with which she asked the question). May smirked.

'She fell asleep, like she always does after a meal apparently, and when she awoke, it was nowhere to be found. Who knows who stole it, assuming it even exists, that is?'

'So, does she remember the names of any of the people in the book, sir?'

'Indeed she does, Viv. Indeed she does. Most of the elders at Salem Chapel, including my father'.

***

Pauline Philbey was more excited than she had been in a long time. This was the day that the local archivist had been preparing for since the previous autumn when the Holme Hill Historical Society had decided on its programme for 2019. She was nervous too, so it was important that the hip flask was full before the tour of Salem Chapel started.

This was it: the very last time anybody would be allowed into the building before Halliday Construction began to rip out the insides of the building ready to convert the place into yet more luxury flats.

It was raining as the HHHS members gathered, so all were sheltering under the elegant Roman portico waiting for Rodney Halliday to arrive and let them in. Perhaps because this was a unique moment for the Society, more people than usual had turned up. There were even some new members. Pauline Philbey introduced herself and her colleague Wallace Walker (who was there to take pictures and record the event for posterity) to the assembled crowd and asked the 'newbies', as she liked to call them, to say 'just a bit' about themselves. Jo Bishop went first; interest was aroused when she talked about her MA project and the work that she was doing on Riddles Mill. Then came Janet and Abbey Harrison, who were just passing through on their narrow boat, had seen the poster by The Bargeman and decided to come along. Finally, having shut the pub after lunch, Linda Welch and Joan Wilberforce had felt they needed to learn more about the building that so dominated the village skyline before it was too late. Joan, much to everyone's horror, said that she was wondering about buying one of the flats (when finished) as an investment.

Rodney Halliday arrived in his BMW 7 series Coupe. He was not alone. The Society members watched while the new owner of Salem got out of his car, skipped around to the passenger side, and opened the door.

'Sorry I'm late. I had to pick Babs up from the beauty parlour in Hartley. She was having her new eyebrow extensions fitted, weren't you, babe?'

Pauline Philbey had never seen anybody quite like Babs Halliday before. But then, neither had anyone else in the HHHS. Philbey was just as intrigued as her fellow members at what had just got out of the car, while the Harrisons would have turned away in disgust if they had been given the chance. But then, as Pauline Philbey mused to herself, a man who can have the word' 'Love' tattooed on the fingers of one hand and 'Hate' on the other was likely to have an 'interesting' wife.

And Babs gave new meaning to the word 'interesting'. Even straightened down, the skirt was the shortest that Pauline Philbey and the others had ever seen, even when they were youngsters in the Swinging Sixties. Then there was the obvious breast augmentation and the 'blonde' hair.

'Sorry, everybody. My fault. Just had to get my eyebrows done. Sorry to keep you all waiting. Isn't this exciting?'

'Yes, Mrs Halliday. It is. Shall we get started?'

Pauline Philbey looked around the Society, sensing their anticipation. Rodney Halliday made his way past the assembled crowd and took out the key to the front doors of Salem. Babs followed immediately behind him.

The chapel smelt like any old, unloved public building. The musk of ages pervaded the air. The double sets of inner entrance doors were half open; cold air rushed out from the main chapel. Halliday told people to stay wrapped up as the roof leaked and a lot of the windows had been broken by the local yobbos. The main notice board still gave details of pew numbers and names (a feature that the new owner was keen to keep), while posters advertising the closing services of December 2009 summoned the faithful from far and wide to celebrate almost 200 years of Methodism (Rodney Halliday said that it sounded more like 'masochism', but nobody laughed at the joke).

Once everyone was in the main part of the chapel, Pauline Philbey began her talk. She had memorised it to the last nuance. Questions were to be asked only at the very end, much to Jo Bishop's frustration as she had seen memorials on the walls that matched with names in her spreadsheets and wanted to know more then and there. Philbey started with the ceiling and its unique decorations; then the galleries and where the choir had once sat; the marble pulpit, paid for by Ernest Riddles himself. The preacher would have towered above the Lord's Table and the brass communion rail, as the local archivist pointed out. The removal of the ground floor pews had increased the echo considerably, and Philbey's voice boomed around the building, much to her satisfaction.

'Any questions before we move on?'

'Is that man going to play for us?'

'Excuse me, Mrs Halliday?'

'That man up there. Is he going to play for us? I love a good tune, eh, Roddy? And call me Babs. That's my name, like Windsor; Barbara, not the Queen, that is'.

The laugh rang out. All eyes were on Babs.

'Come on, is he going to play for us?'

As Babs Halliday pointed, the HHHS members and guests looked up to the back of the pulpit and the choir seats. The intricately painted organ pipes had lost their glitter but still made an impressive backdrop to this former place of worship. Babs walked forward and up the steps to the pulpit.

'Careful, babe, wait for me!'

'I'm fine, Roddy'.

The choirstalls behind the pulpit still had books on the music desks, ready for the next service that would never happen. Babs Halliday sneezed as the dust got up her nostrils. The man at the organ keyboards seemed ready to play. The lights were on and the blower that pumped wind into the instrument hummed.

'Hello. What are you going to play for us?'

Babs Halliday could see the man's face reflected in the mirror at the side of the organ. He must have dozed off, she thought.

Rodney was now beside her and Pauline Philbey not far behind.

Babs tapped the organist on the shoulder, whereupon he slumped over the keys.

'He's dead, Roddy. He's dead'.

'Don't look, babe, don't look'.

Pauline Philbey knew who the player was straight away.

20

May 8, Evening: Bishop to Professor; the Scene at Salem; Elsie Predicts

———— ᴄᴠᴐ ————

Despite being spring, it was cold on Holme Hill railway station. Jo Bishop wished that she had brought an overcoat. Why had she expected Bill Harker's train to be on time? She looked up at the digital display, but the message had not changed since she had last looked; nor the time before; nor the time before that: 'Delayed'. Jo checked her mobile phone to see if the Northern Rail app had any more information; nothing. The same was true of the National Rail Enquiries site.

If I go back to get a coat then the sodding train will arrive, and he will think I have given up on him. If I stay, I will be frozen. Bloody crap service!

The lights in the old mill looked warm and inviting. She could always text him to say that she had gone to The Bargeman and for him to meet her there. But then she realised she didn't have his mobile number; if he had hers, then he would have texted, no doubt of it. He was that kind of person. The next time (if there was a next time) she would make sure that she did have an emergency number. She didn't have a home number either, but then what would his wife make of her phoning Bill there on a Sunday evening?

Jo began to regret having contacted him about the Riddles archives. But then after the events of the afternoon, she was also looking forward to talking to somebody about what she had seen, and never wanted to see again.

Salem Chapel was a hive of activity. Jo counted at least six police cars, two private vehicles, and a large white van all parked around the side of the chapel. Officials came and went. Every light that still worked must have been on inside that old building.

It was now starting to rain; just a few spots, but the damp and the cold made Jo Bishop shiver. Just as she was turning towards the platform exit, Jo heard a train. She looked back up to the display to find that there was now an expected time of arrival: only two more minutes to wait.

She turned back to the platform and watched the two coaches edge slowly into the station. The automatic doors clattered open. She was at the driver end of the train; Bill Harker got off at the other. Jo Bishop decided that she was pleased to see him. She would buy him a drink in The Bargeman and tell him everything she had found out about Riddles in the 1950s and 60s. And the dead body in the chapel, of course.

He walked towards her. She giggled to herself as she thought of a certain scene in The Railway Children, though Bill Harker was no father figure; nor did she intend him to be a lover.

'Hello, Jo. Good to see you. I'm intrigued by what you say you've found in those archives. Fascinating *and* controversial. I'm glad you called me'.

Jo smiled at the lack of pleasantries. No 'how are you' or 'hope you are well' or something similar. Just straight into the topic uppermost in his mind at the time. *That's academics for you!*

'Come on Bill. I'll take you to The Bargeman. They serve good, real ale there, or so I'm told.

***

'Do you have to go Dad? I've just got all the engines ready. The timetable starts in five minutes and must be adhered to in every respect'.

Donald May wondered where his son had got the phrase 'adhered to in every respect'. Some television programme or other that he loved to watch; something on *National Geographic* probably. But that was almost inevitable when you had a child with special needs and who was educated at home. Caz loved Freddie to bits; but he drove her around the bend sometimes. Don wanted to do more, but the job seemed to get in the way all the time.

'Sorry, Fred. You'll have to manage the Hartley and Holme Hill Light Railway without me this evening. I've been called out. It's urgent. Sorry, son'.

Caz put her arm around Freddie as she saw the boy's disappointment. She kissed him on the head.

'Perhaps when Daddy gets back if it's not too late'.

May smiled back, weakly.

'I have to go. Till soon'.

The DCI was out of the front door as quickly as he could manage. The drive to Holme Hill was easy enough at that time of night, despite the roadworks. It began raining as he arrived in the village. The place could look grey and grim on a day like this, he thought. May parked the car on the main road in front of Salem Chapel. Trubshaw and Riggs were standing on the entrance steps talking to uniform.

'Evening, you two'.

'Evening, sir. I presume you'd like to go straight upstairs'.

'Thanks, Viv. Yes, please. I know the way!'

May smiled at Trubshaw. The DCI realised that she would be unaware of how much his early life was bound up with Salem Chapel; how he had sat in the pews near the organ and watched his father as he preached God's Word in that huge pulpit; how he had looked down to see the congregation hanging on his every word. That seemed a different world to Donald May; a world that no longer existed and of which, if truth be known, he had never been a part.

May bounded up the steps two by two and walked along the side galleries towards the front of the building where the vast organ occupied the whole of the far wall. The casing had been designed and decorated to represent the gates of heaven. It seemed odd to have something so decorous in a building that was otherwise so austere.

SOCOs were already well entrenched in the area in front of the organ console, in between the two sets of choir stalls. As May walked past, he saw the open score on the conductor's stand. He stopped to see what the piece was: 'Oh, how glorious', by Basil Harwood. May smiled as he remembered how his Dad had pronounced Harwood as 'Arwood, in good old Yorkshire fashion. Then he thought about what Pauline Philbey had said to him only the previous day. Perhaps his father had not been the saint that everybody in Holme Hill had once thought.

Trubshaw and Riggs were close behind, if out of breath.

'Sir?'

'Ah, yes, Viv. Let's take a look'.

Fizz was already carrying out a preliminary investigation of the body. She seemed pleased to see the three officers arrive.

'Evening, team. This is quite something, isn't it?'

'Do we know who the victim is?

Charlie Riggs was the first to enquire of the doctor.

'It's Peter Smith', said May, 'and I imagine you are going to tell me that his hands are missing'.

'How did you guess, Inspector?'

'Smith was the organist at Salem for many years, and we have recently had a missing person's report filed on him. As to the hands? Call it an educated guess!'

'I'll confirm in the morning, but it would seem reasonable to assume that the hands found in the swamp the other day are those of the deceased'.

Riggs smirked at Felicity Harbord's formal use of language. They all knew she liked to tease them, and this was one of the ways in which she did so: *faux* formality, as she called it.

'A fitting revenge for someone who played an instrument – especially a keyboard instrument, don't you think, Don? Cut off the player's hands; the ultimate torture, I would have said'.

'Was Smith tortured, then, Fizz?'

'Well, if you are wondering, the hands were severed after death, but I was pretty certain of that from when I examined them. But he was tortured. You remember I said that he was restrained, judging by the marks on those wrists, which we shall assume for now are his. Well, he was kept in leg irons as well, by the looks of it'.

'Mode and time of death?'

'Well, he has been dead for at least two days, in my opinion. And judging by the surrounding environment, he was killed somewhere else and then moved here. See how little blood there is, even on the keyboards'.

'And how was he murdered?' interjected May.

'Interesting. It looks like the same *modus operandi* as our last victim. And the same sort of weapon. Which reminds me, May, did you get that email I sent you?'

May nodded.

'You are looking for someone who owns a sabre or a very thin-bladed sword. Perhaps the sort used in fencing in the old days. Not now, of course, when they use rubber tips and all that'.

'Well, that's helpful, Fizz'.

'Just one thing. Last time the murderer was left-handed. This time, they were right-handed, or ambidextrous. Oh, and religious. Same quotation as before, pinned on his lapel. And two more dates. Another week to go before the next victim cops it, and then a fourth the week after that perhaps?'

***

Elsie Wright had pins and needles in her wrist. She had been holding that lace curtain to one side for too long, she realised. In any case, it was getting dark now and there was not so much to see down at Salem. She had observed everything that had been going on since the Historical Society's guided tour of the Chapel had to be aborted.

Elsie remembered how Gordon periodically admonished her for staring out of the window. She smiled as she remembered how happy he was to accept the suggestion that he go down to see what was going on. She had said how easy it would be possible to get a good view from The Bargeman. And she knew that Joan was on duty, Wednesdays.

Elsie watched her son walk to the bottom of the garden and dutifully close the gate after himself. She did not stop checking on his route until he was down the bottom of the hill. Then her attention was drawn to what was happening at Salem. She saw what must have been a body being brought out in a bag and loaded into a large white van. She watched as the doors were closed and the van driven off towards Hartley, for a post-mortem, no doubt.

'Metcalfe next', she whispered.

21

May 9: Some Conclusions Reached

————————⌁————————

The inner cabinet sat in silence, not even drinking coffee, or eating biscuits. Georgie Ellis felt sorry for them as she looked through the glass partition that separated the outer work rooms from DCI May's 'place'. She smiled to herself. *'May's place' sounds more like a coffee shop or a cocktail bar than a senior detective's office. But I want to be in there one day. Whatever my father says, this is the career for me!*

The WPC looked into the inner office, half hoping that the three detectives would invite her to observe again. She had so enjoyed being part of that team, part of any team, for that matter. But she thought that was unlikely today, given the expressions on their faces. *Unless there was some kind of breakthrough, brought about by a talented, ambitious, tenacious, stylish, stunning officer...*

Inside May's office, Trubshaw looked out, wondering what Ellis was grinning at. The Detective Sergeant imagined that George could well be on this side of the door in a few months' time when Riggs had become DS and Don needed a new DC to take his place. And why not? That was where she herself had started, moving across from uniform having served her time on the beat and more, then begun to observe CID proceedings, done the training, and taken her exams. That's how it worked, so good on Georgiana Ponsonby-Ellis, eldest daughter of Sir Noel Ponsonby-Ellis. Not that Donald May would take any notice of the WPC's high-born background. *Quite the opposite, WPC Ellis. You'll have to work twice as hard to prove yourself with him!*

'The ACC wants to see me first thing tomorrow morning, you two, so we'd better have a story to tell. Let's take it from the top!'

Trubshaw and Riggs were surprised at May's sudden energy, to the point where the DC spilt his coffee.

'Sorry, sir, I'll get a cloth'.

'No worries, Charlie. Could you ask Fizz to join us if she is free?'

'Wilco, sir'.

Once Riggs had closed the door on his way out, May spoke.

'What are we going to do, Viv?'

'About what, sir?'

May shrugged.

'About any and all of it, Viv. I've never come across a case like this before'.

'Once in a lifetime, perhaps, sir?'

'What? Oh, yes, once in a lifetime'.

'And what about...?'

'Don't say it, Don. Keep your mind focused on the case. It will help me to go out in style, on a high note'.

May smiled.

'That's if we catch the killer'.

'Indeed, sir. We have a long way to go yet'.

Riggs came back into the room without knocking.

'Sorry, sir, Dr Harbord is in court this morning. She will try and call in later if she is free'.

May nodded, stood up and went over to the murder wall as the DC sat back in his place. The DCI grabbed a marker pen from the holder by the side of the door.

'Rhys Williams was found on the evening of May 1st by Gordon Wright. Wright was on his way back from work. He got off the train at 6.20 pm and went the 'scenic' way home. It had been raining heavily. He told some youths off who were throwing stones at what was left of Salem Chapel's windows. What did they say?'

'They were all interviewed, sir. They could tell us nothing, apart from confirming the time at which Wright told them off'.

'OK. Thanks, Viv. Wright then thought about cutting across the cricket pitch but saw Ted Gelsthorpe watching from his cottage, so he decided to avoid a telling off by going all the way around. As he got to the exit, he noticed a man sitting motionless on the bench by the wall, dressed in coat, hat, and so forth, despite the fact that it was a warm, sultry day in May'.

'Then he mouthed to his mother that he was going to be a few minutes more. Why?'

'Why, Charlie? Why?'

May laughed as he replied.

'Because she puts the fear of God into her son – and everybody else, for that matter. He was already late, thanks to *Northern Fail,* and it was no doubt a toss-up between playing the Good Samaritan and getting bollocked by Mrs Wright when he got in'.

Trubshaw and Riggs joined in. Pitying poor Gordon allowed them to relax into the case conference, even though they could hardly forget that the Assistant Chief Constable was now on their tails.

'Then Wright finds the body. Rhys Williams: an old man with weeks to live; murdered somewhere else, quite some time before being moved to that bench by the cricket pitch'.

May paused so that he could sip his lukewarm coffee.

'And we now know that Williams knew that he was dying. His GP confirms it: Dr Harbord was right; six weeks maximum to live. That was probably why Pauline Philbey was given that folder. But perhaps the notebook, if it really exists, was not supposed to be in there'.

'His throat was slit by a left-handed person using an old-style fencing sword or sabre'.

Viv read from Harbord's post-mortem report.

'Does Elsie Wright have a ceremonial sword, by any chance?'

May and Trubshaw laughed at Riggs's question.

'Well', Riggs replied, 'she hated Williams with a vengeance, didn't she?'

'True. Better put her name and photo on the murder wall, Viv'.

May smirked.

'Only joking. At least for now'.

Trubshaw nodded and smiled back at her boss.

'Then there is the Bible quotation, written on the same sort of paper in both cases: Williams and Smith'.

'We're sure about the paper are we, Viv?'

'According to forensics, sir'.

'And the two bodies were discovered on the first and the eighth of May, the first two dates on the piece of paper'.

May rubbed his chin, then stopped, realising that Trubshaw was watching him, having pointed out that it was one of the little mannerisms that she most loved.

'But not killed on those dates, sir', Riggs interjected.

'No, Charlie; the murders planned and carried out in advance, and the bodies both put in a place where the killer was fairly sure that they would be discovered, and at some point, on the predicted dates'.

'We must be looking for two people, sir. Both Williams and Smith were big, well-built men. The killer must have had assistance, especially to get Smith up to the organ loft'.

Trubshaw got up, walked over to the murder wall, and wrote the point down with her red marker.

'So perhaps we aren't looking for a single murderer. Perhaps there are two people in it together?'

'Yes, sir – one left-handed, and one right-handed!'

Trubshaw again wrote on the murder wall.

'That would make sense of the wounds. And two people ought to be able to move those bodies reasonably easily'.

'I agree, Charlie. And they would more easily be able to capture and torture the victims, in the case of Peter Smith, at least. There's no sign that Williams was tortured is there?'

'No, sir, just murdered'.

'And what about Ted Gelsthorpe? He and Williams were antagonistic to each other. *And* Gelsthorpe was the last person to see Smith alive, as far as we can make out'.

'Yes, sir, and he was the first person to alert us to Smith's disappearance'.

May nodded at Trubshaw. He was about to move the discussion on to Linda Welch when there was a knock at the door.

May waved to WPC Ellis to enter.

'Sir, I've been having a look at those pictures and documents that Mrs Philbey brought in. I think there's something you ought to know. It could be important'.

***

Jo Bishop poured herself another coffee. She had looked through the spreadsheets, just as Bill had told her to. It was best that they had met in the pub; part of her had wished they had come back to her flat, but things might have got awkward. She didn't really know how she felt about him. And how did he feel about her? She had let him kiss her lightly on the lips as his train back had drawn into the station, on time for once. Harker had smiled as he got onto the train and waved back at Jo. 'Till next time', he had mouthed. *Perhaps. Perhaps not. Now is it time I phone the police about these records? Bill thinks not; not yet; not until we are sure. I think I should tell them now. It could be important…*

22

May 9, Rest of the Day: Aftershocks

'Shall I call a doctor? I'm really worried about you!'

'No, I'll be fine'.

'But you're not "fine"! You didn't sleep a wink last night'.

'I'll be alright, Rod. You know me. Good old Babs. Built like a brick sh-… well, you know. It's just seeing that man, with no hands. I've never, never…'

At which point Babs Halliday rushed into the *en suite* to throw up.

Rodney Halliday took out a cigarette from the packet that lay open on the marble coffee table and lit it. Babs would be cross when she saw him smoking inside, but what the hell? She was in no condition to bollock anybody just at the moment.

He looked at his watch; his stomach rumbled. There was no way lunch was a possibility. Babs was still retching in the toilet: perhaps he should ring the doctor; get some pills to calm her down.

Rodney Halliday had seen dead bodies before. He was used to them. And he had watched people die and die horribly in some cases. *But why the fuck did they put that Smith bloke there in the chapel? That was going to mess things up good and proper!*

It had gone quiet in the bedroom. Babs had screamed and then vomited when she saw Smith in Salem. The tour guide had tried to calm her down with a swig of gin, but that had only made her sick again. The police had complained about the contamination of the crime scene when they arrived, but Rodney had defended his wife and the others. How were they to know that someone had been murdered there?

***

Boris was asleep on her lap. The cat and its owner snored loudly, like some kind of grotesque duet from a Donizetti opera. In her dream, Pauline Philbey was reading all the names in the notebook. She had located it in the rhubarb patch at the back of the garden. Thank God, she had found it! There they were all listed: people she had known for years; upstanding pillars of the community that was supposed to be Holme Hill. How could they have been so two-faced? Holier than thou on a Sunday and getting up to their debauchery during the week?

One snore louder than all the others woke Boris, who squawked and dug his claws into Pauline Philbey's legs. The cat's panicked clutching pained her greatly. She pushed her loved one off before he could do any more damage.

'Oh my God! What was that all about?'

As the local archivist came around, it dawned on her that she had not found the black book after all. Relief turned back to despair. May had not believed her for one minute; she could tell from the look on his face when he had interviewed her. Vital evidence stolen and only her word to prove that Rhys

Williams was a bad 'un. Where had it gone? She could only have dropped off for a few moments. Surely someone would have noticed if an intruder had come in while she was asleep.

And now Peter Smith had died. He had been one of the names. Something had to be done. Pauline Philbey decided that she should pay a visit to the other people on the list; or at least the ones who were still alive.

***

'You OK, Jaycee? You still look pale'.

'I'm fine, Abbey. But we had a hell of a fright, didn't we?'

Arthur gurgled happily in his Moses basket. The two women smiled.

'No matter, love. We got each other, ain't we?'

Abbey Harrison laughed at her wife's mockney accent.

'Who's the murderer, Jayce?'

'I don't know. Who do you think I am, Sherlock Holmes?'

'Well, if you are, my love, I'll be your Dr Watson any day'.

They kissed; then kissed again. They were about to embrace more fully when Abbey pulled away from her wife and lover.

'Do you think they suspect us?'

'Excuse me?'

'Do you think they think we might have done it?'

'Abbey! What on earth gives you that idea? Why would anyone think that we murdered an old man, chopped his hands off, threw them in the pond by the cricket pitch, then moved the rest of him into that old chapel and sat him at the organ?'

Janet Christine Harrison laughed so loudly that two passers-by with a dog looked in through the narrow boat porthole to see what was happening. Jaycee shooed the peeping toms away with a flick of her hand and two fingers in particular.

'Well, love, the murders have both happened since we moored up by The Bargeman, didn't they? And you have relatives who used to live here.'

Jaycee stopped laughing.

'Sorry, Jayce. Did I say something I shouldn't have done?'

Janet Christine Harrison turned away and peered out of the other side of the boat, then came back and looked down at Arthur. She took him from the basket and rocked him gently.

'No, babe. No harm done. That was a long, long time ago, and I was a vastly different me then'.

'I know, my love'.

The pair embraced again, but this time with Arthur held in between them.

'But promise me you won't say anything about that to anybody, will you?'

***

'Bugger it. I am going for a drink!'

The new Gordon Wright had decided. His mother could wait. Why should he go straight home just because she had phoned him and said she wanted to talk to him as soon as he had got off the train and walked up the hill to High Windows? It would be something-and-nothing, as always. That bloody woman had such a wonderful knack of making him feel guilty; of spoiling his pleasure; of clipping his wings; of taking away his free will.

Gordon Wright now realised that she had castrated him (or tried to) just like she had done with his father. But no more. *No more will I let that woman rule over me! I know her game; I have found her out; and I will not let it happen ever again.*

Gordon could now see his mother at the bay window. Had she seen him? Probably. Did he care? No, he did not care. He hoped that she was watching as he veered off the pathway by the cricket pitch and made his way into the pub. *Perhaps I shall bring Sally here for a meal sometime. That would upset mother. Or I could take Joan for a drive; we could go up over the Pennines and have a picnic somewhere. Then there are those two on the narrow boat. They enjoyed my company. Except they are a bit butch, doing things like carrying their huge sacks around late at night. Not very ladylike, is it? Still, we do live in an age of sexual equality.*

***

'He looks happy'.

Linda Welch nudged Joan Wilberforce as a beaming Gordon Wright walked into the pub.

'Do you think he's after you, Joan?'

The two women giggled at each other knowingly.

'We shall have to see, won't we, Linda? Men do have their uses from time to time'.

Joan stroked Linda's arm, then traced a finger across her hand.

'I enjoyed the way we thrust and parried last weekend'.

'Oh, stop it, you! Just get on and serve the customers!'

Landlady and barmaid moved apart. Joan turned to serve Gordon now he was at the bar.

'Good evening, young man; a busy day at the office?'

Gordon laughed.

'Well, part of your statement is true, Joan. It was a busy day at the office'.

'Don't do yourself down, Gordon. You're very fit and healthy; and good looking with it! A great catch, I would say. Plenty of women would be interested in you, if you...'

'Oh? If I did what, Joan? If I what?'

Gordon bristled. Joan had by now poured him the whisky that he always had. She didn't need to wait for it to be ordered. It was his comfort drink; no doubt to steel himself for going home to his mother.

'Well, Gordon. If you just relaxed a bit. Chilled out'.

Wright pondered for a moment, then took his whisky and downed it in one go.

'You're right, Joan. Pour me another one. And what are you doing at the weekend? Let's go out for dinner!'

Joan smiled. She knew how to pull a man. She had been able to have any of them when she was younger. Before all the sadness set in.

'Are you asking me on a date?'

'That I am, Joan Wilberforce. And I won't take no for an answer!'

'Then I won't say no. But I may need a favour in return, at some point'.

***

Georgie Ellis closed the door on her flat, threw the car keys onto the coffee table, took off her jacket and put it around the back of her armchair. Once the large glass of red wine had been poured, she lay on the settee and reflected on a good day at the office: the best she had enjoyed since moving to Hartley.

They'll take notice of me now; they didn't spot what was in those photographs. But I did. WPC Ellis, soon to be DC Ellis, I suspect. Once Trubshaw goes and Riggs is promoted, I will be in there, helping them to crack this case wide open. And who gave them their first big break? Me, pointing out what those photos showed about 1976 and that poor little girl. And not discovered until now...

23

May 10, Evening: 'Looking Back, I Could Have Played it Differently'

───◇───

'Enjoy yourselves, you two!'

'We will! Come on, Freddie. Have you got your water bottle?'

Donald May looked at his son as he wheeled his bike out of the garage. Freddie had his helmet on wrong again. Why was he so clumsy and unpractical? The Chief Inspector knew why: because he had Autism Spectrum Condition. It used to be called a 'disorder' and then 'Asperger's' before that. And now it was a condition. Freddie wasn't ill or disabled; just different.

How he and Caz had struggled in the early years before their son had been diagnosed! All the problems at school; the tantrums; the strange habits; the vast vocabulary; the obsessions; the OCD. But now it was under control, mostly.

If only ASC had been 'discovered' when I was young. Life might have been a lot easier. And a lot different. Would I have been a policeman; would I have married Caz? Would I have been a local preacher?

Caz waved father and son off. It was the first time in months that the two of them had spent any real time together. The Holme Hill murders had really set him back. He had been depressed anyway, especially about church and his faith, but now he seemed to be in a permanent bubble. The meeting with the ACC that morning had obviously gone badly. But now Donald and Frederick May were off on a bike ride. It would be good for them both to get some exercise; and to spend some quality time together.

By the time that Catherine May had closed the front door, sat in front of the television, and switched on something mindless to watch, the two bikers were on the old cycle track that had once been the Hartley and Holme Hill Railway. The line had been built in the 1860s to connect Riddles' Mill with the outside world. It had not long been completed when it became a small part of the Lancashire and Yorkshire Railway (in which Ernest Riddles must have had shares) and then in turn part of the LNER and then British Railways. By the time of the Beeching Report, the line had already been earmarked for closure and there was little protest from all but a few die-hard railway enthusiasts when passenger and then freight trains ceased and the metals were torn up. Proposals to turn it into a heritage line had come to naught. May's father had been involved briefly but resigned from the committee in protest at the lack of organisation. At least the trackbed had been preserved, thanks to purchase by the council and it was now a much-loved recreational route. It had thus become a cycle track; and a pleasant one at that. The path was level and the views good to spectacular, especially when it came to the descent into Holme Hill and the impressive viaduct that allowed the railway to cross the river and the canal before it petered out near the remaining train station.

May senior thought how Freddie loved the route. He must have known every inch of it. May junior had studied old maps and got every book on the railway that it was possible to get.

Freddie would take the books out on their cycle rides and compare the old photographs with the scenes as they were now, trying (and usually succeeding) to find the exact spot where a signal or a crossing or a platform or some other piece of industrial archaeology had been.

They reached Holme Hill viaduct quicker than May senior had expected; it had taken just thirty minutes to get there. They would have time to go further before it got dark, but Freddie was keen to stop and study the structure in detail. May smiled as his son recounted the story of the viaduct's construction: the design; the materials; the number of men who had worked, and the names of the people who had died, building it. May could see The Bargeman and the narrow boat; the two women who lived on it looked as though they were in the middle of some heavy lifting: coal for their stove, no doubt.

The DCI rested his bike against the parapet wall and reflected on his meeting with the ACC that morning. May knew that the encounter would be a difficult one, but he had been surprised at the Assistant Chief Constable's anger. It was obvious from the moment that the DCI walked into Alec Rowley's office that his superior was not 'best pleased'. The ACC's monologue must have lasted a good five minutes before May had a chance to say anything.

Eventually Rowley had calmed down. The two men reviewed the case. May realised that the ACC must be under a lot of pressure. One murder was bad enough; but two (and the second in especially dramatic circumstances) was beginning to attract a good deal of attention, locally, regionally, and now nationally. The flames of interest were being fanned by the fact there was a strong chance (not that there had been any kind of official announcement yet) that the murders had been committed by the same person.

That might be the case, but as Rowley and May knew, while there were major similarities between the two cases, there was one fact that suggested different perpetrators: one crime had been carried out by someone who was right-handed; the other by a left-handed person, or so Dr Felicity Harbord maintained. But was one murder a copy-cat of the other? Or were two people involved in both killings, taking it in turns to slaughter their victim? And why the torture and the cutting off the hands? May suggested, as had other members of his team, that Smith's murder, at least, was a revenge killing, and the severing of the hands a fitting punishment for someone who had been such an accomplished keyboard player.

And why were there no witnesses? Neither May nor Rowley had come across a case like this before. Williams must have been put on that seat in broad daylight (especially if Gelsthorpe was telling the truth) and a corpse of his weight and size would not have been the easiest thing to transport from where the murder had taken place, even if it were only around the corner. The two men had agreed that a house-to-house search would have to come next. And what about Smith? Not one single person had seen anything untoward. No vehicles, no people acting suspiciously, no unusual movements. The only thing that anybody had reported was a light left on in the chapel the night before the body was found. But that could have been workmen in the previous couple of days as the downstairs pews had been removed prior to Rodney Halliday's men starting their gutting of the main building before it was turned into apartments. It was almost as if there was a deliberate wall of silence in Holme Hill.

Then there was the biblical quotation. Both Wright and Smith had been associated with Salem. And they had worked at Riddles; but then so had most people of their generation who had lived in the village. Given the text from the psalms, the connection had to be through the Chapel.

May had hesitated to tell Rowley about Philbey's little black book but had decided that, if it turned out to be real, the ACC would find it hard to forgive the DCI for the omission. Rowley had been sceptical, wondering if this was one gin-soaked woman's idea of a joke, or, more likely, a bad dream. Why had Williams been blackmailing other people in the choir? Philbey had said something about wife-swapping, but that sounded more like a surmise than an assertion based in any kind of fact. It all seemed so laughable. May had omitted to mention the reference to his father. After all, if the book was fiction, why start to besmirch reputations unnecessarily, especially that of someone who had been his hero, his role model, and his mentor?

'Dad? Dad! You're not listening to me! You never listen to me. You don't care! You don't love me! I wish I were dead!'

May looked up to see his son leaning over the viaduct.

'Freddie! No!'

May ran over to his son and pulled him away from the edge, much to the surprise of some walkers coming the other way.

'I'm sorry, son. Things have been tough at work. My mind's been elsewhere. I'm sorry. I'm really sorry. But it's dangerous. You mustn't lean over like that!'

Freddie hugged his father and burst into tears. May felt his son's whole body shake. It took him ten minutes to calm him down. The DCI wondered how far the noise would carry, given the wide-open valley. Fortunately, no more people passed until the tantrum was over.

'Tell me about your case'.

'My what?'

'Tell me about your case, Dad'.

'But you're only...'

'No, I am *not*. I don't want to be a child. I want to be a grown-up like you. I want to be a big man. An adult'.

May knew that he would have to tell his son something of what was happening at work, especially if another tantrum was to be avoided.

'Alright. Come on, Freddie. Let's push our bikes a bit further into Holme Hill and then I will point out the places where the murders happened and tell you about our theories on the case.

Freddie smiled.

'Thanks, Dad. I will be like you one day. Detective Chief Inspector Frederick Dawson May, of the Yard'.

May laughed at his son. Where on earth had he got the last bit from? 'Of the Yard?' Some book or old TV programme, no doubt. Freddie never ceased to amaze him. An old man in a thirteen-year old's body.

DCI May told the future detective about the murders, without the gory detail, and began to expound on the theories that May and Rowley had considered, and in one or two cases rejected.

'Tell me about 1976, Dad'.

'Excuse me?'

'The case of the little girl. I read about it in this morning's newspaper. Is there any link between Minnie Hargreaves's death and these two murders?'

May was so taken aback that he began to respond without thinking. As he did so, he had an image of Georgiana Ellis in his head that would not leave him.

'Well, Freddie, it's interesting you should say that, because one of our newish recruits, uniform, at least at the moment, has turned up some interesting new evidence about 1976. The thing is, that new information suggests that back then the police got the wrong man for the murder. We were given a file that had some photographs in it. They were pictures of the May Day procession: Saturday, 1 May 1976. And the thing is… the thing is they show images of the man that was convicted for the murder'.

'And why is that important Dad? He could still have killed her'.

'He could. But at the time (as far as we can tell) that she was murdered, the so-called murderer was in the procession up the main street. You can tell that from the time on the chapel clock'.

***

Pauline Philbey had stopped counting how many times she had refilled her glass. If ever she had had good reason to have a drink and even to get drunk, now was the time. It had been a big mistake to try and visit the people in Williams's notebook, a book that she knew existed. She had not dreamt it, whatever Donald May had implied when she had gone to see him: no, not implied, impugned. It was necessary to be precise in these matters.

The local archivist had thought it strange that Harry Metcalfe had not been at home when she had called. It had been late morning by the time she had walked into Holme Hill, been to the Post Office to collect her magazines and buy some stamps, get a few things from the Co-op and then walk up the road past the cricket ground and The Bargeman. She had shivered as she had remembered her time at Riddles working for Rhys Williams; she felt cold and sick when she thought back to her guided tour of Salem. There was still a police presence there and the entrance was cordoned off by the inevitable police tape. At least, it would mean that Rodney Halliday would not be able to start work on Salem just yet. *O tempora, o mores!* She thought. *Oh, what times, what customs!*

What customs indeed, if men like Metcalfe and Smith and the others were up to no good. She remembered the days of her childhood and the 'holier than thou' attitude of some of the people who went to Salem. That was why she had turned Anglican. Not that they had been much better, though at least she got to sing in St Maurice's choir as a result.

But Harry Metcalfe had not been at home. She had looked through the front room window. It looked as if someone had left in a hurry: a half-finished bowl of cereal on the table by the sofa; an opened letter left on the floor; a radio still talking to itself.

'He's not there. Nobody has seen him for a while now'.

Pauline Philbey had recognised that voice straight away. She turned to see one of Metcalfe's near neighbours standing in her front doorway.

'Hello, Elsie. That's a pity. I wanted a word with Harry Metcalfe. But then I want a word with you too. There's a little book that I have been given, probably by mistake, but I now have it in my possession. It has several names in it. People who live or *used to* live in the village. Your late husband is one of the people listed'.

Pauline Philbey saw how pale Elsie Wright had become.

'You'd better come in. Do you take milk and sugar in your tea?'

24

May 11: Saturday Outings

'What a stupid thing to do!'

'What's that?'

Butch threw down his copy of the *Daily Mail* down onto the bar. Linda Welch picked it up to read the headline.

'I'm no Royalist, but it's kinda sick'.

Welch passed the rag to Joan Wilberforce who read the article out loud.

'Broadcaster Danny Baker has been fired from BBC Radio 5 Live after tweeting a "royal baby" image of a chimpanzee'.

Wilberforce laughed out loud.

'You know, Joan, when I was in Australia, there was a movement to become a republic. I supported it; still do. It's old hat this monarchy stuff. They're no better than we are; worse, in fact, with their holier-than-thou attitude. Just because of an accident of birth, they...'

Welch looked at Wilberforce and Wilberforce looked back. Butch could not work out the secret messaging that was going on between the two women, but he decided that he was needed in the kitchen.

'See you later, Butch', said Welch, without looking around. 'But don't forget to change out of your tracksuit before you get started'.

'Are you OK, Linda?'

Welch nodded and turned away.

Joan came up behind her friend, put her arms on her shoulder and, much to her own and Linda's surprise, kissed the landlady's neck. Welch did not protest; she relaxed her body into the other woman's. Wilberforce stroked Welch's hair.

'I know, Linda, I know. It was awful. The hands. Cut off like that. Who would do such a thing?'

Welch turned around and looked her friend in the eyes. Wilberforce wondered if they were going to kiss. Did she want it or not? She had never been with a woman before; should she be with one now?

Linda broke away from Joan.

'This isn't the end of it, is it?'

Joan Wilberforce shook her head slowly.

'No Linda, this isn't the end of it at all. We are not finished yet, by a long way'.

***

Gordon Wright could see nothing wrong in inviting Joan Wilberforce out on a date. It was only an afternoon drive, after all; but it was an afternoon drive with a difference. Having thought about it, though, he had decided not to tell his mother. Elsie Wright had looked oddly at her son when he told her he was off to work.

'On a Saturday?'

'CPD, mother; CPD. I have to train my colleagues in the new regulations that are coming into force next month'.

'But you have never, ever gone into work on a weekend before'.

'Well, there's always a first time'.

Elsie Wright did not believe her son; Gordon Wright was lying to his mother; she could always tell. Gordon did not care about the fact; Elsie did.

He deliberately walked along the towpath to get to The Bargeman. He looked at his watch. *Plenty of time before I pick Joan up at the end of her shift.* The ground was wet, but Wright deliberately stepped in the puddles, laughing as he did so. *Lancashire Lasses* was still moored where it had been since that fateful day when he had come home from work and discovered Rhys Williams's body. There was no smoke coming out of the chimney, but it was a warm day. The narrow boat was swaying gently as the excess water from the lock flowed past.

Gordon Wright thought back to when he had observed that conversation on the far side of the waterway. *Perhaps I should tell the police about it. Especially now that Peter Smith is dead.* Wright decided against it, again. He might have been mistaken. He could have misheard or misunderstood what was being said. Perhaps the two men were talking about Williams' murder or worrying about who might be next. After all, they weren't actually saying that they were going to murder someone; just that somebody else was going to be murdered, and soon. But why were they talking about 'back then' and 'people should be ashamed' and 'they will pay for it'? Wright remembered those words clearly: 'they will pay for it'.

There was no-one at home on *Lancashire Lasses*. The two women must have decided to take Arthur out for the afternoon. Gordon looked through the porthole into the bedroom area. The double bed was still unmade. It looked as though the

165

occupants had eaten their breakfast and perhaps their lunch in there, judging by the tray, with its plates, mugs, cutlery, and condiments. Someone had half-finished a crossword. Wright could not tell which newspaper it was, but assumed it was the *Daily Mail.* He reminded himself that he was a *Telegraph* reader, through and through: the only rag worth reading, the one thing he and his mother agreed on.

Gordon Wright should have stopped looking, but by now he was fascinated by this window, literally a window, onto two (three, really) other people's lives. He checked to make sure that nobody was watching, then peered through the porthole.

The stove in the corner had nearly gone out; there were just a few embers still glistening red. He took in that wonderful aroma of wood smoke, even though, as he had already noticed, nothing was coming out of the chimney. Then there was the smell of diesel, inevitable on a narrow boat. He had remembered when he and dad had gone sailing on the Norfolk Broads. It was the only time that the two of them had spent together on a holiday. Mother had stayed at home for some reason. Gordon had loved every minute of it. But father had died not long thereafter, and the experience had never been repeated.

The living area was untidy, but even a confirmed bachelor like Gordon Wright could accept that a degree of mess was going to be inevitable with a small child on the premises. There were toys everywhere. Higher up in the cabin was a narrow shelf that was full of knick-knacks; someone was obviously a collector, especially of toby jugs. No wonder they were up there, out of Arthur's reach. Gordon could hear the scrunch of footsteps on the towpath. He would have to go. He just had time to observe two ceremonial swords on display in the entrance to the galley.

Joan likes fencing. I wonder if she has seen these...

***

Boris howled. The food dish was empty. In protest, the cat visited the litter tray and stayed there, pointedly doing his business. Pauline Philbey awoke to the sound of scratching. She really had to go shopping for food, and not just for Boris either: the cupboard was bare for both. Yet the local archivist hardly dared go out; not after the previous day and her encounter with Elsie Wright. What a horrid woman she was! But Elsie was not going to frighten Pauline Philbey off. If only she had the book. She would be on such strong ground then; would have something to show the police. But Elsie was having none of it, with her pointed threats and her cutting remarks about the local archivist's penchant for gin.

Graham Dooley had believed her though. Pauline Philbey was so glad that she had gone to see him. He might be a physical wreck, but, on his good days, he was still all there mentally. Yes, there must have been something going on all those years ago. Dooley had been the minister at Salem in the 1970s and early 80s before he had moved away at the end of his tenure as minister. But Philbey knew that he was not telling her everything when he spoke about Williams and the others listed in the little black book.

'They were different times, Pauline. It was not like it is now. What went on behind closed doors stayed behind closed doors'.

'Should it, Graham? Perhaps if more people had spoken out back then, there would not have been all these problems now, and back in 1976 a thirteen-year old girl would not have lost her life'.

A solitary tear ran down Dooley's face and onto the open Bible that he always had on his lap. He looked at Philbey, then bowed his head as if in prayer. After a few moments, he spoke.

'You are right. I cannot tell you more. I was told things in confidence as a church minister, and I have felt duty bound all these years to keep confidential. But if that was the right thing to do then, it is not the right thing to do now. After you have gone, I will be informing the police. You say that Donald May is the Senior Investigating Officer?'

Philbey nodded.

'I remember him as a little nipper, singing in his Dad's choir. And now a local preacher! He is a good man. If I must tell anybody about all this, then he's the best for me to tell it to'.

Pauline Philbey waved to a nurse to come over to where the two of them were sitting in the lounge.

'The Reverend Dooley would like to make an urgent phone call'.

25

May 12: Sunday Musings

She should not have done it. She knew she should not have done it. Her every instinct told her that she should not have done it. And yet she had done it. The temptation to do it was too strong. It was not that she was weak. Quite the opposite: ambition and the desire to succeed; to be the absolute best; better than anybody and everybody else. That was what drove her. There had been an overwhelming urge to prove herself since she was small, and her father had said she would never make anything of herself.

Finding the evidence that David Harrison could not have killed Minnie Hargreaves had felt oh-so good! The look on Chief Inspector Donald May's face as she showed him the photographs, pointed to the chapel clock, and revealed the significance of the time and that young man's presence in the procession driving one of the floats: that made all the hours she had spent sifting through that folder worthwhile. And now Georgie Ellis was going to do it again and do it so successfully that the DCI would have no option but to make her a DC when Trubshaw left and Riggs was promoted to DS.

When the inner cabinet had dispersed after their Friday morning briefing and nobody else was looking, she had gone into May's office and taken pictures of the murder wall on her mobile phone. Finally off duty, what better way to spend her Sunday than to study those murder wall pictures, now blown up and printed out, and see if she could solve the case? Her father would have no answer then.

WPC Ellis had not bothered to get dressed. She felt comfortable in her white cotton bathrobe, white socks, and nothing else. It was her Sunday, after all, and visitors were unlikely. But she had made herself a good breakfast. Bread newly out of the machine, still warm enough to melt butter on, the crust as thick as it could be while still being edible. Her mother's home-made lemon curd oozed out of the jar and onto the plate. Measure after measure of the best coffee that money could buy.

She looked at the mug and smiled; a present from her sister with the baby's handprints preserved all over it in gaudy red. There were times when she envied Tiggy: adoring, rich husband; two lovely children (though she hated the silly Anglo-Saxon names they had been given); country house in Shropshire and a gite in the Morvan; winter holidays in Verbier or Lech. But Tiggy's life was too easy, she had decided a long time ago. Georgiana Ellis was going to earn her way to the top: all the way to the top. And fast.

She put the half-empty mug down on the breakfast table and studied the pictures of the murder wall. The inner cabinet did not seem to be having much success: there were far too many question marks and not enough linkages across the board.

Let's have a look: two murders, allegedly a week apart, but with seven days between the dates of discovery of the corpses and not of death. Both bodies deliberately left in a location that had some meaning: a cricket field and a chapel. Williams was weeks away from death anyway thanks to the big C; Smith had been a fit older man who was tortured before being killed: hands had been severed after death; cut off and flung into the swampy pond by the cricket pitch. The symbolism was obvious: Smith had been playing the chapel organ perhaps only hours before his death.

WPC Ellis (soon-to-be DC Ellis) sipped pensively on her mug of coffee. She loved her morning brew: rich, strong, nutty, full of caffeine. There was nothing like it! That and a piece of her homemade Bakewell tart; and a second piece...

The same Biblical quotation pinned to both bodies: a reference to children. Or was it one child that was being referred to here? Was it Minnie Hargreaves? She had been part of Salem; a member of the youth group, and a singer in the Chapel choir, along with Williams, and where Smith had conducted them and played the organ.

Thomas Hodgson had been in the choir at Salem too. It could not be coincidence that he had taken his own life yards from the beach bar that Linda Welch owned. Why had he moved out to Australia all those years ago?

Ellis checked the notes that she had made for herself after she had observed the inner cabinet meeting. She found the entry for Hodgson, arranged, like her notes on all the other suspects and victims, in strict alphabetical order.

Twelve months after Minnie had been murdered and David Harrison was convicted of the crime, Hodgson had sailed for Oz. That sounded like an admission of guilt, or at least of some involvement in the girl's death. And what did Linda have to do with Hodgson or the other men, or Minnie Hargreaves or David Harrison?

WPC Ellis put down her book and looked out of the dining room window. *Hodgson left the UK days after Harrison was sentenced to life imprisonment for Minnie's murder. Coincidence or what?*

***

'It's bad for business, Babs. It's oh-so bad'.

'Don't worry, Babe. It will be fine. No news is bad news; no publicity is bad publicity. Remember Skinner and Partners?'

'What about them?'

'Neil Harvey with his hand in the till? They rooted him out, went public on it, and business shot through the roof!'

'But that was different, Babs'.

'Nah. It's just the same. Everybody knows where Holme Hill is now, don't they?'

'Well, yes'.

'And, what has happened to reservations for the new apartments in Salem?'

'Well…'

'Well, what, Rodney, my love?'

Halliday smiled as his wife did one of her mock pouts at him. He could not resist her when she started to bat her eyelids.

'Well, business is booming'.

'Business is booming, is it, my cherub?'

The two of them burst out laughing.

'You're right, as always'.

He sat down on the leather settee and kissed Babs full on the mouth.

'Ooh, Rodney, you are a one!'

More laughter. Halliday was relieved to see that his wife had recovered from her ordeal in the chapel. He knew she would. It was as if it had never happened as far as Barbara Halliday was concerned.

But it *had* happened as far as Rodney Halliday was concerned. And it was a big problem! Delays to the construction work at Salem were one thing, but what if the other little operation was discovered. The police were still snooping around in the Chapel. All the equipment had been removed, just in time, thank God, but there could still be traces. And if those traces were found, then the game would be up. Even if Halliday denied all knowledge of what had been going on, the business might be traced back to him eventually.

If only Williams hadn't interfered. None of these problems would have happened. Damn the old bugger!

'Oh, Rodney? Where are you, Rodney?'

That voice could mean only one thing. Mrs Halliday required Mr Halliday's presence in the bedroom. Mr Halliday was only too willing to oblige.

***

Harry Metcalfe hurt. Every bone, every muscle, every sinew: everywhere ached. It felt just like when he was a boy and had fallen out of the big oak tree in the graveyard at Salem. There had been trouble then! And a broken arm and two cracked ribs. His mother had 'played pop' with him.

Metcalfe shivered. It was not just pain that he felt; but cold, too. Then he realised that he was naked; and strapped to a bed.

It was one of those old-style hospital beds that he remembered from the old fever hospital on the outskirts of Holme Hill. He had gone there as a boy at Christmas with the other members of the Chapel choir to sing carols. The image of rows of beds each containing a white-haired old woman. Some of them were able to sit up and listen to the music; most were on their backs, mouths wide open, mumbling to themselves. Metcalfe thought of Philip Larkin's poem 'Heads in the Women's Ward' as he drifted in and out of consciousness.

What am I doing here? What in God's name am I doing here? Is this a dream?

Metcalfe looked around again, then down at his body; he was an old man, with an old man's skin and bones. It looked like a storeroom. Junk everywhere: old furniture, a typewriter on a roll-top desk, just like the one he remembered from the clerks' office in Riddles. It could have been that same piece of furniture, complete with cracks and ink blotches, sellotape marks and graffiti.

Metcalfe could see his clothes piled neatly in the corner of the room, though he was no longer wearing his glasses. There must have been a window open somewhere; the draft blew across his torso. He pulled at the straps that bound his hands and feet, but to no avail. He thought he could hear voices: women's voices, one deeper than the other. A key turned in a lock; a door opened; footsteps, behind him; then a blindfold, then nothing.

***

DS Vivienne Trubshaw was intrigued to the point where she decided she would follow up the call herself; in person; and on a Sunday. The enquirer had given the Sergeant enough snippets of information to whet her investigative appetite, as her father would have called it. And now, here she was outside the entrance to the old Riddles factory, pressing the buzzer to Jo Bishop's flat.

Trubshaw began to wonder if it was a hoax, as there was no reply over the intercom. After the third time, she decided that it was going to be a wasted journey, but then just as she had decided to go back to her Sunday, a voice crackled at the other end of the line.

'Sorry, I had lost track of time. I was still drying my hair and couldn't hear you. Do come up'.

Trubshaw heard the front door unlock, surprised that there had been no attempt at verification. She looked at her watch: it was only just after the appointed hour, and she was expected. But she doubted if she herself would have been so trusting, especially with a murderer (or murderers) on the loose.

The DS walked into the main entrance area. It looked more like a Greek temple than a factory. She was impressed that the builders had retained so many of the original features: the reception desk, the chandeliers, the staircase, the Corinthian pillars.

A lift pinged and a door opened.

'Hello, Sergeant. Sorry to keep you waiting. I'm Jo Bishop'.

'Pleased to meet you, Ms Bishop'.

The outstretched hand was wet, as was the long silver-blonde hair.

'Please, call me Jo. It was good of you to come, Sergeant Trubshaw'.

'And you call me, Viv. This is just an informal chat, and I was intrigued by what you told me over the phone. It's good of you to see me on a Sunday afternoon'.

'No problem. I'm in the middle of my MA dissertation, so time and schedules mean nothing to me'.

Viv smiled, remembering when she had been writing up her final long essays: lots of black coffee and worse to keep her going through the night.

But it had been worth it. That and the graduate entry into the force.

The lift arrived at the fourth floor.

'What's above this level, Jo?'

'Ah, that's where the owner lives. He created a penthouse suite right at the top of the building. It runs the whole length of this wing of the factory. There's even a swimming pool up there. It can be outdoor in fine weather and then covered over if it rains. I've been up there. He must be worth a packet'.

'And the owner is?'

'Rodney Halliday. He and Babs have it as one of their places. And don't I know it. Noisy people, always arguing with each other'.

'Of course. I met them when she discovered... well, when she found Peter Smith at the Chapel'.

'I was there as well. It was awful, absolutely awful'.

Trubshaw watched Bishop turn away and into her apartment. The DS was surprised how spacious it was, with the original cast iron pillars a key feature of the living area, along with the uncarpeted floorboards. The occupant obviously liked modern art and minimalist furnishings. Apart from a battered old leather sofa, two armchairs and a low-slung coffee table, the room was bare.

'Come and have a look at the view. You can see the cricket pitch and Salem from here. Then there's the pub and the canal over there. It's a great place to be. Just the occasional bit of anti-social behaviour in the park area beyond: loud music, people smoking weed, that kind of thing, but Ted Gelsthorpe is soon after them if they try anything on'.

Trubshaw followed Jo Bishop to the balcony. It was a fine view. And it would not have been a cheap place to buy. Perhaps Bishop had some family money...

'How do you take your coffee, Viv?'

'Oh, black, please'.

'There you are. I hope you like it strong like I do!'

Trubshaw nodded. It was the only way to drink coffee as far as she was concerned.

'Come into my study. It will be easier for me to explain'.

Trubshaw observed that the study area was just a spare bedroom with a large trestle table in the middle on which were piled vast numbers of books and papers. In the far corner, opposite the entrance, was an old roll-top desk on which sat a laptop, a large box of tissues, a grey picture of a couple on their wedding day (the man in uniform), and an old-style, black, telephone. In the other corner was a deck chair.

'Have a seat'.

Trubshaw decided to take the deck chair while Bishop sat at her desk.

'Did you know that Charles Darwin was the first person to attach wheels to the feet of his chair so that he could move about more easily when he was working?'

'No, I didn't'.

The DS was beginning to wonder if the great truth that Bishop was about to reveal would be worth it.

'No. Of course not. Sorry. I have a head full of useless facts'.

Bishop laughed nervously.

'But you might be interested in this one. Here, I have printed out a spreadsheet that I have been working on with Bill, my supervisor, Bill Harker, and I just wondered, *we both* wondered, if the pattern that my research has thrown up is of interest to you'.

Trubshaw grasped the spreadsheet. It took a while for her to work out what the data signified. Then she looked up at Bishop.

'I see what you mean. This pattern of deaths isn't normal. It needs to be investigated'.

Bishop smiled.

'I was hoping you would say that'.

***

It was a long time since Donald May had seen Graham Dooley. He remembered him as a sprightly septuagenarian; remarkably fit for someone of that age. If it had been anybody else, he would have put off the visit until Monday. But because it was his father's old friend and minister and the call from the nursing home had sounded so urgent, he excused himself from playing trains with Freddie and helping Caz with the domestic chores and came straight away.

'I'm here to see the Reverend Graham Dooley'.

The receptionist looked oddly at DCI May as he stood at the desk.

'Are you next of kin, sir?'

'No, I am just a visitor'.

Then I'm sorry, sir, but you can't see him'.

'And that is because?'

'Because he died half an hour ago, sir'.

26

May 13: Re-Writing the Past and Anticipating the Future

'He died before I got there, Viv. He was set to tell me something. Dooley asked for me, and I didn't get there in time'.

'Don't blame yourself, Don. You weren't to know he was dying, and so quickly'.

'At least, he died a natural death'.

You sure, Don?'

'A massive heart attack; but he was old and frail anyway. Perhaps it was the worry of what he wanted to tell me'.

'You think he was connected to these murders in some way?'

May shrugged his shoulders. 'Dooley was Minister at Salem when Minnie Hargreaves was killed; and he would have known Williams and Smith, and my father, for that matter'.

'He would have known a lot of people, Don. He was the local minister'.

'I know, but the message was urgent, and he wanted to tell me something before he died'.

'Well, perhaps we will find out another way'.

'Perhaps we will. And our next interview may tell us what we need to know from 1976'.

Trubshaw knew that May was nervous. Never a man of many words, there were even fewer sentences uttered that morning as they drove to meet former Chief Superintendent Arthur Bradley. Bradley had been the proverbial 'legend in his lifetime'. He had long been given his retirement medal by the time that Vivienne Trubshaw arrived in Hartley, and even Donald May had only a vague recollection of the DCS when he was first a plain clothes officer. But everyone knew Bradley by reputation. And now May and Trubshaw were going to see the great man for one reason and one reason only: to tell him that he had got it wrong in the Minnie Hargreaves' case all those years ago.

Trubshaw decided to take her boss's mind off Dooley and Bradley by telling him about the coffee encounter with Jo Bishop. It worked, up to a point, at least. May was intrigued and shocked at the same time by what Viv said. There had to have been a cover up at Riddles; all those deaths must be related to the contract the firm had been awarded by the Ministry of Defence. A hand-picked group of employees were set to work in a separate part of the factory. They had all been vetted by government officials and told not to tell anyone about the project. After six months, it had finished and the team disbanded. Over the following two years, every one of those workers had been diagnosed with cancer; sooner or later, they had all died. Now that the factory records were public, it had only been a matter of time before a diligent MA student got hold of them and matched up the employee records with the subsequent histories of the workforce.

'So, Riddles has given up its secret'.

'What did you say, Don?'

'There was a rumour about Riddles and the Ministry. I remember it from when I was young. But nobody knew who was on that project; it was supposed to be top secret. But was there any connection to Williams and Smith?'

'That's something we have to find out!'

'Yes, we do, but we need to talk to Detective Chief Superintendent Bradley first'.

May motioned to Trubshaw to look ahead. Neither detective had been to the house before but whatever they had conjured up in their minds as being a fitting home for a retired senior detective and an OBE for services to charity to boot, Bradley Barn was not what either of them had expected. For a start, it was not a barn; or if it had been, it was now so altered that, apart from some of the external stonework, there was nothing farm-like about the structure.

May knew what his father would have said of a place like this: *nouveau riche.* Strange that a man who was so keen to better himself and see his son better himself should be so against people who made their money and then flaunted it in front of everybody else. May senior would certainly not have thought much of Rodney and Barbara Halliday, that was for sure. Donald May smirked at the thought of Roddie and Babs. Especially now he knew that the MD of Halliday Enterprises had done time.

But this was a retired Detective Chief Superintendent's house; and why should the main entrance not take the form of a Grecian temple façade, with non-operational shutters either side of every window, top and bottom? And what better way to while away the hours and days and weeks of retirement than to create and then tend the most immaculate garden that May and Trubshaw had ever seen?

Bradley was in the garden, clipping his topiary, pipe in his mouth and sunhat on his head: he stopped work as soon as the car crunched along the driveway. The Chief Superintendent walked across to greet his visitors.

'DCI May; DS Trubshaw: welcome!'

'Chief Super, good to meet you. I, *we* have heard so much about you!'

'And I you, Donald May. Just because I am retired doesn't mean to say that I am out of touch!'

Bradley laughed.

'Anyway, come in. I have just made a brew, and some cake!'

The two detectives followed Bradley through a set of French windows. Every inch of each wall was lined with shelves, and every shelf was full of books.

'Welcome to my criminology collection. I started it when I became a Detective Constable. And that is quite some time ago now!'

May and Trubshaw looked across at each other as the former Chief Super poured tea and cut his homemade cake.

'I do all the cooking and baking. Have done ever since I retired; still do, even though I am on my own now'.

Bradley nodded towards the smiling couple on the grand piano.

'Cancer. It took her two years to die. I didn't recognise her at the end; she was just skin and bones, and, worse than that, she didn't know who I was'.

'I am sorry to hear that, sir'.

'Please, call me Arthur, and I will call you Viv and Don – OK?'

May and Trubshaw nodded simultaneously.

'So, what can I do for you? I gather you want to talk about the Minnie Hargreaves' case'.

May and Trubshaw nodded again.

'It was a difficult time. There was lots of local anger. She was just a young girl, her whole life ahead of her. And then when David Harrison was arrested and convicted, his family were ostracised. They ended up leaving the area'.

'Arthur, we have new evidence'.

'New evidence? What new evidence?'

Trubshaw took out the photographs from her briefcase and lay them down on the coffee table. May pointed out the image of Harrison on the tractor and the time on Salem clock in the background.

'But that's impossible. It was a watertight case. All the evidence against him: all the witnesses!'

'But what about this photo? When Milly Hargreaves was being murdered, David Harrison was driving a tractor'.

Bradley looked closely at the picture, poring over it for what seemed an age to the two detectives. Then the Chief Super put the photograph down and took off his half-moon spectacles.

'That isn't David Harrison', he snorted.

***

Harry Metcalfe was surprised that he was still alive. Something must have gone wrong. He had thought he was about to be murdered when the door to his prison opened and he heard footsteps; one set, possibly two sets? But then, having been blindfolded, nothing happened. He had heard a car pull up outside. Doors opened and shut; a man and a woman spoke to each other and then to another man. There had been laughter and the noise of another door shutting. By this time, the person or persons in Metcalfe's prison had retreated and he had heard a key turn in the lock.

He could still not see, for the blindfold remained in place. The material felt rough, like a kind of industrial tea towel. As he breathed in and out, he sneezed. He was frightened that he might have drawn attention to himself; that he had reminded his captors he still existed and must be dealt with. And dealt with he was, before the hour was out.

27

May 14: Tensions Rise All Around

—⌇—

'It's you two, isn't it? I've seen you out there late at night, moving things around. Those heavy sacks. I saw you every time! I can tell! I wasn't born yesterday. Now where is it? What have you done with the latest one?'

'Get off our boat and get off now. Otherwise, we call the police!'

'Hah. Beaten you to it there, haven't I? I have already called them. Because I know your game. It's been you two all along. It started the day you arrived. I've been keeping watch and a note in my diary'.

'Jaycee, look after yourself. Come back inside!'

'Leave this to me, Abbey. I won't be scared by a man like him. Just you go back inside and look after Arthur'.

Abbey Harrison decided to do as her wife had asked and went back into the galley of the narrow boat, where Arthur lay amusing himself in his Moses basket. She prayed that her son would not be disturbed by the storm that was blowing up outside between Jaycee and that horrible man from the cricket club.

Abbey moved into the lounge area, from where she could get a better view of proceedings. She knew that her wife's opponent was called Ted, for she had heard others call him that when they went to The Bargeman for a meal the first night they moored up by the pub's lock. He had been at the bar talking very loudly to his mates about the death of Salem Chapel and how it used to be. There had been three others with him. At the time, Abbey had not recognised any of them, but she remembered this one called Ted from when he had so rudely shouted at them about taking up the 24-hour mooring, even though they had permission from Linda Welch. Why had he had a go at them? What didn't he like about her and Jaycee? Because they were lesbians no doubt and, even worse, lesbians with a son. They didn't need a man in their lives, but someone like this Ted would never accept the way they lived. He had even accused them of growing cannabis in the pots on the narrow boat's roof. What a ridiculous idea! He had backed off when they showed him it was parsley.

But this time was different. The man had real rage in his voice and in his body language. Abbey watched as Jaycee kept telling Ted to step off the boat as it was private property. In reply, the groundsman kept pushing at the side of the hull with his boot, as if to move it off its mooring. The boat began to rock, and sway; Arthur murmured. Abbey tried to calm the babe. *Oh, do come inside, Jaycee, my love! Leave him be! He will go away eventually!*

Abbey tried to find her mobile phone. It must be somewhere. *For God's sake, where's my effing phone?* She looked out of the window again. Ted the Turf, as they had started to call him, was now raising his voice. Abbey could see that Jaycee was tense from the way she was holding her body so stiffly.

'How dare you accuse us! We have done nothing to harm you or anyone else in this village! You took against us from the start! How dare you come over here and shout at us! We have every right to be here! We have permission to stay and we are staying! We have done nothing wrong!'

Abbey watched as Jaycee went on the attack, jumping off the narrow boat and going up so close to 'The Turf' that she could have kissed him without needing to move more than half an inch. Her opponent only now realised that Jaycee was taller than him; but not just of a greater height; she was much younger and fitter (thanks to all the working of the locks, no doubt) and would give a better account of herself in a fight than Ted Gelsthorpe could do.

There was silence. Groundsman and Narrow-Boater stared at each other for what seemed an eternity. Eventually, the accuser backed down, knowing that the accused was not going to give way or give in.

Gelsthorpe retreated.

'I'll be back. And if you have any sense, you won't be here tomorrow. I saw you, moving those heavy sacks. And I know what's in 'em. If I see you again...'

But Gelsthorpe did not finish his threat. He thought better of it as he saw Gordon Wright walking along the towpath, a bunch of flowers in his hand. By this time, Jaycee was back inside the narrow boat, comforting the two most important people in her life.

***

'Gelsthorpe's losing it!'

'What do you mean, Gordon?'

'I mean, Joan, that he is going crazy. I just saw him out there by the lock where that boat is moored. You know, the one with those two women on it. They are rather sweet, actually. They sorted me out the other night when I fell and grazed my leg'.

Joan Wilberforce looked across at her date. Gordon Wright was in good shape for his age, though the comb over would have to change. Perhaps he could have hair implants; or cut it really short so that it wouldn't matter that a large part of his scalp was bare underneath the long strands. He had to wear a tie, even though he was supposed to be relaxing. After all, she was only wearing jeans and a poplin shirt; though the latter was from Prada (not that Gordon would ever be able to tell). And his sports jacket looked as though it had not seen the light of day since his father had died and left it to him. Joan decided that she was being unkind in silently critiquing his wardrobe like this. She resolved to stop it (it was a bad habit of hers), smiled at him, and changed the topic of conversation.

'That's enough about old Ted. I suspect he has dementia and it is starting to take its toll on him. Some of the things he comes out with about Riddles and Salem in the old days. And now he's often out late at night, wandering around the cricket pitch as if he is out to catch somebody'.

'Catch somebody doing what?' Gordon coughed on his white wine spritzer as he spoke.

Joan gave Gordon a napkin to wipe up the spilt liquid.

'I don't know; committing murder, perhaps?'

She laughed as she spoke but stopped as soon as she could see that Gordon was not amused. She remembered that he had been the one who discovered Rhys Williams' body. That seemed like a lifetime ago! How much had changed within the village since then, and a second murder!

'Sorry, Gordon, I shouldn't have made a joke then. I realise how traumatic it must have been for you'.

Joan Wilberforce reached out her arm and put her hand on his. She squeezed his palm gently.

Wright looked at her. Tears were in his eyes.

'It was awful. Apart from my father, I had never seen a dead person before. And certainly not someone who was, well, who was *murdered*!'

'It's OK, Gordon. It's OK. I'm here for you. Don't worry'.

Wright squeezed back. Joan traced a finger across his hand.

'Why don't we go for a walk? It's a nice evening. And I want you'.

Wright looked up.

'I mean – I want you to help me with something'.

***

'No, it cannot be! He must be mistaken! I checked those photographs against the police files of the time'.

'Well, he was adamant that it was not, repeat, *not* David Harrison'.

WPC Ellis felt low; lower than she had ever felt since she came to Hartley. The Hon Georgiana had been so sure that she had cracked the Hargreaves case. *It was in the bag, and I had done it!*

'Don't worry, George. These things happen. Let's just call it a false positive'.

Donald May looked at his next DC. He had been like her once: full of enthusiasm; so sure; so confident; absolutely clear what the next career move was going to be. And now? Best not think of now, or the future.

'But I still think that photo shows David Harrison. And I think Bradley is lying. How does he know that it's not Harrison? And how come you just believed him?'

'We didn't just believe him, George, we checked'.

DS Trubshaw was not so sympathetic. Riggs simply sat there, keeping out of it all.

'If you compare that photo with the file on Harrison, yes, there are similarities, but I couldn't say with 100% conviction that they are the same person'.

'I get that, DS Trubshaw, but why was Bradley so sure that it was *not* Harrison?'

'Bradley had a photographic memory. He was well known in the force for it. Nothing escaped him, and nothing was forgotten'.

'I appreciate that DCI May, but it was all a long time ago, and he is an old man. He could be misremembering; he could be mistaken; or he could be trying to mislead you'.

May and Trubshaw looked at each other; Riggs scowled at Ellis.

'He was very convincing, George. He took us all the way through the case. There was far more to Minnie Hargreaves' murder than one grainy photograph of a boy driving a tractor, and an underage boy at that'.

'But why were those photographs in Rhys Williams' folder?'

May and Trubshaw looked at each other again; Riggs smiled at Ellis.

'OK, George. Point taken. I was going to investigate further anyway. You're right about Bradley. I think he's got Parkinson's, for starters. You might like to…

May never finished the sentence. The report of a disturbance at The Bargeman had to be dealt with first.

28

May 15, Morning: Watery Goings-On

— ⌒⌒ —

'Well, he's no loss'.

'Who's that, Viv?'

'Jeremy Kyle'.

'What? Jeremy Kyle's dead?'

DS Trubshaw laughed.

'No, Don, sadly not. His show has been axed. Someone committed suicide after appearing on a programme'.

'Really? Well, I could imagine committing murder after watching that drivel, but not suicide'.

The two detectives laughed. It was the first time they had chuckled together since the Hull Conference. Viv was tempted to put her hand on May's as it rested on the gear lever; she thought better of it. Instead, the DS looked out of the window as the car sped towards Holme Hill. *Here we go again. What next? Where is all this going to end?*

'So, what happened last night, Don?'

'Good question. Well, there was an initial disturbance early evening involving Ted Gelsthorpe and the Harrisons. Uniform dealt with it. I was informed but felt that it should be dealt with by the woodentops, at least in the first instance. But later on, it appears that Gelsthorpe again lost it with the two women. You know, they are living on the narrow boat that's been moored by The Bargeman since the beginning of the month (pure coincidence, we assume, that the murders started the day they arrived). Gelsthorpe had reported them to the police, and they then did the same to him and it just went from bad to worse, all evening, on and off, apparently.

'So, why are we attending this morning?'

'Because during the early hours, after the fracas was supposedly over, when everyone was asleep, allegedly, someone untied the narrow boat from its mooring, pulled it into the lock, shut the gates, let the water out and, lo and behold, the Harrisons and their son were high and dry'.

'That was a stupid thing to do!'

'It was. People can die in circumstances like that. But thankfully, parents and child are fine, if badly shaken. *Lancashire Lasses* is stranded in the lock, with its stern on the cill, if you see what I mean'.

Trubshaw knew what May meant. She and Mike enjoyed (enjoy being the operative word) a canal holiday not long before they finally split up. It was the last time that she had seen him: a futile attempt to rekindle their relationship; but it had not worked. To the point where they returned the boat to the hire place two days early. She remembered how at one point on their journey down the Leeds and Liverpool Canal, they had been sent back because a boat had become jammed up on a lock cill. No-one had been hurt, but it could have been disastrous.

'Couldn't uniform have dealt with it, sir?'

May smiled to himself. Viv always called him sir, even when they were on their own together, when she was unsure of him and how he was feeling. Today was the Fifteenth of May and the two detectives knew the date's significance without having to say or be told. Little had been said in the office that morning. The inner cabinet had reviewed Peter Smith's post-mortem again and compared it with that of Rhys Williams. Riggs had been tasked with going further into the Hargreaves' case and Georgie Ellis had beamed from ear to ear when she had been ordered to help the DC in his work.

But they all knew that May 15th was the third of four dates on the inscriptions: Williams on 1st May; Smith on 8th May; A.N. Other on 15th May; A.N. Other number two on 22nd May. Not that the two victims had been murdered on those dates; Fizz had been categorical about that: Williams and Smith had been dead for one or more days before they were found, with Smith having been tied and tortured for good measure. Williams seemed to have been spared that; but he had been killed in the same way as Salem Chapel's former organist.

'So, why not uniform, sir?'

Trubshaw jolted May out of his thoughts.

'Because, Viv, given everything else that has been going on in that village, I think it needs CID on the case sooner rather than later'.

Trubshaw was about to reply when her mobile phone rang. She put it on speaker.

'Riggs here. Where are you, ma'am?'

The DC always observed protocol when he knew that his DCI would be listening.

'Just outside Holme Hill. What is it, Charlie?'

'I thought you ought to know that Ted Gelsthorpe has just been reported missing. He didn't turn up for a meeting of the Cricket Club Committee this morning and there is no sign of him at his cottage, though his car is still there. One of the Committee members looked through the kitchen window. There are signs of a struggle'.

'Thanks, Charlie. We'll take a look when we get there. Have uniform been informed?'

'Yes, sir, they are trying to get access to the place now'.

Trubshaw acknowledged Riggs's message and, anticipating May's next move, said that they would meet uniform at Gelsthorpe's place. Five minutes later, they were parked outside the groundsman's house. The kitchen door was already open, ready for them. May and Trubshaw kitted themselves out in protective clothing, then entered the cottage. There was a chair on the floor and a milk bottle lay smashed into pieces on the kitchen table. The tablecloth was smeared in blood. May looked around the room, then walked through into the tiny lounge. It smelt of pipe tobacco and felt dank. Over the fireplace was a painting of Gelsthorpe and his wife. May remembered them well from his childhood. But it came as a shock to see a large knife stabbed into the painting and the words of a certain verse from the Psalms spray-painted all over the chimney piece.

***

Joan Wilberforce looked out of The Bargeman's snug window, watching two plain clothes detectives and two uniformed policemen walking across the cricket ground. She grimaced as she saw them stride across Ted Gelsthorpe's beloved pitch. He worshipped that grass; adored every blade. Then she heard a baby cry. She walked back into the lounge where Abbey Harrison had started to breastfeed Arthur. The babe was soon gurgling contentedly.

'What flavour is it today, Arthur?'

Joan laughed at the question and looked encouragingly at Jaycee Harrison.

Jaycee smiled weakly back. Thank goodness that Joan and Linda had heard their cries for help and managed to get them off the boat. They were safe, but their home was flooded, and they had never been able to afford the insurance for it.

'Here, have some more tea, you two. There's nothing like a good cuppa. That will solve any problem'.

Abbey wanted to cry but determined to hold back the tears so that Arthur was not affected. Her son seemed to know when she was unhappy, when both his mothers were unhappy. They had reason to be miserable. The argument with Gelsthorpe had got out of hand. When he had come back after the earlier row and the police caution. The man had been so wild; off his head with anger. Jaycee shouldn't have done it. How would they ever cope now? Losing the boat was their come-uppance, their just dessert.

***

As usual, the 11.15 from Hartley into Holme Hill was overdue, but only by three minutes, according to the display board, so it would not count as a late train when it came to *Northern Rail*'s performance statistics. Jo Bishop looked at her watch, wondering if she would make her connection to Manchester for her supervision with Bill Harker. There was so much to tell him about her meeting with Detective Sergeant Trubshaw and the importance that the data analysis of Riddles' staff records might have for the current murder investigation. Thinking about it all made her nervous, so nervous that she had struck up a conversation with Pauline Philbey, who was off to the John Rylands University Library to do some research.

Jo was never sure what to make of the local archivist, even when she was sober, but the two women got talking about Salem Chapel and its connection to Riddles Mill. Jo decided to ask Philbey about the Mill's more recent history, without, as far as she could, giving the game away about her recent discovery and its reporting to Hartley CID.

'Well, my dear, there were all sorts of rumours about Riddles in the 1960s. The place had fallen on hard times, you know. Cheap imports from the Far East, then cheap labour from Pakistan, just like a lot of the old mill towns in the West Riding: Bradford, Dewsbury, and so on. They had to compete somehow. They had an R&D department that worked for the government at the time; it all was very hush-hush. Scientists brought in from the Ministry of Defence; something to do with a...'

'What is the matter, Pauline?'

Philbey was ashen white; totally transfixed; unable to speak. After a few moments she simply raised a hand and pointed down to the canal below.

Jo Bishop turned around and looked over the station balustrade to see what was wrong. There, motionless in the still water, was the body of a man; completely naked.

29

May 15, Afternoon and Evening: Appearances Can Be Deceptive

———cᴧᴐ———

'What the hell is happening, Don? Who is this? Are we talking about a *third* murder in *three* weeks?'

DCI May listened politely to ACC Alec Rowley, waiting for the point when the Assistant Chief Constable reminded the Detective Chief that the date of May 15th fitted with the predictions pinned on the two previous victims, along with the quotation from psalm 127 verse three: "Children are a heritage from the Lord; offspring a reward from him".

May reassured his superior that he would be kept fully informed of all further developments from now on, but that he did not, at this stage, require additional resources. Vivienne Trubshaw watched the contortions on her boss's face as he tried to explain the actions that had been taken to date. How could May have prevented this from happening, other than by putting a security detail on every possible victim? And how many people would that have been, assuming they could all have been identified? Yes, there were some obvious names to put on the list, but would Ted Gelsthorpe, or Harry Metcalfe, or Pauline

Philbey, or any of a whole number of locals have accepted police advice to be careful? In any case, what did 'taking care' mean in a community like Holme Hill, where everybody knew everybody else? If this serial killer was someone local, then how were they to be identified as a person to be avoided, other than in public?

May sighed as he put his mobile phone away. Trubshaw walked over to him and squeezed his arm gently.

'You are doing a great job, Don. Nobody could do a better one!'

May smiled weakly and wearily.

'Thanks for your support, Viv. It's good to know that someone has confidence in me. I get the impression the ACC doesn't think much of my efforts so far'.

'Has he ever had a case like this?'

May shrugged his shoulders.

'I don't know. But let's get on with it. Fizz might be able to give us something'.

Trubshaw nodded in agreement. The two detectives walked under the railway bridge and past the lock where *Lancashire Lasses* was still stranded. The narrow boat looked largely undamaged apart from scuffing and scrapes to the exterior paintwork. The inside would need a thorough dry out, clean and refurbishment. The DS could see cushions and books and other paraphernalia floating inside the lounge area; it was unlikely that much could be salvaged. At least the occupants had managed to escape. Beyond the lock, the SOCOs had already set up their operation and Dr Felicity Harbord was holding court. In the distance, May and Trubshaw could see the ambulance waiting to take receipt of the corpse once she had finished her initial examination.

'Morning, team. Where's Charlie?'

'He's on a Zoom call with Australia. We are following up a lead down under, as it were. You always manage to be so cheerful, Fizz. You must tell me how you do it sometime!'

'Easy when you enjoy your job, Detective Chief Inspector!'

May and Trubshaw looked at each other, silently agreeing not to pursue the conversation further.

'So, what have we got, Dr Harbord?'

'Another murder, DS Trubshaw; another murder. The victim has been dead for quite some time, and, you've guessed it, throat cut just like the others'.

'Left hand or right hand?'

'Right hand this time, Don; you are looking for a right-handed person, like the second, but not the first'.

May snorted.

'Can I take a look?'

Harbord nodded. The DCI knelt on the canal towpath where the body now lay. May surprised himself by saying a short prayer as he revealed the identity of the latest victim of the Holme Hill Murderer, as the media were now describing the perpetrator.

'Now, I didn't expect it to be him, Viv'.

May looked up at Trubshaw, noticing that his DS must be just as shocked as he now was.

'Neither did I, Don. Neither did I'.

***

Despite the rain, Detective Chief Superintendent Bradley left the French windows open as he sat in his leather swivel chair and smoked his pipe. His wife had hated the stench of his tobacco but had let him do what he wanted in his 'man cave', as she called it. Even now it was the only room in the house in which he lit up. He thought to himself how ridiculous it was to hang on to the home that he had shared with her for all those years. He could not bear to move: it would have been the sensible thing to do at his advanced age; his children kept begging him to downsize; the heating bills alone were far too much. Where would he go? Bradley had been taken by his daughter and her unctuous husband to a new development of sheltered housing near Holme Hill; Ann and Dave had done a good selling job on him, but he could never move there in a million years, not to somewhere within yards of where Minnie Hargreaves was murdered. *What an irony!*

Bradley walked to the window. The downpour would do the garden good, though the bad weather meant that yet again he would not be able to work on the miniature railway that ran around the edge of his property. It was the one thing that he focused on above everything since Jean had died: the one hobby she had not let him pursue while she was alive. And now he was building a scale model of Holme Hill, complete with train station.

He closed the windows. The central heating was blazing away to no avail. He could hear Jean castigating him for wasting money. *Yes, my dear. Just as you say.*

Bradley locked and bolted himself into his study. He walked over to the wall of shelving on the far side of the room, looking with pride at the neat rows of files from floor to ceiling. Every case that he had worked on was represented in those document folders; every single one, arranged chronologically. He traced his right index finger along the section for the 1970s until he reached 1976. He noticed how slim the Hargeaves' file was by comparison with most of the others from that time.

Back at his desk, he sifted through the papers until he found the photograph that he was looking for. It was still there, the one that really did prove David Harrison was not the murderer.

***

'Don't worry, you two. *You three*. You are welcome to stay here for the night. Butch has already prepared a room for you. It's *en suite* and I'll get a cot sorted for Arthur'.

Jaycee squeezed her wife's hand. It was the first piece of good news all day.

'Thanks, Linda. I, *we* appreciate that. We've lost our home'.

Jaycee had always been the strong one, but now it was Abbey who had to comfort her wife as she burst into tears. Linda Welch was not sure what to do or how best to improve the mood. Abbey looked at the landlady of The Bargeman and just shook her head. Linda smiled and motioned to Butch to leave the pot of tea and sandwiches on the table near where the two narrow boaters were sitting. The baby was asleep in Abbey's arms, blissfully ignorant of what had happened to his home and how nearly he might have died, along with his parents.

'When you're ready, Butch will take you up. It's quiet tonight. It seems that nobody wants to eat out, so he is at a loose end. No need for a chef if no-one orders a meal. He's at your disposal. Just shout if you need anything'.

Linda Welch went back into the public bar where Joan Wilberforce was serving 'her Mr Wright', as she liked to describe him.

'Thanks for your help with that little job, Gordon. I owe you big time. Have this drink on me'.

'That's good of you, Joan. Happy to help, though my back is protesting today. What did you have in that box, a body?'

30

May 16: Connections or the Lack of Them

—⌀—

Barbara Louise Halliday looked at herself in the mirror. Rodney loved her when she was dolled up to the nines in all her finery: hair immaculately coiffeured, cleavage tantalisingly revealed, skirt not too short but just short enough, her husband's favourite perfume lingering around her pulse points. She looked at the rings on her fingers: at least £20,000 worth on each hand.

Rod was proud of what he had done for her. For them. 'We made it Babs' were his words when he made his first million. And that had been just the start. More millions soon followed; wealth beyond their wildest dreams. But something didn't add up for Babs; it never had done. Yes, the property development business made money, and big money, but there was another source of income that Rodney Halliday kept to himself, or so he thought. Barbara suspected that he was dealing in drugs on the side, but she never asked him about it: didn't want to ask, didn't dare to ask; knew the answer and didn't want to hear it. *If you don't want to know the answer, don't ask the question!*

And now Rod was dead; murdered. Barbara Halliday looked in the mirror again. The crying had made her face blotchy; her eyes were watery and her skin was pale. She had neither slept nor eaten since the Detective Chief Inspector had knocked on the door the previous evening to give her the news. She had not believed them at first; tried to tell them that there must have been some mistake; that Rod could not be dead. He had only popped out to meet someone at The Bargeman for an urgent meeting about the Salem project. There had been a phone call and Rodney said that he must go then and there.

The woman detective with the DCI had done most of the questioning. She had spoken softly and been very sympathetic. But there was little that Babs Halliday had been able to tell them. She had not known the identity of the caller and Rodney had not told her.

It must have been somebody from work; one of the contractors. They were always phoning him about something or other. He attended to every detail: scaffolding, health and safety, lunch breaks, temporary toilets. Anything and everything. Never wrote anything down; kept all the detail in his head.

She answered the detectives' questions truthfully; all except one, that is. Babs Halliday knew that Rod had enemies. She did not know who they were, and her husband had never mentioned anybody, not outright, anyway. But you don't win too many friends when you run a drugs empire, do you? She kept all that information to herself; that and the strange letter that had been posted through the penthouse letterbox on the morning of Rod's death. Why on earth should anyone send her husband a quotation from the Bible?

***

'So, it's Boris then?'

'What, Pauline Philbey's cat?'

The inner cabinet burst out laughing. At last, the tension was broken. It had been a long and depressing meeting up to that point. Then Charlie Riggs had decided it was time to lighten the mood in response to the coffee break conversation about the leadership of the Conservative Party now that Theresa May had decided to stand down. After all, the mood could not be much more depressed in Hartley's CID team. Another murder had been added to the growing tally of crimes and two people had gone missing: Williams, Smith, and Halliday dead; Metcalfe and Gelsthorpe nowhere to be seen. Crucial evidence had disappeared, assuming it had ever existed in the first place, other than in the local archivist's dream. The breakthrough in the Hargreaves case had turned out not to be a breakthrough after all. Someone who could have helped had died, though at least Dooley had passed away from natural causes before May could get to his bedside. There was no news from Australia: nothing whatsoever that would connect Linda Welch in any shape or form to Thomas Hodgson's 'suicide'. No credible witnesses to any of the recent killings had been identified or volunteered to come forward, despite numerous appeals. The DCI was having to fend off the ACC on a daily basis; the inner cabinet's credibility was on a knife edge.

'Is there any information about Gelsthorpe or Metcalfe?'

'No, sir. We have not had anything'.

May sighed. The moment of mirth over Pauline Philbey's feline companion had passed.

'You know, when we got the call that a body had been found in the canal, I honestly thought that it was going to be Gelsthorpe or Metcalfe. They fit the profile; they were part of the same group as Williams and Smith: the singers, the chapel, Riddles. What is the connection with Halliday? Why him?'

Trubshaw and Riggs looked at each other and then at their boss. They shrugged.

'Come on, you two. We must do better than this!'

'There must be a connection, sir. If Williams and Smith were killed by the same person, then Halliday must be too'.

'Must he, Viv?'

'Same M.O., sir'.

'Yes, in the case of Williams, but not of Smith. Right hand and left hand, remember, Charlie?'

Riggs nodded.

'We haven't ruled out two murderers, sir'.

'No, we have not. It wouldn't be the first time that people have worked in tandem to kill'.

'But why Halliday?'

'Well, there is a connection, sir'.

'Viv?'

'He owns, *owned* and refurbished Riddles, and he was about to turn Salem into apartments. It must have something to do with the factory and the mill'.

May smiled, weakly.

'But where's the quotation from the Bible? You can't pin a piece of paper to a naked body. Where is it; where's that bloody psalm verse?'

***

This was the last chance, the very last chance. Pauline Philbey walked down the side of Salem Chapel to the vestry door. The paving stones were uneven, and she nearly fell twice. The cemetery on the other side of the pathway was overgrown, but she comforted herself that the graves would still be looked after by the Methodist Circuit. She did not know what made her go and look at the family grave. It was not as if she had previously been a regular visitor. There was no need to go and look at headstones when you could look up your family's history online. That was the thing to do nowadays and she smiled to herself as she thought of the family tree that she had put together, right back to the early eighteenth century.

Pauline Philbey never got to the place where her parents were buried, because there, on the edge of the cemetery furthest away from the road, she saw a headstone that made her stop in her tracks. Three names were listed: Arnold, Daisy, and Minnie; the Hargreaves family, all dead within twelve months of each other; the daughter murdered, the parents killed by grief. She read the Bible quotation beneath the names and dates: "Children are a heritage from the Lord; offspring a reward from him".

Philbey decided not to pursue the search for her own father's and mother's grave after all. She took a swig from her hip flask and made her way back to the vestry door. She fumbled in her pocket for the key that Ted Gelsthorpe had let her borrow before he had to give it to the Halliday Enterprises representative in charge of the purchase of the building. She should have returned it sooner; she had promised to do so immediately after the guided tour that had come to such an abrupt end. But the local archivist had so wanted to search through the choir library and the record books, selecting the ones that needed to be sent to Hartley Local Studies Library before the rest were almost certainly thrown in the skip.

Philbey was about to enter the building when she felt a hand on her shoulder. Gentle pressure was applied; then the grip tightened. *Oh my God! It's my turn. I'm for the chop now. I know too much. They must know that I found Williams' book. Oh, dear God, save me from all this.*

31

May 17: Two Men Fall Asleep, One of Them for Good

'Are you alright, Ted? I've brought you a cup of tea'.

Gelsthorpe sat upright with a start.

'Don't worry, we're alone. He's gone to work already and won't be back until late. We'll have sorted something out by then. We have to stick together – people like you and me!'

'Are you sure I am safe here?'

'You are well and truly safe. I will make sure of it'.

Gelsthorpe relaxed and took the proffered cup. Best bone china, he noticed.

'I'm not used to this treatment'.

It was a long time since the Holme Hill cricket club groundsman had been brought tea in bed. Gelsthorpe remembered how it had been the other way around for the last years before his wife died, not that she recognised him, or the food and drink when he had given it to her and tried to engage her in conversation. He had fed and watered the love of his life with a straw and a spoon when he brought her meals up to the bedroom. It had been like feeding a child.

'What's the matter, Ted? Why are you crying?'

'Just remembering Maisie, you know'.

The woman nodded.

'I know. It must have been hard for you. Watching her die like that, especially when you know what caused it'.

Gelsthorpe stopped drinking his tea.

'How did you know about that?'

'Remember that my husband worked at Riddles'.

'So, he worked in the R&D unit as well?'

The woman nodded.

'I never knew. It was all hush-hush at the time. They weren't supposed to talk about it, not to anyone in the mill, not to anyone outside, not to each other and not even to their wives or husbands'.

'You really didn't know? You really always thought that my other half was just an office manager? I am not sure I believe you, Ted'.

'It's true'. Gelsthorpe nodded.

'So, Maisie told you nothing about what they were doing in there, at Riddles?'

Gelsthorpe shook his head.

'It was only after she was diagnosed that I realised what had been happening. Some government officials came and told me I was never to say anything. My wife had apparently signed the Official Secrets Act and there was nothing I could do about it. The government wouldn't accept liability for her illness, but I did receive a handsome payoff'.

'How much?'

'I'm not supposed to say'.

Gelsthorpe paused for a moment, wondering whether to tell his hostess the price of Maisie's life.

'£100,000. It was take it or leave it; I took it'.

The woman sat down on the bed and squeezed Gelsthorpe's hand.

'Not much, is it, Ted? Not much for a life; for your other half; for someone you were married to for forty years'.

'Forty-one, actually'.

'And what about Salem? What did Maisie tell you about the goings-on in the Chapel?'

'What goings-on?' Gelsthorpe replied.

'I think you know what I am talking about now, don't you, Ted? You remember Minnie, don't you?'

Gelsthorpe looked around the room, as if to find an escape route. It had to be the tidiest place he had ever seen; far neater than his own little cottage had ever been, even when Maisie had been alive and still had all her faculties.

'I should be going. I ought to get home'.

'Are you sure, Ted? The police are out looking for you. They think you had something to do with *Lancashire Lasses*'.

'The boat or the two lesbians who live on it?'

The woman laughed.

'Both, I think, Ted. It was you who tried to kill them, wasn't it?'

'Eh? No, it was not me! I just went to see them after they'd defaced my living room'.

'Defaced your living room?'

'They spray-painted some words'.

'What words?'

'I don't know. Some words from the Bible, but it didn't mean anything to me'.

'How do you know it was from the Bible?'

Gelsthorpe laughed.

'Because they said which verse it was'.

'How did you know it was them, Ted?'

'Well, it must have been. Getting back at me for getting cross with them for mooring where they did. It's only supposed to be used for twenty-four hours and they've been there since the beginning of the month!'

'So, you don't understand the significance of that verse? And you know nothing about what went on at Salem?'

Gelsthorpe shook his head.

'What about Dooley?'

Gelsthorpe looked up at the woman.

'You mean, about the secret group?'

His hostess laughed loudly, then nodded.

'I heard the rumours, but I was never part of the inner circle I can assure you. I'll tell you what though, I do feel sleepy. So very, very sleepy. Did you put something in this, this...'

Gelsthorpe fell forward. His last image was of Elsie Wright catching the teacup before it felt to the floor and wet her precious bedroom carpet.

***

There were twelve people at the service: May, Trubshaw, the vicar, the organist, the four pall bearers, the funeral director, and three mourners. May nodded at Elsie Wright as she entered the church, but the dragon of mothers (as Riggs called her) avoided the DCI's gaze. Just as the service was about to start, two more people entered St Maurice's. First came Linda Welch, followed shortly afterwards by Joan Wilberforce. Both women were out of breath, and more than a little flushed. Trubshaw smirked at her boss. The vicar gestured to the landlady of The Bargeman and her friend, who took note of his direction and sat in the front pew opposite all the other worshippers.

'I didn't expect those two to be here, but I thought Pauline Philbey and Ted Gelsthorpe would have turned up'.

It was the funeral director, whispering to herself loudly enough for May to hear. The DCI looked at his DS, nodded slightly, and smiled.

The vicar droned on, trying to make the most of his research into the deceased. May felt sorry for him. As a local preacher in the Methodist Church, he had experienced the slow death of a dire service in front of a congregation who wanted nothing more than an hour's distraction on a Sunday morning; in the building not because they wanted to be in church, but because they always had gone; saying the words not because they meant them, but because they remembered them. Who amongst the attendees today, 17 May 2019, was here because they had feelings for the deceased? Nobody, by the looks of it. Why were there so few people at the funeral? The deceased was an old man and most of his generation were dead. He had not been much liked within the village anyway. May remembered when his own father was buried. Salem Chapel had been full – for the last time – probably.

'I hope there are more people at my funeral, Viv'.

'Don't worry, Don, I'll make sure the place is full'.

For a second, Trubshaw brushed her hand against his. May smiled and squeezed her little finger. The hymn came and the two of them sang lustily – the only mourners to make any sound. The DCI had never heard his DS sing before: she was good, a beautiful soprano voice. *How little I know about her! And she is leaving when this case is over!*

'And now for the committal'. The vicar nodded to the pall bearers to come and move the coffin out of the church and into the graveyard. The funeral director supervised the arrangements with her usual military precision. The congregation followed the vicar as the organist played Handel's *Largo* for the recessional.

It was raining heavily. May looked out over the valley towards Riddles and Salem. The wet mist made it difficult to differentiate between the buildings that made up Holme Hill. He mused on the fact that the deceased, a staunch Methodist, was being buried in a Church of England graveyard. But then, his own father was buried in this cemetery because Salem was full.

Then it was all over. The funeral director said that tea and sandwiches were available in the church hall for anyone that wanted refreshments. The vicar shook everyone's hand and said she had to go to the crematorium to take another service and was already late. Welch and Wilberforce insisted that they had to get ready for opening time and were not hungry or thirsty anyway. Elsie Wright looked at her watch and reminded everybody that Gordon would want his tea as he was coming home early tonight, and she had a guest staying as well. Trubshaw looked at May and the two decided that a quick cuppa was in order, especially as they were getting very wet.

The funeral party departed, and the gravediggers moved in and started to shift soil. They had completed their task and were putting their spades and shovels away when they heard footsteps. As they started their van, they saw a figure in a dark coat and hat holding a black umbrella walk towards the burial site. They thought nothing of it and drove off. The figure stood by the mound of earth, then bent down to read the inscription on the temporary headstone.

'Rhys Ivor Williams. Fell asleep 1 May 2019'.

The figure laughed.

'No, you didn't fall asleep, you miserable old man. I put you in that grave. And you're not the last one that will be buried in this cemetery before the end of the merry month of May'.

The figure stood up, looked once more at the grave, then spat at the cross and walked away, whistling.

32

May 18: A New Detective Constable Ponders the Case

———∿———

Georgie Ellis turned off the television in disgust.

'Last! With eleven points! Why, oh why did I watch it?'

She opened the tin on the coffee table and took out a bar of Old Jamaica Chocolate. She read the label.

'Rich, intense, and fruity. Just like me!'

The WPC laughed. It had been a long and eventful day and, despite the United Kingdom coming last in the Eurovision Song Contest, she was happy. George, as they all called her at the station, and much to her annoyance, was pleased that she was playing a small part in bringing the case of the Holme Hill Murders nearer to a satisfactory conclusion.

The chocolate tasted good; it was her favourite. Georgie Ellis savoured each piece as she popped it into her mouth. Looking at her watch, she realised that it was time for bed and an early start in the morning. Once again, she had been invited to join the inner cabinet at their briefing meeting at 0900 hours on 19 May. This was all looking good! How could she best prepare for the event?

'I'll review today. That's what I'll do! Better than curling up with a book, even a good one!'

She was not at all sleepy, despite being awake since 7.00 am that morning. Her grandfather clock struck 11.00 pm.

'Just one hour to review the case, then I really **will** turn in!'

The chocolate bar was nearly finished as she opened her leather Filofax and turned to the notes pages at the back. She always wrote in pencil; she found it helped her to think, especially when ideas would not come.

First, she thought back to the hospital visit to see Pauline Philbey. The old dear was missing her gin, but there could be no alcohol until all the tests had been completed and she was assessed and found to be ready to be discharged by the consultant. The WPC had been surprised to find Jo Bishop there when she arrived, but the explanation (and the reason for Philbey's presence in hospital) all made sense. Holme Hill's archivist had said what a fool she felt, having a major panic attack because she had thought someone was going to murder her. And it had been nothing more than a playful squeeze on the shoulder.

Jo Bishop had been just as embarrassed, protesting that she had seen Philbey approaching Salem and decided that she would join her in a last look around the Chapel. But the surprise encounter by the vestry door had backfired. Jo had called an ambulance immediately Philbey had keeled over. There had been a few anxious hours while the victim was monitored in intensive care, but now she was sitting up in bed eating grapes and sipping tea.

Georgie Ellis thought back to how she had engaged both women in conversation, initially about the weather and local history, then to do with Salem and its recent past. It didn't take Bishop and Philbey long to reveal all they knew about the mill's secret experiments for the government and the work-related deaths. The WPC had said nothing to her interviewees but resolved to tell Inspector May when she returned to Hartley CID. Ellis smiled as she thought back to how her DCI had been intrigued with the story and called Trubshaw and Riggs into his office to listen to Ellis's theory. Both the DS and the DC were impressed.

'It makes sense, sir. It connects our victims – even our Australian death – and gives us a motive. Now we just need to find someone who was aggrieved enough to want revenge on the managers at Riddles'.

'Yes, Viv, we just need to find a relative of some of the people who died because of that secret project'.

May had laughed at his two subordinates.

'Do you know how many people worked at that factory during the time when that experimental work was being done? Hundreds, thousands, in fact'.

That was the point at which Georgie Ellis (though she said it herself) had come up trumps, reminding the other police officers that Jo Bishop had done a detailed analysis on her computer of all the employees at Riddles and their families. It would be a relatively easy task for the researcher to cross-check the factory deaths against the records of those who had worked on 'Project Earnest' (a joke at the expense of the factory's founder) and to follow up with their families, whose records Jo had also researched on *Ancestry*.

Having relived the day, Ellis now admitted to herself that there was just one problem with the 'Project Earnest' theory. She decided that this was a two-bar problem, so before thinking further about how and why Rodney Halliday's killing fitted in with the deaths of Williams and Smith, more Old Jamaica chocolate was required. Where was the secret stash? She searched every kitchen cupboard; every sideboard drawer; both bedroom cabinets. Nothing; not a single square of chocolate in sight. Even the bar in the old slippers had gone.

'Bugger! Bugger! Bugger! There must be some Old Jamaica somewhere!'

Within minutes, Georgie Ellis had donned an overcoat over her pajamas and dressing gown and was skipping down the steps from her flat and into the lift to the car park. It was cold and she rushed around her BMW Z4 trying to find the missing bar.

'Got it!'

Her giggle echoed around the car park as she ran towards the staircase and lift and back to the warmth of her apartment.

'Now, where was I?'

Rodney Halliday had nothing to do with Riddles, apart from buying the factory and converting it into luxury apartments; and nothing to do with Salem apart from buying the chapel to convert it into yet more luxury apartments. Did somebody have a grudge against Halliday because of his destruction of the village's heritage? But would that justify murder, especially when Riddles had been converted very tastefully and the outline plans for Salem looked eminently respectful of the original architecture, with fittings, pulpit, and even the old organ case (but not pipes) retained as features.

But, as the inner cabinet had found out that morning, Halliday had done time, and more than once. Georgie Ellis had been surprised at the news but noted that it had been mainly petty crime in South London. Then Rodney had suddenly gone off the radar and become very respectable, moving north, and starting his property business, specialising in large, old, industrial, or ecclesiastical buildings. On the face of it, Halliday had become a pillar of Yorkshire society, lavishly giving to Holme Hill organisations: cricket club, rugby club, primary and secondary schools, rotary, freemasons. You name it, he had given, and generously, to these and many more organisations. He was now Chair of Hartley Chamber of Commerce and Vice-Chair of the local Enterprise Board. A tearful Barbara Halliday had told Ellis that her Roddy had even been thinking of standing as a local councillor, for the Tory Party, of course.

He is too good to be true. He cannot be so clean and above board. He must have got his money from somewhere. The construction industry had its 'wide boys': Jo Bishop had said there had been issues with the quality of some of the construction work and especially the gas installation. But nothing especially dodgy, and Halliday himself had taken the penthouse suite at Riddles, so he must have had some confidence in his own builders!

Georgie Ellis recalled the morning conversation about drug dealing near the cricket field. Could Halliday be involved in that? *No, he is too far up the supply chain. The dealers who we've arrested in the village would not even know of his existence.*

Did Halliday have a connection with the killing of Minnie Hargreaves? *Williams and Smith certainly knew the girl – and knew her well: she had sung in the same choir and been the mascot for the singing group with which the two men performed. They had testified at David Harrison's trial and their evidence had helped the prosecution convict the young man of the girl's murder.*

And what about Metcalfe and Gelsthorpe? Both men not seen for days; in Gelsthorpe's case, soon after an altercation with the two women on the boat, who had now taken up residence with Linda Welch at The Bargeman *while their home was fished out of the lock and somehow repaired – if it could be. How were they all linked together, assuming they were, or was it just coincidence?*

And I still believe that I found the evidence that proved Harrison was innocent. The photograph was grainy, but not that grainy. Bradley must be mistaken or lying. But why would he lie? What did he have to gain from letting an innocent teenager go to prison while the real killer remained at large, free to kill again?

Not that there were any further murders in the area like the Hargreaves killing. I checked on all the killings in Hartley Valley for the five years before Minnie died and every one since, right up to 2019. At least DCI May agreed with my analysis: Minnie Hargreaves' murder was a one-off. Her death was bound up with Salem, or Riddles, or both; and Minnie's demise was at the heart of everything that had happened since.

Ellis swallowed the very last piece of chocolate.

'I will get Bradley and the rest. You mark my words, Detective Chief Inspector May'.

33

May 19, Morning: Rise and Shine

———∽———

'Who's a good boy?'

Arthur gurgled. Joan Wilberforce smiled. It was a long time since she had been able to play with a little one.

'Enjoying yourself?'

'I am, Linda. It's nice, isn't it? Being a family, like those three'.

Joan could see the sadness in Linda's eyes. She wondered about asking her boss, and now her friend, if she had any children, but thought better of it.

Jaycee and Abbey came into the dining area. Joan thought they seemed remarkably cheerful, given their home had just been written off. She smiled as she heard Linda offer accommodation to the couple and their baby.

'As I said before, stay for as long as you like, you two – sorry, three. I have plenty of space. The old music room is OK as a sitting room for starters'.

Butch arrived with breakfast: full English. Joan assumed that he must have cooked it straight after his morning run, for he was still in his tracksuit.

'Here we are, ladies. Just what the doctor ordered!'

Joan knew that Butch took great delight in serving up every kind of boiled, poached, grilled, baked, fried food that he had been able to lay his hands on. He had arranged the tables in the snug bar so that the four women, Arthur and he could sit together for the first meal of the day.

There was little conversation, so Butch entertained Arthur, who was fascinated by the man's capacious beard.

'Hey, Arthur, stop pulling at Butch's beard. It must hurt!'

'You're alright, Jaycee. It's no problem at all. I love kids. Always have done!'

'So, why aren't you a dad yourself, Mr Fork Beard?'

Joan Wilberforce winked at Linda Welch as she spoke.

Butch paused, looking down at his half-eaten breakfast. He took a swig from his heavily sugared mug of tea, smacked his lips, and then replied.

'I guess Miss Right never came along'.

'I hope you don't mean Gordon's mum!' Joan laughed.

'I certainly do not! That old witch'.

It was obvious from the look on his face that Butch did not want to talk about his love life – or the lack of it. So, Joan asked Jaycee and Abbey to share their plans for the boat.

In the meantime, Butch played soldiers with Arthur's toast and finished his breakfast. Joan Wilberforce thought about the next death to occur in Holme Hill.

***

Donald May worked out that he had not been to church for three months, well before the first of the Holme Hill murders, as they were now being called. This had happened before when there was an all-consuming case to deal with. May 2019 was different. 'Pressure of work' gave the DCI the ideal excuse not to preach, nor to attend services. He had even stopped praying.

May had always imagined that losing his faith would have worried him more than it did. When had it happened? He could not pinpoint a time when he had stopped believing in God, though as he thought more about it, he realised that falling in love with Detective Sergeant Vivienne Trubshaw had not exactly helped. It was the first time in his life he had been unfaithful to Caz. He had fought off what he now saw as the inevitable break up of his marriage, even if the relationship with his DS did not survive her transfer. It would not be easy to keep in touch once she had left. May shook his head and sighed: if he could sleep with Viv, *and enjoy it so much,* then he did not care enough about his wife, or Freddie.

The bell-ringers were hard at work at Hartley Parish Church. Freddie knew the different peals off by heart and could name them all as they were rung. May reflected on his son's special talent. He would be good in something like forensics when he was older. His meticulousness and his eye for detail and his phenomenal memory would be ideal for a job like that. The DCI looked at his watch. If he hurried, he could still get to the morning service at the Parish Church, but the flesh was far too weak and the spirit was not over-willing, either. He returned to his Sunday paper.

'Dad?'

Freddie appeared in the living room. He carried a locomotive in one hand and was attempting to brush away the spilt milk on his shirt front with the other.

'What's up, Frederick the First?'

'Nothing, Dad. I just wanted to ask you something'.

May put down the newspaper. He had not taken in a single word from his reading of it anyway.

'Fire away, son. I am all ears'.

'No, you are not, Dad!'

'It's just a figure... oh, never mind. What do you want to ask me?'

'What's Helen's law, Dad?'

'Goodness, Fred. Where have you heard about Helen's law?'

'In the newspaper. It's on the front page. It says: "Ministry of Justice announces plans to introduce *Helen's Law*, which would require a person convicted of murder without the presence of a body to reveal the location of their victim's remains before being considered for parole." Will that help you with your case, Dad?'

May laughed. His son never ceased to amaze him.

'I don't think so, Freddie. We have lots of bodies in this case already. We even have a body from 1976 that fits into the Holme Hill murders somewhere, somehow. Unless...'

***

St Maurice's clock struck eleven. Pauline Philbey looked at her watch. Perhaps it was not yet time for a drink. Another hour and then she would get started.

It was good to be home. Jo Bishop had become a real friend since the episode outside Salem and had brought the local archivist home once she had been declared well enough to leave hospital.

It had been a nasty shock. She had to take herself in hand now if she was going to avoid a repetition of the episode.

Pauline Philbey sat down in her favourite armchair and opened her post. Most of it was junk or bills. There was one piece of correspondence that intrigued her. She vaguely recognised the spindly handwriting on the envelope. Whoever had addressed the letter must have shaky hands, she thought. It had a Hartley postmark, so she assumed that it was from someone local. There was a sense of foreboding about the moment as she grabbed hold of her opener and slit the envelope.

It was from the Reverend Graham Dooley. She began to read. Her clock's Westminster chimes sounded. Putting down the letter, she went to see who it was at her door.

'I thought it might be you. You had better come in. I have just been reading some correspondence that will undoubtedly interest you'.

***

The service must be over. The match would start in two hours. The pitch still needed preparing. For a moment, Ted Gelsthorpe thought he was in his own bed, but then, as he fully regained consciousness, he remembered where he was. *What a strange situation!* He got out of bed and walked over to the window, from where he could see across to the cricket pitch and beyond to Salem and Riddles. His head ached. She must have given him something. The pealing bells meant that it was Sunday, but he had no sense of time having passed since he appeared here. How long was it? He looked at his wrist, but his watch was not there. The freshly washed and ironed pyjamas made him itch. They were meant for a taller man and he found it difficult to walk in them. He tried the bedroom door, but it was locked, and he was a prisoner.

What was Elsie Wright after? She had told him that he was with her 'for his own good' and that 'he would come to no harm'. His host had refused to say any more, other than that the danger would pass by the end of the month and that he was to stay calm and enjoy the peace and quiet of being out of circulation for a few days.

Gelsthorpe looked at the cricket pitch once more. It needed mowing before the game. Old Town First Team against Holme Hill First Team. That would be a tight one; two evenly matched sides. He had to get out, go home, and prepare the pitch. He rattled the knob and banged on the door, asking, then shouting, to be let out. There was no answer. He tried to attract the attention of passers-by when he went back to the bay window, but the road was deserted and the double glazing would make it difficult, if not impossible, to be heard.

'Am I next? Is Elsie Wright a murderer? *The* murderer?'

Then Ted Gelsthorpe heard footsteps; two sets of footsteps, in fact.

34

May 19, Afternoon: Four Conversations

———∽———

The room stank of urine and tobacco. The yellowed paintwork bore testimony to the fact that the occupant had been a heavy smoker. DC Charlie Riggs looked around the bookshelves. He sighed as he read the titles: *Christianity and World Order; Christian Unity; The Kingship of Christ; A Plain Account of Christian Perfection; The Holy Spirit and Power.*

'Lots of light reading here, sir, eh?'

'You should try some of it, Charlie. It might do your soul some good: a dose of John Wesley or George Bell'.

'You've read some of this stuff, then?'

'I have indeed, DC Riggs, just about all of it at one time or another! Essential literature for when I trained to become a local preacher'.

'So, you believe in all that stuff, sir?'

'Now there's an interesting question, Sergeant'.

'Sir?'

'It's a long story, Charlie. Another time perhaps? Let's just get on and see if there's anything here that helps us. Dooley wanted to see me urgently, but he was dead by the time I got here. It's a long shot, but I thought if we looked around his room before the care home cleared it away, we might find something: a note, a file, a photograph. Something, anything that helped us find the murderer'.

'Or murderers, sir'.

'Or murderers, Charlie. Indeed. I think it is highly likely that we are looking at more than one killer. But are they working in tandem or what?

May took down a volume of John Wesley's *Sermons* from the top shelf. He dusted off the cobwebs and let the book fall open. He began to read from Sermon 86: 'A call to backsliders'.

> *This is frequently the case with those that began to run well, but soon tired in the heavenly road; with those in particular who once "saw the glory of God in the face of Jesus Christ," but afterwards grieved his Holy Spirit, and made shipwreck of the faith. Indeed, many of these rush into sin, as a horse into the battle. They sin with so high an hand, as utterly to quench the Holy Spirit of God; so that he gives them up to their own heart's lusts, and lets them follow their own imaginations. And those who are thus given up may be quite stupid, without either fear, or sorrow, or care; utterly easy and unconcerned about God, or heaven, or hell; to which the god of this world contributes not a little, by blinding and hardening their hearts. But still even these would not be so careless, were it not for despair. The great reason why they have no sorrow or care is, because they have no hope. They verily believe*

> *they have so provoked God, that "he will be no*
> *more entreated".*

'He will be no more entreated', May whispered, and put the volume back in its correct place. He looked at the shelf below. It contained a series of diaries, one for each year from 1954 until 2019, except 1976.

Then May and Riggs approached the armchair by the window. There was a fine view of the valley: right across to Holme Hill and Hartley beyond. When you knew what to look for, you could make out Salem and Riddles and St Maurice's. On the table next to the armchair was a big leather Bible. May watched as his DC skim-read the open pages. One verse had been ringed several times with a biro.

'Children are a heritage from the Lord; offspring a reward from him'.

'Quoting from the Bible, Charlie?'

'Yes, sir, from this one here'.

***

'That was wonderful. I never knew it could be so good'.

Joan Wilberforce laughed and cried at the same time. It was such an obvious thing to say, but it was true. Now, at the tender age of 55, she had finally found out how good it could be; wonderful, in fact; the best thing she had ever experienced. Joan had read books and watched films; that had been fiction, though. Real life was never like that; at least, not with her husband. Derek: a boring name for a boring man.

'Thank you for this afternoon. It was gorgeous'.

'My pleasure'.

'No, my pleasure. I have finally found out what it is like to have a proper bath'.

Joan's lover laughed.

'What *do* you mean?'

Joan sat up in bed, not afraid to let her naked breasts be seen.

'Well, when I was small, my parents made me sit in the bath with my head at the tap end. They didn't want me to enjoy being in the water, so that was the way around that I had to be. I thought everybody had a bath that way around. It was only when I married Derek that I found out which way you were supposed to sit. Mind you, that was the only thing I learnt from him'.

'So, you never saw films and tv programmes where people were having a bath the right way around?'

'Well, yes, I did, but that didn't seem right. My mum and dad had made sitting in the bath the other way feel sinful. I couldn't do it for years. And that's what I meant about sex. I thought making love and it being enjoyable and fun and erotic and mind blowing and all the other things that it has been today… well, I thought that was for other people; that it wasn't real, just a fantasy put about by novelists and filmmakers and all that; while real life was…'

'At the tap end?'

'Yes. But it doesn't have to be like that, does it?'

Joan's lover simply smiled.

You have shown me that. Think of all the years I thought making love was just a chore; just something you had to do to get pregnant. Derek never seemed that bothered, even when we were 'courting', as they used to say. His definition of 'ardent' was a quick fumble, over in five minutes, on a Saturday night after he'd come home from the pub, then he'd turn over, with his back to me and read his bloody car magazine or, if he was really drunk, just fall asleep and snore. Never a thought about my needs; nothing!'

Joan looked down at her body.

'Not much is it?'

'You look lovely. And I fancy you something rotten'.

'Do you?'

'Yup. From the moment that I laid eyes on you, as they say'.

'Liar!'

'Absolutely true'.

'Look, today was out of this world'.

'You deserve it'.

'So do you, my love'.

They kissed.

'It all sounds to have been so shitty for you, what happened back in the 1970s, you know'.

'That was then, this is now'.

'But what happened then fits in with what's happening now, doesn't it?'

Joan's lover said nothing.

'And you know something about these murders, don't you?'

Again, Joan's lover said nothing.

'I'd understand if you said you were involved. Those men back then. They deserve what they're now getting for what they did in 1976. I won't tell anybody if you are involved. Are you?'

Joan's lover said nothing for a third time, got out of bed and started to get dressed. At last, there was a reply.

'Come on, Joan, let's get dressed. We have a pub to run'.

***

Jo Bishop lit a cigarette. It was her first in three months. She poured herself a big whisky while she decided whether to go back into the bedroom. It had been a big, big mistake. Why, oh why had she done it?

The snoring got louder. *Bloody hell! Over in five minutes then the bugger rolls onto his back and falls asleep! No wonder his wife doesn't 'understand him'. I'm going to have to change my supervisor. I can't have Bill; not now I've slept with him. At least, he gave me the courage to talk to that Detective Trubshaw, not that she was very sympathetic, and then that nice WPC. She knew what I was talking about, took me seriously, and took it further!*

Jo looked at the bedroom door and decided to make a coffee instead of going back in. To add insult to injury, there was an awful racket upstairs. *So much for the grieving widow. What the hell is going on?*

The noise got louder. Jo stubbed out her cigarette and went to the balcony to see what was happening. Unlocking the patio door, she tried to slide it open without making too much of a noise, just in case the occupants of the penthouse realised that somebody was listening in.

The shouting continued.

'You were supposed to do him over! Frighten him! Make him scared enough to pay up! You weren't meant to kill him!'

'But we didn't kill him! We had nothing to do with his death! Honest, Babs! As I swear on my mother's grave!'

'I'll be swearing on your grave before I have finished with you! And what's this letter all about?'

'I dunno, Babs. Can't be me, LOL!'

Jo had worked out that there were three voices arguing above: one woman (Babs, presumably) and two men, one with a light voice, the other speaking gruffly with a thick Cockney accent. At least, that was what it sounded like.

'So, this had nothing to do with you, either of you?'

'No, boss. We were nowhere near when he was murdered'.

'You sure?'

'And what did you do with all Rodney's stuff?'

'Don't worry boss, it's all taken care of'.

'You sure?'

'Yup. Sure'.

'So, who killed my husband then?'

The conversation stopped, suddenly. Jo tiptoed back inside her apartment so as not to be detected. Bill Harker was waiting to greet her with open arms.

***

'It was for your own good, Ted. We had to make you disappear, otherwise, you would have been dead by now. I am sure of it'.

Gelsthorpe snorted.

'You've had a very funny way of protecting me. Locking me up like this. Wasn't there an easier way?'

Elsie and Gordon Wright looked at each other and shook their heads.

'I don't think so, Ted. Mother has filled me in on what has been happening and what she has found out, thanks to Pauline Philbey and this little book. These are dark days for Holme Hill'.

35

May 19, Evening and Night: An Adventure Goes Horribly Wrong

---cⱴɔ---

The BMW Z4 purred to a halt. Georgie Ellis switched off engine and headlights, got out of the car and quietly shut the door. She looked up and down the country lane to see if she had been noticed. There was not a sound, apart from the hoot of an owl in the tree near to where her beloved motor was now parked. The lack of any moon made it difficult to see the way ahead, but she had studied the map in detail before she had left home, memorising the way to Bradley Barn.

This will either make or break my career. But somebody has to do it. I just know that Bradley is lying! David Harrison was innocent, and I shall, must *prove it.*

WPC Ellis walked slowly down the lane towards DCS Arthur Bradley's home. *Arthur? That was the name of that baby on the boat, wasn't it? How names go out of fashion and then come back as all the rage! Not that I should worry. I don't want children to get in the way of my career! It's bad enough having to put up with Tiggy's two! God, why call them Throthgar and Aethelwald! I'd rather have Arthur any day.*

Georgie Ellis switched off the small pocket torch that she had been using to guide her way. Bradley Barn was in sight. There were lights at the double-gated entrance and another one over the front porch door.

This is an impressive house, even on a Chief Superintendent's pension!

Ellis rummaged in her pocket for some Old Jamaica, bought at a garage on her way over. How good it tasted! For a moment she wished she were back in her warm flat, snuggled up with a good book. *Arthur and George* by Julian Barnes was currently sitting on her bedside table, half read.

Get a grip woman! If you are going to get to the top, you must do this; you really have to, Georgiana Ellis!

There was a security camera above the portico and another one at the corner of the house, by the triple garage. She walked further down the lane, on the opposite side of the road to Bradley Barn. Beyond the end of the boundary wall was a dirt track that looked as though it led to a farmhouse; its lights glistened in the distance. The owl hooted again; WPC Ellis turned back in the direction from where she had come. She could just make out the shape of the Z4, still where she had parked it.

She looked at her watch. Only five minutes had elapsed since she had arrived. It seemed more like an hour. Walking down the track, Ellis noticed a side entrance to the grounds of Bradley Barn. It appeared less well protected than the front of the house; she decided to investigate.

First came what must have been a small milking shed when these outbuildings were part of the original farm. She looked through the window: no dead bodies; no glaringly obvious evidence; no killer lurking in the shadows ready to be captured and convicted; just a ride-on lawn mower.

There was a second outbuilding next to it, heavily padlocked, but nothing of especial interest inside, as far as she could make out, other than a half-finished kit-car. She remembered her father building one of those. It had taken him years, but he had done it. Georgie Ellis was like her father: determined to see something through to the end, almost whatever the cost. When she was a little girl, he had often called her Magnus (like Magnusson, the host of *Mastermind*): 'Magnus, I've started, so I'll finish' Ellis.

Ahead, she could see a light go off on the ground floor and, a moment later, one come on upstairs. Bradley was presumably going to bed. She looked at her watch: ten past midnight. *Hmmm, another night owl!* She crept up to the French windows of what was obviously the study, judging by the book-lined walls. It was remarkably easy to pick the two locks on the double doors. She eased herself through the narrowest possible opening, making sure that she made no noise. Once inside the study, she listened carefully, in case she had disturbed Bradley. She was in the clear. So far.

Ellis turned on the pocket torch and began her search. The library of books was of little interest, but the rows of neat box files offered much more potential. Not a single folder was of any consequence, however.

She turned to the mahogany desk. All but one of its capacious drawers was unlocked but contained nothing other than stationery, empty notepads, a stapler, a hole punch, dividers. The last drawer that she tried was locked; she eventually managed to pick the lock.

Here at last was what she was looking for. A file marked 'David Harrison'. As quickly as she could, Georgie Ellis photographed all the documents and pictures. This surely proved the young man's innocence and Bradley's duplicity. Having completed the filming, she put the file back as she had found it, locked the drawer, then looked around the room to make sure that there was no evidence of her visit left behind. She had closed and locked the French windows and was about to head back the way she had come when a car turned into the side entrance. It was heading straight towards the French doors.

WPC Ellis ran along the side of the house, staying in the shadows to avoid detection. The car stopped, someone got out and knocked at the French windows. After a few minutes, Georgie heard the windows being opened and two men talk. But instead of going inside Bradley's house, the host came out and began to walk with his visitor around to where Ellis was hiding. A light came on: she had to think quickly. At the far end of the back wall of Bradley's Barn were some steps down to a basement room.

Ellis ran down the steps. To her surprise, the door was unlocked. She went inside. The musky smell overwhelmed her to the point where she had to put a gloved hand to her mouth. The footsteps and the voices got louder. The two men were coming down into the basement room. The door opened and they entered. She took shelter behind an old filing cabinet.

'So, you'll be back in the morning?'

'Yes, I'll have everything ready. Can I take a look?'

'Over here. I thought it best to store it down here. But it will be just as it should be by the time we need to put things in place'.

The two men laughed.

'OK. What time shall I call back in the morning?'

'About 11, I would say. Then we'll get everything ready for the discovery on Wednesday'.

'You look tired'.

'Yes, I feel it. I will be glad when it's all over. Not long to go now'.

'I know. I feel the same way. But we can put an end to it all then. Once and for all. I had better go. I have an early shift in the morning. So, 11 will be good for me. I should be able to get here for then. And don't worry, everything is ready at the other end'.

Georgie Ellis heard the two men walk out of the cellar. The door closed behind them, then a key in the door. She waited until the footsteps had died away completely, then came out from behind the filing cabinet and went to pick the door lock. It was easy enough to do. There was just one problem, the door was also now bolted and padlocked from the outside.

She remained calm and took her mobile out of her pocket. Ellis sighed. Wherever she went in the basement room, there was no signal.

No way of getting out and no way of phoning. Think, think, think, woman!

The excitement was now turning to fear; the adrenalin rush had faded. Suddenly, the Hon. Georgiana Lucinda Ponsonby-Ellis felt cold and afraid. She should not have come; not have acted like this. What would happen when DCI May found out?

That's if I am alive to report back to Hartley CID.

Ellis regained some of her confidence and composure. She walked over to the bulky equipment near which the two men had stood talking. There was a faint hum. Taking the tarpaulin off the top of the machinery, she discovered a large freezer.

The lid was heavier than expected. It creaked as she opened it. Much to her surprise, Georgie Ellis found frozen food of all varieties: ice cream, pizzas, a large turkey, meals-for-one. There must have been at least six months' worth of food in there. The WPC was about to close the lid when she noticed something glinting. She peered down. It was a ring, and the ring was attached to a hand. Scrabbling to move the meals out of the way, Ellis found an arm, attached to a torso and then a head.

'Harry Metcalfe', she cried.

36

May 20, Morning: An Inspired DCI; a Bemused Widow

'Where's George? I would have expected tea and biscuits by now!'

Charlie Riggs looked at the murder wall, full of photographs, diagrams, post-it notes, and much more.

DCI May looked at his watch.

'She normally brings our drinks in at 10.30, doesn't she, Viv?'

'Yes, sir, regular as the proverbial clockwork'.

May looked at his DS, wondering what she thought of the ambitious WPC. He decided 'not very much'; but then he had never really understood women and how they might envy each other, or not.

'I still don't understand why Halliday was killed, at least not as part of this sequence of murders'.

'I agree, Viv. Rodney Halliday undoubtedly has a lot to answer for, but I don't see any real connection with the other two murders, where the victims knew each other, lived in the same village, worked at Riddles, worshipped and sang at Salem, and performed in the same barber shop group'.

'Halliday had converted the Riddles building and was about to start work doing the same to Salem. So, there is a connection, sir'.

'Yes, Charlie: Riddles and Salem. It all comes back to those two buildings and what went on inside them. What about Project Earnest? Is there a link there?'

May went over to the murder wall as he spoke, tracing the various connecting lines; nothing stood out.

'Williams and Smith were definitely both involved in the secret project. The staff records from the period and the work that Jo Bishop did on all the documentation prove that. But I can find no reference, no link, nothing that connects Rodney Halliday to that work for the government'.

'There has to be a link. Perhaps Halliday had a relative who was involved in the project: what about a father or some other relation? Somebody who was central to the work; someone who was culpable for the deaths of all those factory workers because the side effects of that "wonder material" were not considered – just like asbestos, only even more lethal'.

'I know, sir. Asbestos was bad enough, but if you read the medical reports for the people who worked on Earnest, what horrible deaths they had!'

'And that would be enough for any family member to want revenge on the people responsible!'

'But, sir, why was there so little in the newspapers at the time or since? Why was there no official inquiry? Something so blatantly wrong should have been fully investigated!'

May smiled at his Detective Sergeant. She could be so passionate when she got the bit between her teeth. *I was just as moral once.*

'Government cover-up, Viv. There would have been hush money from the government of the day. People would have been paid to keep quiet. But that gives me an idea. Charlie, when we've finished this morning, see what you can find out from the relevant ministry... defence, was it? By now the records should be available, shouldn't they?'

'It depends, sir. They may have been embargoed for longer if it was top secret. But I will make it my top priority today'.

'Thanks, Charlie'.

May smiled at the way in which his Detective Constable used that phrase: everything was a 'top priority' to Riggs; not that he always got the order of his priorities right. But he was a good copper and deserved promotion to DS when Trubshaw left.

'Let's hope that your research links Halliday to the other two murders, then'.

'Viv?'

'Yes, sir?'

'Get me a tea and a biscuit, would you?'

Trubshaw grimaced, said nothing and left the room to get the boss his morning cuppa and a rich tea. Once the DS had left the room, May spoke.

'I'd like you to take over from Viv when she moves to Lancashire, Charlie. I want you to be my DS'.

Riggs smiled, having known that this was coming ever since Trubshaw had accepted the DI job on the other side of the Pennines.

'Great. Of course, sir. It will be an honour and a privilege to serve under you as your Detective Sergeant, sir!'

May was taken aback by the response. He didn't feel he had been much of a role model or provided any real leadership over the last few months, not since he had lost his faith and gone to bed with Vivienne Trubshaw.

The DS appeared with a tray on which there were three mugs: one of tea and two of coffee. Milk in the tea and one of the coffees; Riggs took his black; no-one had sugar.

May took the biscuit offered. Perhaps rich tea and tannin would inspire him.

'Viv, remind me what Fizz said in her PM report about Halliday's murder'.

'Same MO as the other two, almost certainly by someone right-handed'.

'So two right-handed; one left-handed?'

Trubshaw nodded.

'And two of the bodies with a Bible reference attached to their persons. One not?'

Trubshaw and Riggs nodded in tandem.

'What if the murders aren't linked? What if there are three separate murders, made to look as if they were all perpetrated by the same person?'

Trubshaw and Riggs looked at each other and then at their DCI. May folded his arms and smiled.

'Now, there's a thought...'

***

The penthouse felt so empty and silent. Rodney had been such a noisy so-and-so. Babs Halliday remembered all the times when he had entered a room and immediately everyone realised he was there; he filled every space that he occupied.

She would miss him. He had been the only man for her since they had been at secondary school together in the east end of London. She had never looked at anyone else; ever. Babs Halliday knew that her husband had been a bad boy; but she still loved him, for all his faults. She had known about the drug dealing and the extortion; she had stood by him when he was sent down; she had even turned a blind eye to the affairs.

He had been good to her. They had wanted for nothing: nice houses; cars; holidays; jewellery; fine clothes; an expensive nose job; all the Clarins that she could fit in every one of her bathroom cabinets, and more. Despite everything, he had loved her and she had loved him.

But she could never forgive him for what he really was; what he must have been for the whole of their married life. It sickened her to think of him looking at those pictures; doing things that no decent man should even think about doing. And when his henchmen had discovered Rodney Halliday's perversion, they had been just as determined as she was to bring him to justice; to put an end to his activities once and for all. But not by going to the police; that would be too easy for him and he would find a way out thanks to his fancy lawyers, his peculiar handshakes, and the officials in his pocket. This would be old-style east end punishment. Everything had been arranged; the die had been cast.

There was just one problem: somebody else had got there first. Barbara Halliday opened the envelope inside which was a piece of text cut out from some book or other. She failed to understand why she had been sent it, but read the words out loud, just in case it gave her some inspiration.

"Children are a heritage from the Lord; offspring a reward from him".

She was none the wiser.

37

May 20, Afternoon: Letters from the Past; a Book Reappears

———o⅄o———

Pauline Philbey went into the kitchen and poured what was left of her gin down the sink. She looked at the empty glass and wished that she could find the book. That little volume held the key to the murders. She was sure of it; not just who had been murdered, but who *would* be. Even Halliday was in there: Dr Ernest Halliday, BSc, PhD, FRS.

It had been a short but delicious affair. She had been working for Rhys Williams; Halliday had breezed in and out of the office, always making some chirpy comment. She had laughed at his jokes; listened carefully as he explained his work; smiled as he ruffled his hair when he couldn't solve a problem with the wonder formula; delighted at his enthusiasm when there had been some breakthrough or other; tried to find out what he was doing, all in secret, for the Ministry of Defence.

Then one morning he had simply told her that they were going out for a meal: that evening, no messing about. There was a new restaurant in Hartley; he wanted to try it out, and he was going to take her, Pauline Philbey. 'No' would not be taken for an answer.

'Meet you at 7.00 at the railway station; we'll go by train; then I can drink'.

She had met him. They sat opposite each other in the single carriage that trundled from Holme Hill into town every evening and had eaten at the Chinese on Market Street. He had insisted they use chopsticks even though it took twice as long to eat the food and he had spilt down his front. But then that was nothing new; he was such a messy eater, but she loved him for it. She loved him full stop. She had done from the first time he had walked into the office at Riddles.

He had told her his life story in that one evening: about his love of learning and his fascination with chemistry; about his scholarship to Cambridge from his east end school; about the alienation from his family because he had turned his back on their criminal way of life; how he loved singing in choirs from when he had been at university and how he had joined the Select Seven as a 'supernumerary'. She had called him 'the eighth man' in the singing group. He had laughed like only he could laugh. Then he had told her his worries about that group; that there was something wrong that he couldn't put his finger on. If he could just find out what they were up to. There was something strange about them. Sad, lonely men; that's what they were. All they wanted was love, and nobody was giving it to them.

Whatever else they discussed that evening, that night, and the following morning as they dressed for work, Dr Halliday could not be persuaded to say anything about the secret project. He just clammed up whenever she tried to raise the subject; but then he had signed the Official Secrets Act and he could not break his oath, even for his precious Pauline.

The relationship had not lasted. Ernie had been called away to London and Philbey had never seen him again. He had left no address, no telephone number, no contact details of any kind. When she had asked Rhys Williams what had happened, there was simply silence. Williams had started to make things difficult for Philbey: deriding her work; criticising her in front of other workers in the office; making lewd suggestions when she was on her own with him. So, she had resigned and been paid off in lieu of notice. Then a series of letters had arrived; one a day for three weeks, and one day, nothing. The correspondence had stopped as abruptly as it had started.

Pauline Philbey went upstairs to her bedroom and got down on her hands and knees. Her back ached as she did so. She prayed sitting nowadays because of her arthritis. But she had to stoop on this occasion to look under the bed. Part of her wondered if it would still be there after all those years.

But it was, with the key in the lock. Philbey laughed. Why did people do that? What was the point of locking a box and then not removing the key? It was not easy to turn; rust had fused the mechanism, so she took the container down to the kitchen, got a knife and forced the lid open. It smelt musty. She took the letters out and read them; each and every one. There were tears in her eyes as she got to the final piece of correspondence.

Dear Philbers,

I miss you so. I have never felt about anybody like I feel about you, honestly! Wish I was back in Yorkshire; wish we were together! I hope to be there before long! Then we can pick up where we left off!

The trouble is, the MoD want this thing finished and I need specialist equipment that isn't available at Riddles. Sorry I couldn't say anything when I left, and I'm not supposed to say anything now. I shouldn't even be writing these letters. So hush, hush, all this. Nobody must know where I am. People would kill to get the secret now that I am so close!

And what do you think has happened? Bloody Rodney has gone and got himself arrested. Just when I thought I had earned enough money for everyone to move out of that shithole in London and I could give up this project and live the life that I want to live, with you, my love!

'So, they were related! Rodney must be the younger brother that he used to talk about! The black sheep of the family!'

It won't be long now, I promise you! Can't wait to get my hands on my Philly!

Your Electronic Random Number Indicator Equipment!

XXXX

Pauline Philbey folded the letter back into its envelope. She brushed her thumb over the address. They had spent some wonderful days, and nights, in Hartley. It was all so obvious now. Rodney looked so like him: same floppy hair, same lop-sided grin; they even cleared their throats the same way. She had hardly been able to contain her emotions that day at Salem. When Halliday junior had turned up at the guided tour, she couldn't believe it. For an instant, her heart leapt for joy, thinking it was her Ernie. Then she saw the blousy wife and the tattoos on his hands. That was no eminent researcher; that was not the man she had been in love with all those years ago!

Philbey closed and locked the box and put it on the bottom stair, ready to take it back upstairs when she went to bed. She looked at the gin bottle but decided to have a coffee instead. The clock struck three. She felt tired but could not doze off like she usually did. She tried to read the newspaper but could not concentrate. Daytime television was no distraction either. Perhaps she could do some cataloguing of material from the local archive. Her laptop was just warming up when the doorbell rang.

Pauline Philbey opened the door.

Elsie Wright smiled as she handed over a little book.

'I think this is yours'.

38

May 20, Evening: Freddie Makes a Breakthrough; Ellis Has an Adventure

―――cho―――

DCI Donald May was not supposed to drink. His father had held true to the Methodist tradition of not consuming alcohol. It was only when the Chief Inspector was at university that he first became a heavy drinker. Then he saw the light. It was too easy to consume too much; and the greater his capacity, the harder it seemed to be to get drunk. He stopped drinking. For many years, he did not miss it either. Caz was a good Methodist, and therefore there was never any alcohol in the house. May became known in the force as a tee-totaller, and after periodic ribbing when he was in the junior ranks, his approach had been accepted and, indeed, respected.

Refusing drink had been part of who Donald May was, just as he was never going to accept an invitation to join the Freemasons. He often mused on the fact that he had got so far in the force despite being so un-clubbable; graduate fast-track entry and then his PhD had probably helped.

The whisky was the annual Christmas present from the neighbours; Caz never had the heart to tell the Spencers that the Mays didn't drink, so the bottles went in the sideboard.

'Don't you think you've had enough, Don? That must be at least your third'.

'I know, Caz, I know'.

'I haven't seen you like this in ages, if ever. What's wrong?'

May shook his head. Caz sat down and put her arm around her husband. She kissed his forehead gently. He smiled and looked at her. She noticed the tears in his eyes.

'A bad day at work?'

The DCI nodded.

'Tell me, Don. I want to help'.

Caz stroked her husband's hair.

May put his glass down. He said nothing for what seemed an eternity, then cleared his throat and spoke.

'I have a week to sort this unholy mess'.

'A week? Who says so?'

'The ACC. I got called into his office this afternoon. If I can't show significant progress by next Monday, then I am off the case and it gets escalated to division'.

'But that's so unfair. You've worked your butt off on this case, *these cases*. What's happening is unprecedented, especially in sleepy Holme Hill. What did people call it? "The Rip Van Winkle Village of Yorkshire!"'

May laughed.

'They did indeed, Caz, they did indeed. I remember Dad being so indignant when he read that description in the *Yorkshire Post'*.

May went silent again.

'What have I said, Don? Don't say your father is implicated in all this!'

The DCI nodded.

'Apparently, he is listed in the little book that Pauline Philbey has, or said she had'.

'But she lost it, didn't she? Or you thought she never had it. You said it was just her imagination, after too much gin!'

May nodded.

'I'm not sure. She said too much that rang true for it to have been an old woman's befuddled dream. But that's just one of my problems'.

'And the others are?'

'How long have you got, Caz?'

Caz May ruffled the DCI's hair, then kissed him on the lips.

'All evening and more'.

May smiled back at his wife.

'Thanks. We haven't talked like this in ages, have we?'

Catherine May shook her head.

'I'm sorry, Caz. There's something else I need to tell you'.

'Shhh. One thing at a time. Tell me about the case first. You never know, just talking about it could make you see it from a different perspective. Freddie's always going on about it. Goodness knows why it fascinates him so!'

'He's incredible, that son of ours! He'll be head of Scotland Yard before you know it!'

'I know. Only the other day he was saying he had solved the murders'.

'What?'

'Yup! He has this conspiracy theory, as he calls it. No single person is the perpetrator. Rather, it's a whole group of people carrying out the murders. They are acting as a kind of cartel. So, if person A wants someone dead, then person B carries out the crime; then person B reciprocates for A; C does the same for D and then, if there is more to come, as you suspect, D is going to murder someone soon on behalf of C. More than that, though, Freddie has this idea that there is someone behind A, B, C, D and however many more murderers there are queuing up to kill; a mastermind, who is planning and scheduling it all, organising the killings to make them look as if they were by the same person'.

'My God, Caz! That would explain a lot!'

'Wouldn't it just?'

DCI smiled and whispered to himself.

'Thanks, Freddie, you're a star!'

***

The Honorable Georgiana Lucinda Ponsonby-Ellis opened her second bar of Old Jamaica and supped her third (large) glass of red wine. She watched the late regional tv news but, for once, there was nothing about the Holme Hill murders.

There will be soon, thanks to me!

WPC Ellis shivered.

But it could have been so different. I might have been the next victim of the Holme Hill murderer – no, murderers – if they had caught me.

She felt so weary but could not give in to sleep until she had written up a full report of her adventure. It was time for coffee – strong black coffee. Pouring the remainder of her wine back into the bottle, she corked it and put it on the dining table. She switched the coffee machine on and gloried in the smell as her drink came to the boil. Ellis sank back on the sofa, opened the document she was writing, reminded herself where she had got to, then began typing again.

Having been locked in the cellar, and with no means of escape, I had no option but to wait until daylight, when I imagined that Bradley and the other person would return to move Metcalfe's body, as they had previously discussed. I took the opportunity to look around the space. I opened the freezer and examined the body, making sure that I was wearing my gloves and that I did not leave evidence of my search. The victim had been killed – as far as I could tell – in the same way as Williams, Smith, and Halliday. The body seemed to be fully dressed, though I did not uncover it all.

Having done that, I searched the whole of the cellar to see if there was anything else of interest. There were various filing cabinets, but all were empty. The wine racks contained nothing worth drinking! Then I found an old doll's house. Inside, in what must have been the living room, were a whole series of figures. Four of the figures had miniature swords pushed through their necks. Three more figures were in the room, but there were no swords. The seven figures were all male, arranged in a circle around a final figure: that of a young girl.

Ellis poured more coffee as she thought about the figurines.

'The Select Seven and Minnie', she said aloud, swilling the drink in her mouth, as if to suck the caffeine straight into her system.

Having completed my search of the cellar, I tried to keep warm and get some sleep, but not before I reviewed the pictures that I had taken of Bradley's file on Harrison. Bradley must have had doubts about David Harrison's conviction from the start. After his retirement, he must have gone back and investigated Minnie Hargreaves' murder off his own bat and not only concluded that Harrison was innocent but also who had murdered the young girl, hence his involvement in the recent killings.

As I bedded down for the night, I made sure that I was out of sight as far as possible so that if Bradley and the other person came back while I was asleep, they were unlikely to find me.

I didn't get much sleep. There was an old blood-stained mattress in one corner of the cellar, but I decided to lie on the floor, just in case it was evidence. Was it Metcalfe's blood? Or one of the other victims?

They came back early the following morning. I heard the door being unlocked and two people come in. I assume that it was Bradley and his accomplice from the previous evening, but they said little and spoke quietly. To avoid being detected, I was right at the back of the room, behind the filing cabinets. I wanted to sneeze because of the dust but I managed to stop myself.

Ellis paused and made another coffee. Did she need to include details such as sneezing? Not really, but the WPC (who might still become a DC if she could retrieve the situation that she was now in) somehow felt it was therapeutic to set down what had happened, including every detail as far as she could remember. She could always edit the text before submitting the final version to DCI May. It was late but she was no longer tired as she relived the great adventure.

I heard them open the freezer and remove the packets on top of Metcalfe's body. Then they talked to each other as they heaved the corpse onto what I later discovered was a trolley. There was a lot of huffing and puffing at that point and some arguing as to how best to carry out the task.

As they wheeled the trolley to the door, I looked out from behind the filing cabinets. I assumed that the older man (he had white hair) was Bradley. I did not recognise the other person and only ever saw him from behind. But he was well built, thick set (like a rugby player) and did the heavy lifting as they got out of the door and had to pull the trolley up the steps. He wore a red tracksuit.

Because they were busy doing that, I was able to get out of the cellar once they had got the trolley onto the garden path and were wheeling it towards the same van that I had seen the previous evening.

I went the other way around the house and made my way over a gate into the fields behind Bradley Barn and then back onto the road where my car was parked, but not before I had got the vehicle registration.

I waited in my car until the van went past and then I followed it as cautiously as I could. I do not believe I was detected in any way.

It was difficult at times to trail them because it was by now rush hour through Hartley and into Holme Hill. But I managed to keep them in sight at all times. The van finally stopped at The Bargeman where the two men got out and unloaded a large sack in which I assume was the body of Harry Metcalfe.

I left my car at Salem Chapel, and walked to the pub. By the time I arrived, the van had driven off. I thought about following it but decided that it was more important to see what had happened to the corpse.

Everything was locked up. I went around the back of The Bargeman where the van must have delivered its contents but could see nothing. I was looking through the kitchen windows when I was attacked, a hood was put over my head, rope tied around my arms, hands, and feet, and I was bundled into another vehicle (or had the same van returned? I do not think so, as the engine sound was different). At some point on the journey to wherever, I was drugged and fell unconscious.

The next thing I knew it was evening and I was bound and gagged underneath the viaduct of the old Hartley branch line to Holme Hill. They had taken my mobile phone, but I managed to crawl to the canal towpath and waited until someone came along, untied me, and took me back to my car.

I then went home and decided that it was too late to call anybody and that it was best to write up what had happened before I reported in for work on 21 May.

The strange thing was, the person who 'rescued' me was from Holme Hill, and I have long had my suspicions about him. It was Gordon Wright.

39

May 21, Morning: Nothing Is as It Seems

―∽―

'Linda Harrison Welch: licensed in pursuance of Act of Parliament to sell intoxicating liquor on or off the premises'.

Detective Sergeant Vivienne Trubshaw read the sign over the front door of The Bargeman as she waited for a reply to her call to DCI Donald May. The pub had seen better days. When the DS pressed the doorbell, there was no sound. As she lifted the old brass knocker, it came away in her hand. Paint and plaster peeled off the walls. The old sash windows looked rotten. She remembered that Linda Welch had talked of her plans for Holme Hill's pub when DS Trubshaw and DCI May had first met her.

That seems like a different life now! An eternity! And it was just a couple of weeks ago!

Trubshaw felt weary at the thought of all this death. Three people had been killed already and at least two more were scheduled to be murdered by the end of the month, if you believed the notes that had been left with each body – or at least two of the bodies: was there a note relating to Rodney Halliday somewhere?

Why should we not believe the notes? They have been right so far! And then we have Gelsthorpe and Metcalfe missing, presumed, well, who knows what? Not to mention bloody George. Gone AWOL with her latest boyfriend, no doubt. Too cocky for her own good, that one. A right smarty-pants, just like I used to be!

Trubshaw began to wish May were over, the month, as well as the man, and that she could get on with preparing to move to Lancashire. Don had asked her to meet him off duty again. She had resisted so far but knew that she would give in before much longer. The DS should really keep saying no, but she wanted to spend time with him before it was too late. She could not help herself. She loved him; she always would. But then, so did Caz and Freddie. It would be wrong to take the man away from his wife and child; and, if the truth be known, he was never going to leave them either, despite all his protestations to the contrary. She determined not to meet with May; then she changed her mind and decided that the air had to be cleared.

Just one last time. Then it will be over. For good.

Trubshaw walked around the front of *The Bargeman* and towards the canal, hoping to see some sign of life. She walked past the delivery bay where barrels were unloaded and unloaded regularly. The stale smell of beer made her feel nauseous. She had never liked ale of any kind; that was her dad's drink. Dry white wine was preferable. The DS looked at her watch yet again: after 10 o'clock in the morning.

Surely somebody should be stirring by now!

Beyond the lock gates a crane was parked ready to lift *Lancashire Lasses* out of the water and onto a waiting low loader. Two men were scratching their heads trying to work out how to get the chains underneath the boat. Trubshaw stood at the end of the lock and stared down into the abyss below. Water was still pouring through the paddles. She could see how damaged the boat was: a large gash in the side of the hull; part of the cabin roof torn off; the contents drenched and ruined. *Lancashire Lasses* would need a great deal of TLC to be fit for human habitation. This was deliberate destruction, but to what end? Were those two women and their baby really in danger? Trubshaw decided that they must have been, if the narrow boat had filled with water before they had escaped. If anybody had fallen in, then they might have been sucked down and out through the paddles.

The DS shivered as she turned back towards The Bargeman; still no sign of life. Then a car arrived. A woman got out, went to the front of the pub, took out a key, unlocked the door, and went inside. Trubshaw thought how Joan Wilberforce was always so well dressed; Jaeger from top to toe; Mulberry document case; not a hair out of place. She could almost smell the Clarins even right over by the lock.

Now that there was someone to talk to back at the pub, DS Trubshaw left the canal side and returned to where her car was parked in readiness for the interview alongside her SIO.

A second car drew up; DCI May, at last. Trubshaw thought about asking him where he had been and telling him off for being late, but then decided just to smile thinly instead; that would have the same effect.

'Sorry, Viv. Problems at home. Freddie threw a real tantrum this morning. Caz just couldn't do anything with him. I had to go back home on my way here to help'.

'And now?'

'Things are OK. But he is in a funny mood. He has got a thing about these murders. He thinks he knows the answer and says he has worked out who is going to be killed next'.

The Detective Sergeant smiled and said nothing.

'And not just that, but he says there is a whole group of murderers – one per death – and a mastermind behind it all'.

'Well, I'll give your son full marks for imagination'.

May laughed; Trubshaw giggled.

I will meet up with him – just for old time's sake – definitely.

As Joan Wilberforce could be heard unbolting the front door of The Bargeman, Trubshaw pointed up above the doorframe.

'What do you always say about there being no room for coincidence in police work, sir?'

May nodded and winked.

***

WPC Ellis simply could not get up and out of bed. Her eyes must have looked like piss-holes in the snow, as her father would say. She should have gone to bed sooner, and not drunk so much, but that report had to be finished. Why could she hear DCI May and DS Trubshaw talking to each other? She was not up and dressed yet, and they were here ready to receive her briefing about the trip to Bradley Barn and what she had found there.

Ellis opened her eyes more fully. Her two superior officers were still talking. It was definitely their voices. She had heard the Chief Inspector and his Sergeant in conversation often enough, but she could not make out what they were saying. She detected the word 'coincidence'. That was one of May's favourite phrases: 'police don't believe in coincidences'. Trubshaw went on to say something like 'line of enquiry' and the two of them laughed.

There is definitely something going on between those two: everybody in the station knows it, but nobody dare say anything. I have seen them though!

May referred to the CPS only giving them 36 hours and they would need to get on with it.

She heard footsteps. Must be one of her noisy neighbours in the flat above. She had to tell them off regularly. They didn't like it when she went out onto her balcony and shouted: 'which part of shut the fuck up don't you understand?' That usually did the trick.

Ellis looked more closely at the ceiling. She really would have to get that crack fixed.

But there is no crack in my ceiling!

The WPC tried again to get up but she could not move. She looked down and around her. Georgie Ellis was tighly laced up to the bedposts, hands and feet, with a gag around her mouth. This was not her warm and welcoming flat.

Where the hell am I? What about my report?

Ellis blinked and tried to focus. Within the confines of her bondage, she attempted to move her body so she could look around the room. Apart from the bed there was just broken furniture, with an old piano in the far corner; boxes of what looked like music scores stood on top. This was definitely not her flat. Had she ever been back there after her night in Bradley Barn? But it wasn't the place where she had hidden in the cellar either. What could she actually remember?

I was definitely at Bradley Barn. I saw Metcalfe's body in the fridge. Then I hid. I fell asleep and then…

And then…

Gordon Wright took me home. Or did he?

Why was Gordon Wright on the towpath? How could I get from the viaduct to there when I was tied up?

By now, the Hon. Georgiana Lucinda Ponsonby-Ellis had realised not only that she was no longer in her flat, but also that the last time she had been there was the previous day, before she left for Superintendent Bradley's place.

It was all a sodding dream! I never got out of that cellar! It was so real! I never woke up! Somebody must have drugged me!

The WPC pulled at her bonds, but there was little movement.

Bugger! You're well and truly scuppered, now, Ellis!

May and Trubshaw were still talking, but now with a third person involved in the conversation: a woman, a familiar voice. Ellis realised that these sounds were not part of her dream; they came from above. The discussion must be going on at the entrance to the building which contained her prison. After a few moments there were footsteps and a door closed. Her fellow police officers must be right above. She could hear creaking as the people sat down. Ellis recognised May's distinctive cough. The interrogation began, at which point the WPC realised who was being interviewed upstairs and whose cellar she was in.

As she struggled to free herself and tried to open her mouth behind the gag, Ellis realised that there was someone else in her prison cell; Harry Metcalfe was sitting next to her in his Sunday best. Then the door opened, and Darth Vader appeared.

Perhaps this is a dream after all...

***

Pauline Philbey was about to make one of the biggest decisions of her life. She could put it off no longer. But first, she had to go over her previous day's discussions with Elsie Wright one more time.

Thank God, the book really had existed! She was relieved rather than aggrieved when Elsie Wright had admitted she 'temporarily removed' it. Wright had known about the log of names long before it had dropped out of Rhys Williams' folder of photographs: Williams had told Philbey all about it and what he was going to do with the information it contained. Elsie Wright had not meant to steal it, but when she came visiting the first time, the front door was open, Pauline was snoring happily, and the book was in her hand. Wright realised what it was straight away, for Williams had gleefully described its appearance to her on more than one occasion. She just had to see what was inside.

'I'm sorry, Pauline. I should have given it back when you came to see me the other day, but I didn't know what to do. There has been so much death in Holme Hill, not just now, but all those years ago: you know, the people at Riddles, Minnie, her parents, David Harrison. They all deserve something better. We have to right the wrongs that took place all those years ago'.

Pauline Philbey nodded as she remembered Elsie Wright's words and could not help but agree with her. But did 'righting those wrongs' mean committing murder?

She opened the gin bottle to help her decide.

40

May 21, Afternoon: Pieces of the Jigsaw Begin to Fit, but Where's George?

'Well, what did you make of that, Viv?'

'Hard going, sir'. Trubshaw grimaced.

DC Charlie Riggs joined the other two detectives in May's office. The DCI was already on his second coffee of the afternoon. Riggs decided not to speak, sensing that his Senior Investigating Officer was not in a good mood. He always looked out of the window when he was depressed.

'Coffee, Charlie?'

'No thanks, Viv, I'm tanked up already. I've been drinking the stuff all day while I've been catching up on paperwork. Paperwork that has led nowhere. There is absolutely no evidence to link Linda Welch to Thomas Hodgson's death. Perhaps it was, *is* just coincidence that he was found just yards away from her bar'.

May snorted, eyes still fixed on the car parked down below. Two people sat inside talking. He recognised one of them. By his watch they had been there for at least an hour. The DCI turned back to the two officers sitting at his conference table.

'What were we saying earlier, Viv? "Police don't believe in coincidences"'.

'I know, sir, and I would normally agree, but Charlie's been working on the Hodgson case for days now, and we are no further forward than we were last week'.

May, Trubshaw, and Riggs looked at each other.

'Let's forget about Australia, but not about Linda Welch. She knows more than she is saying. A lot more'.

'Sir?'

'Viv, fill Charlie in on what happened this morning. I'll just listen in'.

Trubshaw smiled. May often did that; it gave him time to think and review an encounter with a possible suspect. Sometimes, like now, he would go over to the whiteboard and write things down as she was speaking. The DS had got to know her boss so well over the previous three-and-a-half years that she could predict with almost 100% accuracy when and what he was going to write on these occasions. Sometimes, the DCI even asked her what he was going to write. Her answers had never been wrong.

'Well, they were all there. Not just Linda, but Joan Wilberforce. She arrived while I was waiting for Don... I mean, Inspector May to arrive. Then the Lancashire Lasses, you know, Jaycee and Abbey and their baby, were still in residence'.

'What of the other *Lancashire Lasses*? The boat, I mean'.

'Good question, Charlie. I watched two men trying to decide how to get the thing out of the lock where it seems to be very stuck, much to the annoyance of all the boaters wanting to get past The Bargeman and out onto Hartley Canal'.

'Where does the trashing of the boat fit in, Viv? Another coincidence? And how come that boat arrived on 1st May and is booked to be there for the whole month? A third coincidence, perhaps?'

May played with the marker pen as he stood and stared at the blank whiteboard.

'Gelsthorpe had threated them, hadn't he? And now he's disappeared'.

'Just like Harry Metcalfe', mumbled Riggs.

'Why did he threaten them? And why damage the boat like that? He must have been angry!'

Trubshaw thought back to her inspection of the badly damaged narrow boat.

'The lasses' earlier statement said that Gelsthorpe had told them they had to move on from the mooring, even though Linda Welch had given them permission to stay for the month. They wondered if he had a problem with two women living together'.

May shrugged his shoulders.

'Well, he is of that generation. My father had a problem with homosexuality, I know that, not least because of his strict upbringing. And mine, for that matter'.

Trubshaw and Riggs looked at each. They knew that May was worried about the reference to his father in the book that Philbey had supposedly discovered. It had yet to turn up, and both detectives though that it was a figment of the old dear's imagination, but the Detective Chief Inspector couldn't quite convince himself that the local archivist had dreamt it. Any of it; or all of it.

'Was Gelsthorpe capable of doing the damage, sir? He seemed quite frail, the times that I have seen him'.

'I think he is very fit for his age. What about all the physical work he does, looking after that cricket pitch? And he keeps a very neat garden, complete with a decent vegetable patch. And it wouldn't take that much to push the boat into the lock. It would be quite easy once you got the thing moving, pull it into the lock, tie it up too tight against the lock gates so that it is resting on the cill, then empty the lock, and beat a hasty retreat'.

Riggs looked quizzically at his DCI.

'Don't worry, Charlie, I have done a fair amount of narrow-boating in my time. It's easy enough to do if you follow the basic safety rules. If you get the balance right, the boat is easy to move, as are the lock gates. Even an old man wouldn't have a problem with it'.

Trubshaw poured herself more coffee.

'I don't believe it was Gelsthorpe, sir. I think Jaycee and Abbey did it'.

'What, deliberately trashed their own boat?'

'Why, Viv?'

'To implicate Gelsthorpe and to camouflage his disappearance. I don't think Ted ran off after sinking the boat and trying to murder the women; I think they abducted him and *then* scuttled their home'.

'And your evidence, DS Trubshaw?'

The Detective Sergeant smiled. Riggs always addressed her formally when he was not convinced her theories were sound.

'Well, if they were taken by total surprise when the boat was sinking in the lock, and they were in danger of drowning, why is it that they had all Arthur's things, changes of clothes, baby food, nappies, etc.? You name it, they had it. I asked Joan if she and Linda had supplied anything to help out Abbey and Jaycee after the boat sank, but she confirmed that the Lancashire lasses had all they needed when they arrived'.

'So, that's why you were questioning Wilberforce!'

'Indeed'.

'And what about Welch?'

'Well, Charlie, we have one clue that was hiding in plain sight all the time. And we have walked underneath it every time we have been to The Bargeman'.

'Yes, Viv noticed it while she was waiting for me to arrive. *Linda Harrison Welch licensed in pursuance of Act of Parliament to sell intoxicating liquor on or off the premises.* Check it out, Charlie. Surely, we cannot have another coincidence here, can we? Harrison as her middle name and David Harrison as the lad convicted of murdering Minnie Hargreaves all those years ago?'

'And what about Welch and the lasses? Did you notice how affectionate she was with Arthur? That was more than just a woman playing with a baby. That was a grandmother playing with her grandson'.

The speculation went no further. Another matter intervened. WPC Georgiana Ellis had not reported for duty since the previous Friday. It may only have been Tuesday afternoon, but this was not like George. George was always the first in the office every morning, ready to work, day and night, determined to prove herself and desperate to succeed. And she had been so delighted when May had involved her in the current murder investigations. She said good night to everybody in the office on 17 May and nobody had seen or heard of her since.

The inner cabinet's discussions on the afternoon of 21 May had been curtailed by a report that a BMW Z4, with the registration plate matching that of the vehicle owned by one

Georgiana Lucinda Ponsonby-Ellis had been found abandoned in a country lane some quarter of a mile from Superintendent Arthur Bradley's home.

'This is not going to end well, folks. I suspect that idiot has been taking the law into her own hands. What on earth possessed her to do that?'

***

'If I still smoked, I would have finished a whole fag packet by now'.

'What, in a single morning?'

'You should have seen me in my youth. I was quite the party girl then. Smoking, drinking, partying. You name it, I did it! Don't let the grey hair fool you!'

'Oh, I don't, Pauline. I bet you were a real goer!'

Philbey's smile lasted but an instant. The great weight of her immense and deepening dilemma pressed down on her once more, as it had been doing for every second, every minute, and every hour since Elsie Wright had called. She could not forget the fateful moment when the dreaded woman had handed back Williams's notebook and invited Pauline to join the conspiracy.

But it was not as easy as that. There were loyalties and principles to be considered; old friendships to be remembered and future consequences to be thought through.

Which was why she was now sitting in a car with Jo Bishop waiting to go into Hartley Police Station and talk to DCI Donald May.

She had not told Jo everything that had transpired at the meeting with Elsie Wright, but in recent weeks she had become close to her fellow local history researcher, not only because they shared a love of heritage and archives, but also as a result of their joint interest in the dark secret of Riddles's research department. Philbey had told Bishop about Ernie, what she knew of his work, of his supernumerary membership of the Select Seven and his wariness of the other singers in the group. She had been much less forthcoming to Jo Bishop about who she suspected had committed the recent murders.

Jo Bishop looked at her friend in the front passenger seat. Philbey was staring ahead, looking at everything and nothing on the other side of the windscreen. Bishop knew enough of the dilemma to feel sorry for the older woman, torn between friends and duty as she obviously was.

'Well, are you going to go in or not?'

Philbey looked at Bishop and smiled weakly.

41

May 21, Evening: A Handkerchief and a Chart

'You look dead beat. Why don't you stay the night?'

'I shouldn't really'.

'Why not? You're over 21 and there's nobody waiting for you at home'.

'No, I ought to go'.

'Come on, Joan. Stay. You know you want to. We could have a repeat performance...'

Linda Welch giggled and stroked Joan Wilberforce's forearm. The barmaid stopped her work for a moment, put the empty beer glasses down on the bar and turned to her boss.

'You know I want to. But should we?'

'Why not? It's perfectly legal. And we have feelings for each other. Why bloody not?'

'Well, the police, that's why bloody not!'

'How do you mean? We were just "helping them with their enquiries". They have nothing on us. We have nothing to hide'.

Linda took Joan's hands, pulled her close and kissed her lightly on the lips. They were entwined in a deeper embrace when Butch walked through from the kitchens.

'Sorry to interrupt, you two ladies. I hadn't realised you were… well, you were "busy". I'll lock up and leave you two to it'.

Welch and Wilberforce giggled.

'Thanks for all your help today, Butch. I couldn't have done it without you. But I do wish you would wear something other than your damn track suit. Joan will sort you out. She's a real *fashionista* you know!'

'No thanks boss. I must be going. I'll finish the latest job off tomorrow. Everything is secure for now'.

Welch and Wilberforce watched as The Bargeman's head chef walked out of the back door, shut, and locked it behind him, walked to his van, got in, turned the engine and drove off.

'Now, where were we?'

'I think I ought to go, Linda'.

'Nonsense. Come on. I bought you a toothbrush, so you didn't have to use mine this time'.

Joan shivered as Linda smiled.

'But I don't have any pyjamas'.

'You won't need any, my love'.

They giggled again. Joan Wilberforce looked down at her hands. Linda was fiddling with her wedding ring.

'I don't know why I still wear it. Force of habit, I suppose. It's five years since Captain Underpants left the Wilberforce household. And you know what? I haven't missed him for a single day'.

'So?'

Linda raised her eyebrows inquisitively.

'OK. I'll stay. But I want to talk first'.

'Talk? I want to do something other than talk! Just you wait till I get my hands on you!'

'I know you do, Mrs Linda Harrison Welch. But I have to ask you something first, and I want you to promise to answer me truthfully'.

'The truth, the whole truth, and nothing but the truth, so help me God'.

Welch raised her right hand; Wilberforce slapped it down.

'Linda! I'm being serious'.

Wilberforce stopped smiling.

'OK, Joan. I'll answer but come to bed first'.

'No, down here, we might disturb Arthur if we go upstairs'.

'He's such a sweetie, isn't he?'

'He is. He looks like you!'

'Pull the other one, Joan! Looks like me? You mean all crumpled up and liable to belch and fart at the first opportunity?'

The two of them smiled and stroked each other's arms.

Linda Welch tried to kiss Joan Wilberforce, but Joan turned away at the last minute.

'I have to ask you this, Linda. Did you murder Thomas Hodgson?'

Welch coughed, uncontrollably.

'What's the matter, Linda? Are you OK?'

'It's nothing, Joan. I have a bad chest, that's all. Too many years of smoking. It will catch up with the old girl one day!'

'Here, have some water!'

'I'd prefer some whiskey with it!'

'Not now. It makes you snore!'

'No, it doesn't!'

'Anyway, you haven't answered my question. The police were asking you about your time in Australia and Thomas Hodgson. He was one of those singers, those men who used to have the room upstairs. He was linked to that girl's murder, wasn't he?'

'And you are linked to that girl as well, aren't you?'

'If you don't want to know the answer, Joan, don't ask the question!'

'But I do want to know. I *must* know!'

Linda Welch coughed again, wiping her mouth as she spoke.

'I did not know anything about Thomas Hodgson in Australia. I had no link to him; I had nothing to do with his death. I swear to you; I really do. Cross my heart and hope to die'.

Joan Wilberforce smiled weakly and nodded.

'OK. I'll believe you. But you ought to get that cough seen to'.

'I know, my love. I will. I have already made an appointment to see the doctor. Now let's go to bed'.

They went up the stairs together, holding hands. Linda made sure that her blood-stained handkerchief was well hidden as they did so.

***

'Dad, will you take a look?'

'Not now, Freddie, your Dad is very tired'.

273

'Yes, Fred, I am going to go to bed soon. It's been a hell of a day'.

'But, Dad, I've drawn you a picture'.

'Is it a tree, Frederick?'

'You only call me Frederick when you aren't taking me seriously!'

'But that's not true, Freddie. Your Daddy always takes you seriously!'

'No, he doesn't! It's not fair! He's always busy. His mind is elsewhere, thinking about the case!'

Detective Chief Inspector Donald May burst out laughing.

'Oh, Freddie! Come here! Let me give you a hug!'

'No, I won't!'

But Frederick the Great wanted a hug, and he got one from both his parents. Sobs and cries were soon replaced by a lecture from May junior on the best way to solve the Holme Hill murders.

'I know, Freddie. You have already told me all about your theory. And you know what? I shared it with DS Trubshaw and DC Riggs. You remember them? Charlie is a great fan of yours!'

Freddie smiled.

'Is he really? Let me show you my picture, Dad'.

'Go on, Don. Just five minutes. I know you are tired, but it will mean such a lot to Fred'.

May nodded.

'OK, Caz. OK, Fred. Come on, show me your picture'.

Frederick May ran off to his room and came back five minutes later with a piece of A3 paper.

'We need to put this on the table so that I can explain it all to you properly'.

Freddie ran off into the dining room without waiting for his DCI father. By the time May senior had joined his son, the sheet was spread out and weighted down with a condiment at each corner so, as May junior insisted on explaining, the diagram did not curl up.

At first Detective Chief Inspector Donald May did not really listen to the future Commissioner Frederick May (of the Yard); rather he was wondering if he should give his job up, just as he had abandoned his preaching and his faith. After all, he did not seem to be especially good at it; and in another few days, he would be taken off the case. It was as simple as that. What pained the DCI most of all was the fact that he was not sure he cared any more.

May senior decided that he really ought to look at May junior's diagram. Not only was it a work of art, but it was also a minutely engineered chart of all the key details of the Holme Hill murders. What's more, as father and son pored over the linkages and the affinities together, DCI Donald May began to wake up to the fact that he should start to take his commissioner-elect son more seriously.

Everything that Freddie had deduced and laid out on the chart made sense. In fact, it was the only plausible explanation that brought everything together; the most coherent reasoning that he had come across so far in the last month of murder.

There was just one problem: proving it.

42

May 22, Morning: Another Death; More Revelations

'Well, that was inevitable, wasn't it, Viv?'

Detective Sergeant Trubshaw nodded.

'Same MO, Fizz?'

'Looks like it, team'.

Riggs grimaced.

'Don't look at me like that, Detective Constable!'

'Sorry, Fizz. I mean, Dr Harbord'.

'Enough, you two. We have a dead body – our fourth – and right on time: the twenty-second of May 2019'.

'I thought it was going to be Harry Metcalfe'.

'So did I, Viv, so did I'.

Detective Chief Inspector May surveyed the body laid out before him. He decided to take one last look at the corpse before Dr Felicity Harbord had the victim shipped off to the mortuary in Hartley.

'Left hand or right hand, Fizz?'

'Right hand this time, Don'.

'Could it be one person who is… well, who is ambidextrous?'

Harbord shrugged.

'I suppose so, but it's unlikely. The force with which the throat is slit each time militates against it. I will take a look when I have carried out the post-mortem; no promises though'.

'Thanks, Fizz. I appreciate that'.

Harbord nodded to the waiting men to zip up the body bag and load the murdered man into the ambulance.

May's mobile phone started to vibrate. He checked the caller's identity and then chose not to answer.

Trubshaw looked at her boss and watched him shake his head. *That will be the ACC. He's off the case for sure. We have to make a breakthrough and make it today!*

The DS watched Riggs follow the trolley to the ambulance, where he helped load the body.

'I'm sorry, Don'.

'Sorry? For what?'

'For being taken off the case'.

May laughed.

'I still have a week, Viv'.

'But I thought that…'

'That the phone call was from the ACC?'

May laughed some more.

'No, it was Caz'.

Trubshaw looked away.

'I imagine she wanted to tell Freddie how the case was going and was ringing me to find out more'.

'Freddie?'

'Yes. You know I told you a while back that he has this theory about the Holme Hill murders?'

Trubshaw smiled and nodded.

'I do, sir'.

'Well, Commander Frederick May of the Yard has been doing a lot of work since he first discussed his explanation of the crimes to me. And I have to say, I am beginning to take what the great man says seriously; very seriously'.

The DS snorted.

'I know, Detective Sergeant. A thirteen-year-old boy with Asberger's cracks the case where three seasoned coppers, no, the whole of Hartley CID cannot make any headway. But he is a very unusual lad. He sees patterns where nobody else does; he never gives up until he has analysed information from every angle'.

'Isn't that what we have been doing for the past three weeks, sir?'

'Welcome back, Charlie. You seemed especially shaken by this latest victim. Any particular reason why?'

Riggs looked around the village, across to Riddles, down to Salem, up to *High Windows*, then back to The Bargeman.

'I didn't expect it to be him, sir'.

'I know, Charlie. I, *we* all thought it was going to be Harry Metcalfe'.

'Well, sir, at least he died where he wanted to die, I suppose'.

'At the cricket pitch?'

'A fitting end, in one sense, sir, after all the time he spent lovingly cultivating that square of grass'.

'I hadn't thought of that, Charlie, but I doubt Ted Gelsthorpe would have expected to have his throat slashed and then his body flattened by the heavy roller, would he?'

'No sir, that's true. At least, we have the Bible quotation again, unlike with Halliday'.

May turned to Trubshaw and smiled.

'Freddie has an explanation for that, too!'

***

'What happened to him, mother?'

'He must have decided to leave. The fool! I told him that it was for the best if we kept him here out of harm's way'.

'But where can he have gone and why did he not want to stay?'

Gordon Wright looked out of the bay window. He noticed police cars and an ambulance by the cricket pavilion.

'You don't think the fracas down there has anything to do with Ted's departure, do you, mother?'

Elsie Wright went pale. She held on to the bedpost.

'What is it, Gordon? Is it the police?'

'It looks like it, mother; a whole lot of them as well. I can see some men putting something into the ambulance'.

'When did you realise that Ted had gone?'

'Well, I brought him his early morning cup of tea and left it by the bedside. He seemed fast asleep, so I left him to it. Then an hour later I came back to see what he wanted for breakfast and there was no reply, so I went over to the bed and noticed that there was no movement, no sound at all. Then I worked out that it was just his pillows made up to look like a body. That's when I called you, mother'.

'What time was it when we said goodnight to him?'

'Just after ten, mother. I heard the church clock strike the hour'.

'Did he say anything to you about wanting to go?'

'Nothing at all, mother; did he mention it to you? He seemed happy to be here, that we were looking after him!'

'I knew we should have kept the bedroom door locked. I should have known he was only pretending to go along with our plan to keep him safe. And look what happened the moment he gets out'.

'But we don't know it's him over there, mother. It could be somebody else'.

'Well, whoever it is, assuming that it is a dead body in that ambulance, it's the right day for it, just a week after Halliday was found, a fortnight after Smith turned up and three weeks since you discovered Williams sitting on that bench'.

Gordon Wright felt sick. He needed no reminding of the dead body in the park; not the kind of thing you expect to find on your way home from work; nor something you want to see, ever. And Williams was but the first corpse. Now it looked as though there was a fourth. Was it Ted Gelsthorpe, the man that his mother had been shielding? Gordon had accepted her explanation, based on Rhys Williams's little black book that she had shown him. It made sense in the wake of all the fallout from the dark experiments that had gone on at Riddles. But why Ted? His own wife had died from coming into contact with that strange material that the research group had been working on. Gelsthorpe had told him all about the goings-on back in the seventies. But had there been more to it than just a hush-hush experiment gone horribly wrong? There must be, surely!

Gordon Wright looked at his mother.

'You have told me everything, haven't you? You're not hiding anything, are you?'

'Of course not, Gordon! How could you ever think that? I would never do anything like that to you, my only son!'

Elsie Wright fiddled with her pearl earring as she spoke. Her husband always knew it was a sign of her deceit; son Gordon remained blissfully unaware, or so she hoped.

***

Gin had long lost its taste for Pauline Philbey, but she still drank it to try and forget all the things that she kept remembering. It was as if her subconscious had devised a rota that churned up all the dark memories in turn; just as she had managed to suppress one ugly reminiscence, another one popped up, right on cue.

The local archivist felt especially guilty for the way she had conned Jo Bishop into thinking that she had reported the reappearance of Williams's book. Yes, she had gone to Hartley in Bishop's car. Yes, she had entered the police station while her fellow local historian had waited for her.

That was as far as it had gone. Once inside the building and out of Bishop's sight, Philbey had left by a different exit, wandered around the town centre for what she thought was long enough to constitute the time that would elapse in an interview with May or Trubshaw or Riggs, and then returned by the same route, in and then back out of the police station.

Jo Bishop had asked Philbey how it had gone. The local archivist had expressed disappointment at the seeming lack of interest about the book and the meeting with Elsie Wright.

'I don't think they took me seriously, Jo. It's only my word against Elsie's'.

'But what about the book, Pauline? Surely that's vital evidence, and it proves that you were telling the truth all along!'

'I know, Jo, but it doesn't really tell you anything. It's only a list of names and dates. It could have been something innocent, like dues paid to one of these men's societies. There used to be one called The Grand United Order of Oddfellows. My father was in it; very much an association for aspiring northern working-class men, a poor man's freemasonry, you could call it!'

'What did they say, Pauline?'

'Nothing, really. They thanked me and said they would be in touch in due course'.

Jo Bishop had been disappointed with the outcome of the visit to Hartley CID. Replaying the conversation in her mind, Philbey thought how saddened Bishop would be if she realised what had actually happened. Why had she done it? Why had she not given May the little book? Why had she not reported the conversation with Elsie Wright?

Pauline Philbey could not give an answer. She just knew that it was not the right thing to do: to go inside that police station; to ask for the officer leading the investigations into the Holme Hill murders; to hand over Williams's book; to report the conversations with Elsie Wright.

Elsie Wright: Pauline Philbey and she had never been friends. There was even a time when Elsie had wondered if Philbey was having an affair with her husband during that brief time when she had worked at Riddles. But there had been only one person that Pauline Philbey had been interested in, and he was long gone.

Philbey thought back over the two recent meetings that she had had with Wright. The first had been an away match: Philbey had visited High Windows to report the discovery and subsequent loss of the book and to tell Elsie about those parts of Williams' log that had implicated her husband and the other members of the singing group. Wright had denied everything and virtually shown Philbey the door.

The rematch, on home ground, had been much more amicable. Starting with the return of Williams's book and an admission of theft, Elsie Wright had gone on to admit that Williams was a bad man, a blackmailer, not just of the men on his little list, but of others who had sought to tell the truth about the experiments at Riddles. Not that any had done, because Rhys Williams had got dirt on all of them, and especially those who had been complicit in the experiments, even though they knew of the side effects that it was likely to cause through continued close contact with the so-called "wonder material".

Philbey had not been able to countenance Williams's murder for being a blackmailer. But she could condone his killing as a just reparation for the death of her beloved Ernie Halliday. And that was something she would never have said to Hartley CID. Not now, not ever.

43

May 22, Afternoon: People and Deductions

———⌒⌒———

Nothing, absolutely nothing. Babs Halliday had ransacked the penthouse and found nothing. But then, what was she looking for? There must be something to explain Rodney's murder.

How can I love him and hate him at the same time?

Babs had rifled through every drawer, every cupboard, every nook, every cranny of that penthouse. She would have to go out to the holiday home in Fuerteventura and look there if all else failed. But it was unlikely that Rodney had left anything incriminating in their other place. He was so careful to cover his tracks and leaving something dodgy somewhere that was not occupied all the time and where he could keep an eye on it was not the way he operated.

*That is why I never knew his other side. The side that I hate now that I do know. I would never wish him dead, but I understand why others would want to kill him for what he was. But that was not my Rodney. I will always love **my** Rodney.*

Babs believed the boys when they had sworn that they were innocent of Rodney's death, but she didn't believe Butch. He was a different kind of animal altogether. John Butcher would be able to explain his way out of anything, anywhere, anytime, a real smooth talker.

Why would someone like Butch have got mixed up in the drug ring? Did Rod have something on him? Perhaps that was the connection.

Babs poured herself another drink, sat down on the sofa, and pressed the button to unfold the seating so that she could half lie down.

Rod used to love it when we sat on this sofa watching the telly. He never minded when I watched Strictly Come Dancing, *but I could tell he wasn't interested. He humoured me, my Rodney.*

Babs Halliday switched on the television. It was still tuned to the BBC News 24 Channel.

That's what Rod was watching the last time he was here. Bloody news programmes! Always had to watch the news, as if he was waiting for someone to mention his name.

She half listened to the newsreader: Andrea Leadsom had resigned as Leader of the House of Commons because she no longer believed that the Government would deliver Brexit; British Steel had collapsed into administration with the loss of 5,000 jobs and another 20,000 under threat in supply chain organisations.

Babs sighed and reached for the remote. As she did so, she looked at the papers spread out on the coffee table in front of her. Rodney had been poring over them the last time they were together. Even she recognised what they were: plans of Salem Chapel. She gathered up all the documents and took them over to the dining table where she would have the space to spread them all out.

Having done that, Babs realised that the plans were not just of Salem, but of Riddles, The Bargeman, High Windows *(that's the place where that old hag and her mummy's boy son live, isn't it?)* and a smaller house whose plan was not labelled.

I understand why Rod would be studying a plan of Salem, and even of Riddles (though why before it was converted to flats? We finished that project two years ago!). But what's the point of having plans of the local pub and Ernest Riddles' old house?

Babs Halliday stood up and leaned over the dining table. She smiled, remembering what Rod used to say when she bent over like that. She shuffled the plans, then shuffled them again. It was not easy to do, given the size of each sheet, but eventually they were in an arrangement that made sense. Even the plan of the unnamed house could be fitted in.

Babs stood back and surveyed her handiwork. The jigsaw came alive as she looked at it. And though it did not tell her who had got rid of Rodney or why, it did show how the perpetrators were able to get away with murder so easily.

***

'OK, let's look at our latest victim'.

May looked at the newly extended murder wall as Charlie Riggs added as much information as had been amassed about Ted Gelsthorpe.

'Fact number one: Gelsthorpe lives, *lived* near where all the bodies were found. He was supposedly out for the day that Rhys Williams was found but was certainly home by the time that Gordon Wright discovered the body on the park bench, and he is, *was* certainly around the area a lot of the time tending his beloved cricket pitch. He guarded it with his... well, you both know what he guarded it with'.

May looked at Trubshaw and Riggs, who nodded in confirmation of the fact.

'So, he might have been murdered because he had seen something that would identify the murderer or murderers?'

Trubshaw and Riggs shrugged.

'Gelsthorpe and Williams both worked at Riddles and occasionally drank together in The Bargeman. Though, if you remember, Elsie Wright said that the two of them had not spoken to each other for at least two years and Gelsthorpe "wished he had never known Williams", to quote the lady of High Windows'.

The three of them smirked at the description of Elsie Wright.

'Gelsthorpe was one of the last, perhaps *the* last person to see Peter Smith alive. They went into Salem Chapel together supposedly so that Gelsthorpe could hear the organ one last time before Halliday and his contractors moved in. *And* he discovered Smith's hands in the swamp by the edge of the cricket pitch, though we have to assume that was coincidence, but a strange and gruesome one at that!'

Detective Sergeant Trubshaw got up and went to the murder wall to add a dotted line between the photographs of Gelsthorpe and Smith. She half turned around when she had finished writing.

'There is a link with the Lancashire lasses as well, Viv. Best write that on'.

Charlie poured himself a coffee. Then spoke.

'The intimidation that they complained about; you remember he had a go at them. Then there was the trashing of his house and the daubing of that slogan'.

'It's not a slogan, Charlie. It's a verse from the Bible!'

'Sorry, sir'.

'And he was a good friend of Arnold and Doris Hargreaves, Minnie Hargreaves' parents'.

DCI May thought back to his youth in Holme Hill. He knew Arnold and Doris; two good, ordinary, working people driven to an early grave by the death of their daughter. *Nobody should live to see their children die, especially not as a result of being murdered.*

'We mustn't forget that, Viv. There has to be a link with Minnie Hargreaves's killing'.

'But we also need to remember, sir, that Gelsthorpe's wife died thanks to working with that "wonder material" that turned out to be highly carcinogenic'.

'Indeed, Charlie. Plenty of motive for Ted to commit murder'.

'Except that someone murdered him first, sir'.

DS Trubshaw was now back in her seat at the conference table. She poured coffee and took a digestive biscuit from the plate. She looked at May and Riggs as she ate and drank.

'And when we have finished talking about Gelsthorpe, we need to determine what we are going to do about WPC Ellis's disappearance'.

***

Georgie Ellis heard a toilet flush. She was still in the same room, but her companion was nowhere to be seen. They must have moved Metcalfe's body while she had been unconscious. The drugs were wearing off again and she realised where she was: not in a dream, but not fully in the land of the living either.

It had to be the cellars of The Bargeman. The clang of beer barrels rolling down into the next room told her that; and the visit of her superior officers the other day, whenever that was. She had recognised May and Trubshaw's voices, and also that of Linda Welch. She had heard the baby crying – that must be Arthur – and the discussions, sometimes with raised voices, between Welch and Wilberforce when the two younger women had gone to bed.

That much was real. *It must be real! I cannot have dreamt all of it!*

Ellis thought back to when she had left the BMW Z4 down the lane from Bradley Barn. *That was real! That really was real! They will find my car soon! That will alert them!*

But what about after that? What about sneaking into Bradley's study? The file? The doll's house? The body in the freezer? The pictures on her mobile phone? *Where is my mobile phone? If they can trace the signal… but then it will be in the canal or smashed or anywhere except where it will be useful. They will have seen the pictures and got rid of it somehow.*

Ellis felt her pulse quicken. *Calm down! You are still alive. They haven't killed you yet. They could have done anytime! But they haven't. They **might** but they haven't. So, start thinking. Relax, breathe, work out a plan.*

Ellis's plan was not the one she was hoping for. It was a plan alright, but it was the murderer's – or murderers' – plan, or at least the bits she could piece together. Lying there, bound, and gagged, she had time to work it out: if not why or who, she was beginning to understand the 'how' of the Holme Hill murders. Now she needed to stay alive long enough to make sure her deductions could be put to the test. If only she could find a means of escape. That would be one way of seeing if her new theory 'had legs', as DCI May would say.

44

May 22, Evening: Hardly a Whitewash

'Bugger and double bugger!'

Pauline Philbey looked down at the upturned pot of paint. Emulsion oozed in all directions. Boris watched the liquid flow towards him. He gingerly pawed at the paint then decided to beat a hasty retreat before his owner lost her temper and threw something at him.

The local archivist slowly descended the step ladder and assessed the damage. *Why on earth did I decide to redecorate the living room? What a stupid thing to do and look what has happened now! Think, woman! Think!*

Boris looked at his owner then at her attempt at abstract art from the safety of his fluffy cat basket. Pauline Philbey laughed. It was the first time that she had done so for a long time.

'Hardly Jackson Pollock, is it, Boris?'

Boris licked his paws, sneezed, yawned his mouth almost inside out, circled inside his basket and then settled himself back down. He had hardly begun to snooze when there was a loud knock at the door.

Pauline Philbey decided to ignore it. Mopping up the paint was a far higher priority than receiving visitors. In any case it was either the postman or an Amazon delivery driver wanting to leave a parcel for the next-door neighbour. They were the only callers that she received these days. Apart from Elsie Wright, that is, and she was hardly the most welcome visitor.

The local archivist wished that Elsie had never visited – not once, but twice – and that she herself had not returned the compliment. But they had met and conversed, and now Pauline Philbey knew far more than she ever thought was possible to know about Riddles, the Select Seven, Minnie Hargreaves and, most poignantly of all, the death – no, the *murder* of Ernie Halliday.

She should have told the police what she had learned – mostly from Elsie Wright – though Jo Bishop had filled in some of the detail about Riddles from all her archive research. *I feel bad about her. I like her. I am not the person of integrity that she thinks I am. But I couldn't tell the police; not yet anyway. Not until I have found out more.*

The knocking at the door intensified. *If I don't get this mess cleared up now, this carpet is ruined! Bugger off!*

'Hello?'

Pauline Philbey turned around.

'What the hell are you doing in my house?'

'The door was unlocked, and… well, you weren't answering'.

'That is no excuse for letting yourself in. This is private property, so please, leave my house!'

'But I need to talk to you. Urgently!'

'Can't you see I'm busy? Now please leave. Go!'

'But you'll want to hear what I have to say'.

Pauline Philbey stopped her mopping up and looked her unwanted guest up and down. The visitor leaned over. *The woman has no shame! Cleavage down to her navel and legs up to her armpits.*

'I know you! You were at the guided tour of Salem!'

'With my husband. My late husband'.

'I'm sorry. I heard. Saw the body floating down the canal'.

'I am sorry too, despite everything about him'.

'Despite everything?'

Pauline Philbey could see that Barbara Halliday was 'filling up'.

'Come on, help me clean up this mess. Then I'll make a cup of tea – or perhaps something stronger – and we'll talk'.

'I'd like that, Pauline. And I'll tell you what really happened to Ernie Halliday'.

***

Detective Chief Superintendent Arthur Bradley poured himself another whisky. It was his third; or his fourth. He didn't think it was his fifth, but he had stopped counting – and caring. Despite the amount of alcohol consumed, he was not at all inebriated; quite the opposite, he was stone-cold sober. Gelsthorpe was not supposed to be dead. Metcalfe was. Now there were two bodies for the price of one. And a third lay – alive if not well – in the cellars of The Bargeman. And there was still one other person to be called to account. But that was another story.

Bradley got up from the old leather armchair and walked over to the French windows. It was still light, despite the hour, though the sun was nothing but a thin strip of yellow and orange on the horizon. Emley Moor's mast stood erect in the near distance. The DCS remembered when the original had fallen down: 1969.

'I was a DS then. Promoted to DI five years later. Then came 1976 and I was in charge of the Minnie Hargreaves' case.

My first murder investigation as the SIO. What a way to start! And now she is avenged. More or less. But Gelsthorpe? No, that was wrong!'

'Have another drink Arthur and let's move on. Gelsthorpe was "collateral damage", as they say in those cop shows'.

Bradley snorted at his companion as he poured himself another drink and returned to his chair. The man seated opposite was half his age and twice as strong. *Thank goodness, given all the moving that has been necessary over the last few weeks.*

'Have another yourself, John'.

'No thanks, Arthur. I should be driving back to Holme Hill, and I expect I am already over the limit'.

'You'll be fine. Just give them the handshake if they stop you'.

Bradley laughed; John Butcher raised his eyebrow.

'Only joking'.

'Ha–bloody–ha'.

'So, we're agreed then?'

'We're agreed, Detective Chief Superintendent Bradley'.

Now it was Bradley's turn to raise an eyebrow at Butcher's attempt at humour.

'Metcalfe, then Ellis?'

'Yup, Metcalfe, then Ellis. We have to sort her, stupid interfering woman, and then the last one on the list. That will be quite something, if we can get away with it! But I really must away, Arthur. See you tomorrow'.

***

'So, you have to decide whether I am the one to believe'.

'Or if Elsie Wright is telling the truth'.

Babs nodded.

'Yup; or if Elsie Wright is telling the truth. It's your choice: take your pick!'

Pauline Philbey looked at her uninvited guest. Despite her initial reaction to this blousy, tarty woman, she had warmed to Barbara "just-call-me-Babs" Halliday.

'Have another gin, Barb…, *Babs*'.

'Don't mind if I do, Pauline, don't mind if I do. Glad the paint's all gone now. Thank God for that!'

Boris meowed in agreement, walked across the recently cleaned floor and jumped up onto Babs Halliday's lap.

'I'm not really a cat lover, Pauline'.

'He won't bite, Babs. Just let him be and stroke him now and again'.

'Rodney liked dogs. Didn't like pussies, except…'

The two women looked at each other and smiled.

'So, Babs, do I believe you? You say that my Ernest was murdered all those years ago?'

Barbara Halliday nodded.

'So far, so good. That's what Elsie Wright said. But then the stories diverge'.

Babs pondered for a moment, trying to work out what the word "diverge" meant.

'Now, Elsie says that Ernie was murdered by the Select Seven because he knew too much about what they were up to with their shenanigans. You say that he was murdered by the Russians because of his "wonder material"'.

Babs nodded, tentatively stroking Boris as she did so. Pauline Philbey decided that both stories were plausible. Ernie had continued to write to her after he left Riddles and then the correspondence stopped. Suddenly. *Surely, the Select Seven would not have killed him after he had left the area. Unless the letters were forgeries… No, that was not so, they were his writing and his style and used their special language to each other. Or he had been forced into writing them… Again no, Ernie being Ernie he would have got some kind of code to her if he was writing from captivity.*

Babs' explanation made sense, especially when she had said that Rodney had reported how Ernest had feared for his life because of the secret project. Pauline Philbey knew that Project Earnest had been hush-hush, but it was only now, as Barbara Halliday described it to her (as best she could) how important Ernie's work really was and what impact it might have had for future national security if the formulae had got into the wrong hands. But what was Babs Halliday's motive, and what did she know about Elsie Wright, and what did she have against her?

'Trust me, Pauline. I've no axe to grind. Honest'.

Philbey sipped her gin. She believed Babs Halliday; she really did. But she also remembered what Ernie had said about the Select Seven. What was it? "Sad men". Had they murdered Minnie Hargreaves? And why had they killed her? Elsie Wright had never said; only that Ernie had been murdered to stop him reporting the Select Seven to the police. Wright had then offered Pauline Philbey a chance to get even: "an eye for an eye", she had said.

'Don't believe her, Pauline. Ernie would have said something to Rod. And he would have told me. I just know it'.

And yet, as Pauline Philbey looked at her cleavaged new friend, she could not believe everything that Babs Halliday said either. Not least because of what Ernie had said about his brother, all those years ago.

Time for another gin.

45

May 23, Morning: Minds Are Made Up

'Does it really matter?'

'I don't think it does'.

'Neither do I'.

'Well, I do. We agreed a schedule and we should stick to it'.

'But our "schedule", as you call it, is all to pot anyway thanks to the bloody cock-up with Gelsthorpe'.

'How was I to know that he had a weak heart?'

'Because he's a bloody old codger, that's why! You were supposed to keep him out of the way while we did the final murders, not kill the bugger!'

'I did not kill him; he died!'

'Same difference!'

'Anyway, I say we stick to the original plan'.

'All very well, but *you* don't have a dead body in your basement. We can't keep him in that freezer much longer.

Anyway, why did he have to be moved here in the first place. What was wrong with keeping him in your freezer?'

'We had to move him here so that we could put him out on the day'.

'So why couldn't we put Metcalfe out as originally planned and keep Gelsthorpe in the freezer?'

'Because I didn't want him in my house any longer and he was going off!'

Two of the group burst out laughing.

'I still think we could have put him in the freezer and sorted him out later'.

'Well, it's done now. I don't care anymore. I just want it to be over. Then I can get on with my life'.

'We can all get on with our lives'.

'But it's not as simple as that, is it?'

'What do you mean?'

'Well, how many more murders are we prepared to commit, apart from the ones we planned?'

'But Gelsthorpe doesn't count!'

'Well, perhaps he does, perhaps he doesn't. But just at the moment he is not the person I am worried about'.

There was silence. Children could be heard playing, then the school bell rang. Workmen chatted as they erected scaffolding. A baby cried and a mother tried to hush it. A police siren wailed past down the road. Every member of the group held their breath until the noise was long past and their fear of being apprehended had subsided.

'You mean her'.

'I do mean her'.

'We can't keep her imprisoned forever'.

'And we can't kill her'.

'Can't we?'

'That would be two policemen killed then'.

'Hang on, we haven't killed the other one yet!'

'No, but we have to if we are going to complete the plan – we agreed that we would. We can't back out now. Everybody – and I mean everybody – has to play their part'.

There was more silence. Someone coughed; someone else shuffled.

'I have an idea'.

'Yes?'

'What is it?'

'Yes, come on, solve the problem!'

'We kill two birds with one stone, or rather two police in one go'.

'Go on'.

'And make it look like a terrible accident. We could work something out. We have the expertise'.

'So, we get rid of Ellis and May together?'

'That would be the idea'.

***

Pauline Philbey's gin supply had run completely dry since Babs Halliday's visit and never had she been less motivated to go and buy some more, even though the local off-licence was only a brisk walk away. Boris had disappeared. The local archivist smiled as she remembered when they had moved into the house on the hill. Boris had had a field day – literally. The morning after Pickfords had departed, Philbey had come down to breakfast to find the living room floor littered with rodents of various shapes and sizes. Boris was in the middle of the carnage, admiring his work. There was never a problem with rats or mice ever thereafter.

If only real life were as simple. Someone was having a field day now; except this was with real people, not rodents.

'Of mice and men', she mumbled.

Pauline Philbey jumped and then caught her breath as she realised it was only the noise of Boris coming back in through the cat flap. The moggy mewed loudly, pitter-pattered over the carpet, leaving a muddy imprint as he went, then jumped up and onto her lap. He was wet through and made the most of curling up against his owner, rubbing himself dry in the process. Philbey tried to stroke him but his fur felt horrible.

'What am I to do, Boris?'

Boris yawned, wriggled, adjusted himself, then fell asleep, purring all the while.

It was time to go to the police and tell them everything. They could decide where the truth lay and what had to be done. This killing spree had to be over and the perpetrators brought to justice. Ultimately, she believed neither Elsie Wright nor Babs Halliday; ultimately, Pauline Philbey believed only one person: herself.

She pushed Boris off her lap, reached over for her mobile phone, and dialled Hartley CID.

'I need to speak to Detective Inspector Donald May, personally and urgently'.

46

May 23, Afternoon: Wright Makes a Clean Breast of It

———— ⌁ ————

'Are you sure you're OK?'

Gordon Wright nodded.

'I don't believe you'.

'I'm OK, Sally, honest. Just need to sort some things out at home, that's all'.

'Looks like a lot to me'.

'How do you mean?'

'Your face says it all, Gordon, my lovely'.

Wright blushed at the thought of his workmate calling him 'lovely'. It was the first time he had smiled in days.

'You can tell me, Gordon. Honest. I can keep a secret'.

'You don't want to know my secret, Sally. Some things are best not shared'.

'Try me, Gordon'.

Gordon had 'tried' other women recently, and where had it got him? Into a lot of trouble. *How I long to go back to April 30th! Back to my quiet, dull, mundane, boring, unexciting life!'*

'Come on, Gordon, how long have we worked together now? I can tell that something is very wrong. Let's have a coffee break – we are owed one – and walk around the park'.

Sally Matheson got up from her seat and went to Gordon's desk.

'Come on, Flash, you need help, big time'.

Wright smiled. It was a long time since Sally had called him that. He had taken his colleague for granted since Joan Wilberforce had walked into his life. He suddenly remembered that it had been Sally he was itching to go out with. She was no Joan – no Clarins, no Jaeger, no immaculate hair and makeup, no being constantly late, no endless fixation with her appearance. No, Sally Matheson was no Joan Wilberforce. She was a good friend; always had been, always would be.

'OK. But you might not like what I have to say. I can't unsay it when I have told you my story'.

Sally put her hand on Gordon's shoulder and squeezed it gently.

'I can cope. How long have you and I worked together, in this very building?'

The two of them looked around the open plan office in which it seemed they had spent much of their adult lives.

Wright stood up, took his jacket off the back of his chair, and walked to the exit. Sally followed eagerly behind.

It was warm enough outside not to need overcoats and the park was only just across the road from the office building. Much to Wright's surprise, Sally linked arms with him. He did not resist. It was the first genuine physical contact he had experienced in a long time. Tears welled up.

'What's the matter, Gordon?'

'Nothing, Sal. Problems with my contact lenses'.

Matheson smiled thinly.

'Let's sit down. Over there'.

She pointed to the old bandstand that stood in the centre of Hartley Memorial Park. It was a place of many happy memories for her, when her father had played in the local brass band and a group from Holme Hill called the Select Seven had joined as special guest singers. The choirmen had sometimes brought a young girl with them. 'She has the voice of an angel', her father had often said.

'So, come on, Gordon. Let's have it all out'.

Wright looked at Matheson, knowing that he would tell her everything and that nothing would ever be the same again between them. But then nothing in any part of his life would ever be the same again.

'OK', he sighed, 'here goes'.

'That's fine, Gordon. I'm listening. Take your time. Mary will cover for us if we need more than half an hour'.

'Right. You remember that I discovered a dead body?'

Matheson nodded.

'Well, that was just the beginning of the weirdest month of life. And it isn't over yet!'

She looked at her watch to check the date.

'Another week to go yet, Gordon!'

'Don't, Sally. I don't think I can take anymore!'

Wright buried his head in his hands and cried. Matheson put her arms around him.

'There, there, Gordon. It's alright. It'll all be alright. I'm sorry, I shouldn't have joked'.

She looked around the park to make sure that nobody was watching them. A man like Gordon should be allowed to cry unobserved.

After a few moments, Gordon Wright leaned back on the park seat, blew his nose, dried his eyes, and began again.

'My mother and I have never got on. She and my father were never happy. As you know, I am an only child, and after I was born, I don't think they were ever... well, you know what I mean'.

'Go on, Gordon. I understand'.

'My father was involved with a group called the Select Seven'.

Matheson laughed.

'I was just thinking about them. My father knew them. They used to sing here in the summer, back in the 1970s when I was a child. I played with their 'mascot', as they called her. What was her name?'

'Minnie Hargreaves'.

'Yes, that's her. Gosh. That's a long time ago!'

'And you know what happened to her, don't you, Sally?'

Wright clasped his colleague's hand. Matheson stopped smiling.

'Yes, I remember now'.

'Well, she is part of the story'.

'Go on, then. Tell me. I promise your secret is safe with me'.

'The man whose body I discovered was one of them too. Rhys Williams. He was sort of the leader of the group. They all worked at the local mill'.

'You mean Riddles? Where those luxury flats are now?'

Wright nodded.

'Riddles comes into it as well, and Salem Chapel. There's a connection there; and with my house, or rather my mother's house'.

'What's it called again? It's got a funny name, hasn't it?'

'I wouldn't say it was funny, but it's called High Windows. It has these very tall windows, you see. It was built by Ernest Riddles, the founder of the factory, in the nineteenth century, and it is said that the house was sited and designed so that he could see everything that was going on in Holme Hill – his village'.

'And can you?'

Wright laughed.

'You can. Just ask my mother'.

'I would rather ask you, Gordon'.

Matheson put her hand on top of Wright's.

'Well, I think my mother is involved in the murder – no, the murders'.

Matheson gasped.

'Your mother? You must be joking! A strait-laced old...'

'Go on, say it. I don't mind. I think the same of her, believe me, and worse!'

'Not my place to say, Gordon. She's your mother!'

'And don't I know it. I should have left Holme Hill and her years ago. No wonder my father spent all his time with that singing group and the chapel, and work'.

'Go on, Gordon. Keep going with you story'.

'The trouble is... the trouble is, Sally, I'm involved in it now. She's got me involved'.

'What? You're imagining things, Gordon'.

'I only wish I were. It started after the first murder, when the police came to see us. And I didn't really believe my mother when she said that she had not seen anything all day, even though she stares out of those front windows for hours on end and, thanks to Ernest Riddles, she doesn't miss a thing. So, she must have seen what happened to Williams. And then when that organist's hands were found by the cricket field, she didn't seem surprised'.

'He was the one who was found in Salem Chapel, sitting at the organ?'

'Yes, minus his hands'.

'How gruesome!'

'Thank God I didn't see that one'.

'I agree!'

'Peter Smith – that was the organist's name – he was a member of that singing group as well'.

'OK. The plot thickens'.

Matheson regretted making light of Gordon's story.

'Sorry, Gordon. I didn't mean to sound facetious'.

'Well, Sally, the plot does thicken, in more ways than one'.

'In what way?'

'Well, my mother seemed to be on the phone a lot, all of a sudden. Then she had callers: a woman called Pauline Philbey came and I heard them arguing. Then somebody called Babs Halliday, and *she* was the wife of another of the victims'.

'And he was?'

'Rodney Halliday. He wasn't one of the Select Seven, at least, but he owns, *owned* Riddles Mill and had just bought Salem Chapel to convert that into more luxury flats, just like the old factory'.

'And do you know who she kept talking to on the phone?'

'I think it was several people, but I know that one of them was called Graham'.

'Graham who?'

'Well, if you look in the recent obituaries, I think it can only be Graham Dooley. Reverend Graham Dooley, that is'.

'And he is… or was?'

'Minister at Salem Chapel when the Select Seven were the core of the choir and Peter Smith was organist'.

'So what? None of that means anything. Your mother would have known Dooley anyway, wouldn't she, if your Dad was so involved in the chapel back then?'

'Well, yes, I suppose so, but there's a lot more to it than that. And this is where I start to be involved. And I so, so wish that I never had been. It's all going crazy!'

'I am sure there is some logical explanation for it all'.

'I need to tell you something else before I tell you about my mother and the next victim'.

'The next victim?'

Gordon Wright could see Matheson's eyes widen. *She must be wondering how much more there is of all this. But I can't stop now. It feels so good to get it off my chest, to tell somebody else. And if she tells the police, well, so be it. I am tired of all the lies and the deceit. I just want it to end.*

'I have made friends with, well, with two women who live on a boat, with a baby'.

'Two women on a boat with a baby?'

'Yes. They are married to each other and the boy is called Arthur'.

'And where is there boat now?'

'Well, it was by the local pub. You know, The Bargeman, the one that I keep saying I am going to take you to one day'.

'Chance would be a fine thing, Gordon. Sorry, I shouldn't have said that'.

'No matter, Sally. I should have taken you there a long time ago. And we should have had this conversation a lot sooner, too!'

'Keep going, Gordon. I can tell what a release all this is to you'.

Wright nodded.

Well, I got friendly with them. They took me onto their narrow boat one night when I had an accident on the towpath. They sorted me out and – I don't know why – I took to them. While I was there, I saw two people arguing on the other side of the canal and I heard the word 'murder'.

'And did you recognise them?'

Wright nodded slowly.

'Yes, I did. One of them is now dead and the other has disappeared'.

307

'And their names?'

'Ted Gelsthorpe and Harry Metcalfe. Gelsthorpe's dead and Metcalfe's nowhere to be seen'.

'Don't tell me, and they were both members of the Select Seven'.

'Don't joke, Sally. Metcalfe certainly was. And Gelsthorpe found the hands – well, at least one of them. The police found the other one if I remember rightly'.

But there's more to my time on the boat. The women asked me to help them – to help them move things'.

'What things, Gordon?'

'I don't know. I thought at the time it was sacks of coal, but with all the goings-on in Holme Hill, I just wonder if it was a body'.

Sally Matheson bit her lip hard in a bid to stay quiet. She just about managed not to laugh.

'But there's far worse. Ted Gelsthorpe came and stayed with us for a couple of nights before he died. My mother said that he was frightened that he was next on the list. That's why she locked him in the bedroom at night, just in case. Then one morning he was gone, and the next thing I knew, he was dead, *murdered*, by all accounts'.

Matheson exhaled breath like she had never exhaled breath.

'And then I need to tell you about Joan'.

'Ah, I remember her; you told me. She's the one who persuaded you to dress up as Darth Vader for the fancy dress evening at The Bargeman'.

'That's the one'.

47

May 23, Evening: May and Trubshaw Take Tea; Linda Reveals a Secret

———⟶∿⟵———

'We have to find a way in. We know what's where and how the various sites interlink, thanks to Pauline Philbey, but her plans don't show any access points'.

Detective Sergeant Vivienne Trubshaw looked across at her boss. DCI Don May stared out of the window of their favourite tea shop. She knew that look; he often gazed into space when he was thinking how best to move forward on a case.

Trubshaw took in her surroundings. This might be the last time they would be together in the *Speckled Teapot*. May turned back to face his DS.

'The intriguing thing for me is that Freddie was saying all along that there had to be a series of tunnels linking Riddles and Salem, which is how bodies could appear and disappear without anyone noticing'.

'Indeed, sir. And thanks to their recent archival research, Jo Bishop and Pauline Philbey have shown just how far those tunnels go'.

May looked quizzically at Trubshaw, but then realised that she had to keep up the pretense of formality; the café was full of Hartley residents, some of whom might well know the Chief Inspector, especially given his recent high profile in the Holme Hill murders.

'And Philbey even produced some pictures when she came to see me. But that was nothing like the other stuff she revealed about Riddles and Ernie Halliday and Elsie Wright and the Select Seven, was it now?'

'No, sir. It was not! I was not expecting anything like that to come out when she said she had to speak to you urgently'.

'At least, we now have a way forward'.

'What do you make of Fizz's news on Gelsthorpe, sir?'

May looked around, conscious of the fact that they were talking, however *sotto voce*, in a public place.

'Gelsthorpe was obviously not the planned victim. That's what. He may have died under duress, but he wasn't murdered *per se*. At least, not in the customary way. So, those wounds were inflicted *post mortem* to make it look as if he was the next person on the list'.

'And you were expecting Harry Metcalfe'.

'I was. He was the obvious person. He fitted the profile along with Williams and Smith'.

'And Hodgson, even though we will never pin anything on Linda Welch for that one'.

'It could have been an accident, I suppose. Swimming in strong currents, got out of his depth, sheer exhaustion followed by collapse, and inability to get back to shore'.

'Or he did commit suicide?'

'Why then, though? Did something cause him to kill himself all those years ago, when he had left the country?'

'Who knows what causes someone to take their own life? Perhaps he did meet Linda Welch, and realised who she was, or she told him. Or saw her and recognised her, and that brought all his feelings of guilt back about the Hargreaves' murder and Harrison's possible wrongful conviction and that pushed him over the edge. I guess we will never know unless she confesses'.

The two officers nodded at each other. May signalled the waitress for the bill.

'Whatever happened to Hodgson, I think he was on the list, or would have been if he had still been alive when this month of murder started'.

'I agree. What begins to give this case shape, though, Viv, is what Pauline Philbey told us about Rodney Halliday. He is no longer the odd one out; his murder makes perfect sense, given the various motives behind these killings'.

'And, dare I say it, sir, proves the other part of your Freddie's theory!'

May laughed.

'It does!'

The DCI's smile quickly subsided.

'I just wish we could find Georgie. I have a bad feeling about her'.

'We all do, sir. Everyone in the station is on the case in their spare time. I think they have her somewhere. And now we know about those tunnels, we can perhaps catch them at their own game. We just need an access point'.

'That's for first thing in the morning. I should go home and talk some more with Commander Frederick May of the Yard. He's my best hope of a further break in this case!'

May squeezed Trubshaw's hand as they stood up and left the *Speckled Teapot*. She squeezed back. Then they went their separate ways.

***

'So, did you do it?'

'Do you really want to know?'

'Yes, I do. If we are going to make this relationship work, then I need to know everything about you'.

'But if I tell you, that will be it. You will not be able to un-know any of my history. And then you will be implicated in all that I have done, and anything that I might still be planning to do'.

Joan Wilberforce rolled over and away from her lover. These had been the best weeks of her life. She had never known anybody like Linda Welch.

'You have shown me what love can be – not just the physical side of things either. Everything. I want us to be together. Just the two of us'.

Welch laughed.

'Oh, my love! You are such a sweetie! I wish it were that simple'.

'Don't you love me back?'

'Of course I do. Haven't I made that obvious? I fell for you as soon as you walked into The Bargeman and said you wanted that barmaid's job I was advertising for'.

Joan stroked her lover's back, drawing a big heart with her index finger in and out of her spine. Linda's body trembled as she began to cough.

'What's wrong? What is it, my love?'

'It's nothing. Honest. Just a smoker's cough'.

Welch held the handkerchief to her mouth, making sure that Joan Wilberforce did not see the rust-red bloodstains.

'Very well', she sighed. 'I will tell you'.

'Go on, then, Linda'.

'No, I did not kill Thomas Hodgson. But I wanted to. As soon as I saw him all those years ago. I couldn't believe it when he walked into my bar. There was I, on the other side of the world, trying to get away from everything about my past and build a new life and who should come back into it when I was least expecting it?'

'And the reason?'

'You know really, don't you?'

'He was responsible for David's conviction, wasn't he?'

'Him and the others. David would never have hurt a fly. He loved Minnie, could not have killed her. But they framed him, and he went to prison. It broke his parents' – my aunt and uncle's – hearts. And I loved them like they were my mum and dad. My real dad was a wastrel and my mum had no time for me. But they looked after me. And I loved Minnie too, like as if she was my big sister'.

'So, what did you do to Hodgson?'

'Nothing. Just confronted him with the truth'.

'And what did he say, Linda?'

Welch laughed.

'He denied it all at first. Denied who he was, what he was, what he had done. Then he left the bar. But I saw him again not long afterwards and I followed him and found out where he lived. I went to see him one night. I told him I was going to report him to the police. Then he admitted he was Thomas Hodgson. Said he knew what had happened but hadn't been the main person responsible for Minnie's death, just that he had gone along with the others. I gave him twenty-four hours to think it over before I reported him to the police. Then I left his house'.

'He lived alone?'

'Yes, Joan, as far as I am aware'.

'So, then what happened?'

'He came to my bar after closing time the following evening. Said he was sorry for what he had done. He shouldn't have let it happen. He promised that he would go to the police himself the following morning and tell everything, including the names of everybody involved back in the UK'.

'And then?'

'Then he left. And that was the last time I saw Thomas Hodgson. The next day I heard police and ambulance sirens and found out that he had committed suicide. So, I swear to you, Joan, I had nothing to do with his death – well, not really'.

'And what about all the other deaths since?'

Linda Welch shook her head.

'Come here, my love. Enough talking. I have something else in mind before bed'.

48

May 24, Morning: Ellis
Relents and Vows Revenge

—ᴄᴠᴏ—

The Hon. Georgiana Lucinda Ponsonby-Ellis had never had a problem keeping her weight down. Indeed, mother had often commented how easily she lost weight. But what would Davina Ponsonby-Ellis think of her daughter now?

Georgie had lost a stone since she had been caught, drugged, bound, and imprisoned. Her captors had regularly brought her food and drink; had let her use the old bathroom in the corner of the basement where they were keeping her; had said that no harm would come to her if she followed their instructions to the letter.

She had various theories as to who her captors were, though they had never revealed themselves to her. Whenever anyone came to her prison cell, they were always masked. She had grown accustomed to the regular visits from Darth Vader. But while the appearance might be the same, WPC Ellis could tell that different people were using that mask. Some were thick set; others were slim; some were male; others were female.

It was after four, five, six days – she had lost count – that something different happened. This time, two Darth Vaders came into the basement room. Georgie guessed that both had visited her – separately – before; now they came together on some special errand, no doubt. The one with the deeper voice did most of the talking. The taller, thinner one mostly nodded in agreement, occasionally coughed and wheezed, but rarely spoke. *That one doesn't sound well.*

'So, you want me to write a letter?'

Darth number 1 nodded and breathed heavily.

Darth number 2 cleared their throat.

'A letter to Don. I mean, Detective Chief Inspector May?'

Darth number 2 spoke this time.

'Yes. You just have to write out the words that are printed on this sheet and we will do the rest'.

Darth number 1 held a piece of paper up to Ellis's face.

'You're too close. I can't read it!'

Darth 1 withdrew the sheet.

'That better?'

Ellis nodded.

'So, read it!'

Darth 1 snapped.

'But I can't write this! I won't! It's a trap!'

'If you want to save yourself, then you will write it!'

Outside Georgie Ellis could hear cars and people talking; normal life was happening: people going about their business; children off to school; men and women off to work; old people going to the chemist or the church coffee morning, or whatever else people did on yet another ordinary day.

Not WPC Georgie Ellis though. Here she was in this dank, cold basement, tied up at the mercy of unknown captors. *Perhaps this is the dream! Perhaps I will wake up soon and go into work and make tea and bring biscuits for the inner cabinet like I always do. I want to wake up now! Please can I wake up? Surely, they have realised what has happened. Surely, they are searching for me. It is only a matter of time, only a matter of time before I am discovered and freed!*

'And what happens if I refuse?'

The two Darths looked at each other, then spoke as one.

'Then you and he will both die'.

'I won't do it. There is no way you will make me betray a fellow officer!'

'And what about Tiggy?'

'What do you mean?'

'You know what, *who* we mean'.

'Tiggy, your sister. The one you used to hotbox with when you were away at boarding school together'.

That was a different world. Me and my elder sister at Roedean! The things we did then! Thank God, we didn't get caught! We would have been expelled – and worse – especially when we had boys in the car with us as well!

'You don't want anything to happen to her or the children, do you?'

Darth 1 was dominating the conversation again.

'You bastards! You absolute bastards!'

'If you do as we say, you and Tiggy will be fine. Nothing will happen to you. We don't want you. We have no grudge against you. It's your boss we are after'.

Darth 2 spoke softly, despite the strange sound that came through the mouth of that hideous mask.

'Why Donald May?'

'You don't need to know. Just do as we say and nobody will get hurt'.

Darth 1 turned to Darth 2.

'What time will Tiggy be picking the children up from school?'

'The usual time, I imagine'.

'Such lovely children, aren't they? Pity if any harm should come their way. Mother and Aunt would be so distraught'.

'Alright, I will do as you ask! But I will get you for this! You'll be sorry you ever crossed me! Don't you forget it!'

Darth 1 laughed; Darth 2 remained silent. Once the letter was written, they left her alone. May would recognise her handwriting even though she had been shaking when she penned the letter. What would he think? What would he say? What would he do? WPC Ellis just hoped that May – or Trubshaw or Riggs – would spot the hidden message. In the meantime, she would work on her escape plan, now that she had worked out where the tunnel entrance must be and where it might lead, if not how she could free herself.

49

May 24, Afternoon: Truth Will Out; Final Plans Are Agreed

'I'm scared, Jayce. Scared and upset. We have lost our home and now we are going to go to prison!'

'Oh, my love, of course we aren't going to go to prison!'

'But what have you done, Jaycee?'

'Don't worry, my sweetheart! Leave it all to me!'

'But our boat, why did you have to do that to our boat?'

'What do you mean, Abbey?'

'I'm not totally stupid, my love. I know it was you that trashed the boat'.

'But...'

'But nothing, Jayce. You **must** tell me what's going on! I know it's something to do with Linda and Joan. And that girl's murder all those years ago. You're involved, aren't you? Have you killed somebody?'

Jaycee laughed and hugged her partner tightly.

'Oh, my love! What do you think I am? An axe murderer?'

'Well, perhaps you are, Jayce. How can I tell? I don't trust you anymore. I thought we were special; no secrets; two in one. I was the happiest person in the world when Arthur was born. And now...'

'Don't cry, Abbey. I can explain everything'.

Abbey looked over at the makeshift cot in their room at The Bargeman. Arthur was fast asleep, blissfully unaware of the many dramas that were unfolding around his parents.

'Go on, then, explain everything'.

Jaycee joined her wife on the sagging sofa in front of the double bed that had been their refuge since *Lancashire Lasses* had been damaged; beyond repair, it now turned out. From where the two women were they could see across the cricket field and up to where Gordon Wright and his mother lived; and across to Salem Chapel where the handless organist had been found; over to the canal and the railway bridge where Rodney Halliday's body had floated past one morning; then back to the pond and the roller, where Smith's hands and Gelsthorpe's flattened corpse had turned up. And finally, the bench on which Rhys Williams' lifeless body had sat.

Jaycee took Abbey's hand in hers.

'OK. Here goes. You sure you want to know what happened?'

Abbey nodded.

'No secrets, Jayce. Remember?'

'I know, Abs. No secrets'.

There were tears in both women's eyes now.

'Linda Welch is my mother'.

Abbey Harrison smirked.

'I had more or less guessed that Jayce. The way you two were with each other and the way she looked at Arthur. Just like a grandparent does at their grandchild'.

'I should have told you'.

'Why didn't you?'

'I was told not to tell you. And I didn't want you to get involved!'

'Not involved! Not involved?'

'I know, I know. But this is a very serious business'.

'Oh, Jayce, can anything be more serious than you and me?'

'I know, my sweet. Which is why I didn't want you to get involved in these murders'.

'I knew it. You killed them! You killed all those men!'

Jaycee laughed.

'Oh, my love. I didn't kill them'.

'You didn't?'

'No, I did not. But... but I helped the others to kill them'.

***

Elsie Wright liked Earl Grey, with lemon, not milk. Milk just ruined it; she did not understand how anyone could do such a thing to a wonderful brew like that.

Everything was ready for the tea party. The teapots full. The scones and cakes baked and ready. The chairs arranged as they should be for a gathering like this.

The grandfather clock struck four. They should have been here by now. What could have happened? Had any of them been detained by the police? They were getting careless. Too many slips. People not following instructions like they should have done. Not playing by the rules.

Elsie Wright could feel her pulse quickening. If only people did as they were told. As she had told them to do. Everything would have been fine.

Except for Ted Gelsthorpe. That was her own fault. She should have known that he had a weak heart. But it had been so necessary to get him out of the cottage, so that they could use the secret entrance to the tunnels that led to and from the groundsman's cellar. Gordon had believed her when she told him that Gelsthorpe was in danger and needed to be protected from the group that was committing the murders.

Or so she thought. He had been acting very strangely since Ted had died and the body found. She had tried to tell him that he had left early one morning of his own accord and the murderers must have got him. But he had been carried out of the house after dying of a heart attack in Elsie Wright's front bedroom.

She had disagreed with making it look like one of the murders. But then, how would his disappearance have been explained otherwise? Especially in the light of the faked trashing of the boat in order to throw suspicion on Gelsthorpe and the scuttling of the Lancashire Lasses to make it look as though the groundsman had sought retaliation and then gone into hiding. That was a beautiful plan, and Ted had been blissfully ignorant of it all, given that he was already in Elsie Wright's bed. Not that Elsie had shared it with him, of course. No, she had been in the spare room.

Elsie went into the hallway to check the time. She remembered that the clock was always ten minutes fast, so only now was the hour approaching. There was a knock at the door. The first member of the group arrived and was ushered into the front room and offered tea and refreshments. Then two more people arrived. Before long, the group was all present and correct. Once everyone had been fed and watered (as Elsie liked to describe it), the meeting began.

The plans for the remaining murders were well on the way to being finalised.

'Only another week to go now, everybody'.

50

May 24, Evening: Commander and Inspector

—⌐∿⌐—

'Why are you doing that?'

'Doing what?'

'Why are you straightening out those paper clips?'

'Am I?'

Detective Chief Inspector Donald May looked down at the slim silver lines on the coffee table.

'Are you sad?'

May stroked his son's head.

'Don't be. It will be OK. Honest'.

'I know, Commander Frederick May of the Yard'.

May laughed.

'Why are you laughing, Dad?'

'I should have put you in charge right at the start of this investigation, Frederick the Great. You were right about the tunnels. I didn't believe you, and you were right. A woman called Pauline Philbey came to see me at the station recently. She is the local archivist and has all these plans and maps of the area. She and a friend of hers 'put two and two together' about a series of passageways between Salem and Riddles and High Windows and The Bargeman'.

'Can I see the plans?'

Freddie May jumped up and down on the sofa.

'Calm down, Fred. Don't disturb Mum. She's had a long day. She might hear you!'

'Sorry, Dad. You're still my commanding officer'.

'At ease, May junior. At ease. You know that I can't bring material home from the station'.

'So, who did it? Was I right?'

'It looks like it, Commander'.

'You mean that there was more than one murderer, like I always thought?'

'Yup, right on, bud'.

Freddie May snorted at his father's false American accent.

'And that there was a ringleader who was organising it all?'

'Hmmm. Not so sure about that one, Commander'.

'But it all seems to have been planned out with military precision'.

'Indeed, it does, son'.

'Bradley?'

'How did you know about him?'

'I just do. Is it Bradley? Is it him, Dad? Is he the mastermind behind it all?'

May looked down at his empty whisky glass.

'He must have had something to do with it all. I agree. He would know how to carry out a plan like this'.

'On behalf of a whole group of people, each of whom wanted someone murdered'.

May thought how grown up his son sounded. But then Fred had never been a child; had never played with toys; had never had friends. Frederick May was born middle aged; talked like an adult; thought like a detective. Had done since he was a baby, or so it seemed.

'And what about Minnie Hargreaves, Dad? It must all start with her murder'.

'And David Harrison's conviction'.

'Rodney Halliday seems to be a different kettle of fish'.

May senior tried not to laugh at his son's old-man-isms, as Caz called them. Only the previous day the boy had said that he was reading the 'ante-penultimate chapter' of his latest book, a detective story, of course. Mum and Dad had smiled quietly as their son had spoken. Freddie was even talking about wanting to wear a waistcoat. Age thirteen.

'Well, Pauline Philbey helped me to join the dots on that one, Fred'.

May junior sat bolt upright.

'Dad, you should have told me about that! How can I solve these crimes if I am not in full possession of the facts?'

DCI May burst out laughing.

'Oh, Freddie! You are such a love'.

May junior gave his father 'that look'.

'Sorry, Commander. It won't happen again, sir. Now let's get on with our case review'.

'What did this Philbey woman say, then?'

'Rodney Halliday had a brother, Ernest, better known as Ernie, at least to her'.

'When was that?'

'A long time ago, Fred. When Riddles was still open. Ernest – Ernie – Halliday was a research scientist leading a team at the factory. They were working on a top-secret project to develop a new "wonder material" for the government'.

'Did she have a 'fling' with him, Dad?'

'Er, yes, she did have a 'fling', as you put it, with Ernest'.

'Then what happened?'

'Ernest went away, allegedly to do with the project, and was never seen again'.

'Murdered?'

'Well, son, according to Pauline Philbey, Ernie Halliday was murdered because of the secrets surrounding the "wonder material"'.

'And how does she know that?'

'Because Babs Halliday told her so'.

'Babs Halliday? That's Rodney Halliday's wife, isn't it?'

'It is indeed, Freddie. Commander. Sir'.

'And do you believe her?'

'Which one? Pauline or Babs?'

'Dad, why is she called Babs?'

'It's short for Barbara, Freddie'.

'Ah. I meant either, or both. Does Pauline Philbey believe Barbara Halliday's story about Ernie's death?'

'Well, it's interesting you say that. She doesn't'.

'Why is that?'

'Because Elsie Wright told Philbey a different tale'.

'A different tale?'

'Yes. Elsie Wright came to see Pauline Philbey after she had previously demanded to know what had happened to Ernie. It was all to do with a little black book that belonged to Rhys Williams. It contained all the details of his blackmailing'.

'And who did Wright say killed Ernie Halliday?'

'Well, she...'

The doorbell rang.

May looked at his watch. 9 pm. He went to the door and opened it without thinking.

There standing in front of him was Detective Sergeant Trubshaw.

'Sorry, sir. Can I come in? We've had a letter. It's from Georgie'.

51

May 25, Morning: Breakfast Musings

———⌀⌀⌀———

Joan Wilberforce felt sick. She really wanted to throw up, to rid herself of the lead in her stomach and the pressure in her lungs. That would mean sticking two fingers down her throat, but it would not work: wrong kind of nausea. This sickness encompassed your whole body; pervaded your mind; drove right into your very soul.

As she lay in her own bed for the first time in a week, Joan thought back over her life. Now that she had experienced love properly (as she had told Linda), the time with anybody else had been a pale imitation of the feelings she was now experiencing.

There was just one problem: Linda Harrison Welch was a murderer. Joan was sure of it. She had killed Thomas Hodgson. There had been something in Linda's eyes. That was no suicide. Joan's lover had killed Hodgson.

It was understandable. Joan was sure she would have done the same if one of her close family members had been wrongly convicted because of a conspiracy. She had overheard the interview when May and Trubshaw asked Linda about her time in Australia.

Hodgson's death was the least of Joan's worries. It was the recent killings that concerned her. For some ridiculous reason she started singing the madrigal *Now Is the Month of Maying,* one of the songs that she had seen painted on the walls of that upstairs music room at The Bargeman. Linda would never answer her questions about the month of May. There were no *merry lads playing.* There never had been, just a group of men who had sung together, with a young girl as their mascot. Then this girl, Minnie, had died, and Linda was wreaking her revenge for David Harrison's wrongful conviction and subsequent death, along with those of his parents.

How could I love a murderer? How could I?

Joan Wilberforce got up and went into the kitchen where she made herself a coffee – strong and black. She looked at her mobile: there were no messages from Linda. Joan thought back to the blazing row. Linda had a duty to tell the truth if they were to be a couple. There was no room for lies and deceit. Her men friends had given her enough to last a lifetime. *Two failed relationships – and I thought I was going to be third time lucky with a woman!*

Joan sipped her coffee and went back to bed. The sickness had subsided.

Perhaps Hodgson really did commit suicide. People do feel remorse. Perhaps he thought he had put it all behind him; started a new life down under. Then who turns up but somebody from his past who reminds him of everything that he was trying to escape?

Joan looked at her watch. She decided to give herself another half an hour and then attempt to start the day. A shower with that wonderful Clarins body wash would do the trick!

Whatever the truth is with Hodgson, it can't be a coincidence that after Linda arrives back in Holme Hill and her daughter and wife moor up by the pub, the other members of the Select Seven are murdered, one by one.

The sickness returned as Joan Wilberforce began to wonder if she had assisted any of the crimes. She thought back to her appointment to the pub: just a few hours a week to earn some extra cash and to get out of the house after her ex had finally walked out, *the useless sod.* She smiled as she thought back to the first encounter with Linda. She thought of Gordon Wright. He had tried in his mummy's boy way to 'get off' with her, but she had only met up with him because Linda had told her to.

Why did I have to do that? He was OK, but I could never have had him as a boyfriend – ugh! Not my type at all! Though it was so funny when I had to persuade him to dress up as Darth Vader for that fancy dress evening Linda organised at The Bargeman. *What an idiot he looked! And how uncomfortable he was! But he would do anything for me. The ninny. That's what Linda said. It was odd that there were three other Darth Vaders at the party. Why three?*

52

May 25, Afternoon: Philbey's Greatest Shock – to Date

––––––⌒⌒––––––

'Well, I've done it now! I just hope that they don't find out I have shopped them'.

Boris looked up at his owner, yawned, burped, licked his front paws one after the other, and then turned and headed for the cat flap. The food bowl had been licked cleaned of its breakfast contents.

The little black book was now in the hands of the police, where it should have been all along. Pauline Philbey continually castigated herself for not handing Williams's log over to DCI May sooner. Then there would have been none of the issues to do with its loss and eventual return, with all the altercations with Elsie Wright in the meantime.

'And who knows? Some people might still be alive'.

Pauline Philbey looked at the LibDem election leaflet still on the front doormat. She had thought about voting in the European elections the previous day, then decided that there was little point. That would have meant going out and into Holme Hill.

'Who would have thought that the Rip-Van-Winkle village of Yorkshire could be home to all these murders and murderers?'

Boris was staring at the cat flap, wondering whether to venture out. It was raining; it seemed to rain perpetually. So much so that the council had instigated a system of flood warnings and was even considering the installation of a siren.

Thought of sirens took Pauline Philbey back to the time when she worked at Riddles and the warning klaxons had sounded because one of the experiments on Ernie's "wonder material" had gone wrong. She had felt sick at the thought of his being hurt. But it had been a false alarm. One of the machines had overheated; nothing more. Rhys Williams had told her in no uncertain terms to get back to her work and stop looking out the window. It was not long after that incident that she had left Riddles, as had Ernie.

Pauline Philbey had waited for Ernie until all hope was lost and her life had continued much as before. Now she had to wait for the events of the last three weeks to reach their inevitable conclusion; and nobody's life would ever be the same again.

The doorbell rang. The local archivist looked at the clock then the half-empty gin bottle. For a moment she wondered about taking a swig to give her some Dutch courage but decided against it, especially given the hour.

The bell sounded again, continuously this time. Boris looked at his mistress. Philbey shook her head.

'I'm not going out there. If we wait long enough, they will go away', she whispered to her beloved cat.

But the visitor did not go away; the bell kept sounding.

Boris bawled. Philbey held her face in her hands.

'Go away! Please, go away!'

Philbey went into the kitchen to make a cup of tea. It was as if she was back at Riddles listening to the alarm. She looked down at the teapot and at the tea leaves dropped inside. The kettle boiled and she poured the hot water out. She stirred and stirred, but the sound would not leave her head.

'Enough. I am coming. Whoever you are, I am ready for you'.

Philbey strode across the living room and out into the porch. She took the house keys down from their hook and unlocked the door. A familiar face greeted her.

'Hello, stranger! Gosh, I haven't seen you for ages. How are you?'

The stranger stared back at Pauline Philbey. A trickle of blood ran out of the visitor's mouth and down onto her immaculate Barbour jacket over head-to-toe Jaeger. The bell stopped sounding as Joan Wilberforce collapsed into her long-time friend's arms. She was quite dead.

53

May 25, Evening: A Final Message?

—⦅∿⦆—

Pauline Philbey watched while Joan Wilberforce's shrouded body was stretchered out of the living room. Boris observed from the safety of his basket, licking the blood off his paws as he did so. There was a whiff of the signature Clarins as the corpse departed the house.

How long was it since the two women had met and chatted over a cup of tea and a scone at *The Speckled Teapot*? Weeks; months even. Philbey regretted the fact that she had not been more supportive after Joan's husband had traded her in for a younger model, as he had scornfully and cynically described it. There had been few tears when it had happened. Indeed, most of Holme Hill had seen it coming for years. Terry Wilberforce's twice-weekly walks along the old railway line or the canal towpath into Hartley had been not only for exercise, but also to meet someone.

Joan had never discovered the identity of the mystery woman – assuming it *was* a woman (there was little doubt of that, she had often stressed) – or if she did know the identity of her rival for Terence Alexander Wilberforce's affections, she had never informed Pauline Philbey. And if she were going to tell anybody, it would be her best friend, surely.

DCI May and DS Trubshaw followed Dr Felicity Harbord out of the house. All three remained silent until the vehicle carrying Wilberforce's mortal remains away to the mortuary.

'Stabbed, with a long thin blade'.

'Same weapon as before, Fizz?'

'Could well be, Don. I will know more on Monday morning when we do the post-mortem'.

'How long did she take to die?'

'She had lost a lot of blood by the time she got to Philbey's house, DS Trubshaw. You can tell that by the state of her car. God knows how she managed to drive here. Why the hell didn't she phone for an ambulance or call for help somehow?'

May cleared his throat.

'Perhaps something or somebody was preventing her from doing so. Perhaps she was escaping and turned to her best friend to help her. People do strange and illogical things in emergencies.

'Or perhaps she was trying to get to Philbey to tell her something'.

'Poor Pauline. The old girl's really shaken up. She keeps saying it's all her fault. That if she had answered the door straight away and not kept Wilberforce waiting, she might have saved her'.

'Very unlikely, Don. She was only a couple of minutes from death when she arrived, by the looks of it. And Mrs Philbey's description of the events after the door was opened suggest that Joan was already dead and beyond saving by the time she fell into her friend's arms'.

'Anyway, folks, I am off back to enjoy my weekend. I leave you to your investigations. See you Monday'.

The coroner nodded and went to retrieve her car from where it had been perilously parked on the blind corner just outside the imposing gates of Philbey's house. May and Trubshaw turned back towards the front door, walking past Wilberforce's Range Rover, the driver's door still untidily open. The SOCOs did their work in silence.

'May we come in, Mrs Philbey?'

Philbey nodded. The Detective Chief Inspector thought how red her cheeks were; she must always have been a drinker.

The two detectives took the liberty of sitting down on the ample sofa, now that the SOCOs had finished their work. Trubshaw was soon joined by Boris, who planted himself firmly on her lap. May smiled quietly, knowing how much Viv hated felines. Freddie loved them and played with any and every pet that Mum and Dad allowed him to have. Indeed, he often said how much he preferred them to humans. Given all that had been going on in Holme Hill in recent weeks, Donald May began to realise that his son had a point.

'Tea?'

'Sorry, Mrs Philbey?'

'Tea? Would you like a cup of tea?'

'Not for me'.

'And not for me, Mrs Philbey'.

'Come on, Donald, no need to Mrs Philbey me! I remember when you were in Sunday School at Salem. I even taught you! Call me Pauline!'

'Sorry, Pauline. I remember too now you mention it! My father said that you were his best Sunday School teacher ever!'

'That I was! Those were the days! But then you are not here to reminisce, are you?'

'No, we are not, but we can come back tomorrow if you would prefer it. And we have someone keeping an eye on you tonight'.

'So, you think I am in danger, Don?'

'Just taking precautions, given all that has happened here'.

'Not like it used to be, DCI May and DS Trubshaw, is it? I remember when you could leave your front door unlocked and no-one would even think of stealing anything while you were out'.

Donald May nodded. His father used to say much the same in his later years, especially after he had been burgled, though they took memorabilia rather than valuables. That never did make any sense.

'I think we will come back tomorrow morning, if we may, Pauline. We already have your initial statement, and we can talk with you about it all on our return'.

Pauline Philbey nodded. The two detectives got up. May noticed that some colour had returned to the old woman's face. He could not tell whether she wanted her visitors to stay or go.

Once outside, May looked up at the clear sky.

'He telleth the number of the stars, and calleth them all by their names'.

'Sir?'

'It's just a quote from the Bible – that book that I haven't been reading for a while now'.

'Oh right, sir'.

Trubshaw took May's hand and squeezed it hard.

'If you want to talk, Don...'

'I know, Viv. Perhaps tomorrow. I should get home. I'm dead beat. We all are'.

The two of them turned back to look at the house, as if to make sure its occupant was safely inside. There were no lights in the living room but there was one upstairs. The porch light beamed down across the old oak door.

Trubshaw nudged May.

'Do you see what I see, sir?'

'I do, Viv. Somebody – Joan Wilberforce, I assume – has written something in blood. A message, perhaps?'

54

May 26, Morning: A Mistaken Identity and an Examined Letter

—⦿—

'May has resigned'.

'What?'

'May has resigned; effective next month'.

'Pull the other one, Charlie'.

'I mean it, Viv. It's in the newspaper; and in the other media'.

DS Vivienne Trubshaw looked at her fellow detective and wondered. *Don has been under a hell of a lot of stress lately. He doesn't have much time left before they bring in the big boys and girls. He's lost his faith. He has a flakey marriage. He's wondering what to do about me. Perhaps I should leave sooner, but I am not sure that would help. I need to stay until he goes. But… why has he said nothing to me? Donald May owes me an explanation.*

'Morning, both. Thanks for coming in on a Sunday morning, but this case conference couldn't wait till Monday morning, for obvious reasons!'

Trubshaw looked at her pasty-faced boss. There were large bags under his eyes; not surprising when they were at Pauline Philbey's house until after 10.00 pm the previous evening. *I bet he would have had to deal with Freddie when he got home as well. The boy's tantrums were unbelievable when they came, and Caz could no longer cope.*

'I've never known anything like it, sir. We are the talk of the county – and the country. The village has been renamed Holme Hell by the tabloids!'

DS Trubshaw snorted, still wondering why the DCI had not said anything to her about his resignation; and yet everybody else seemed to know. *I had thought better of Don.*

'But no publicity is bad publicity', Riggs continued. 'We have had reports of people coming from far and wide. All the hotels are full, thanks to the reporters and media people crowding into the area. There's even a rumour that a film director is scouting for possible locations for a film about it all'.

'For the love of God! What are these people on?'

May banged the conference table hard. Trubshaw sighed. The DS looked at her DCI. *Can this shitstorm get any worse?*

'Anyway, you two, let's focus on Georgie's letter for now. We can concentrate on Joan Wilberforce's murder tomorrow morning unless there's something that we need to deal with right now'.

'No, sir. We have uniform combing the area and doing a door-to-door'.

'Thanks, Charlie. Viv and I will go back for a full interview with Pauline Philbey this afternoon'.

May looked at Trubshaw. Trubshaw nodded in reply. *Why, why, why does he have to resign? He has done nothing wrong!*

'OK, Charlie. Put the letter on screen'.

Riggs obliged. Just as the three detectives were about to look at the WPC's spindly handwriting, coffee and pastries arrived. The timing seemed ironic, given Ellis's coffee routine. They all thought it; no one said it.

'Pastries, sir?'

'The least I could do on a Sunday morning, Viv'.

Charlie was the first to choose, but then realised protocol dictated that he should have let the DCI select first.

'Go on, Charlie. I know that you love the ones with the custard inside. And I don't like custard'.

'Is it proven that this is Georgie's handwriting, sir?'

'That's the expert opinion we have. And it looks good to me, given the other examples of her script that we have to compare the letter with'.

'Written under duress, do we think?'

'Georgie is a real toughie beneath that Roedean exterior of hers, but she must have had little choice. What would any of us do in such circumstances?'

'Good point, Viv. The same, I imagine. What do you think, Charlie?'

Riggs quickly swallowed the last of his pastry, wiping his mouth and hands with the tissues provided along with the food.

'Send a coded message. That's what I would do'.

All three looked at the letter displayed on the screen at the far end of May's office. Ellis was being well treated but was hostage to a group calling themselves the New Select Seven. We know where that nametag comes from, don't we? Georgie will be released in exchange for Detective Chief Inspector May on the evening of the 28th. More information as to when and where the swap would take place will follow. The DCI is to come on his own, unarmed and with no wiretap. If it is a no show, then WPC Ellis will never be seen alive again.

'I've called in extra forces. I'm not waiting for the ACC to take the decision over my head'.

'Good call, Don. Sorry! Good call, sir'.

There was a brief spark in the DCI's eyes as he looked at Trubshaw, then the curtain came down again.

Charlie Riggs noticed that the DS had only broken off a small piece of her pastry and left half of that morsel. May had not touched his.

'Go on, Charlie You're a growing lad, have mine'.

'And mine'.

'Thanks, sir! Thanks, Viv!'

The plate was soon empty; only a few crumbs remained on the conference table to suggest that anything had been eaten in the DCI's office that morning.

'Charlie, is there anything about the paper on which the letter was written or the envelope in which it was posted?'

'No, sir. The letter was hand delivered, as far as we can tell, but nothing on CCTV and no witnesses. The paper and the envelope are standard WH Smith issue. It could have been bought from the store in Hartley. It could have been purchased anywhere!'

'And any time'.

'Thanks, both. Fingerprints?'

'Only Georgie's, sir'.

'And have either of you seen any special coded message from George?'

'Nothing, sir'.

'No, nothing, sir'.

'Then all we can do is wait for the next communication. What are you two doing next Tuesday evening?'

'I'm going to catch up on some paperwork if that's OK with you, sir?'

'Fine, Charlie. Are you off, Viv?'

'Well, sir, I would quite like a word with you in private if I could'.

Riggs nodded and closed the office door as he left.

'Don, I'm just a bit surprised that you didn't tell me. Charlie knew, and it's all over the newspapers this morning. With respect, I don't think you should do it. I know things have been hard over the last few weeks, but you are a good copper, and you have done a first-rate job in difficult circumstances, especially with all the recent cuts to budgets'.

May nodded.

'It has been hard, and I have seriously thought about throwing in the towel'.

'But think of all that you have achieved, especially in this area!'

May nodded again.

'Think again, sir. I know it can't work between us, for all sorts of reasons, but you have a lot more to give the force. It has given you so much satisfaction in the past and will do so again'.

'What are you on about, Viv?'

Trubshaw hesitated.

'Your resignation, sir. Don't do it!'

'Well, thanks for your concern. When I do come to think about it, I will remember what you said!'

'How do you mean, Don?'

'Well, I haven't resigned, and I am not planning to – at least, not until these murders have been solved!'

'But Charlie said that you had resigned and it was in all the media!'

Detective Chief Inspector Donald May burst out laughing. DS Trubshaw had never seen him laugh so loudly. There were tears in his eyes.

'Yes, Viv, May has resigned. But not this May. *Theresa* May as leader of the Conservative Party!'

55

May 26, Afternoon: Welch Reflects; Philbey Is Interviewed

———— ❧ ————

Linda Harrison Welch looked out of her bedroom window from behind the lace curtains that her lover had insisted be hung there. The cricket square was being mowed ready for the Sunday afternoon match. Linda could still smell Joan Wilberforce's perfume.

How she loved her Clarins! And her Jaeger!

The owner of The Bargeman turned around; back to the four-poster bed that she had been sharing with Joan every night for the past week or so. How they had enjoyed being together! What pleasure they had brought each other!

I have loved like I never loved!

But not the previous evening; and not this morning.

I wish I could turn back time! I wish none of this had happened! I wish Joan had not found out!

Linda sat on the edge of the bed and wept.

Why now? Why not ten years ago? When I had a life?

Welch coughed. And coughed. And coughed. She covered her face with her palms. When she had stopped spluttering, she took them away and looked.

'*Now* I really do have blood on my hands'.

The owner of The Bargeman laughed like she had never laughed.

***

Detective Chief Inspector Donald May wished he could be home with Freddie. They could have been playing trains or out on a bike ride or even discussing the case. But talking about the Holme Hill Murders was not the same as having to investigate them for real.

May thought about Vivienne Trubshaw. He could also have been with his Detective Sergeant, but not here, as they were now, standing in front of Pauline Philbey's house waiting for the local archivist to answer the door.

The word written in Joan Wilberforce's blood was still there. Photographs had been taken from every angle; the significance of the letters C-O-O remained unknown.

Trubshaw looked at May. Only the previous evening they had held hands; only a finger touch, but enough to make them both tingle. She had wanted to kiss him; and he had wanted to kiss her. Nothing had happened; nothing would happen, not now, not ever.

'What do you think, sir? C-O-O?'

'That's assuming those are the letters. It's just a scrawl really. Could it be S-I-O?'

'What? You mean Senior Investigating Officer? You mean you?'

May snorted and shrugged.

Trubshaw knew that look. She knew that her boss – and lover – was worried: about the murders; about Georgie; about what was going to happen to him when he went to the hostage exchange meeting that was being proposed.

A second letter had appeared out of nowhere; just like the first. Nothing had been traceable – very clever! – or at least, nothing yet. *Iacta alea est* May had said when he had read the communication. Viv had to translate it for Riggs. 'It's Latin, Charlie', she had said. 'It means *the die is cast*. It's a quote attributed to Julius Caesar'. The DC had grunted, the working-class chip still pressing down heavily on his shoulders.

The three of them would be spending much of the following day working out how to prepare for the encounter on the evening of May 28th, now that they knew when and where. For the time being, they had to focus on the job in hand. Assuming, that is, Pauline Philbey ever answered her door.

May and Trubshaw looked at the bloody writing, but no further inspiration came. It was just as well that they could hear a key in the door and two bolts being slid back.

'I am sorry to have been so long, Inspector, Sergeant. I fell asleep. It's the first rest I have had since... well, you know what'.

'We do, Pauline. May we come in?'

Trubshaw looked at Philbey and tried to smile reassuringly. The local archivist was beyond any kind of reassurance.

The woman nodded, turned away from her visitors, and walked back inside. The two detectives followed, in silence.

'I would offer you tea, but...'

'I'll make it, Mrs Philbey. You talk to DCI May. Just point me in the direction of the kitchen'.

The hostess pointed to the door at the far side of the ample living room. Boris followed, as if to make sure that the Detective Sergeant found what she was looking for.

'I'm sorry, Pauline. I'm so sorry. I know you and Joan were close'.

Philbey took out a handkerchief from her sleeve and blew her nose.

'We were close, yes. But not recently. I had seen less and less of Joan over the last few months, and then nothing at all since she got that job at The Bargeman.

'Why do you think that was, Pauline?'

Philbey waited until the Detective Sergeant had returned with tea and biscuits before giving her answer. Boris followed, waiting until Trubshaw had sat down, whereupon he jumped up on her lap, circled around, and then sat down, immovably.

'That's an easy question to answer, Donald. She was in love, madly in love. Had no time for anyone else but her *paramour*'.

'How do you know, Mrs Philbey?' Trubshaw poured tea.

'Call me Pauline, dear. Everybody else does, especially your boss. Mind you, I have known Donald May since he was in short trousers'.

Trubshaw looked at May; May blushed slightly.

'How do you know, Pauline? How do you know about Joan?'

'I know, dears, because she told me. She rang me up a few nights ago. I can't remember when. I think I had probably had too much to drink. But I do remember that she sounded more alive than I had heard her sound in years. She talked about how she was in love like she had never been in love before; how everything was better than it had ever been. She had two rotten marriages. Awful men – God knows why she married them; I could never understand what she saw in either of them. She said that there was some business that her new partner had to complete and then they were moving abroad to begin a new life together'.

'So, this lover, who was it?'

Philbey laughed.

'She wouldn't say, DS Trubshaw. Joan just talked about how surprised I would be if I found out'.

'Was that because her lover was married?'

Philbey shrugged.

'Joan wasn't one for infidelity, Don. She abhorred men being unfaithful to their wives. She had suffered too much at the hands of her exes'.

'Could she have been a woman?'

'Could who have been a woman, Detective Sergeant?'

'Joan's lover'.

Philbey laughed.

'I very much doubt it. She was a very feminine lady. A real looker. She used to do part-time modelling in her younger days. Knew every detail of her body; knew just what wear to look so very elegant. We used to call her "The Queen of Jaeger". That was our nickname for her. But she didn't deserve to die'.

'What do you make of the message written in blood on your door?'

'I don't know, Sergeant. I am not even sure I can make the letters out'.

'We think they might be C-O-O. Does that mean anything to you?'

Philbey shook her head.

'Who would want to kill her, Pauline?'

Silence.

'Pauline?'

'Well, she did say that she was beginning to worry about her safety, but when I quizzed her further, she just said that it was a general feeling in the village with all the murders'.

'Nothing more than that?'

Philbey shook her head.

'Did Joan say where she and her lover were going to move to, when the unfinished business was done?'

'She did, actually'.

'And?'

'It was Australia'.

The interview concluded; the two detectives left. Pauline Philbey placed her back to the door once she had closed it, as if to make doubly sure that no-one would get in. Then she realised that she knew what the letters C-O-O signified.

56

May 26, Evening: Conclusions Begin to Be Reached

---cᴧɔ---

Arthur burped and hiccupped, then gurgled merrily.

Linda Welch looked at her grandson and smiled. *This little bag of sugar is the best thing to come out of all this mess. At least we are now back together: me, my daughter, my grandson.*

Welch looked up. There in the newly decorated sitting room on the first floor at *The Bargeman* sat her daughter and her daughter's wife.

'It's good to have you three here, it really is'.

'Thanks, Mum. It's good to be here'.

Jaycee put a hand on her wife's thigh and squeezed gently.

'And what do *you* think, Abbey?'

'I want what Jaycee wants. I want what is best for her and for Arthur. I'll do whatever you want, Linda'.

'You don't have to, Abbey. You could walk away now, with your son, and you would not have done anything wrong'.

'Wouldn't I?'

'No, Abs. You could get away scot-free. Why don't you? You could take Arthur and have a life. You have no need to be mixed up in any of this business'.

'But I do, my love. We are in this together, for all time'.

Jaycee and Abbey kissed as Linda Welch watched.

Once upon a time I would have found it hard to watch two women kiss like that. It wasn't easy when I heard that Janet had come out and, to top it all, had got married, and her wife had given birth. But who am I to talk? Who am I to cast the first stone? Look at me now! I found the love of my life back in Holme Hill; and that love was a woman! Who would have thought?

'This is where they used to meet. It looked a lot different when I first moved in. Joan and I completely redecorated the room. But I can still feel them here. Those men'.

'You mean the Select Seven?'

'I hadn't realised you knew about the group, Abbey'.

'Jaycee told me everything, Linda. We agreed that we would have no secrets, and eventually she filled me in on the history of this room, this place, this village. I just wish that she had done so sooner. A lot sooner'.

'I'm sorry, my love'.

'It's OK, Jayce. I understand. I know you were only trying to protect me. And I'm not cross with you anymore. Honest'.

Abbey Harrison looked at the photograph of the music room as it had been in its heyday, complete with musical quotations painted on the walls and the ceiling. Now it was just a comfortable lounge, with its standard three-piece suite, coffee table, bookcases, wall-mounted television: all the trappings of normal life in a sleepy village in West Yorkshire.

'You're sure you want to carry on with this, you two?'

Abbey and Jaycee both nodded. Linda Welch looked at her watch.

'What's wrong, Mum?'

'It's Joan. She should have been here by now. She's already an hour late'.

'I thought you said that Joan was never on time!'

Linda Welch smiled, remembering their first date.

'No, she's not. But even for Joan, this is late'.

'Do you think the police have got her?'

Jaycee laughed.

'Oh, my darling Abbey, it's all OK. Joan doesn't know anything about what's been happening and our involvement in it'.

Linda Welch sighed.

'Well, actually, she does now'.

'How do you mean, Mum?'

'She asked me about Thomas Hodgson'.

'So?'

'So I told her'.

'But, Mum, there was nothing to tell. It was years and years ago and the guy killed himself'.

'Well..'.

'Well, what? He did kill himself, didn't he?'

'Not exactly, Janet. There's more to it than that'.

'And you have only helped with the other murders, haven't you? You're only an accessory, like we are now. I mean, you didn't do the actual killing, did you?'

***

'What do you think, Commander May, sir? What do you think C-O-O means?'

'Not sure, DCI May. I will have to think about it. My best guess so far is that it is an acronym'.

'Good point, sir. I shall have to consider that at the team briefing tomorrow morning'.

Donald May smiled at his son. Freddie so enjoyed these conversations; was desperate to be treated like a grown up. Then there were times when it was as if you were dealing with a two-year old. Those uncontrollable rages; the total unreasonableness. Caz couldn't cope with it. She had had enough; she really had. Even the school found it difficult. They were going to have to decide soon about what to do with him. But then he was such a bright child. There had to be a role in society for someone as intelligent as Freddie.

'You OK, Dad? You look tired. Your eyes are bloodshot'.

'I'm OK, son. It's been a long day. Perhaps it's time we both went to bed'.

'But we haven't finished our case review for the day yet! And I don't have to go to school tomorrow. It's the late May Bank Holiday!'

Donald May smiled thinly. Caz arrived with a welcome tea and biscuit for her husband and a glass of milk and a slice of Battenberg for her son. She sat down opposite the two men in her life.

'Why don't you both pool your thoughts on the latest murder and give me a summary? That might help you to see more clearly. I often find it helps to share your ideas with someone who is outside the environment in which you are working. After all, it isn't as though I am a work colleague, is it? Not like your DC, or even your DS, for example.

She knows. Now I know she knows. But Caz being Caz, she will never say anything.

'Come on then, you two. Fill me in, Commander, Detective Chief Inspector'.

May senior and May junior both smiled and saluted. Commander May took the lead in filling in the newly appointed Chief Constable on the latest murder and then its predecessors. The DCI added the occasional detail to assist with the briefing. The CC asked a small number of questions, all of which were highly pertinent in the opinion of her two senior officers. Eventually the briefing was over. The grandfather clock – a twelfth birthday for Freddie from his grandmother – struck 11.00 pm. The case review had lasted nearly forty minutes.

The room fell silent. Eventually Chief Constable Caz spoke.

'Interesting, gentlemen. Very interesting. Thank you for the briefing. I think I have worked out what C-O-O stands for'.

57

May 27, Morning:
Research Turns Risky

―◈―

Gordon Wright looked out of his study bedroom, across the cricket field and towards the railway embankment. A train pulled into Holme Hill station: no-one got off, and no-one got on. If it had been a normal Monday morning the platform would have been teeming with workers clambering onto the soon-to-be-pensioned-off pacer trains to get into Hartley, Halifax, and Leeds or, going the other way, across to Manchester. The contra-flow of teenagers alighting the train to attend Holme Hill Academy would have made the fight for a seat all the harder.

Northern Rail really are useless! Thank God, it is a Bank Holiday!

Gordon rearranged the folders on his desk and tried to work. This little area was his sanctuary. Not even his mother was allowed in. It must have been the maid's room when old Riddles had lived here, given the connecting door to the master bedroom. Wright's thoughts turned to Ted Gelsthorpe.

I must go to the police. My mother has something to do with these murders! It all became clear to me when I was talking to Sally. I could see the look on her face as she listened to my admission. Or was it a confession? What will the police think? Will they believe me? Except what am I telling them? That my mother, a woman in her late seventies, someone regarded by all the village as a respected member of the community, is a mass murderer? What evidence do I have? Will they accept my story about Gelsthorpe?

But it isn't a story: it's a non-story. Ted came to stay with us; rescued by my mother; protected from those who were out to murder him. Except then he left us suddenly; perhaps something (or someone) frightened him, and the next thing we knew was that he was dead, laid out flat under his beloved cricket roller. So, what would the police want to know?

'What do I care? I am going to get my own place soon, away from this village, and my mother!'

Wright cleared his throat and went back to his research, putting aside all thought of contacting Donald May. Wright opened his files and cleaned his computer screen. It seemed ironic that for all his correspondence with other genealogists around the world, the person who had helped him most to close the gaps in his family tree lived in Holme Hill. It had been a while since he had corresponded with J76. Gordon eagerly powered up his laptop and waited for his email to load. As he waited, he heard the front door slam. He peered over the top of his computer screen, looked out of the window again, and saw his mother walk across the road and towards Salem Chapel. For a moment, he thought about following her, but the tiredness that he had been experiencing since Gelsthorpe's death overwhelmed him. Wright yawned suddenly and uncontrollably.

Most of the unread messages were from work. A few were spam and one was from Sally. Gordon scrolled back through the inbox: little or nothing else of interest. Then he saw it: an email from J76. He should have read the one from his colleague first, but his anonymous fellow genealogist intrigued him. Sally was safe, a thoroughly decent woman. J76 was an unknown; they might be dangerous, but it was about time there was some excitement in his life. For all the awfulness of the last few weeks, beginning with his first sight of a dead body, Gordon Wright had come alive. He had met Jaycee and Abbey and, much to his surprise, enjoyed playing with Arthur; had taken the gorgeous Joan Wilberforce to dinner and dressed up as Darth Vader at a fancy-dress party at The Bargeman; had witnessed a conversation about a murder; had helped shield Ted Gelsthorpe; had confided in Sally, who had responded to his plea for help: all this and a thousand other things, all in a single month. And it was not over yet.

Gordon clicked on the email. J76 was not their usual chatty self. The message was so curt he wondered if he was corresponding with the same person as he had been doing over the last few weeks. All the previous messages about his ancestors had been so comprehensive, so detailed, so knowledgeable. There was an urgency about the two sentences that were now displayed on the centre of his screen. He resolved to reply straightaway, agreeing to what was being asked of him. It was a decision he was to regret for the rest of his life.

58

May 27, Afternoon: Demands for Justice Begin to Mount

—⌒◦⌒—

'Thank God, you're OK. Where the hell have you been? I have been worried sick about you. Why didn't you answer the phone? Where were you last night? Look I'm sorry; I am *so* sorry. But I love you!'

The caller could hear breathing. Someone – a man – was talking in the background.

'Hello? Who's there? Is that you?'

Linda Welch put the phone down, ran to the toilet in her *en suite* and threw up. There was blood in the vomit, but that was the least of her worries.

Something has happened. I know something has happened. She wouldn't have left me like that; without saying a word. She would have got in touch.

Linda Welch flushed the toilet, splashed cold water on her face, gargled with mouthwash, then walked back into the bedroom, and sat down on the bed. She took one of the pillows and pressed it to her face. She could still smell Joan on the material.

'If only I could turn the clock back'.

The phone rang. For a brief instant, Linda thought it might be Joan ringing back, but then she remembered that this was her private, ex-directory number. Not even her lover knew about it.

She let it ring and ring and ring. Then the noise stopped.

I don't think I can go on with this. Has Joan been arrested?

The phone rang again. Linda did not answer immediately, but then decided she had to deal with the world. Perhaps the caller had news.

'Hello?'

'Linda. It's me. Have you heard about Joan?'

'No. What about her?'

'I'm sorry. I am *so* sorry'.

'When? How?'

***

Detective Chief Superintendent Arthur Bradley downed his second whisky and poured himself a third.

'You sure you won't join me?'

Bradley's guest shook their head.

'No, I suppose not. You've got a lot to do today *and* tomorrow'.

'And the day after', the visitor replied.

'Indeed. Especially the day after. We'll be finished then'.

'The 29th of May. Everything will have come together'.

Bradley put the glass to his mouth, sipping the single malt like the connoisseur he was. He let the liquid flow gently into his mouth; it trickled into every corner so that he could appreciate the taste.

48 hours and it will all be over. Will it have been worth it?

'Are you having second thoughts, Arthur?'

Bradley snorted.

'It's a bit late now, isn't it?'

'That look on your face. I know you too well not to recognise that you are having doubts'.

The Superintendent shook his head slowly.

'Anyone would have doubts. But it's far too late to change course. I am in this too deep. We all are'.

Bradley's visitor nodded.

'No, we have to finish what we started. We owe it to Minnie and David'.

'There's something you're not telling me, though, Arthur. What is it?'

The visitor stood up and walked over to Bradley's desk. The Superintendent looked up as his guest as they placed their hands on the files marked 'Hargreaves and Harrison'.

Bradley smirked.

'I find it ironic that you used blackmail to get me involved in all this. And there was no need, no need at all: I would have agreed to your plan anyway. Those two and Ernest Halliday deserved, and still deserve, justice'.

***

The photographs were torn, or crinkled, or both. Not one of them gave Barbara Halliday what she wanted. Except what was she looking for? She had tried everything else and all she had left was a shoebox full of old pictures.

I thought I was onto something when I found this stash of photos. But they tell me nothing; nothing at all. Why were there no pictures of Ernie? Yes, Rod's brother had escaped his background and his early upbringing; had made something of himself; but why was there not one photo of him in any of these boxes? And why were they in that old desk that came from the chapel? What else don't I know about my late husband?

Barbara Halliday looked over at the cocktail bar. She ought to start thinking about Rod's funeral: that would require another drink before she looked at the funeral director's brochure. Would she go ahead with Rodney's wishes? Or would she just have him cremated and be done with it?

The vodka and orange tasted good. She remembered the first time she had been out with Rod and he had suggested she try it. He had got her tipsy and they had done it in his car after their night out. She had never been with anybody else before, or since. She had waited for him patiently since he had done time. And then from rags to riches; wealth beyond her wildest dreams.

Anything and everything for you, Babs. Anything and everything. You just say the word and it's yours. We've arrived!

Barbara Halliday looked at the photographs once more. Still nothing came to her.

Right. There are no family pictures with Ernest and Rodney together. But then there are no pictures of Ernest at all. Did he really exist? He must have done. Who was that man that Pauline Philbey went out with? Why did Rodney tell me about having a brother? What about all those stories about him and Ernest when they were kids? About how Ernie was the clever one, always with his nose in a book. What else did Rod say? The scholarship to the grammar school; university; research; then secret work for the MoD; then disappearance. Killed because of his knowledge of the "wonder material".

David Baker

It was time for a refill; a large one.

If he ever did exist, it is as if someone has tried to erase all memory of Ernest Halliday. Were these people now trying to do the same with those other people who had all worked at Riddles with Ernie back in 1976? But why Rod? Did he know something about the "wonder material" that meant he had to die? And how many more deaths were there going to be before all this was over?

59

May 27, Evening: Ellis Is Back in Control, or so She Thinks

—◦◦◦—

Georgie Ellis took pride in having been successful in befriending her captors. She had read so many books about hostage situations, the WPC knew what should be done in the event of capture. Except that the Hon. Georgiana Lucinda Ponsonby-Ellis had always assumed she would be the one negotiating the hostages' release, not the victim.

She had nevertheless adapted the advice given in her texts, and, somewhat to her surprise, the various Darth Vaders who kept her fed, watered, abluted, toileted, and well, had released her to move about her room freely on condition there were no escape attempts from that basement prison.

Georgie had sensed the growing tension among the Organised Crime Group members. There was an argument about the wording of the letter she had been forced to write. She had overheard the heated conversations between two men and then a man and a woman; all about the mess they were in.

WPC Ellis had worked out where she was and how she could escape. One Darth had let slip enough for her to work out how to access the tunnel. It all fitted with the discussions she had with Jo Bishop. Thank goodness!

Thank God, I have a photographic memory! I know every access point. I could give them all the slip! I know how to do it as well. Now that I have their confidence, it would just be a matter of timing, when there are the fewest of them around, when the pub is open, when I can merge into the crowd, when I can...

But WPC Georgie Ellis had decided some time ago that escaping now was not the best course of action, no way. It would be necessary to go along with the OCG until the very last minute. That would mean this crime group – and they were certainly well organised – could be caught in the act and her DCI would be saved.

Will they have got my message? Will they have understood it? That's what I need to know. Surely, Trubshaw will spot it, even if nobody else does.

***

'Is everything in place?'

'As far as it can be. The final arrangements will be made tomorrow'.

'Sir, permission to speak freely?'

Detective Chief Inspector May looked at his Detective Sergeant.

'Of course, Viv. You have always been able to speak freely with me'.

DC Riggs averted his gaze while his two senior officers looked at each other.

'I think what you are going to do tomorrow evening is completely wrong headed. You are putting your life in grave danger with no obvious guarantee that you will stay safe or WPC Ellis will be freed'.

'What alternative do I, *we* have?'

'We could issue search warrants for The Bargeman, High Windows and Bradley's place, sir'.

'Don't you think I haven't considered that, Charlie?'

'Sorry, sir'.

'Not enough evidence, is there? For all our suspicions, we would find it difficult to get a warrant for all three locations. In any case, as I have said many times, Charlie, none of that is going to help us find and free George, is it?'

'No, sir, it is not. But I agree with Viv. I don't like it, this spy-thriller intrigue. Doing a hostage swap, you for her'.

'But every angle has been covered, Charlie, and you know it. What could go wrong?'

Riggs grimaced.

'How do we even know she is still alive?'

'They wouldn't dare murder a police officer, surely!'

'Well, sir, what do they have to lose? They've murdered plenty of people already. One more isn't going to make much difference, is it?

'Perhaps it's two more, Viv, Charlie. We haven't found out what happened to Harry Metcalfe yet, have we? He fits the pattern of murders, unlike Halliday and Wilberforce. Remember, we never found the biblical quotation on Rodney's body, and there was no sign of any such reference on Joan Wilberforce, was there?'

'Just her writing C-O-O in her own blood on Pauline Philbey's front porch. Is that a Biblical quotation?'

Riggs poured his fellow officers more coffee as he spoke. He did the same for himself and took two chocolate biscuits for good measure.

How is it that my DC never puts on weight?

'What do we make of the M.O. of Joan's murder?'

'Well, sir, that seems to fit with the others, according to Dr Harbord's initial findings. Don't forget we have the post-mortem tomorrow morning'.

'Yet another sword attack'.

'Yet another sword attack, Charlie, except that this one seemed to have been less calculated and more frenzied. Is that right, Viv?'

Trubshaw nodded.

'So it seems, sir'.

'As if there was a haste about the killing, perhaps?'

'Which could be passion or anger kicking in?'

'It could, Charlie. Or perhaps the perpetrator, or perpetrators, had to get to Joan Wilberforce before she could spill the beans'.

Riggs nodded.

'But why go to Pauline Philbey?'

'You heard what she said, Viv. Joan and Pauline had been best friends until the new love interest had kicked in'.

'I guess so, and where would you go if you were bleeding to death and needed to tell someone what you needed to tell them before it was too late?'

'Your best friend'. Charlie Riggs had a marvellous knack of eating chocolate biscuits and speaking at the same time.

'Yup. Even though they hadn't seen each other for a while, thanks to the new love of Joan's life'.

'We need to get on to that. Who was the new love interest? Tomorrow morning, Viv'.

'On it, sir'.

'OK, you two, let's call it a day'.

Riggs took the last biscuit as he agreed with his SIO.

'Sir, just before we go, can we take another look at Georgie's letter? There's something that's been bugging me about her writing, and I think I know what it is'.

60

May 28, Morning: A Code Deciphered

—∽—

'Take care, Dad!'

'What makes you say that Freddie?'

'No reason'.

Detective Chief Inspector May looked at his son sitting glumly at the foot of the stairs.

Freddie never says anything for no reason.

'It's just another day at the office, son'.

'So, why are you going to be home late?'

'There will be a... a special operation this evening that needs my attention'.

'Have you told your commanding officer about this, DCI May?'

'Er, no, sir'.

'Then a sitrep at once, May!'

'But, sir...'

'Enough, DCI May. I need a briefing immediately'.

May looked at his watch. He had time to talk to Freddie before he set off to work and his son knew it. Caz was unaware of what was planned for later that day, though May senior suspected that she suspected. And Commander Frederick May of the Yard certainly suspected.

'Very well, sir, ten minutes for a briefing before I set off for Hartley CID'.

'Understood, Detective Chief Inspector'.

Caz looked through the serving hatch that linked kitchen to dining room as she heard the two men in her life sit down at the table. She motioned to May senior to ask him if he wanted a drink; there was no answer, apart from the closing of the hatch door. Caz thought better than to listen in.

'Well, Freddie, *Commander May*, it's like this'.

Sensing his father's reluctance to speak, May junior smiled.

'Go on, Dad. I can take it'.

May senior smiled back.

'I know you can, Fred. I know you can'.

The DCI took a deep breath and began his sitrep.

'The story… I mean, the situation report begins with a very silly act by an incredibly stupid officer'.

'WPC Ellis, I assume?'

'Indeed. WPC Ellis, who took it upon herself to investigate Superintendent Bradley, or so it would seem'.

'She's quite posh, isn't she?'

DCI May laughed at his son.

'She is true blue blood, Freddie. But she doesn't want people to know. Or so she claims!'

Commander Frederick May of the Yard snorted in disbelief.

'And, Dad, remind me what evidence there is that Ellis was investigating Bradley'.

'Her car was found abandoned about half a mile away from Bradley's house'.

'But there is no proof that she went inside his place and nothing to suggest that Bradley kidnapped her'.

'Spot on, Freddie. All evidence is circumstantial. But why else would her car be where it was?'

'And she didn't tell anybody else about what she was up to?'

'Nope. Not a soul. Well, at least, nobody at the station. But then she was, *is* a bit of a loner. No close colleagues at work, and, as far as we can tell, no boyfriend. Her family lives a long way away and they are estranged. At least, her and her dad are.

'I thought you said there was a sister. Tiger?'

DCI May laughed.

'Tiggy. The sister is called Tiggy. We informed her of Georgie's disappearance. Tiggy couldn't help us much. They are hardly ever in contact now. Apart from Christmas cards, that is'.

'So, nobody would miss the WPC?'

'Not apart from us. She was good at bringing the senior officers drinks and biscuits in the morning'.

'Should you be saying things like that, Dad, in this day and age?'

DCI May blushed and smiled sheepishly.

'Not really, son. I'm sorry. I will try and do better in the future'.

'Now, what about the ransom note?'

'How do you know about the note?'

'I heard you and Mum talking last night'.

'Fred! You should have been asleep! You shouldn't listen in to private conversations like that!'

'I couldn't help it, Dad. I couldn't sleep. And you and Mum were talking quite loudly, especially when I sat on the landing'.

Donald May sighed, deciding that there was no point in castigating his son.

'It's not so much a ransom note, Fred, as a proposal for a hostage exchange. Her for me!'

May could see the shock in his son's face.

'I am OK, Dad. Don't worry about me. I can take it. Honest. I want to know. I want to help you. We are fellow officers, remember?'

'WPC Ellis will be released this evening at 10.00 pm if I offer myself up as a replacement hostage'.

'And what if you don't?'

'Then she will join the other victims and there will be one more dead body on our hands tomorrow'.

'How do you know that the message is real?'

'Well, it is in her handwriting'.

'The work of a clever forger?'

'Unlikely, son. We have had the handwriting checked by an expert. It's almost certainly hers'.

'And no clues or secret messages in the text?'

'It's interesting you say that. We spent a lot of time at our case conference the other day looking to see if there was anything unusual about the letter or her handwriting or anything that might give us a clue'.

'And was there?'

DCI May laughed.

'It may seem odd, Freddie – though I think you would understand – but Georgie Ellis was a real stickler for grammar and punctuation and English (rather than American) spelling of words. And this letter was awful, not the sort of writing you would expect from someone who went to Roedean'.

'What's Roedean, Dad?'

'A posh independent school for girls. And before you ask, Freddie, we don't have time for me to explain that!'

Frederick May said nothing.

'There were commas and full stops where there shouldn't have been, and they weren't there when they should have been. And words spelt with a z rather than an s...'

'Like organize instead of organise?'

'Exactly so. Georgie hates that. She tells everybody off – even me, though I'm her commanding officer – just like you are mine!'

'What does this tell you?'

'It was DS Trubshaw who spotted it. I am surprised that Georgie's captors didn't notice, but perhaps grammar and punctuation are not their strong points. Not everybody is like you and me, are they, Fred?'

May junior smiled, thinly.

'You had better tell me what the secret message said, Dad'.

'It says... if you isolate the words that are between these extra commas and full stops, it says: "don't come, you will be killed if you do"'.

61

May 28, Afternoon: Preparations Continue

She had to go through with it. It had been planned for long enough. And now it was nearly over. She had mourned all she could mourn. There had been a few weeks of blissful pleasure like she had never known before and would never know again.

Linda Welch felt more tired than she had ever felt. Months had become weeks; weeks were now turning into days.

I only need three days: three more days and it is done.

'Did she really have to die? For God's sake, tell me! Did she have to die?'

Welch's guest nodded.

'She was about to tell the police everything. She had worked it all out and she was going to Hartley to spill every bean in the tin'.

'But I loved her!'

'Love? What's that? I stopped being able to love years ago. And you know why, Linda. You know full well, why'.

'So why are you here? Why are you doing all this? You must know what love is!'

The guest laughed.

'I did. Oh yes, I did. And I knew what trust was. I trusted and I loved'.

'Like I loved Joan. She was the love of my life. In just a few short weeks, I came to love her like I never loved'.

'I know you did, Linda. And I am sorry for that. But we simply could not afford to be caught now. We are so near to completing our task'.

'Did she have to be murdered like that? So horribly?'

'There was no alternative. If she hadn't been killed when she was...'

'Couldn't she just have been kept under lock and key until we've finished? If it's good enough for Ellis, why wasn't it good enough for Joan?'

'We need Ellis alive, remember? We don't get May without Ellis!'

Welch lit a cigarette. *How Joan hated my smoking!*

'Alright, alright. We had our few weeks. And they were wonderful!'

'It was going to end soon anyway, wasn't it, Linda?'

'What do you mean by that?'

'You know full well what I mean'.

Linda Welch put her head in her hands. She could still smell Joan's Clarins from the last time they had embraced.

Is there an afterlife? What will you be doing now, Joan? Shopping for new clothes, knowing you! I so hope there is: I'll be joining you soon, and I can't wait!

'No, I don't know what you mean. I don't know at all'.

***

Pauline Philbey threw down her *Guardian* so violently that Boris mewled in shock. The cat stared back at his owner, as if waiting for an apology; none came.

'What is the world coming to? Alistair Campbell expelled from the Labour Party for voting Liberal Democrat in the European Elections?'

She thought back to her time at Riddles.

Those were the days. That's when the Labour Party really was the **Labour** *Party. All the fights with the bosses over workers' rights. They were bastards to the shop floor workers. Sending them into that laboratory without proper protection. Ernie could see that. Perhaps that was why they got rid of him.*

The local archivist looked at the half-empty gin bottle on the side board.

When did I last have a drink? When did I last enjoy a drink? When did I last want a drink?

She made a coffee: strong and black. It tasted awful, but she downed it.

I need my wits about me.

She made another coffee: strong and black. It tasted even worse; but she downed it. She studied the plans once again. Even enlarged to four times the size of the original, some of the lines were faded.

I suppose we should be lucky that these plans of Riddles, Salem, and so on survive at all! Have I got it right, though? Was I correct? The numbering of these sheets doesn't add up. What if there is a plan missing? One that gives details of more tunnels and secret passageways? Donald May could die tonight if I have made a mistake.

***

Why am I here? What am I doing? It was wrong when I first did it, and it is wrong now! It will always be wrong!

Jo Bishop enjoyed afternoon sex. It was her favourite time of day to do anything and everything; especially making love.

It had got better with Bill Harker; much better. She was even able to forget for most of the time not only that he was her MA supervisor, but also that the Professor and Head of Department was married. Jo Bishop had even met Mrs Harker at a reception for new postgraduate students.

That all seemed such a long time ago.

She listened to Bill's light breathing as they lay in bed together. In the short time that she had known him, his hair had got much greyer, though he was still in good shape for an older man. Jo traced her hands across his torso just to make sure.

It had been quiet in the penthouse flat since that time she had overheard voices talking about murder and more. Bill had cautioned her from going to the police. It would have been her word against theirs and she wasn't even sure who *they* were. One of the voices had to be Barbara Halliday's: it was a woman speaking in a Cockney (or perhaps even a Mockney) accent, that was for sure. But Jo was not convinced by Babs. Surely, people like that didn't really exist. And yet there she was, along with her *nouveau riche* husband and his beringed hands.

Jo thought of the day when they arrived at Philbey's history tour of Salem. Pauline had nudged her and whispered how Babs and Rodney must both have had plastic surgery.

What a way to spend your money!

The second voice that Jo heard that day had sounded odd. She couldn't place the accent at all, but that was not important. Bill had asked her to describe how this man – it had to be a man because of the deepness – spoke. All she could say in reply was that Barbara Halliday's visitor spoke slowly and deliberately, as if he had special education needs.

The other visitor had been just the opposite: articulate, speaking quickly, and confidently in clipped phrases. Bill had wondered if this was someone ex-military. Babs – if it was her – had taken more notice of him than the slowly spoken one.

Rustling under the duvet signified that Jo Bishop's supervisor and lover was waking up.

'Tea?'

Professor Harker nodded.

'You enjoyed that, didn't you?'

Jo kissed her lover's forehead. Harker grunted.

'I'll go and put the kettle on'.

She looked out of the kitchen window as she made Bill his cuppa. Never had she encountered anyone who drank so much tea. The cricket square was starting to look untidy, now that Ted Gelsthorpe was no more. Jo Bishop missed the groundsman's regular cutting of the grass, his painting of the white lines, his pulling – despite his age – the heavy roller, and the thousand and one other jobs that he busied himself with before, during, and after the cricket season.

The silence still surprised Jo Bishop. Not because there was no lawn mower and no shouting at children – or adults, for that matter – who dared to trespass even one inch onto Gelsthorpe's precious pitch. Today was different; it was as if the area had been cordoned off prior to some activity that warranted additional security or an absence of people.

Jo felt two hands on her upper arms. The hands moved up to her shoulders and then her neck.

'Stop it, Bill. I'm making your tea'.

62

May 28, Evening: An Exchange Takes Place

———— ⌒ ————

'Is everything ready?'

'Yes. Nothing can go wrong'.

'You sure?'

'Relax. I said that everything is ready, and I mean everything is R-E-A-D-Y'.

'Everybody in place?'

'Everybody in place'.

'The exit route in place?'

'Yup'.

'I'm sorry to ask all these questions. We have come so far. I don't want anything, *anything* to stop us now!'

'It won't. I really do promise. Now let's go and get our man!'

***

Gordon Wright wondered if he had done wrong by going to the chapel as requested. The query had seemed innocent enough and he was happy to share his specialist knowledge with a fellow enthusiast. JB76 was not what or who he had expected, but the face was vaguely familiar to him. It would not be long before all the furnishings were stripped out, so it made sense for someone to take detailed photographs and measurements of the mechanism while it was both *in situ* and – tribute to Victorian engineering and ingenuity that it was – still in good working order, despite age and lack of maintenance. Indeed, Gordon was not sure how many people knew of the curious system's existence; not Pauline Philbey.

But why had JB76 wanted to know all about the system, how it worked, and what was its potential? The idea of a research paper did not quite ring true, not least because of his fellow enthusiast's interest. Perhaps there was an ulterior motive.

It was too late now. Wright looked out of his study window. He tried again to message JB76 and ask if they could meet again. There was no reply. There had been no contact since that meeting at Salem.

***

'Are you OK about this, Don?'

Detective Chief Inspector Donald May nodded.

'I'm OK, Viv. It's got to be done. It goes with the territory, remember?'

Detective Sergeant Trubshaw looked at her boss, her friend, her lover.

'I couldn't bear it if anything happened to you'.

'It won't, Viv. I'll be fine. Honest'.

'Can I give you a good luck kiss?'

May smiled at his DS for a moment that seemed to last for eternity.

'I'd like that'.

She pecked him on the cheek. They both wished for more; wished they could be somewhere else; wished they were free to express their feelings for each other.

But they were not free. They would never be free.

The DCI and his DS looked at each other, then got out of the car. Trubshaw squeezed May's hand one last time. She walked behind him as he moved towards Salem Chapel.

The Detective Chief Inspector looked up at the vast temple. This had been the place where he and his family had worshipped. His father in the choir; his grandfather the organist; his great grandfather the senior steward. Donald May still had the books from those early days when the present building had been designed. Freddie had poured over the accounts; had made up a spreadsheet logging all the people who had given money to the appeal. From pence and shillings and pounds to hundreds. And at the head of the list: Ernest Edwin Riddles, who had given £1,000. Freddie had worked that out as £82,049.30 at 2019 prices.

That's my Freddie!

May walked up the steps. Trubshaw turned back to the car as he did so and took up her place alongside Charlie Riggs. He smiled at her and nodded.

The DCI took the chapel's front door key out of his jacket pocket and unlocked it. He coughed as he did so: a signal to his colleagues listening in.

'He's inside. Everybody is in place. Don't worry, Viv. He will be fine. He's been in difficult situations like this before'.

Nothing quite like this!

Trubshaw looked at Riggs.

I'll miss old Charlie. Not the brightest DC on the force, but he's kept us all cheerful, especially over the last month.

Trubshaw and Riggs saw the huge oak door close.

'He didn't tell the ACC what he was going to do, Charlie. Do you think he should have done?'

Riggs shrugged and turned away from the DS.

'I know this is personal for the boss, but I wonder sometimes if he hasn't done it wrong'.

The Detective Constable looked at Trubshaw in amazement but decided not to speak. Instead, he checked his firearm and advised her to do the same, even though they had both done so a hundred times already that evening.

They could hear May's footsteps inside the building, despite the occasional crackling from the wire. The other officers were stationed at every exit from Salem Chapel, and inside the tunnels that linked it to The Bargeman, Riddles' Mill and High Windows. They would catch the perpetrators red-handed. There was no escape, no way out.

Donald May looked up at the pulpit. The marble gleamed in the semi-darkness. He smiled at the monogram 'EER'. It was everywhere; all around the gallery edge; on the ceiling; painted on the organ pipes; it was even on the cloth that covered the Lord's table.

People weren't worshipping God here. They were lauding Ernest Edwin Riddles. He was their Lord and Master.

As instructed, Donald May sat in the front row of pews, as if waiting for a sermon that would never be delivered. The last time his father had preached here, he had used the Parable of the Sower as his text. The Detective Chief Inspector had quoted from that homily many times.

I don't suppose I will be doing any more preaching anywhere now.

May looked at his watch. It was nearly time.

Is this a hoax? It can't be. That was definitely Georgie's writing, and she wouldn't write that letter as a joke; she must be under duress and in fear of her life.

May heard the Parish Church clock strike the hour. He thought of Freddie, sitting at home waiting for him. He tried to think of Caz, but each time her face appeared before him, it immediately turned into that of Vivienne Trubshaw.

As the last bell tolled, he heard a noise. As if from nowhere, WPC Georgiana Lucinda Ponsonby-Ellis stood before him in the pulpit.

'Ellis? Georgie? Are you alright?'

There was no reply. Then May noticed that there was a gag over her mouth. He could only see the upper part of her body, but from the way she was holding her arms, the DCI surmised that Ellis's hands had been tied behind her back.

'Don't worry, Georgie, you'll soon be free!'

Two figures appeared from either side of the lower pulpit and stood either side of the Lord's table. May laughed.

'What is this? Some kind of *Star Wars* convention?'

The two Darth Vaders said nothing.

'Alright, I'm here. Detective Chief Inspector Donald May. You've got me. I'm here at your request. Now let WPC Ellis go. You've had her for long enough. It's me you want. So, let her go and take me'.

'You have come alone?'

Darth number 1 pointed at May. The DCI found it difficult to make out what the creature was saying, given the distortion of the voice.

It must be some kind of device in the headdress. That means I won't recognise who is behind the mask. Which means it could be someone I know; someone from the village perhaps. It could even be Elsie Wright!

'Have you come alone?'

Darth number 2 joined the conversation.

'I have come alone, yes'.

'Are you armed?'

The Vaders spoke in unison.

'No'.

A third Darth appeared from the old choir vestry and frisked May.

'He's clean'.

'What about WPC Ellis? Untie her; let her go!'

'Very well'.

May decided that Darth number 1 was in command.

A fourth Vader came up behind Ellis and made to untie her. The WPC clasped her wrists, trying to soothe the pain of the bonds that she had endured for so long now.

'Now take the gag off! I want to talk to her before we go any further!'

'No can do, Don. You can ask her questions, but only yes or no answers from the Hon. Georgiana Lucinda'.

They must know everything about her, given how long she has been their prisoner; even her blue-blood background.

'Have they treated you well, Georgie?'

The WPC nodded.

'Are you OK now?'

Ellis nodded again.

'Now we are going to walk the WPC round to the front of the building'.

May watched while Darth 4 walked George from the pulpit, across the gallery, and down the stairs at the back of the chapel. For a moment he lost sight of the WPC and her guard, but Darth 3 opened the inner porch doors so that the DCI could see Ellis step off the stairs, walk through the Chapel entrance, and out into the fresh air. She turned round to look at her boss briefly, shaking her head as she did so. Darths 3 and 4 pushed the WPC out of the door and closed and locked it behind her.

'We have kept our side of the bargain, Detective Chief Superintendent May. Now you must keep yours'.

63

May 29, Morning: After the Night Before

─────o╲o─────

'A body has been found'.

'Where?'

'On the canal towpath midway between The Bargeman and High Windows'.

Vivienne Trubshaw wanted to retch.

How could it all have gone so horribly wrong?

Riggs offered the DS some coffee. She declined.

'We'll have to inform the ACC now, Viv'.

'You mean about Don?'

Riggs nodded.

'Yes; and about Ellis'.

This wasn't supposed to happen.

'We'll find him, Viv. And we'll find Georgie. I promise!'

'Tell me, Charlie, how could the boss go into the chapel without being sure that Georgie was being set free?'

'He must have been deceived somehow. There's nothing that we picked up from the wire that suggests he wasn't satisfied that Ellis was not being released. You heard him, Viv'.

'I know I did, Charlie. You're right. The conversation that he was having with those men, women, or whatever suggested that Georgie was being released. Not only that, but Don, the boss, said he **saw** her leave by the front doors. And yet she never appeared. It makes no sense, Charlie'.

'I know, Viv'.

Riggs squeezed Trubshaw's arm.

'And where are they now? We had every exit from that chapel covered. All the secret exits and entrances had been mapped out and guarded. It was impossible for anybody to leave Salem without one of our people apprehending them. But they just vanished into thin air'.

'And yet they can't be still in the building'.

'We searched and we searched. Nothing, absolutely nothing'.

'We'd better go, Viv. SOCOs are already on the towpath and Dr Harbord will be there shortly, no doubt.

***

A small crowd had gathered by the canal bridge. Trains rumbled overhead; the sound magnified a hundred times by the resonant acoustic below. Trubshaw looked up at the patterned brickwork as it arched over the water.

How Don would have loved that! He was so interested in industrial archeology. Genuinely, not just because of Freddie. Freddie... what are we going to tell him? And Caz?

'Well, what a surprise! Another body by the canal; one more to add to the list of Holme Hill murders!'

'It's not funny, Felicity'.

'I'm not really laughing, Viv. It's tragic, actually. Absolutely tragic'.

Vivienne Trubshaw steeled herself. Charlie Riggs did the talking.

'Can we take a look, Dr Harbord?'

The physician smirked, knowing that she now had the Detective Constable well trained in how to address her properly.

'Of course. I thought you'd never ask. Can't give you time of death as yet, but I can tell you how he died'.

'Was it the same as the others?'

'It was. But what's wrong, Viv? I know it's a dead body, but you look as white as a sheet'.

'Let us see, please'.

DS Trubshaw held her hand to her mouth. DC Riggs clenched his fists.

Harbord lowered the sheet to reveal the victim's face.

Trubshaw and Riggs looked at each other and smiled.

'What's so funny, you two?'

'Well, it's not... it's not... never mind. Tell us more'.

'I assume you have some idea of who the victim is?'

'We do, Dr Harbord. We do indeed. It's Harry Metcalfe'.

'The one who has been missing for some time? The one you were expecting before, when it turned out to be Gelsthorpe, was it? Or the other one. The ex-spiv and barrow boy from the East End? I am getting confused with all these dead bodies!'

'Metcalfe was one of the Select Seven and in Williams's little black book'.

'Ah, right. I remember now. Let me see, along with Williams and Smith. But not Halliday. Or Gelsthorpe?'

Trubshaw looked at her watch.

'Don't worry, Detective Sergeant. Time to move the body. By the way, where's your boss this morning? I thought he would have been here by now!'

***

'So, where do we go from here?'

Detective Sergeant Trubshaw looked at Detective Constable Riggs. For a moment, she did not reply. Then she stood up from her seat at the conference table, looked over to Detective Chief Inspector May's desk, then out of the glass partition into the main office.

'They blame themselves. Every man and woman in that office feels that they let the boss down. I feel I let him down. And I know you do!'

Riggs nodded.

'And Georgie. Let's not forget her. To lose one officer is...'

'Alright, Charlie. Cut the literary allusion'.

'The literary what?'

'Never mind. We all know that they are in danger. Georgie was threatened with being murdered. And her warning letter to DCI May said that he would be killed if he turned up at Salem'.

'Look on the bright side, Viv. When we heard about that body on the towpath, we thought it was one or other of them, didn't we? Let's face it'.

'You're right, Charlie, I thought it was the DCI. It never occurred to me that it could be our favourite WPC'.

'But it wasn't. It wasn't either of them'.

'No, it wasn't. But it could be one or other or *both* of them next'.

'There has to be a simple explanation for all of this. What did Sherlock Holmes say?'

Trubshaw snorted.

'Sherlock Holmes? What are you on, Riggsy?'

'Seriously, Viv. If we rule out the impossible, then whatever is left, however improbable, must be the truth'.

'God, Charlie! What have we come to? Quoting bloody Sherlock Holmes!'

And yet I'll try anything if it means we find Don and Georgie alive.

'It is impossible for Don and Georgie to have vanished into thin air. There must be some other way out of that chapel in addition to the secret entrance on Philbey's plans. That is the only way they could have left Salem; not just Don and Georgie, but their captors. We heard the boss talking to at least three other voices last night'.

'And Georgie? Why did Don think that she was safe? He saw her leaving the building by the front door'.

'He *thought* he saw her leaving by the front door. Smoke and mirrors, Viv. Smoke and mirrors. Well, *mirrors* at least'.

'Some kind of optical illusion? That's the only thing that makes any sense in this crazy, nonsensical world'.

64

May 29, Afternoon: Deception All Around

⌒✦⌒

In the back galleries, worshippers heads touched the ceiling. People peered over the balustrade, looking at hats, partings, bald patches. Pew doors squeaked open and shut, as late arrivals were shown to ever smaller squares of seating. Cross-legged children squeezed against the communion cushions. Singers shuffled onto seats. The organist played movements from *Messiah*. The preacher took his place in the pulpit.

Silence.

Banners and standards were lowered.

A thousand pairs of eyes turned towards the marble podium.

'Psalm 127, verse 3: "Children are a heritage from the Lord; offspring a reward from him". That is our text for today'.

The multitude murmured. The preacher pored over his papers.

No more words came. The choir rose and covered the preacher with their robes. They screamed at him.

'We have no King but Williams! Crucify him! Crucify him!'

The preacher man vanished. The organist turned round from his keyboards to conduct the choir in their continuing cacophony. The congregation gasped when they saw the organ grinder wave two bloodied stumps.

'Follow the beat! Follow the beat!'

"Children are a heritage from the Lord; offspring a reward from him".

'Faster! Faster!'

The congregation joined in.

'Louder! Louder!'

The preacher reappeared with two ceremonial swords.

'Is he ready? Have you got him ready?'

The congregation waved their banners and shouted.

'Crucify him! Crucify him!'

The swords were held aloft.

Silence.

'Bring him here!'

Vivienne Trubshaw, Charlie Riggs, and Georgie Ellis appeared from underneath the pulpit. Behind them, in handcuffs, walked Detective Chief Inspector Donald May.

'He is here. He is with us!' The three of them cried.

May said nothing.

"Children are a heritage from the Lord; offspring a reward from him".

The DCI was pushed up the steps to where the preacher stood, swords aloft.

Ellis unlocked the handcuffs and stood next to her boss. May thought how smart she looked in her WPC uniform. He turned away as Detective Sergeant Trubshaw opened her arms to him, but DC Riggs stopped her from coming forward.

'They are waiting for you'.

The lights had been turned so low in the chapel that May could not see the preacher's face. The DCI moved closer.

'Graham! Graham Dooley! Help me! I am innocent!'

Dooley laughed.

'None of you is innocent!'

Dooley turned away from May and pointed his swords towards the congregation.

'See them all before you. You are next!'

May looked down. There in the front row sat Rhys Williams, Peter Smith, Rodney Halliday, Ted Gelsthorpe, Harry Metcalfe, and the DCI's own father.

'Dad! Dad? What are you doing here?'

The man shook his head in reply then looked down at his feet.

The DCI felt a hand on his arm.

'It's over, Don. This is it. This is the end'.

'But Viv! Do *you* think I am guilty as well?'

'Yes, Don. Yes, I do!'

'But I have done nothing!'

'That's just it, sir, you did nothing!'

'But Charlie, what was I supposed to do?'

'Stop all this happening!'

'All what, Charlie?'

'Look down there, Donald'.

The Reverend Graham Dooley pointed his swords at the front row once more.

'See those two young people?'

May saw a boy and a girl holding hands.

'Do you know who they are?'

The DCI looked at Riggs and Trubshaw. They shrugged. May shook his head.

'Those two young people down there are David Harrison and Minnie Hargreaves. They are both dead thanks to you!'

'Don't be ridiculous! I was only young when Minnie was murdered!'

'Sir. Sir!'

May turned away from the boy and the girl.

'What do you want, Ellis?'

'Sir! Sir! We must escape now!'

The WPC grabbed May's arm, pulling him down the stairs and past the men in the front row. The DCI looked back to see that they were running after him and Georgie: all of them, even Viv Trubshaw and Charlie Riggs.

'We're nearly there, sir!'

May saw the open doors and felt the cool air on his face.

Free, at last!

The DCI tripped as he ran down the steps. WPC Ellis held out a hand to break her boss's fall, but he hit his head hard on one of the Corinthian pillars.

'Sir! Wake up! Wake up! They are coming for you!'

***

'Are you sure this is the right thing to do?'

'I have never been surer'.

'You've always been sure about all this, haven't you?'

The man nodded.

'Do you have no conscience?'

'Why should I have a conscience? Did those men have a conscience?'

The woman paused for a moment before answering.

'I believe they did. In the end'.

'You mean after they were so shit-scared that they would say anything to be spared the sword?'

'Well, there was that, yes. But I think they all carried a lot of guilt inside well before we got hold of them'.

'You think what you like. I think they were just a set of cold-hearted bastards. What's the matter with you, anyway? Are you going soft? Next thing you'll be saying that we shouldn't have executed them'.

'No, I am not saying that. I would never say that. It's just...'

'Just what?'

'It's just that I want it to be over. So much death; so many murders'.

'Nearly over. It will soon be 31st May and then our project will be complete'.

The woman nodded.

'Just one more to go. In fact, it's time that we caught up with Detective Chief Inspector Donald May and his sidekick'.

'But that's the bit that is worrying me. Ellis has done nothing wrong. Why do we have to kill her as well?'

'Oh yes she has. She knows too much. If we are to have any chance of having a future after this, then she has to be snuffed out as well'.

'Like Joan had to be snuffed out?'

'Afraid so'.

***

'Nothing?'

'Nothing. Absolutely nothing'.

DS Trubshaw shook her head and downed yet more black coffee. The biscuits remained untouched on the conference table.

'We have checked every exit and entrance to Salem Chapel, including every inlet and outlet to and from the secret passageways that are marked on those plans that Pauline Philbey gave us. We have done the same at Ted Gelsthorpe's house. They all join up, but no sign of activity there; certainly not over the last 48 hours'.

'There must be another passageway, Charlie. It's the only explanation. One that is not on Philbey's plans'.

'A super-secret one perhaps?'

Trubshaw nodded.

'By the way, Viv, how did the DCI's wife take it when you told her?'

'You mean told her that her husband was missing, possibly murdered, because of police incompetence? And, just to add insult to injury, the WPC that her husband was meant to be saving in exchange was nowhere to be found either?'

'Sorry, Ma'am'.

The DS buried her head in her hands.

'No, Charlie, I'm the one who should be sorry. It's got to me has this. We let the boss down. We should have been more protective. We shouldn't have let him go'.

'I know, Viv. It's getting to all of us. But, but haven't we had our murder for today?'

'How do you mean, Charlie?'

'Well, today is the 29th, a week after the last murder, and we found Harry Metcalfe. And the pattern was the same as before. Same likely M.O. and same biblical quotation. There has only been one killing on each of those days; so, no more murder for today'.

'I would like to believe in your logic, Charlie, but just because the bodies have appeared on 1, 8, 15, 22, 29 May doesn't mean that Don hasn't already been killed. Or Georgie, for that matter. Dr Harbord has said more than once that she thinks some of the bodies have been stored in a freezer; so, who knows what could have happened to him?'

'I know, Viv, I know. Anyway, what did Mrs May say when you told her?'

'Not much, actually. It was her son that did most of the talking?'

'You mean Freddie? He's a strange one: an old man in a thirteen-year old's body'.

'A very clever thirteen-year-old'.

'I know. I think he knows more about modern policing methods than I do!'

'Charlie?'

'Yes, Viv'.

'What does *camera obscura* mean?'

'Why on earth would you ask me that?'

'Well, Freddie said that he knew that his Dad would be captured and that we had to check out the *camera obscura* in Salem Chapel'.

***

'Sir, wake up! Detective Chief Inspector May! Wake up! Please!'

'Where am I?'

'You're underneath the Chapel'.

Donald May opened his eyes.

'What? Salem Chapel?'

'Yes'.

'But, Georgie, why are you here? They should have freed you!'

'Yes, they should. But you were tricked, sir. I wasn't being let out of the Chapel at all. It really was smoke and mirrors – well, *mirrors*, at least'.

'I don't understand. God! My head!'

'They drugged you, sir. And they will be back for you soon. For me too'.

'Who is they?'

'They wear masks all the time. But I think I know who at least one of them is. The one who keeps coughing'.

'I just feel so sleepy'.

'There's no time to sleep, sir. We must go now. They are coming back to kill us. I just know it'.

65

May 29, Early Evening: Enquiries and Solutions

———∽∽———

Pauline Philbey was getting used to police interview rooms. Not being able to speak to Donald May was a worry to her, though. She didn't trust the woman and she thought the young man was too flippant. Or at least he had been on her previous visit to Hartley Police station.

'Now, Mrs Philbey, you said that you had more information for us'.

The local archivist clutched at her handbag, wishing she had taken out the flask and had a swig before the interview began.

At least, I am not a suspect. I really am "helping police with their enquiries".

'Is there any news? Is there any news of Donald? I feel it's all my fault, you see'.

'Not as yet, Mrs Philbey. But Detective Sergeant Trubshaw and I have put every available resource onto finding him'.

'Why do you think it's your fault, Pauline? You don't mind if I, *we* call you Pauline, do you?'

Philbey shook her head.

'You have been so helpful to us. Without your knowledge and understanding of the archives, we simply wouldn't have known about the underground tunnels'.

'But I have gone over the documentation again. Including with my friend Jo Bishop. Do you know her?'

The two detectives nodded their heads.

'Well, there must be more. The plans are all numbered. I realise that now. Jo pointed it out to me. But there is one missing. There is a gap in the sequence'.

Trubshaw and Riggs looked at each other.

'We thought there might be more tunnels. That's the only way we can explain the disappearances'.

'*Disappearances*. Plural?'

'Yes, Pauline. WPC Ellis has not turned up either'.

'Oh, dear. Oh, dear. Oh, dear. Oh, dear'.

Philbey clutched her handbag. She could feel the flask.

'That is another puzzle that we have yet to solve, Pauline'.

'How do you mean, Constable?'

Riggs cleared his throat.

'We find it difficult to believe that the DCI would hand himself over in exchange for WPC Ellis without being satisfied that she had been freed'.

'It's not something Detective Chief Inspector May would ever do. You see, we wire tapped him and the conversation that we heard strongly suggested that Georgie had been freed'.

'But obviously not', Riggs added.

'So, let me get this right. Detective Chief Inspector May thought he saw the WPC leave the building, but she hadn't?'

'Nope. We were waiting outside. Nobody appeared'.

Pauline Philbey looked down at her handbag. She crossed and uncrossed the straps.

'Well, you see, I meant to talk to you about that'.

'How so, Pauline?'

Philbey opened her handbag, looked briefly at the flask, and then pulled out a long brown envelope.

'You had better have this. Perhaps it is going to be more useful than I originally thought'.

***

'I don't like it, Jayce. I know I said we were in this together. But it's got out of hand. This project of theirs is out of control. Look at all the deaths!'

'Oh, my pretty one. I'm sorry. I told you to leave. You still can, it's not too late!'

Jaycee took Abbey in her arms.

'Don't cry. It's alright'.

'But it's not alright, Jayce. How many more murders are there going to be?'

'I don't know. I really don't know'.

'Your mother is mad'.

'Oh Abbey, no, she's not mad'.

'I have seen her. I have seen that look in her eyes. She's not sane. Nobody could be sane and do what she has done'.

Jaycee sighed.

'She's dying, Abbey'.

'What do you mean, dying?'

'Just that, Abs. She's got weeks to live'.

'Why didn't you tell me before?'

'I've told you more than enough already, my love. But I guess you need to know what drives Linda Welch'.

'She has lung cancer. Terminal lung cancer'.

'So, that's why she coughs so much'.

Jaycee nodded, putting her arm around Abbey.

'I'm sorry. That's your mum!'

'Yes. For all her faults, that's my mum!'

'So, why all this? Why is she involved with this gang?'

Jaycee laughed.

'She has some old scores to settle before she... before she dies'.

'And that involves killing people?'

'I don't know about that'.

'Yes, you do, Jayce. You know full well that your mother is involved in those murders. And she has got you involved. And now me!'

'But, my love, I told you before. You could walk away from it all. I can't, but you could; you *really* still could'.

Abbey got up and paced around the room. She checked Arthur, still fast asleep in his cot.

'What about Arthur? What will happen to him if his parents are both in prison?'

'Then leave now, Abbey! There is no proof that you were involved. *No* proof at all!'

'Come with me! I can't live without you, Jaycee. You, me, and Arthur: we were the perfect family. Until all this happened. And now it's ruined!'

Jaycee tried to embrace her wife but Abbey pulled away.

'Do you love me, Jayce?'

'Of course, I love you'.

'How much do you love me?'

'Why ask, Abbey? You know I love you more than anything'.

'You really love me more than anything? Truly?'

Jaycee wiped the tears from her eyes.

'Yes, I truly do. You are the love of my life, but...'

'But what, Jayce?'

'But there are family loyalties. My mother...'

'Your mother will soon be dead and out of it. We have a life to look forward to. Or, at least, we *had*!'

'Abbey...'

'Don't you Abbey me! If your mother had cared for you, she wouldn't have got you into this. Is her revenge so important that it counts for more than your happiness? My happiness? Arthur's happiness?'

Jaycee stared at the floor in silence.

'If you love me, if you *really* love me, Janet Christine Harrison, then you will do as I ask. For my sake, for Arthur's sake, and for your sake. And you will do it now!'

'Very well, Abs. You know I love you. You know that I could never say no to you. I agree. It's time to call a halt to all this'.

***

At first, Gordon Wright chose not to answer the phone. It was almost certain for mother, just like all the other telephone calls over the last few weeks; those and the incessant visitors, and the meetings in the drawing room. The house had never been so busy. Ever since May 1st and that awful evening when he had discovered Rhys Williams' body.

Now all was quiet. Apart from the telephone ringing. Again.

Gordon Wright looked out of his study window. It was still light.

I like this time of year. The warmth; the smell of newly mown grass; children playing outside.

He thought back to the winter months and the many times he had phoned the police about the flash cars parked by the cricket pavilion late at night, with their lights on and their engines running.

Drug dealers, every one of them! And nothing done about them!

Wright watched people enter and exit The Bargeman. He thought back to the chats with Joan Wilberforce and the "date" they had been on.

I thought there might have been more. But she was just playing with me. Making me run those errands for her. Buying all that Clarins stuff in amongst. Then there was that stupid fancy dress party at the pub. What was all that about? Sally said Joan was too old for me. But that never bothered me. Nothing bothers me now. Well, almost nothing.

Gordon Wright determined to answer the phone this time. He got up from his desk, strode along the landing, and ran down the heavily carpeted stairs.

'I thought you were never going to answer the telephone!'

'Sorry, Pauline. I have been avoiding contact. Most of the calls on this number are for my beloved mother. Why didn't you ring me on my mobile?'

'I didn't know your number, Gordon. But no matter. I have told them, just like you asked me to'.

Wright sighed.

'Thank you, Pauline. I really appreciate that'.

'And you really think it has a bearing on what happened last night?'

'Yes. And if I had come clean sooner, Donald May wouldn't be in so much trouble'.

'You can't be certain of that, Gordon'.

'Oh yes, I can. JB76 didn't know enough about the mechanism to operate it. Until I met him at the chapel and showed him'.

'And you think they used the *camera obscura* to fool May and the others?'

'I do. So, it's all my fault. Without that device they would not have been able to whisk Ellis and May out of the Chapel as they did'.

'You have to admit that Ernest Riddles was a clever old so-and-so, if a mischievous one, setting up all those gimmicks in his chapel'.

'How can I make amends? I will never forgive myself. I should never have told mother about the *camera obscura*. That's when JB76 started to get in touch'.

'You mean your mother told this JB76 about the system and the trapdoors?'

'Yes. She told me not to tell anybody else. And I didn't, until now, when I decided I had to tell you. It must have been her who told JB76'.

'And who is JB76?'

'You'd be surprised'.

***

Detective Chief Inspector Donald May hurt everywhere: head, arms, legs, stomach.

'Is this a dream?'

'No. They drugged you, sir. You didn't see them. It was all so sudden. They had some kind of device that fooled you into thinking I was leaving the building when I was actually going back down into my prison; this place, in fact. Then the trap door in front of the communion table or whatever you call it. You were in absolutely the perfect spot'.

'But what about Trubshaw and Riggs and everybody on the outside?'

'By the time they had twigged what was happening – or rather not happening – the group had all vanished'.

May could now see the WPC's face clearly. She was thinner than he remembered.

'How have they been treating you, George?'

'Alright, sir. But that's not important now. We need to get out of here'.

The DCI looked around the room.

'I don't see how. For starters, we are both shackled at the ankles. And then, even if we could free ourselves, how the hell do we get out?'

'I have a way around it, sir'.

'You do? Like you had a way around due process when you decided to investigate DCS Bradley?'

Ellis blushed.

'Sorry about that, sir. I was just...'

'Enough, WPC Ellis. If we ever get out of this alive, then you will have to face the consequences of your actions'.

'Yes, sir'.

'In any case, how come Trubshaw, Riggs, and the rest of the team haven't done a search of the premises? We have the plans for the Chapel and the links to the other buildings around the cricket square'.

'Well, you have most of them. But there is one set of plans that they cannot have had'.

'And what do they show?'

'Well, if they exist at all, those plans will show the secret network of rooms *underneath the chapel itself*!'

'Good God. We've been looking everywhere but the obvious place: Salem!'

'But I think I know a way out'.

'All very well, WPC Ellis, but we still have to find the key to these shackles!'

DCI May lifted his leg to emphasise his point and their predicament.

'Not a problem, sir. I have a key'.

66

May 29, Mid-Evening: Wilberforce's Killer May Be Revealed; May and Ellis Meet Their Fate

'Have you told them then?'

'It's only an idea, Freddie'.

'But I think it's a good idea, Mum. A really good idea. And we need to help Dad'.

He's really worried, but he's trying not to show it. Classic Freddie. Always trying to be the grown-up.

'But you seemed so sure when you were talking with Dad and me the other night'.

Dad and me. That's my Freddie. He would be grammatically correct. Not "Dad and I" like most kids.

'They're so busy, Fred. DS Trubshaw, DC Riggs, and their people. They are doing everything that they can to make sure Dad *and* that WPC are safe. They don't want me ringing them at this time of night with some cock-and-bull story about who killed Joan Wilberforce'.

'But whoever killed her is probably behind the other murders *and* Dad's capture'.

'Come on, Commander May, it's time for bed. I'll get your milk'.

'I'm not going to bed. I'm not going anywhere until you ring Detective Sergeant Trubshaw and tell her what you think! What *I* think! It could be really, really important'.

'But your Dad thought it was a daft idea'.

'He didn't really! Or if he did, I didn't. It makes sense. C-O-O. That was all she had time to write'.

Caz looked at Freddie.

He won't give up until I have rung. He will go on and on and on. I know him of old. He has so worn me down over the years. Don doesn't know the half of it.

'Alright. I will ring once you are in bed'.

'I don't believe you, Mum. You are trying to fob me off'.

'Freddie, I would never...'

'But you would. You have done. And I won't stand for it. I will not go to bed until you have rung and told them. Please!'

'Alright, I will. I will do it right now'.

Frederick May watched his mother dial the number and then made her put the phone on loudspeaker so that he could be sure that she really was talking to the police.

'Hello, is that Detective Sergeant Trubshaw?'

'Yes. Who is this?'

'It's Caz, Caroline May. We have met, if you remember'.

'I remember. I'm afraid we have no more news. But we are doing everything that we can to find your husband. Absolutely everything, believe me'.

'I know, I know. But that's not why I am ringing'.

'Oh? What is it then?'

'Well, Don and I – *and* Freddie, of course – we were talking about the case the other evening. And...'

'Yes, Mrs May?'

'Call me Caz. Everybody else does!'

'OK, Caz. You were telling me that you and Don... *DCI May* and Freddie were talking about the case'.

'Well, specifically about Joan Wilberforce's murder'.

'We're following up a number of leads on that one at the moment'.

'I know that you can't tell me anything more but... well, I think I know what C-O-O stands for'.

'Well, Caz, any assistance you can give us will be gratefully received'.

'Go on, Mum! Tell her! Tell her now!

'Sorry, DS Trubshaw. Freddie is insistent that I share my theory with you'.

'And your theory is?'

My theory is... my theory is that they aren't initials or an acronym. My theory is that she was spelling the word cook: C-O-O-K. But she died before she could finish'.

'Cook? As in someone who cooks?'

'As in someone who cooks, especially at The Bargeman pub, where Joan Wilberforce worked'.

***

Donald May thought back to his visit to the Jersey War Tunnels. He must have been about ten. His father was keen to go but his mother and sister were 'agog with indifference', as his grandfather used to say. It was damp, dark, cold, forbidding. The scent of disease, misery, and death still pervaded the place. Dad had to take him outside to be sick. They had not gone back inside.

The same nausea overcame the DCI as he realised where he now was. The cell had the same painted brick; the same strip lighting; the same musty smell. The place was soulless; utterly soulless.

'Are you OK, sir?'

May nodded.

'The drugs have worn off; the hangover has abated'.

God! I sound just like Freddie!

'We have to go now, sir. We really do!'

'How did you get the key to the chains?'

Ellis smiled.

'I just befriended one of my captors. Then I picked their pocket when I was on one of my toilet runs'.

May laughed.

'You're starting to redeem yourself, WPC Ellis. But you've a long way to go yet. What's next?'

'Well, we have to wait until they come for us, and then, when the time is right, we make a run for it'.

'And when will that be?'

'I don't know when, sir, but I think I know *where* we will need to try and escape'.

'Something else you worked out on your toilet runs, by any chance?'

'Yes, sir! When I was first captured, I am almost certain that I was in the basement of The Bargeman. I even heard you and DS Trubshaw talking as you waited for somebody to answer the front door. I seem to remember that you and she were talking about Linda Welch's middle name being Harrison'.

'Yes, I remember that. A lot has happened since then!'

'What, sir?'

There isn't time for that now, Georgie'.

'No, of course not, sir. After a couple of days, I was brought here. I was blindfolded, of course, but I could retrace my steps back to the pub basement and then I think we could get out from there!'

'Well, George, you have given us a chance. Even if it's only a slim one!'

'Thank you, sir. By the way, sir. I am so sorry that I got us… well, *you* into this mess, but I am going to do my best to get us out of it'.

'I know. I'll remember that'.

Ellis turned away from the DCI.

I just hope to goodness that I can do this!

'Shush! Sorry to shush you, sir. But they are coming! They are coming for us!'

May heard a clock strike 10.

Ten in the morning? Ten in the evening? What day?

'They are coming for me, aren't they, Georgie?'

'Well, yes, sir. But they are coming for me too, I am sure!'

413

May squeezed the WPC's arm as the cell door was unlocked.

Darth Vader appeared. May found it difficult to understand the mutated voice. Georgie Ellis interpreted.

'He says it is time. We are being taken to the place of execution. Before you ask, I am used to the sound now; I can make it out. I can even tell them apart'.

May thought about rushing the Sith Lord then and there, but Ellis drew the DCI's attention to the gun in Darth's hand.

The barrel-roofed corridor stretched for at least half a mile. May and Ellis looked straight ahead, aware that Darth was behind them, watching their every move. The DCI and the WPC counted doors – more cells, presumably – and corridors off at right angles to the main avenue down which the two police officers were now walking.

The march to the scaffold paused in front of a pair of thick metal doors.

'Nuclear shelter', May whispered to Ellis. 'I have seen these before. They were constructed all over the country during the Cold War. But I didn't know there was one here in Holme Hill, right under Salem Chapel!'

Did my father know about this? Did the other members of the Select Seven?

Ellis sighed.

That suggests there is no means of escape once we are inside there.

The doors inched open.

'This must have been the War Room'.

'Keep quiet!'

May and Ellis gasped at the scene that now greeted them. Neither had ever seen anything like it.

67

May 29, Late Evening: First Revelations and Last Wishes

'So, John Butcher has form?'

'He does, Ma'am. He does, indeed'.

Riggsy always calls me Ma'am when he's worried. It's as if he can't bear the familiarity. But then I am his boss, especially now that the ACC has promoted me to acting DI in Don's absence. God, I wish he were here. I wish this was all sorted. I will never be able to live with myself if anything happens to him; nobody here will.

'He's been under the radar for a long time now, but it definitely fits with the theory that "the cook did it"'.

Riggs smiled at his joke; Trubshaw ignored her DC.

'What do we have on him?'

'Well, it's early days, but so far I've found out that he's done time: drugs, burglary, ABH'.

'Where did he operate?'

'London area, mainly'.

'London? Drugs?

'Yes. Quite sad, really'.

'How come, Charlie?'

'Well, before he ended up in prison, he was in the military. Something of a hero. First Gulf War. Ended up in the SAS'.

'So, trained to kill?'

'Definitely. And by all accounts he was quite a killing machine. I guess it helped, being ambidextrous'.

'Ambidextrous as in being able to use your left hand as well as your right'.

Riggs looked at the acting SIO and nodded slowly. Trubshaw walked over to the window, just like her boss often did when he wanted to think. Outside all was quiet. It was raining, as it usually did in Hartley at this time of year. Two uniformed officers were escorting a noisy, drunken youth into the station.

There are times when I wish I was back on the beat. That was a simple life compared with now!

'What's he doing in Holme Hill, working at The Bargeman?'

'That's what we don't know. Yet. After he got out of prison, he disappears. Until earlier this year, that is'.

'When he rocks up on our patch'.

'Yes, Ma'am'.

The two detectives smiled at each other. They both knew that time was not on their side. It was now nearly midnight and there was no sign of May or Ellis, nor any trace of their movements after the botched hostage exchange.

How could we have got it so wrong?

'Any links with our other suspects? Bradley? Welch? Elsie Wright?'

'Not obviously with any of them, but he does have a link to Salem Chapel?'

'What? Come off it, Charlie!'

'Well, not with Salem, exactly, but with the Methodist Church'.

'Really'.

'Butcher was adopted through a Methodist adoption agency. And guess who was the Chairman of the Board at the time he was adopted?'

'Go on, Detective Constable Riggs, surprise me!'

'Donald May's father'.

***

'You won't get away with this! I promise you!'

'But we already have done, Detective Chief Inspector'.

It was difficult to tell if Darth 1 was laughing or clearing his (or her) throat.

'No, you haven't! There are police all around this building, searching every inch of Holme Hill. It won't be long before they find us and apprehend you!

The other Darths joined number one in riotous throat clearing. Ellis looked at May.

I hope the DCI knows what he is doing. These people don't like to be provoked.

'Your colleagues will never discover this place! Never! Your position is hopeless'.

May looked around the bunker.

This complex place was designed to withstand a nuclear holocaust. It's not on any plans that I have ever seen. Perhaps there's something in the MoD files; but Viv and Charlie won't think to look here. Why should they?

By now, the four Darths had seated themselves at the large table in the middle of the room. Ellis noticed how the top was covered with a map of the British Isles. Flags were littered about the country, a remnant from the last practice run for World War III.

'Do be seated, Detective Chief Inspector May and WPC Ellis'.

'Can we cut the *Star Wars* stuff? At least show me who you are! Don't I, don't *we* deserve that?'

Darth 1 looked at his fellow Sith Lords. They nodded back.

'Very well. You should at least see who your executioners are. But do sit down. You might as well be comfortable for your last hour'.

Darth 4 was the first to unmask.

'Hello, Detective Inspector. I assume you had your suspicions about me'.

'Yes, Mrs Wright. We have had our eye on you for some time now. We were just unable to prove it'.

Georgie Ellis noticed how the old woman's eyes glowed.

Is it rage? Excitement? Satisfaction? Or just the glaucoma?

'But why, Elsie? Why is someone like you mixed up in all this?

'Someone like me, Donald? What does that mean? What am I like?'

'An upstanding member of the community, Elsie'.

Wright laughed at the WPC's remark.

'What? You mean, like my husband and his cronies in that singing group?'

'What were they, then, Elsie?'

Elsie Wright looked at the other three Darths. Darth 1 nodded.

'They betrayed this country'.

'How do you mean, Elsie?'

'Mrs Wright, to you, Ponsonby-Ellis, or whatever your name is'.

'How do you mean "betrayed"?'

'Perhaps I should explain, Detective Chief Inspector'.

Darth 3 unmasked.

'You! I knew it!'

'Yes, WPC Ellis. You were very stupid to do what you did. Snooping around my house. You were bound to get caught!'

'I expected better of you, Arthur Bradley'.

'You need to know the full story, DCI May. It's not what you think. None of it is'.

'Go on then. Explain it to me. To us'.

Detective Chief Superintendent Arthur Bradley clasped his hands and leaned forward, as if briefing his officers during a murder investigation.

'The Select Seven were more than a singing group, Donald. They were spies. But worse than that, they were double agents'.

'Double agents? Even my father? You must be joking!'

Georgie Ellis had never seen the DCI laugh like he was laughing now. It was a laughter born of fear and hatred.

'It's true, Detective Chief Inspector! Those men betrayed this country, lock, stock, and barrel. They were supposed to be working on the new "wonder material" at Riddles and they were passing secrets to the Russians all the time'.

'What secrets?'

'You're too young to remember the Cold War, Ellis, but they were dark times. This country could have gone under back then, if men like the Select Seven had got their way'.

'I just don't believe you, Bradley. My father would never do anything like that! He was a God-fearing man!'

'He might have been, DCI May, but he was also being blackmailed by Rhys Williams. Like the rest of them. Except for Hodgson, that is, and he died a long time ago'.

'A revenge killing?'

'Hodgson took his own life, by all accounts'.

Bradley looked at one of the two remaining Darths and nodded slowly.

'Blackmailed over what?'

May banged the conference table as he spoke.

'Over Minnie Hargreaves' death and David Harrison's framing for her murder'.

It was Darth 3. The mask was difficult to remove, given all the hair that was tucked inside the helmet.

'We have known it was you for some time, Linda. We only had to read that you were "licensed in pursuance of Act of Parliament" to make the connection'.

'I changed my name, but I didn't have the heart to drop 'Harrison' completely. That was a bit of a giveaway, wasn't it?'

'But you had David Harrison convicted Detective Chief Superintendent!'

Bradley shook his head.

'I did. And not a day has gone past since when I have not bitterly regretted what I did back then'.

'So, why did you not speak out? Why did you let such a gross miscarriage of justice happen?'

'I was ordered to. By the very highest authority. I was under the strictest instructions to protect those men'.

'Protect them from what?'

'From being revealed. At the time, they were meant to be on "our" side. The secret of the "wonder material" had to be kept safe at all costs. It was only later that we realised that they had been selling secrets to the Russians'.

'And what was the "wonder material" supposed to do?'

'Think about it, Don. Given the Cold War and this place, it had to do with nuclear war. Ernie Halliday had perfected a thin covering that protected the wearer from radioactive environments, however harsh. It would have made life after World War III possible'.

'Where does Minnie Hargreaves fit in? Why did she have to be killed?'

'Because, Don, she found out their secret. She was their mascot, remember?'

May nodded at Linda Welch as WPC Ellis kept her eyes on Bradley and Wright.

'They thought she was too young to understand, so they let their guard down: too much careless talk. Over time she worked out what was going on and said that she was going to go to the police. Except that she came to me, and I warned them off'.

'Was Ted Gelsthorpe one of them?'

Bradley and Welch looked at Wright, who then replied.

'That was unfortunate, Detective Chief Inspector. We had to get Ted out of the way so that we could access the secret passageways to and from his cottage. But sadly, he died on us. A massive heart attack'.

'So, why dress his death up to look as though he had been murdered?'

'Because... because it would have aroused more suspicion if he had been found dead than if it looked as if he was a victim of the Holme Hill Murderer'.

May looked at Ellis and then back at Bradley, Welch, and Wright'.

'Who actually killed Minnie, Detective Chief Superintendent?'

'We don't know. We tried to find out when we captured each of them, but none of them would give up the secret. Right to the bitter end, they protected each other. But in a way, they all killed her and they were all responsible for David Harrison's death. He was just a young innocent who was in the wrong place at the wrong time. It was easy to pick him to take the blame'.

'Why now? Why wait all this time?'

'I can explain that'.

It was Linda Welch.

'I was the one who started it all. You see, I was diagnosed with terminal cancer not long ago. I have nothing left to live for and nothing to lose. I won't live long enough to be tried, let alone go to prison. I researched all about the case and went to see Arthur. He filled me in on his own work, how he had found out what the Select Seven really were, and how he had been a stooge for them. That's when we came up with our plan'.

'What about you, Elsie? Why are you involved in all this?'

'Why not, Don? I hated the Select Seven from the day they were formed. Hated what they did to my husband. Hated what he became as a result of Rhys Williams' influence. Like Arthur here, I am a patriot and, for all my faults, I am a mother. I knew Minnie's parents; and David Harrison's too. I saw them killed by grief and remorse. They needed to be avenged. When Arthur and Linda approached me, it was easy to say yes'.

'Which one of you killed them?'

'I did'.

The last Darth now spoke for the first time.

'So, are you going to show yourself?'

May and Ellis waited in anticipation as the mask was removed.

68

May 30, Early Morning: Awakening Truths

—✦—

The machine motored menacingly. What had begun as a distant hum was gradually growing into a growl. Two grey-green eyes stared unblinkingly. Pauline Philbey felt a weight on her chest: probing, pressing. She found it difficult to breathe. Her whole face was being enveloped.

Is it my turn? Is it the end?

'Ow! Oh, it's you! For God's sake, Boris!'

The local archivist sat upright in bed, knocking her beloved moggy off the pillow. The cat landed in the middle of Philbey's evening tea tray, splattering bread, butter, jam, milk, sugar everywhere.

'Sorry, Boris. I didn't mean it! Boris?'

Despite Philbey's entreaties, Boris had scuttled out of the boudoir, down the stairs, and out of the kitchen door cat flap.

God, I feel awful! When will all this end? Murder on my doorstep. Literally!

She looked at the alarm clock by her bedside.

'Half past one! Will I never get to sleep ever again?'

Silence. Nothing. Not even an owl hooting.

Pauline Philbey got out of bed and put her nightgown on.

Perhaps Boris will be back by now.

Having switched on the landing light, she walked gingerly down the stairs.

Why am I tiptoeing around? It isn't as though I have a houseful!

Boris was nowhere to be found. Not even in his favourite cat basket in the kitchen. Pauline Philbey decided to make a hot drink and sit in the lounge, waiting for her pet to return.

Sitting in her favourite armchair, she looked around the room. This was the family home; Philbeys had lived here for generations. And would for many more years to come, no doubt.

What will they think of these murders in the future? What a lovely peaceful place this used to be! It will never be the same again.

Philbey's gaze alighted on the small bureau by the side of the fireplace. She decided to look at the family albums that were in the bottom drawer.

Perhaps that will send me to sleep!

The tatty brown paper envelope was dusty. Unravelling the string, she took out the leather-bound album and began to flick through the pages. A passport-sized picture fell out. Pauline Philbey reached down to the floor to pick the photo up, taking care not to disturb her whisky-fortified mug of hot milk.

On the back of the picture was a date: 'May 1976'. She turned it over. The face was familiar to her. Tears began to form as she realised who it was.

He was such a handsome man. And so funny. He could make me laugh like nobody else could.

'Oh, Ernie! What happened? Where did you go? Why didn't you come back for me? I would have gone just about anywhere with you! What a wonderful life we could have had together!'

Do I believe Babs? Or Elsie? Neither? Both?

Pauline Philbey could hardly keep her eyes open. The picture fell to the floor. Boris returned, leapt up onto his owner's lap, and circled round until he had found an appropriate sleeping position. The local archivist was already whiffling away, not to be awakened until a surprise visitor later that day.

***

The identity of the last Darth came as a surprise to May. Ellis, never having seen the man before, looked quizzically at her boss then across at the fourth member of the gang.

The WPC thought him to be different from the rest. For a start, he was younger – and fitter – as far as she could tell. His hair was cropped short, the sort of style that you got in the army or the marines. The nose was that of a boxer; but the hands were those of an artist or even a surgeon: soft, delicate, capable of finely judged movements. His red tracksuit was a strange contrast with the setting and his mask, now removed and lying on the table.

It looks as though he has been out for a run. And yet now here he is, sitting in judgement over a frightened little WPC and her boss. I never expected to be in a situation like this when I joined the police. And I never thought I would die in a nuclear bunker executed by four Darth Vaders!

Wait! Didn't Gordon Wright say that he had seen someone in a red tracksuit the day Rhys Williams' body was found?

'You! You were under the radar all this time!'

426

May turned to Ellis. The DCI looked disgusted with himself. The WPC looked at the four people sitting in judgement on the far side of the table and then back at her boss.

'Who is this man? Who are you? I have never seen you before!'

'Haven't you, Georgie? Are you so sure?'

Ellis looked at Bradley, then at the younger man sitting next to him. The policewoman nodded as the realisation dawned.

'You are the man I heard talking to the Detective Chief Superintendent here that night. You were wondering what to do with Harry Metcalfe's body, the one you had put in the freezer!'

'Very clever, WPC Ellis. You should go far, or rather you would have gone far in the force'.

'We're not done yet, Bradley. You won't get away with this. Any of you!'

The Detective Chief Superintendent laughed.

'But we already have, Don. No one has been arrested; not even interviewed under caution. And how will your colleagues be able to trace the murders back to us? Would anyone believe that we all did it?'

'Except you didn't all do it, did you? What I don't understand is why you are involved in this escapade. Why are you here, John Butcher? Why did you murder all those people?'

Ellis looked at May.

'The cook from The Bargeman. I do recognise you, now!'

'Welch and Wright, I get their involvement. And I now understand why DCS Bradley is here. But who or what are you to this place and these people?'

'Far more than you could ever imagine, Donald May'.

'Do we get to hear why, then?'

Butcher stood up and walked to the head of the conference table.

'Of course. You have a right to know everything before I kill you and your over-inquisitive colleague there'.

69

May 30, Dawn: In Tandem if not in Chorus

'I love you'.

'I love you too'.

'I'm sorry, Jayce'.

'No need to be, Abs. I'm the one who should be sorry'.

'How so?'

'Well, I should never have got you into this in the first place'.

'Well, no, perhaps not, Jayce. But you did and here we are. We will make amends for all that's happened'.

Janet Christine Harrison got out of the bed she loved sharing with her wife. Comfortable though it was, thanks to Linda Welch's ministrations, the temporary accommodation at The Bargeman was beginning to pall.

Oh, to be back on our boat. I wish we had never come here. All this blood; all this death.

'You're not having second thoughts, are you, Jayce?'

Abbey's wife smiled weakly, then shook her head.

'No, not really, Abs. I just wish… I just wish none of this had ever happened'.

'But it did, Jaycee. You were loyal to your family: to Linda, to David, to Minnie, and her parents. Yes, it was awful, but that is no reason to kill others. Innocent peo…'

'Innocent people? There is no way any of those people were innocent. They all knew what they were doing. And innocent, *really* innocent people lost their lives because of those men'.

'Two wrongs don't make a right, Jaycee. Not even a Gordon Wright'.

The two women laughed for the first time in a long time. It was a silly, stupid joke, but it broke the tension between them.

'So, we are agreed?'

'Yes, Abs. We are agreed. I know what I have to do, and I will do it'.

The two women kissed. St Maurice's church clock struck four. The dawn chorus began. Janet Christine Harrison dressed, kissed the sleeping Arthur, embraced Abbey, and walked out into the morning.

***

'You wonder why I am here. I will tell you why I am here, Detective Chief Inspector Donald May. Your father. That's why I am here!'

'What does my father have to do with you, Butcher? With any of you?'

'Your father was not a good man, Don. Believe me. I knew him. Him and my husband. They were part of it'. It was Elsie Wright.

'Don't believe her or any of them, sir! I wouldn't believe a word of it. Any of it!'

'I suppose you're going to tell me that you killed your husband as well, aren't you, Elsie?'

'Well, I did, actually. It was easy. He had a weak heart anyway. Nobody suspected. Not only were those men passing secrets to the Russians, but they also knew, they *knew* all along that the material was carcinogenic. They sent hundreds of people to their deaths; not just the people at Riddles who worked on the project but also the people who wore the clothes. Every one of them died sooner or later and died a horrid death, including people in this village. People who were my friends'.

'And my father, May senior. Did you kill him as well?'

The four Darths laughed.

'Sadly, no'. Butcher and Bradley spoke in unison.

'He really did die of natural causes, unfortunately. That's why you are going to pay his debt'.

'What do you mean, Butcher?'

'Well, not only was he one of the Select Seven – and you have heard what they did – but he trafficked children. Children like me'.

'What. You're mad, Butcher, totally mad. My father would never do anything like that!'

'But he did, Detective Chief Inspector. And did it systematically over a number of years'.

'This is pure fantasy. A Russian spy and a child trafficker? How do you know?'

'Because, WPC Ellis, John Butcher became my son. I paid a high price for him, but it was the only way my wife and I could have a child. We even bought a daughter as well'.

'What do you mean, Bradley?'

'I mean through the Methodist Children's Home that he used to run. He laundered children like others launder money. Him and the very Reverend Graham Dooley'.

'None of this is true! I just don't believe you!'

'And why should I, *we* pay for anything my father did? "Why should the son bear the punishment for the father's iniquity?' When the son has practiced justice and righteousness and has observed all My statutes and done them, he shall surely live"'.

'Very good, Detective Chief Inspector May, very good indeed. You certainly know your Bible. Ezekiel, chapter 18, verse 19, if I remember correctly'.

The voice came over a loudspeaker. The four Darths smiled at each other.

'Who are you? What do you want?'

The voice spoke again; the sound came from every corner of the conference room.

'I want nothing but your death, DCI May'.

'I have done nothing wrong. Nothing!'

May and Ellis looked around again but could see nothing. The four Darths continued to smile.

'What about this? "Prepare for his sons a place of slaughter because of the iniquity of their fathers. They must not arise and take possession of the earth. And fill the face of the world with cities"'.

'Isaiah, chapter 14, verse 21'.

'Very good, Detective Chief Inspector. Most impressive. The Bible is so full of contradictions, is it not? Just like real life. All those men, pillars of the local community; staunch members of Salem Chapel. All of them, each and every one of them rotten to the core. And now you and your little WPC here are going to pay the final debt'.

After a moment's silence, the doors opened behind May and Ellis. Who should appear but Darth number five?

***

Vivienne Trubshaw counted the cracks in the ceiling for the third time. She had not slept since Donald May had been abducted, but Riggs had made her go home nevertheless.

What's the point, though? I am not going to sleep; there is no way I can sleep; sleep is the last thing on my mind until this is all over!

Riggs had not listened to Trubshaw's protests, instead ordering his boss out of the office.

Trubshaw stroked the empty half of her double bed.

I wish Don were here now. Nothing would matter. Life is too short.

Trubshaw's mobile vibrated on the bedside table.

'Yes?'

'We have a lead, Ma'am. A tip-off. I've assembled a team already. Get to Salem as quickly as you can and I will brief you there'.

70

May 30, Breakfast Time: Two Police Officers Prepare for Their Fate

———∽———

Jo Bishop gasped for air. She pulled at her top, hoping to escape the unbearable suffocation. The weight pressed down on her.

I am going to die! They have found me out! They know I did it!

Bishop's breathing grew shallower. There was a final exhalation, then stillness: no sound; no movement.

'JB! JB! What's the matter?'

'What? What do you mean?'

'You were having a bad dream!'

'Was I?'

'Yes, you were! I'm surprised you weren't heard at the other side of the cricket ground!'

Jo Bishop pulled herself up and looked at Bill Harker lying next to her. She had grown used to having him share her bed.

I never thought he would have the guts to leave his wife. But here he is.

'Was it bad?'

'Bad?'

'Yes. Your dream, or rather your nightmare'.

Bishop lay her head on Harker's chest.

'I thought I was being murdered'.

'Another Holme Hill murder!' Harker snorted.

'Bill!'

'Sorry, Jo. Sympathy never was my strong point'.

Harker kissed his lover's cheek.

How did I get into this? I vowed never to become involved again! And here I am, living with one of my students!

'Bill?'

'Yes, my love'.

'Why were you so interested in those plans I found of the nuclear bunker?'

'A fascinating period, the Cold War. It's one of my specialist interests. Always has been. Remember I am old enough to have been there! You weren't even born until 1976!'

'I guess so, Bill. But why did you force me not to tell Pauline Philbey or the police about my discovery? You weren't bothered about the old factory tunnels'.

'Still hush-hush, JB; official secrets and all that. The bunker plan shouldn't have been where it was. It's top-secret information even now. People might kill if they thought we knew something we shouldn't'.

Harker pulled his student on top of him and began to kiss her roughly.

***

435

'So, why won't you show your face like the others?'

'Why do you need to see my face?'

'Because I want to know the identity of every single one of this group!'

'You have seen enough, DCI May, you and your WPC. More than enough!'

'And why the Darth Vader masks?'

Georgie Ellis was too tired to feel fear.

*How many days and nights have I been incarcerated down here? We have to do something **now**! Can't DCI May **do something?***

'I can answer that, WPC Ellis'.

Linda Welch sounded weak; her voice was thin and gravelly.

That must be the cancer.

'We both can'.

Welch looked at Elsie Wright, who took and squeezed Linda's hand.

'*Star Wars* was David Harrison's favourite film and Darth Vader was the character he most loved'.

'You dress up as a tribute to him?'

'Yes, we do, Detective Chief Inspector; and to disguise our appearances and the sound of our voices'.

Georgie Ellis snorted.

'It's not funny, Woman Police Constable'.

'I think you are all pathetic!'

'Georgie!'

'Well, sir. This isn't the way to behave!'

'Behave? What do you know?'

Darth number five shouted at the two police officers.

'Anyway, I am tired of all this talking. You have had plenty of time to hear about our cause. Enough now! We must get on with it! Butcher! Bradley! Take them!'

May and Ellis both noticed how the other four Darths snapped to attention when Darth number five spoke. The others looked to this one as their leader. May even expected Butcher and Bradley to call him 'sir'.

Elsie Wright drew two swords from underneath the conference table and gave them to Butcher, who took one in each hand. The weapons reminded Georgie Ellis of the one that hung over the fireplace in her ancestral home.

'Ab ipso ferro': from the same iron. The Ponsonby-Ellis clan have had that motto for hundreds of years. They lived and died by the sword in the old days. And now it is my turn to do the same.

Butcher lay the two swords in front of the police officers, then proceeded to help Bradley shackle the prisoners once more and move them to the far end of the conference room, where they were each tied to an iron pillar supporting the ceiling.

Donald May stared at Darth number five.

'Tell me something. Where does Rodney Halliday fit into all this? I understand the others – in a perverse sort of way – but what about Rodney Halliday, *your* brother?'

71

May 30, Travel to Work Time: Some Will Never Arrive

— ∾ —

Gordon Wright looked up and down the platform.

Another journey where I will have to stand all the way.

He looked at his watch. Not only had "his" train been cancelled, but the next one was now "delayed" at Hebden Bridge.

Wright looked at his watch again.

30 May. 30 days in which my life has changed; in which this village has changed; in which everything has changed. Nothing will ever be the same again.

'Train services between Holme Hill and Hartley, Halifax, Bradford and Leeds and Rochdale and Manchester are currently suspended owing to a major incident'.

Gordon Wright joined in the collective groan. He could feel the joint despondency. It would be the bus to Hartley and then beyond.

On a normal day, I would have gone home, phoned the office, and worked on my archival research instead. But this isn't a normal day. This is the day my beloved mother gets arrested for murder. And good riddance!

***

Janet Christine Harrison had never been so nervous in all her life. She had vomited outside the back steps of The Bargeman and then again when she arrived at Salem Chapel. She thought back to her goodbye to Abbey and Arthur as she turned the key in the vestry door lock.

Can I remember the way? I was with Butch. I should not have helped him hide those drugs on the boat. But that was as nothing to what else I have done: helping Linda with killing all those people. Nobody deserves to die. Not even evil people like that. Especially not using the family's ceremonial swords. Why did Butch want them? Why kill them that way?

'But I will make it up to you, Abs; you and Arthur!'

Jaycee thought it was somehow fitting that she should be making this promise in front of the altar. She stood looking at the cross for a moment before proceeding around the back of the pulpit.

Why did I bow my head? It's not as if I believe in anything! And yet, it's as if there is somebody else in this chapel with me. Lots of people, in fact.

Janet Christine Harrison still said a prayer as she activated the mechanism on the secret door and went down the steps into the complex of rooms. She took in the scene. Once upon a time this was where Ernest Riddles's secret society had met, according to Linda. The secret service had taken over the premises in the late 1960s. After the end of the Cold War, when Salem had been sold, Rodney Halliday had used it for his drug trafficking operations until he had the cash to turn it into luxury flats. Jaycee had played her part well, as the understudy to John Butcher; she had enjoyed the role, the disguise, and the extra money. As long as Abbey never found out what had been going on…

Why would that matter now? Abbey knows the serious stuff. She knows what I have done and how I am going to make amends, even though it is killing me inside!

Jaycee went to the board that hung on the far wall. She looked down the list of Sunday School Superintendents and found the name of Ernest Edwin Riddles. The letters were at least twice as big as anybody else listed. She pushed the large, curled-round 'E' for Ernest and waited.

Nothing.

She pushed again.

Still nothing.

She pushed a third time; harder. There was a click, then a low, moaning noise.

Jaycee looked behind her. Pressing the 'E' activated a hatch in the floor by the old harmonium that had once – a very long time ago – accompanied children singing their Moody & Sankey. She peered down into the void that was revealed.

I should have brought a torch. Think! How can I see down there? I know: mobile!

Jaycee Harrison took out her phone and switched it on. There was no signal, like last time.

The torch app was sufficient to guide her down the metal steps and into the tunnel below the chapel. The brick vaulting was a work of art in its own way; cleverly put together by Victorian workmen.

They could never have known what would happen with their secret passageways! Those engineers. Now which way?

Jaycee prided herself on having a good memory, but all the routes looked the same. She closed her eyes and thought back to when she and Butch were moving those sacks. *Whose bodies were inside them? Did it matter?*

It's this way. I remember now! It must be this way.

Janet Christine Harrison felt cold. Her steps echoed down the tunnel. Periodically she stopped and turned around to make sure that she was not being followed.

Who could be following me? Who would know about these tunnels? If I can sort this out before the police discover the truth, then Abbey and I can put all this behind us. We can be a family again! Why, oh why did I listen to Linda; to my mother, of all people?

***

'Any last wishes, Detective Chief Inspector May? Or you, WPC Ellis?'

'Linda. Stop this now! You and the others have done enough damage already. Save yourselves!'

Welch laughed.

'Not when we have come this far and our work is nearly complete'.

Georgie Ellis watched the woman's eyes as she spoke.

'Sir, there is something wrong with Linda Welch. With all of them, in fact. Look at their eyes; listen to the way they speak. It is almost as if they are in a... well, some kind of a... I don't know how to say it. I can only think of the word... a trance'.

'I know what you mean, George. They aren't quite "all there", are they? Except perhaps Ernest Halliday; but we can't see his face. Not yet, anyway'.

'Sir?'

'Yes, Georgie?'

'Will we ever get out of this alive?'

'If I have anything to do with it, we will. And I know that everybody back at Hartley CID will be on the case and doing their darndest'.

Georgie Ellis thought what an old-fashioned phrase 'doing their darndest' was. It reminded her of Dad.

How I wish I could see him again! Make up with him after all the years of distance!

'There is no escape, Donald'.

It was Darth number five, standing right in front of them; John Butcher was just behind him, a ceremonial sword in each hand.

'It is time now. I have just one question before you are executed. You will be first, WPC Ellis, so that your boss can see you die'.

'And your question, Ernest?'

'How did you know it was me?'

May laughed.

'I will tell you if you take your mask off'.

'Why do you need to see my face?'

'You know why, Ernie Halliday. Living proof, you could say'.

'Very well, Detective Chief Inspector May, very well. Let's say that this is your last wish; and I am only too willing to give it to you'.

Darth number five reached up to the back of his head to unclasp his headgear. Just as he was about to show his face, the doors burst open.

'Freeze! Nobody moves! Hands up!'

A dozen armed police in body armour rushed into the conference room.

'Viv! Thank God, I thought you would never get here'.

'Are you alright, Don? Georgie?'

'We are now! How did you find us?'

'An anonymous tip-off; backed up by following this woman down the tunnels. That made it easier to find this place. We wouldn't have found it otherwise'.

'Harrison! You!'

A sheepish Jaycee was led into the room by two uniformed officers and made to sit down alongside the other culprits. Linda Welch looked across at her, but there was no response.

Freed from her shackles, Georgie Ellis collapsed into Charlie Riggs's arms. Paramedics were waiting outside the conference room to treat her and then get her airlifted off to hospital.

'What about you, Don? Do you want to go as well?'

May shook his head.

'No, I want to make sure that these people are locked up back at Hartley CID. And I will take great pleasure in interviewing them all!'

Vivienne Trubshaw looked at her boss. For all the ordeals he had been through over the last few days and before, he looked more alive than he had done for months.

Don is on fire. He is angry. I know that look.

DCI May looked around the conference table: Bradley, Welch, Wright, Butcher. He came last to Darth five.

'Take your mask off! Now!'

Ernie Halliday stood up and continued unclasping his mask. He pushed up the visor front and took the disguise up off his head.

Trubshaw felt sick as the face was revealed. Riggs and May turned away to hide their reactions.

72

May 30, Lunchtime, Afternoon, Evening: Brief Encounters

―――⌁―――

The radio had been on all morning. Pauline Philbey had not heard a word of it for hours; until now.

'Trains on the Leeds to Manchester line have been severely disrupted as a result of a police chase in the Holme Hill area, where an armed and dangerous man is on the run. The general public is advised to exercise extreme caution. Do not approach him if identified. Please stay indoors as far as possible until further notice'.

Whatever next? He'll be at my door before you know it.

Having fed a noisome Boris, Philbey wondered about returning to her armchair to slumber on but thought better of it and went to her study to do more work on the 19th and early 20th century plans of Holme Hill that she and Jo Bishop had been studying. Philbey had grown to like Bishop, though she was not sure about her taste in men, certainly not if Bill Harker was meant to be an exemplar. The Professor seemed to have developed an unhealthy hold over his student: telling her what she could not do, who she could and could not see.

I would have told him where to get off a long time ago! I would never let a man tell me what to do! Well, there was one, but that was different...

The kettle boiled. Pauline Philbey made herself a strong coffee and added a dash of her favourite whisky. She was about to sit down to attempt *The Times* crossword when the doorbell rang. The local archivist tensed immediately. The last person to come calling had been Joan Wilberforce.

Philbey looked out of the bay window to see who it was. She could only see a tall thin figure wearing an anorak. The hood was up.

What did the radio announcer say?

The doorbell sounded again.

Exercise extreme caution.

Philbey looked at the telephone in the hallway.

Shall I call the police? What will I say? I am just being overanxious!

The doorbell rang a third time. This time, Pauline Philbey answered it. To be on the safe side, she put the security chain on as she inched open the door.

'Who are you?'

'I need your help. Will you let me in?'

'Who are you? What happened?'

'I've been in an accident. I need help'.

'Please, I need help'.

'Pauline Philbey's visitor stretched out their bloodied hands. Please, let me in'.

'But I don't know you! You could be anybody. You could be that escapee'.

'For the love of God, Pauline, let me in!'

'You know my name!'

'Of course, I know your name. It's Ernie! Do you remember me?'

Philbey turned away. She recoiled, walking backwards into the hat stand.

'No! This is some kind of a joke! It can't be you after all these years. I am going to call the police!'

'Don't do that, Pauline. I need your help. I need it now, and fast. Now let me in, will you, Pauline? Please!'

Halliday slumped to the ground on Philbey's doorstep. She relented and opened the door.

***

'How did you know it was him, Don?'

DCI May smiled at his Detective Sergeant.

'It had to be him. He was the link between them all: the singing group; the "wonder material"; Riddles; he was the one who would most want his brother killed'.

'But why?'

'Well, Charlie, it was something that Pauline Philbey told me; that and looking at Rodney's past history'.

'How do you mean, sir?'

'Well, you remember that Ernie Halliday disappeared suddenly and never returned, but wrote to Pauline Philbey for a while. She showed me the letters. He was trying to give her a message, but she didn't notice; she didn't realise that that there was a secret code in his writing. It was actually George who gave me the idea when she did the same; except we spotted what she was trying to tell us in time. I went back and looked at Ernie's correspondence with Pauline. He was trying to tell her that he was being kept captive by the Select Seven. They were forcing him to write to her to throw her and others off the scent. The sad thing for Ernest Halliday was that his brother was the one doing the dirty work. And he was very handsomely paid for getting rid of his brother'.

'Except Rodney didn't get rid of Ernest, did he?'

'No. He didn't. I don't understand that. Though given how Ernie looks now, he might wish he were dead'.

'Why does he look like that? Why is he so disfigured?'

'Pauline Philbey told me that in the records she found, there was a note about a horrific accident in the laboratory. It must have been Halliday – Ernest Halliday that is, who was injured. I suspect there were others who may have died, but we don't know who they were – yet. That must be the reason why he disappeared and never came back for Philbey. And he was somehow able to avoid being killed by his brother until such time as he could get his revenge'.

'And cleverly using Welch, Wright, Bradley and Butcher to do his dirty work!'

'Indeed. With a bit of help from some of the drugs that his brother was trafficking!'

'What are we going to do now, sir?'

'Catch him, that's what! We should never have let him escape! He can't have got far. You wounded him, Charlie, I am sure of that!'

'I know, sir, but how were we to know there was yet another secret passage out of the nuclear shelter?'

'Well, Ernest Halliday did. Somebody must have told him at some point!'

***

'I have to go, JB. I am supposed to be giving a lecture this afternoon'.

'On what?'

'The usual. I won't be back this evening. I won't be through in time. I'll stay in Manchester. I'll see you tomorrow. ABW'.

He always says ABW. I can't work out whether or not I like it. I think I could find it very irritating.

'Bill?'

'Yes?'

'Before you go there's something I want to ask you'.

Harker looked at his watch.

'OK. I don't need to leave for another ten minutes. The trains seem to be running late anyway for some reason. No surprise there, thanks to *Northern Fail*'.

'Sit down, Bill'.

Harker thought for a moment then put his briefcase down by the apartment door and sat on the sofa. Jo Bishop positioned herself on the armchair opposite.

'What do you know about these murders?'

'What?'

'These murders in Holme Hill'.

'Oh, come on, Jo! Who do you think I am?'

'Don't give me that crap, Bill. I think you have an interest in this case beyond local history. You are linked to these killings somehow'.

'No. Well, no, not really'.

'What do you mean, no, not really?'

'Well, I may have passed some information on to some people'.

'Some people?'

'Yes. They were enquiring about Riddles and I may have given them your research notes'.

'What? Why?'

'Well, no reason, really'.

'No reason? No reason? There's always a reason, Bill'.

Jo Bishop lit a cigarette.

Professor William Harker looked down at his feet, then his watch, and then his lover.

'They gave me rather a lot of money for the information. And especially about the nuclear shelter. And the trapdoor and the *camera obscura*'.

'The what?'

'It's a series of mechanisms in Salem Chapel. Ernest Riddles had them installed as part of his occult worship. The effects were meant to startle his followers. It was all hush-hush, but I found out. Then I... well, I encouraged you to research the Chapel and its architecture'.

'And who paid you for this information? And keeping it quiet?'

'It was a man called Gordon Wright'.

'What? Gormless Gordon? He wouldn't say boo to a goose!'

'I think he was only the messenger'.

'For what? All your information?'

Harker nodded.

'Is there something else, Bill?'

Harker nodded.

'I used your University ID to contact him'.

'What, you mean JB76?'

***

The man had lost a lot of blood. Pauline Philbey's brief career as a nurse meant that she could stem the flow, but he needed to be taken to hospital.

'I am going to call 999 now'.

'No. You mustn't! There's no time!'

'Are you really Ernie? What happened to your face? It's awful!'

The man looked up at Pauline Philbey, then took her hand in his.

'It *really* is me. PP – *per procurationem*, remember?'

'God, it really is you. Nobody else would know that!'

'Don't cry, PP. I just wanted to see you one last time'.

'But I thought you were dead!'

'So did I!'

'What happened then?'

'There was an accident in the laboratory. That's where I got this face. I wanted to shut the project down, but the Select Seven wouldn't let me. They insisted I continue; but I couldn't be seen looking like this, could I?'

'It wouldn't have mattered to me, Ernie'.

Pauline Philbey stroked the marks on Halliday's face. Tears began to roll down his cheeks.

'I never stopped thinking about you, PP. Honest'.

'We must get you to a hospital, Ernie'.

Halliday shook his head.

'I've done bad things, Pauline. Very bad things'.

'You mean the murders?'

Halliday nodded.

'All of them?'

More nodding.

'I organised it all. It started when I saw an advert in *Private Eye* about the Select Seven. I knew what it referred to straight away. I answered the ad; it was Linda Welch. She told me about how she had met and murdered Thomas Hodgson in Australia for being one of the Select Seven and putting David Harrison away. And that she was dying and wanted to avenge David's death, and Minnie's too. Then I did some more research and found out about Superintendent Bradley. I turned him. He was so guilty about framing David and letting the Select Seven off – including Donald May's father, who was running a racket of his own – that Bradley was only too willing to help bring them to justice'.

'What about Elsie Wright?'

'Ah, good old Elsie. Fine upstanding Elsie. She was the group's conscience. I wish I had never invented that "wonder material". And I wish even more that the Select Seven hadn't kept going with the experiments; and then selling the secrets to the Soviet Union. It wasn't just the people over here who died because of it; it was even worse there. All hushed up of course, but thousands, tens of thousands, if not more, died'.

'And what about Rodney? What about your brother?'

'He was the worst of all. He tried to murder me. He was the Seven's henchman. They got to know him through me. And then he betrayed me for money. They 'took out a contract' on me. But I managed to escape. And I have been on the run ever since. Until Linda Welch put that advertisement in the magazine'.

'And you were able to persuade them to murder all those people, including my friend, Joan Wilberforce?'

'Joan had to die. She was going to the police. She found out through Linda Welch. I reinforced their courage with... with some medication. Nothing more. But it helped to get the job done.

'Was it worth it, Ernie?'

'They had to pay for what they did, PP. Right from Minnie Hargreaves through to all the men, women, and children – yes, children – that died because of their greed'.

'Please let me phone for an ambulance'.

Halliday shook his head.

'Pauline, "Children are a heritage from the Lord; offspring a reward from him", and I love you'.

With that, Professor Ernest Halliday, BSc, PhD, FRS, breathed his last.

73

May 31: A High-Ranking Officer Visits Hartley CID

—⌀—

'I've never known anything like it'.

'None of us has, Viv. I can't believe any of it'.

DS Trubshaw looked at her boss. In a few days' time, she would be gone; their relationship would be over, and that's the way it had to be.

May smiled back.

'So, Butcher murdered the lot? We weren't looking for more than one person after all. It was just one person who could use either hand. To fool us, no doubt!'

'Yes, he actually killed every one of them; apart from Gelsthorpe, that is. Poor old Ted just got in the way and died of a heart attack in the process'.

'And I wonder about Hodgson, sir. I don't suppose we will ever know about him. I still think Linda Welch did it'.

'She hasn't said anything about that one so far. I doubt she ever will, given her health'.

The three police officers nodded to each other as they looked at the completed murder wall.

'Butcher killed them, but Ernest Halliday was the mastermind behind it all. He convinced the others – not that Linda Welch, Arthur Bradley or Elsie Wright needed much convincing – that "the Lord's work" had to be done'.

May used a marker to link all the five murderers on the wall before continuing.

'According to Pauline Philbey's statement it sounded as though he had 'got religion' and was wreaking revenge on the Select Seven and their associates because of all the deaths that they had caused. Strangely enough, as you have probably guessed, I lost my faith a while back. But through the last couple of days, I have felt an inner strength grow back inside me, despite everything, including what I have discovered – and I suspect there is more to come – about my father'.

Trubshaw could see the moistness in the DCI's eyes as he turned away to look out of his office window.

'I am pleased to hear it, sir. It meant, *means* a lot to you, I know'.

'Though Rodney Halliday was not just about "an eye for an eye", was it? It must have been personal as well. Imagine, your own brother trying to kill you, just because the price was right. Greed has a lot to answer for'.

The smell of freshly ground coffee was irresistible, the plate of biscuits beyond temptation.

'Have they all confessed, then?'

'Georgie! We didn't expect to see you back so soon!'

'Well, I thought I had better get back into harness and uniform while I still could. I've had a check-up and, apparently, I am none the worse for my ordeal'.

The WPC looked at her boss as she brought in the refreshments. May gave nothing away.

'Yes, they have, Georgie. Though they may say they were acting under duress, given the drugs that Ernest Halliday had been giving them'.

Vivienne Trubshaw looked at the WPC. *What will happen to her? A major disciplinary perhaps? But then she did help to solve the murders, in a way. I suspect Don will make sure they go easy on her.*

'Oh, sir, Professor Harker wants to make a statement as well. He's coming in with Jo Bishop later today'.

'Thanks, Charlie. I imagine that will have something to do with the nuclear bunker, but let's wait and see'.

DCI May's phone rang.

'OK, thank you, Sergeant. Send them up'.

'Well, everybody. Look sharp. A VIP is about to inspect our office'.

Trubshaw, Riggs, and Ellis looked at each other. There had been no announcement.

After a few moments, Caroline May appeared, followed by her son.

'Fellow officers, I would like you to meet Commander Frederick May of the Yard, the brains behind this investigation, as far as I am concerned'.

'Thank you. It was nothing really', said Freddie. 'Just good old-fashioned policing'.

Lightning Source UK Ltd.
Milton Keynes UK
UKHW010220210721
387488UK00002B/17/J